P9-CFS-453

*"The Lords of the Storm are not dead: I believe they will never die. They live on through the power of the bloodstones.*

*"We should have approached them with the care and caution of anthropologists studying a new species, not as a group of intoxicated treasure-hunters.*

*"Of one thing I am certain: The bloodstones should never have been disturbed. . . ."*

—From the diary of Erika Weller,
   Co-leader of the Chapman/Weller Expedition

"AN UPDATED H. RIDER HAGGARD OCCULT–ADVENTURE . . . A CROSS BE-TWEEN *SHE* AND *KING SOLOMON'S MINES*."

—*Kirkus Reviews*

# CATACOMBS

## John Farris

A DELL BOOK

Published by
Dell Publishing Co., Inc.
1 Dag Hammarskjold Plaza
New York, New York 10017

Copyright © 1981 by John Farris

All rights reserved. No part of this book may be reproduced
or transmitted in any form or by any means, electronic
or mechanical, including photocopying, recording or by
any information storage and retrieval system, without the
written permission of the Publisher, except where permitted
by law. For information address Delacorte Press, New
York, New York.

Dell ® TM 681510, Dell Publishing Co., Inc.

ISBN: 0-440-11580-9

Reprinted by arrangement with Delacorte Press
Printed in the United States of America
First Dell printing—June 1982

*Catacombs* is dedicated to
Mary Ann,
Julie,
John,
Jeff,
and Peter.
My friends, partners, and fellow explorers
of adventures unknown,
lives not yet lived.

The pictographs in this book have been adapted from drawings made by Jonathan Kingdon and published in *East African Mammals: An Atlas of Evolution in Africa*, Volume 3, Part A (Carnivores) by Academic Press, Inc.

# PROLOGUE

# THE DIARY OF ERIKA WELLER

**March 19/0930 hours**
**Day 173**

*For the first time since we arrived nearly six months ago, I feel afraid of the Catacombs: this enormous burial ground of an elite society, carved into our familiar rock of Earth. Yet they are as distant from what we regard as human as the alien life forms of a planet a million light years across the galaxy.*

*The Priests of Zan are not dead: I believe they will never die. We have just begun, after exhausting exploration, to grasp the idea of their continuing power, a mastery of eternity. They stand mute but dreaming in a reliquary of their fabulous civilization. All has been revealed to us; too little we understand. They have not been waiting for us. We don't matter. We are transient, vulnerable, inferior, possessed by the smoke of their dreams, helpless to divine the meaning of their continuing existence.*

*Of one thing I am certain: They live on through the power of the bloodstones. And the bloodstones should never have been disturbed, despite their accessibility and immeasurable value. We should have approached them with the care and caution of anthropologists studying a new species, not as a group of intoxicated treasure-hunters.*

*Jack Portline is dead, the back of his head shattered by repeated blows from a mattock.*

*He had been missing for five days. We found his*

body in a previously uninvestigated chamber on the
seventh level of the Catacombs, near the Repository.
He was dragged there in a clumsy attempt to hide the
remains, but the trail of blood, still fresh after several
days, wasn't difficult to follow even in the available
light from the central core. (It is worth noting again,
despite the horrible circumstances, that nothing seems
to spoil in the Catacombs. Fresh milk remains fresh
after weeks without refrigeration. Growth—hair, fin-
gernails—is severely retarded.)

We concluded that Jack had surprised his assailant
at work, looting the Repository. There was a small
pool of blood on the stone floor near one of the crystal
vaults, and more spots on the vault itself. From this
vault as many as fifty bloodstones have been removed: Chips and I didn't take the time to count all
of the empty sockets. One man could carry, without
difficulty, that many stones down the mountain in a
rucksack. They would weigh only about seventeen
ounces. In what passes for civilization in our time, the
red diamonds would have a value well in excess of
one hundred million dollars. So much for motive.

One of our friends and associates is demented, a
murderer. Which one? There was nothing to do but
summon all the members of the Chapman/Weller expedition, by beeper, from the depths where they have
been working in numerous chambers of the Catacombs, and from the base camp on the mountain. It
will be hours before we are sure who else is missing;
and that man will have Jack Portline's blood on his
hands.

We are in the expedition's "common room," if indeed you can describe space the size of a zeppelin
hangar, hewn from solid rock, as a room. Level One,
Sector One (our destination) of the Catacombs, which
we chose because there are no tombs here, no open
feline eyes to study our every move from deep within

*their flawless crystal sarcophagi. In a lonely area of Sector One that takes up as much space as a table-cloth on a football field are the Mylar mushrooms that comprise our home in the Catacombs: privacy for work, study, recuperation. The costly paraphernalia of expeditions on spaceship Earth. Cadmium fuel cells, fluid recyclers, field-grade microelectronics for every type of data processing.*

*Chips is asleep on the pneumatic mattress next to mine, a hand flung out against my side for compan-ionship and reassurance. I know I should sleep now, before the next ordeal, but I can't. In the beginning, months ago, was the agony of acclimatization: The Catacombs lie many thousands of feet above the mi-graine level for all but the most seasoned and hardy alpinists, and few of our middle-aged scientists quali-fied as such despite rigorous preconditioning before the expedition was assembled. After we adjusted to the altitude, sleep was still a fitful experience at best, disturbed by the nervous excitement from our con-tinuing, phenomenal discoveries. In a place where there is no day or night, only an unvarying level of illumination several footcandles brighter than the light of the full moon, we've all wanted to work be-yond our capacities to make the most of the available time. Sleep and food too often seem to be expendable, and we've suffered from this neglect ourselves.*

*Now, after weeks of the eerie silence of tombs, there are earthshocks, occurring more frequently dur-ing the past few days. We are, after all, in the Great Rift Valley, an area of ongoing seismic activity, of ir-resistible forces slowly splitting a continent apart. It's as if the bloodstones are the heart of this mountain, a heart which has been severely damaged by the trans-gressions of a greedy maniac. I think it may be too late already, but we must try to get the stones back to where they belong. . . .*

Continued.

By 1400 hours we were all assembled. All but two: Jack Portline and his murderer. I must say Chips did not seem surprised. But he was deeply shaken by guilt and rage at himself for having twice placed his trust in a man whose essential faithlessness is well known to the world. Privately I reminded him that we'd never had a choice. Yet I too feel guilty. Is a unique discovery like the Catacombs worth the bargain we are forced to make, the senseless death of a colleague?

After only six months our work here is drastically incomplete, but clearly none of us has the heart, or the stamina, to continue for now. Our sensors and computers now predict the likelihood of a major volcanic eruption; temperatures have been rising slowly inside the Catacombs, from a previously consistent 62.8 degrees. The decision was made to pack it in. Chips has gone down to the base camp to signal for helicopters. He feels it is best not to say anything about the murder, or the theft of the bloodstones, until he can speak to Kinyati.

Jumbe Kinyati will see to it that justice is done. And quickly.


## Day 174

Time for only a few notes; but the habit dies hard. And I'm concerned that these tapes of mine might be the only surviving evidence of the Chapman/Weller expedition.

The helicopters, both personnel carriers, came early, just after sunrise. One landed at the base camp and another in the cul-de-sac outside. We had removed our equipment and computerized data from the chambers—and Jack Portline's body, sewn into a sleeping blanket and weighing more than the rest of *our gear put together. Now there is virtually no trace of our months-long sojourn in the Catacombs.*

The Tanzanian Air Force in charge of the airlift, a bearded man named Timbaroo, ignored Chips' protests and loaded all of our data into a single helicopter. He and his soldiers obviously came equipped to make short work of the evacuation. They carried portable oxygen with them to nullify the effects of the extremely thin, cold air. And they had guns, for which there was no necessity. None of us were allowed aboard; the helicopter took off almost immediately. It's a valuable find, of course, unprecedented, and the government is jealous of its prerogatives, but this amounts to confiscation—or outright theft.

When Chips continued to argue, too vehemently, with the general, he was placed under arrest, at gunpoint, and taken away to the base camp. It was obvious they had intended from the beginning to make us prisoners.

I was only a few yards from the entrance to the Catacombs. They weren't watching me. I slipped back inside. By now I've been missed. Will they search the Catacombs? I don't think so. It is measurable in square miles, and I could evade them easily. But without food or the means to recycle urine, I have no chance of surviving.

If they leave without me I might try to escape down the mountain. Difficult, even if I were strong, at a peak of conditioning. But anything could kill me out there—a misstep, a rockslide, the biting cold of night. Oh, God!

. . . Later. The earth was shaking so strongly I found it difficult to stand, let alone walk. I vomited, and have a severe headache.

Fireballs are more in evidence. They're clustered around the core of the Catacombs, each as bright as a miniature sun. They are frightening, but harmless.

So I hope is the transformation, quite unlike any I've experienced here.

I made the mistake of making eye contact with one of the entombed creatures—and abruptly I was striding across the storm-darkened Serengeti Plain, solitary, like most of my kind, in search of a morning kill: wildebeeste, Tommy. The transformation was astonishing. I knew who I really was, yet I felt the smooth power of another body, of unsheathed claws and spotted coat, of hunger burning in a lean belly. I had the ability, unique among animals of the world, to sprint at an incredible speed in pursuit of game. I spotted my prey, accelerated, overtook the gazelle, and slowly strangled it with the bite of jaws that were too weak for dealing quick deaths. I feasted, then returned miles across the plain to the hiding place of my cubs. I found nothing left but hanks of black birth-hair: While I had eaten, they were eaten. By hyenas.

The transformation abruptly was reversed, as they all were, and I stood weeping in the chamber, unaware of how much time had passed.

. . . Chips is calling me now, pleading with me to come out. General Timbaroo must have put him up to it but he does sound worried, for my sake. He knows what I'm capable of. Chips says that I am only making more trouble. He may be right; I only know I have no more time to think about it. I don't know why we're under arrest, why the data collected by the expedition was taken. But surely Chips will straighten everything out.

In the meantime, it's unthinkable that any harm will come to us.

# ONE

# THE POWER
# OF THE STONES

"The Lords of the Storm. They sound like gods. Think of that, Matthew. They have looked upon mankind and seen that we are assholes. From their infinite wisdom and compassion is distilled a drop of pity. A blood-red drop. Maybe FIREKILL is a gift from the gods."

"On the other hand," Jade said, "they may have a godlike sense of humor we won't appreciate at all."

Excerpted from the archival tapes of
President Douglas Jaret Creighton,
cross-file reference N640-1715,
The *Hondo* series.

# KINGDOM MISSION

In the late afternoon Erika awoke from exhausted sleep to find herself shivering, and for a few moments she was horrified, thinking that she too had come down with the fever.

She sat up in her creaking bed, bagged in mosquito netting that had turned brown from the sun and was weighted with the dust of drought. Except for a violent pulse and heartbeat she discovered no other symptoms of a possible viral infection. The tremors were a reaction to a dream which, recurring, always found her vulnerable: a chilly bath of terror to purge the frustration and anxiety of her waking hours. In her dream magisterial men with the savage, flat-skulled heads and yellow faces of cheetahs came vividly to life in their crystal tombs, shattering barriers that had lasted ten thousand years. The cat people of the Catacombs—always they brought her back to the months of the expedition, and the bloodstones.

In retrospect, as she sat huddled on the bed with her head close to her knees, coughing a bitter taste of unassimilated dust from the back of her throat, the Lords of the Storm were less threatening than concerned in their attitudes toward her; they reached out as she slow-stepped through the ritual of the dream as if to bestow power which she so sadly lacked in her present circumstances. But as they touched her with slender hands nearly doubled in length by hooked fin-

gernails, their expressions became static, simplified:
The faces vanished slowly, leaving just the bold
strokes of pictographs, a dead language she could only
partially read after weeks of study.

The afternoon wind was blowing from the north,
from the shrunken soda lake of Rukwa, across the
miles of glazed savannah, and through the upland
bush and acacia trees that surrounded the deteriorating old mission. Erika, in her misery, wrapped her
arms around her thin knees to diminish the trembling;
darkened by the sun, viewed through layers of netting, she was like the uneasy seed in a strange, transparent fruit.

She heard footsteps in the bungalow and looked up.

Alice Sinoyi filled the door space of the little bedroom; there had never been a door. Alice's cropped
head was the color and texture of burnt sugar. The
lower half of her face was covered with a surgical
mask, a protection against dust aerosols which they all
were observing. Beside her head, on the wall, was a
stark, slightly askew pale shadow of a cross that had
been removed when the mother superior of the white
sisters who had taught in the mission school departed
for another assignment.

"Erika?"

"Oh, Alice. What time is it? How long have I slept?"

"About four hours. You are coming with me?
Bwana Chapman now is having the fever." There was
no tone of urgency in her voice. She seemed fatalistic,
unmoved.

"Oh, my God."

Erika tumbled from the bed, flinging the cumber-
some net aside, and reached for her sandals. She
thought she heard an airplane circling above them,
the twice-weekly Beechcraft from Mbeya that carried
supplies and, occasionally, more help from the district
hospital to the quarantined mission and village. And

she heard something else: a surge of orchestral horns, the scratchy but still-powerful voice of Maria Callas. The aria was in French, issuing from the hi-fi equipment of Father Varnhalt, the half-crazed old priest who presided over the largely defunct mission. He was a serious opera buff and was given to playing his records for hours, often in the middle of the night, and at full volume.

> Divinités du Styx, ministres de la mort!
> Je n'invoquerai point votre pitié cruelle.

*Gods of the Styx, ministers of death! I shall call upon your cruel pity.* . . . . Erika shuddered again; today his choice of *Alceste* seemed dismally appropriate. She took a fresh mask from a carton on top of the dresser, which was dark and ugly and typical of mission furniture, and airy from wormholes. As she followed Alice through shaded but stifling brick arcades, she tied the mask behind her head. Her fingers were a trifle clumsy; she felt dizzy and dreamlike, the world falling into soft focus at the edges of her vision.

Erika stopped and glanced up as the plane, throwing off needles of light, made another low pass over the mission buildings. Something, apparently, was obstructing the salt-pan landings strip half a mile downhill. A herd of zebu, cattle, or perhaps one of the thinning bands of topi seeking what was left of the brackish water in the Songwe River.

By the stockade gate the masked soldiers slouching under dust-caked but still-green mango trees also looked up, shielding their eyes and making feeble jokes about the prowess of the bush pilot. But he was free to come and go and they were not. The soldiers were of tribes other than the Fipa or the Nyika, stationed far away from their own districts. They were afraid of the plague, but more afraid of running away.

If they were caught, Colonel Ukumtara, a Masai whom they all feared, would personally shoot them. And few of the conscripted soldiers had any idea of how to make their ways home from the southern highlands, through empty hostile country which they knew to be populated by sorcerers, vampires, and werewolf hyenas.

The hospital was a long, two-story building with high ceilings; it had been built in 1912, a few years after the end of the devastating Maji-Maji rebellion, during which the Germans had killed seventy-five thousand blacks and gained a firm hold on the southern tribal districts. Only about half of the original stucco remained on the brick walls, and a wooden gallery was in serious disrepair. There was an overhanging tin roof topped with thatch that had been riddled by rats.

The rats had become so numerous and threatening as the mission population dwindled that a quartet of tough young tomcats recently had been flown in from Mbeya. They patrolled together, for their own safety, and had succeeded in driving the rats from the living and eating areas of the mission grounds. The ecology of Africa is exceptionally fragile, habitat and migratory patterns depending almost entirely on the erratic monsoons. It was now the season of the long rains in East Africa, but even in a good year this crescent of the Rukwa Valley received only about twenty inches of rainfall. This year, so far, there had been almost none; brief showers did little more than settle the laterite dust. With every humid drizzle the sky seemed to bleed.

For three weeks the hospital had been crowded with the seriously ill. Surrounding it, almost like a halo, was a corrupt, nauseating odor which Erika had become somewhat accustomed to: She had spent most of her time there since the outbreak of the fever. An abandoned school building nearby was now rapidly filling with blacks from the surrounding villages; in another day or two there would be no more room at the mission.

Alice left her and went, flat-footed, heavy in the haunch, toward the auxiliary ward, where a woman's despairing *lulloo* had interrupted Mme. Callas' passionate mezzo air. Already nearly one hundred fifty cases of the fever of unknown origin had been diagnosed. Sixteen patients, unresponsive to broadspectrum antibiotics and serums for known fevers such as Rift Valley and Congo, had died. A few victims, those under thirty years of age who had contracted the disease, seemed to be recovering. No children had been brought in as yet, and only two of the young soldiers assigned to the mission had been stricken, not seriously. The older you were, the more deadly the fever.

Raymond Poincarré had come out onto the gallery in his short-sleeved smock to drink a cup of fruit juice and smoke a strong cigarette. He was the only doctor the Tanzanian government had sent to them in this emergency. For nearly a month he had worked eighteen hours a day with a staff of native nurses from the Mbeya hospital to contain and attempt to identify the fever. His father was a Belgian, his mother had been a Fipa woman from the valley south of Muse. He'd been out of medical college for less than a year, but Erika thought he would become an outstanding doctor if he wasn't worked to death. His only fault, as she saw it, was a steadfast refusal to discuss or even acknowledge the fact of their involuntary sequestration.

Poincarré looked at Erika as she negotiated the tilting, creaking stairs to the second floor. He had a high, light-brown forehead and wore gold-rimmed glasses, a miniature gold ring in the lobe of one ear. His face was too youthful to be lined, but these days it had fallen into a pucker of weariness, or resignation. He spoke to her in French, his voice still strained from laryngitis caused by the dust.

"I'm sorry to get you up so soon; but he was asking for you."

"Are you sure it's the fever?" Erika said, still in shock. "Chips has had malaria for many years—he could be having a flareup in spite of the chloroquine."

"No, he's not malarial. It's a fulminating febrile sickness. Lymphadenopathy is evident. Time will tell." Poincarré didn't sound hopeful. The pitch of the airplane engine had changed as the pilot sought to land. He glanced from the descending aircraft to the livid hollows beneath her eyes. "They should have sent me a good supply of gamma globulin this time. I've asked for it nearly every day. For your safety I suggest that you have an injection. Why haven't you been eating? You mustn't lose any more weight. You'll surely collapse if you keep on at this pace—you were up all of last night."

"I feel fine." In truth she had experienced dancing spots before her eyes, and palpitations, as a result of jumping too quickly out of bed. Erika blinked hotly at the frieze of lizards around the screen door, and heard someone groaning inside the ward. "Shouldn't we know what it is by now? You sent the blood and sputum samples to Mbeya over three weeks ago."

He shrugged. "The laboratory there is primitive. The samples may have been mishandled; they often are. Or perhaps they were spoiled in transit to the virus lab in Dar."

"This can't be an isolated outbreak; there must have been something like this fever before. There must be a vaccine."

"I don't know, Erika. Mutations of deadly viruses are common in Africa. It takes a very long time to isolate the new strains and cultivate antiviruses. By the time that happens, the disease may run its course."

"Leaving how many dead?" She was panting for breath. She leaned against the wall; the lizards rearranged themselves watchfully. "But that's it, isn't it? That's why the government can only spare us one doctor and a few nurses when what we really need are virologists, epidemiologists, a well-equipped field laboratory. Does USAID or the World Health Organization know what's happening in Ivututu? No. Because someone in power in this country will be bloody well pleased if every single member of the Chapman/Weller expedition dies here!"

Whenever she touched on this sensitive subject, he pretended to have great difficulty in understanding her Swiss-accented French.

"Virologists are scarce in East Africa. But I must admit I would welcome some help, if only for a few days." He dragged on his cigarette, then stubbed it out on the railing and pocketed what was left. "They'll be coming with the supplies soon enough; I want to be sure my requisition slips are in order. Even then it's a guessing game each time I open a parcel."

Erika, her face flushed, turned without another word and went inside. They had received supplies on a steady basis, some of which were still in Red Cross crates airlifted to East Africa to combat health emergencies nearly a decade ago. They had ample fuel for the generators and more than enough food, but she knew she was right: No one in authority really cared that they were being slowly wiped out.

Edith Esmond, an archaeologist from the University of Chicago, had been the first to sicken and then to die, her throat impassably swollen, her tongue black, her skullbones soft as a baby's. Then Brant Luradale, the expedition's photographer, and the epigrapher Evangelos Trimakis succumbed within a week after symptoms appeared. Each man was past fifty and Edith, a robust fifty-seven, had been the senior member

of their group. Of the thirty-two nonnative members
of Chapman/Weller, all alive and well six weeks ago,
one was missing and unaccounted for—Jack Portline's
murderer—and seven were dead (their bodies, presumably on someone's orders, had immediately been
packed in dry ice and removed, by military helicopter,
from the mission; but Erika had no idea to where the
bodies were taken, and Raymond Poincarré, if he
knew, wouldn't talk).

Twenty more of the explorers and scientists had
fallen ill. Paul Boneparth, a forty-six-year-old computer programmer, had been at the point of death for
two days, then rallied. His symptoms had abated mysteriously, but his mind seemed to be gone. Of the four
members of the expedition so far untouched by the
bug, Erika at thirty-six was the oldest.

In the high room dimmed by shutters where the
sick lay sweltering, nearly naked, bronzy from fever
like fallen pharaohs in temporary pyramids of net, she
found another black nurse asleep sitting up, head pil-
lowed against her chubby hands on the back of a
metal chair. She had a lollipop secure in one cheek,
and nursed it unconsciously between dragging snores.
The victims of the fever announced their distress in
mutters, rattles, and low groans. Those most badly off
were in old-fashioned oxygen tents fed from tall,
nipple-topped metal bottles. Buckets and bedpans
wanted emptying, sheets changing; there was an acrid
stench of insecticide and Lysol in the air. Erika's steps
dragged as she searched the faces of friends for signs
of improvement or further dissolution.

"Erika."

They'd found another bed somewhere and put it at
one end of the aisle, beneath the windows, then extended it with a bench, but still his ankles and feet
protruded, creating a bulge in the netting. He was at
an angle in the narrow bed, pillows behind his back;

his eyes were half open. His shirt was unbuttoned, and his chest was bare and sweaty. The first thing she wanted to do was bathe him.

"Oh, Chips."

He licked his lips with a slow tongue. "Under the weather," he said, smiling. His breath was bad, he had vomited, his beard was still matted. He waved her away as she was about to part the netting and sit beside him—as if it made any difference now. Only children were *ilombwe*. There was no sure way to avoid the fever—she would get it in due course. Now that Chips was sick she didn't care; she would just as soon die with him. They had long been partners in expeditions—Chekiang, Titacaca, Palenque—but lovers for only a little more than a year.

Instead of sitting, Erika brought him a drink, a can of cool Pepsi from the little kerosene refrigerator beside the single sink in the ward. He was able to sip some of it through a straw.

Chips had in one hand a creased, faded color photo of a tall young man, beardless but in his father's image: Toby Chapman. From time to time Chips glanced at his son's face, and his own face softened—with longing, with love and despair.

To distract him Erika said, "I've been wondering about this bug. If it's something we brought with us from the Catacombs, why did it take so long to incubate? Some of us would have fallen sick while we were still there."

Chips nodded. "Deliberately introduced once we arrived in Ivututu."

"By whom?"

"The only one of us—who's missing." It was difficult for Chips to talk, to swallow. The Pepsi ran out of a corner of his mouth as he pulled at the straw. He stopped drinking and with clumsy fingers tucked the photograph of his son into a shirt pocket. His hand lingered over his heart but he looked sternly at her, all business.

"Erika, my being laid up doesn't change anything—"

"What? Oh, no, you're not serious!"

"One of us . . . still has to get out of here. Get help. When I realized how sick I was, I . . . talked to Bob Connetta. Told him just what to do to the plane while he was helping to unload it. Tonight you'll have a chance to get out of here. Odds don't favor you, but you have to make it. You're a damned good pilot, my lady. Take Bobby with you. Head straight for Nairobi. North northeast from here, maybe six hundred miles. Piece of cake in that Bonanza."

"Leave you?" she said, too loudly, outraged by the suggestion.

"Only chance, Erika. Do what I tell you." He looked past her, at the rows of beds. "Have another look at them. Help you to make up your mind. Seven dead. Maybe tomorrow it'll be Vinnie, or Lennart, or Tsutomu."

Erika bowed her head; she was shaking again. She pressed her long hands together. Most of the time she wore surgical gloves, despite the inconvenience and the humidity; she knew what could result from even a minor cut or an unnoticed pinprick. Defying the conditions under which she worked, she had stayed scrupulously clean and tried to see that everyone else did the same, though the fresh-water supply was a trickle and it was necessary to throw a bucket of scrub water into the toilets to flush them into the overburdened drain fields.

She was determined not to shake Chips' morale by demonstrating nerves in front of him. She looked up, smiling. But Chips wasn't watching her; he had put his Pepsi down and was straining to clear his throat.

Her own chest ached in response to his efforts. A

week ago, in a rage, he had struck Colonel Ukumtara, and had been placed in confinement in a windowless room behind the chapel. There his endurance had crumbled. Now he was very nearly helpless.

"One thing . . . in our favor. The bloody colonel has relaxed now. He doesn't expect much of you, or any woman. He's bored . . . with this duty. His boys are careless."

Erika ran a hand through her short haircut. "How would I get down to the plane after dark?"

"We'll think of something."

Chips was short of breath. She felt as if she were needlessly irritating him; he had placed his trust in her. She said, with a confidence she forced herself to feel, "I'll be back for all of you, darling, no later than tomorrow. After I've raised hell with the embassies and the news services."

"We should be . . . front page all over the world. A bit shoddy and premature, considering the work still to be done. But necessary."

"If only we'd been allowed to keep something, some scrap of proof of what we've found in the Catacombs. A photo, a latex mold, a single bloodstone." Erika thought of the cat people in their transparent tombs, alone once more, waiting, as they had waited for a hundred centuries, still guarding their hoard of red diamonds—a hoard now reduced, perhaps critically, by as many as fifty stones. She shuddered. Once she had savored the impact she anticipated their find would have on the world. Now she could only shrug, feeling defeated. "There'll be outraged cries of hoax."

"Muted skepticism, perhaps," Chips said, trying to encourage her. "But your credentials demand respect. Publicity is what we must have now, an uproar of . . . volcanic proportions."

Erika flinched.

"Sorry. Bad choice of words. Almost no time left, if we're right in our assumptions about the bloody mountain. So . . . over the wall with you, and God bless."

He jackknifed in a fit of coughing, but Erika for once was oblivious to his distress; she had heard the creak of boards outside and glanced at the half-shuttered window only a few feet away, beyond which the afternoon blazed with the volatile white-ness of tropic sun. In that blaze something dark mo-mentarily floated, like a gourd-shaped spot of eclipse. *Creak, creak.* A thoughtful tread. Light was reflected in a thin arc from the spectacles of Dr. Raymond Poincarré, as if he had glanced at her in passing. They had kept their voices low, but he was too close not to have overheard.

For a few moments Erika nearly panicked. These past weeks she had worked closely with Raymond to save the lives of her friends and associates, and she could never question his dedication to them. On a per-sonal level he was almost aloof, but he had shown flashes of interest in her. His mother was dead, his father was a rummy who was in the monkey business in the highlands of Iringa. Raymond owed his career to his sponsor, Dr. Robeson Kumenyere, who held no cabinet post but exerted a major influence on the des-tinies of this rigidly structured socialist country. At the mission Raymond shared, or was forced to share, quarters with Colonel Ukumtara, who had a primitive faith that the presence of the doctor helped to keep the fever from visiting him.

Perhaps Raymond was afraid that if she escaped, the government would charge him as well as the colo-nel with the responsibility. He was a young man, and he knew that the jails of his country held more politi-cal prisoners than South Africa's jails. But he also knew what was going to happen at the mission if more help wasn't forthcoming. Before the fever burned itself out in this isolated valley, hundreds might be dead.

There was only one way to proceed: She had to confront him at once, try to reason with him, put him to a test of loyalties.

Erika went quickly outside, but Raymond had already gone down the steps and called for a Land-Rover that was parked near the gate.

"Raymond!"

The first time he pretended not to hear her; along the path that circled the yard the Land-Rover came grinding to pick him up. She called again. This time he looked back, silently. Erika could not tell much from his expression except that he seemed withdrawn, troubled. He swung aboard and dropped into the nearside seat of the Rover, and Erika helplessly watched him go. Outside the stockade the Rover took the track down to the landing strip, where the plane from Mbeya was being unloaded.

She knew then he had made his choice: a lingering death for those who were left from the Chapman/Weller expedition.

# CHANVAI,

## Momela Lakes, Tanzania
## April 29

As the Boeing 707 banked gently right and the Chinese captain began his final descent to the airport on the Sanya Juu plains, the glare of the lowering sun on the window awakened Len Atterbury. He looked up and saw the mountain.

"Hey, Dad—is that Kilimanjaro?"

Morgan Atterbury put aside his three-day-old copy of *The Guardian* and took off his reading glasses. In the front of the VIP compartment of the plane, which belonged to the Republic of Tanzania, a typewriter was clacking. Ron Burgess, Morgan's senior administrative assistant at D.O.D., an indispensable man even when the secretary took a brief holiday, was making the best of the unorthodox and (he probably thought) tacky arrangements. In Tanzania, working with the small U.S. embassy staff, Ron would have to establish a rapid communications link with the Pentagon, to keep Morgan informed whenever the brass decided something important was breaking around the world. Ron was bent over his machine like a nearsighted stork in a fishpool, typing with three fingers. The advent of some spectacular scenery outside intrigued him not at all.

Morgan smiled and crossed the wide aisle. His son's nose was almost against the window. Morgan leaned down to have a look for himself.

What he saw was rare: the high glaciers of Kilimanjaro, cloudless, flame-edged peaks fully exposed against a cobalt-blue sky. There was not another mountain in sight. Kilimanjaro stood alone, eternally in snow, just three degrees south of the equator.

"That's it, Len. I've never seen it so clearly at this time of the year. Usually it's raining. But they haven't had a good rain here in months. The drought's almost as bad as it was in 'sixty-one."

While the plane curved around the hard, broken, basaltic eastern flank of Mawenzi, it began bucketing slightly in turbulent air. Morgan held on to the back of his son's seat and saw a haze near the summit of the famous, often-photographed center peak, which was Kibo, the only one of the three volcanoes considered to be active. Fumarole gases were common in the caldera, but seldom was there enough of the escaped gas to be visible from any distance.

And he noticed something else that was out of the ordinary: Water apparently was running off the glaciers, twisting in numerous flashing streams through the rocky alpine desert between Kibo and Mawenzi peaks and the montane forest below. A prolonged absence of clouds might have resulted in the runoff as the sun's rays, unoccluded, struck the glaciers day after day.

"You have to see it from up here to appreciate how big it is," Morgan said. "The base of the mountain covers an area of fifteen hundred square miles."

"How much is that?"

"Oh, about four times the size of Los Angeles."

"Dad, did you ever climb it?"

"A long time ago."

"Can we climb it while we're here?"

Len turned his face eagerly toward his father; and Morgan was sadly stunned, as he often was, by the sight of the boy's opalescent right eye. It lay, beneath a dark and drooping lid, like a dead, waxen lake congested with dreams; all of Len's dreams of wholeness.

He was sixteen, the youngest of Morgan's three children, and the most athletic. Two years ago on a Boy Scout outing in the White Mountains of New Hampshire, he had fallen a long way down a nearly vertical slope. After three months in a coma he recovered slowly from the extensive brain damage he'd suffered. He could just manage to walk now without the aid of his leg brace, which he hated. His right hand was frozen shut, probably forever. The doctors had said he could improve only so much through willpower. But Len was determined to walk without limping, then to run, then to win all the races that he ran.

"You don't think I could make it," he said flatly, when Morgan was slow to answer.

"If we had the time I know you'd make it. But the climb takes about five days, up and back. We'll just be at Chanvai long enough to hop over to Serengeti for a day. I told Jumbe you wanted to see lions. Someday we'll come back for a real vacation."

Len nodded; he was stubborn but not argumentative. He turned and eyed Kilimanjaro again. They were lower, nearer. There was a vivid green belt of cultivation and hardwood forest; he thought he saw a herd of elephants, black as raisins in a clearing. He gazed up again at the austere peak, sizing up the mountain, filing away the challenge it afforded.

"Does Jumbe have any children?"

"He had two sons. But they were killed fighting in a guerrilla action in Rhodesia several years ago."

Len nodded, still absorbed by the view. The plane shuddered again as if in a crosswind. The pilot made a right rudder correction, then the landing gear rumbled down. One of the flight attendants, elegant and ebony, slender as bone, entered the compartment.

"Please preparing now for arrival, Mr. Secretary."

"Thank you, Adami."

She turned on the closed-circuit TV for Len; it gave him a pilot's-eye view of the approach, over the greenish-yellow plain, to Kilimanjaro International Airport.

"*Ashante,*" he murmured. During the long and tedious flight from Saudi Arabia, Adami had taught him about twenty words and a few phrases in Swahili. His gaze returned to the mountain as she reached down to buckle his seatbelt for him.

"You are hearing about the famous *chui*—the leopard?"

Len nodded again; lately he'd been reading Hemingway's stories.

"I'd sure like to see it. Is it still there? Frozen just like new?"

"*Laba,*" she said, shrugging. Perhaps. "There is another legend of Kilimanjaro. Incredibly interesting, I think. Concerning the son of Solomon and Sheba, you are knowing about them? His name Menelik, Ethiopian, they buried him in the crater of Kibo with his fabulous treasure. Buried also his ring with the seal of Solomon. Oh, many years since. If one is black, like you and I, and fortunate to find the ring of Solomon, the wise ring as they say, putting it on your finger is also making you wise, a king of men."

She looked from Len's face to the dense purpling folds of the great mountain.

"*Ni nzuri kama nini*—meaning how beautiful. Our national symbol. All around the world, peoples knowing Kilimanjaro. Welcome to our beautiful land, and being happy as long as you are staying." Adami flashed a big shy smile at Morgan too, and retreated.

Ron Burgess had packed up his typewriter. Morgan picked up the folded *Guardian* again, but out of the corner of his eye he saw a dark spearpoint of fighter-interceptor aircraft thrusting upward from the end of the single long runway at the airport. He knew at a glance exactly what they were: MiG-21 fighter-interceptors, NATO designation Fishbed. They had a combat radius of 350 miles and they were part of the small but potent Tanzanian People's Defense Force Air Wing. More than likely the fighters were copies built in China, and were being flown by Chinese pilots. Morgan wondered where they were off to: They didn't have the range to be effective in the small but serious border war Jumbe Kinyati had been waging with the neighboring state of Zambia.

Or, perhaps, they were airborne now to put on some show of welcome for the United States Secretary of Defense, to politicize an occasion which Morgan had tried very hard to keep on a personal, friendship level.

Morgan felt like groaning. He'd had problems trying to explain his sudden change of plans to the members of the small press corps that had accompanied him to Riyadh. Nothing of great interest had happened at the conferences. The Arabs had been as rude as they dared. The newsmen were bored and surly from the desert heat and no one had brought enough liquor along. They sensed something news-worthy and thought that, as usual, they were being lied to. Bill Bowers, Pentagon correspondent for *The New York Times*, had been irritatingly persistent.

*Mr. Secretary, isn't there a connection between Jumbe's recent erratic behavior and your decision to pay him a visit at this time?*

*I wasn't aware that he'd been behaving erratically.*

*Out of character, then. He invaded Zambia, and he's refused to meet with a mediation team from the O.A.U.*

*That's properly a question of diplomacy, and because I'm not in possession of all the facts I wouldn't*

*want to comment. Bill, Jumbe and I were friends be-
fore Jamhuri. It's been too long between visits. When
he heard I was in Riyadh he invited me down for a
long weekend, and I was delighted to accept. I welcome the opportunity to show my son a little of Africa.*

*Do you plan serious political discussions with
Jumbe? He can hardly avoid asking your advice about
the war—*

*Let me repeat, this is not an official visit. But we're
both statesmen, and Jumbe loves a good debate.*

*Nowadays instead of debating, he seems to be more
fond of taking provocative stances. "Peace does not
come except by the point of a sword." He was talking
about apartheid. You've read the* Guardian *interview?*

*No, I haven't had the opportunity.*

But too much of his conversation with Jumbe had
been cause for lingering concern: The President, who
spoke English well, retained his Cambridgian elo-
quence but lapsed into stressful pauses and seemed
muffled by sorrow.

"I appeal to you, Morgan. In the course of events it
may well be our last opportunity to see each other."

"Jumbe, that sounds ominous. You're not sick?"

"My days are filled with sickness . . . the educated
African's malaise, an intellectual pox that disfigures
while we deliberate, in one quarrelsome council after
another, on the fate of our continent."

"I don't understand."

"Morgan, I've been too good a student of prehistory, the patient unfolding of epochs, and a dull student of my own tinderflash times. I've learned terrifying lessons of statecraft that unfortunately . . . I may
lack the time to apply. But that's another matter. It's
our friendship that most matters at this hour. You
can't imagine my joy at hearing your voice again. I'm
at Chanvai for the weekend. Say you'll come."

His voice faded down the daylong distance, becoming indistinct. Morgan wasn't sure he heard him correctly:

"Perhaps, in passing, I can be of some use to you and the nation you serve so ably. Some intelligence has come my way, just out of the blue. I think you'll be grateful."

The 707 settled down on the runway, with only a mild thump, and the engines braked thunderously. Morgan quickly read through the last paragraphs of *The Guardian*'s interview with Jumbe Kinyati.

He sits on the verandah of the rambling but unpretentious estate house in Chanvai, where he now spends most of his time, smoking an old Meerschaum pipe and gazing across one of the world's loveliest lakes at the solitary might of Kilimanjaro. For two decades Jumbe has been acclaimed as a truly progressive leader, unafraid to criticize Africans for their lack of vision and self-righteousness, adamant in his insistence that what Africa needs today is sound economic planning and creative statesmen, not revolutionaries.

"For my people," Jumbe has said, "Utopia is not to be found in an imitation of European social norms, but in a childhood free of disease, a well-filled belly, and peace of mind."

But peace of mind, and freedom to speak one's mind, are becoming rare in Tanzania. It is known that Jumbe has been shopping for sophisticated weaponry which the Chinese are reluctant or unable to provide. The army and air force have undergone massive buildups. For what purpose? Jumbe speaks of enemies and traitors among the leaders of neighboring states, particularly Zambia, whose president, Hugh Manchere, has advocated a multiracial solution in South Africa. Jumbe is flatly opposed to any such accommodation, and apparently obsessed with the need for what he terms a "final solution."

"There is *no* alternative to the end of white minority rule in South Africa. A negotiated settlement with racist devils is impossible. Economic sanctions will not prevail. Conventional means of revolution, however bloody, cannot succeed. Their government can be removed only by power, an overwhelming, destructive force." Such force, he concedes, black Africans do not possess and are not likely to acquire in the foreseeable—

"Dad, there's a Russian plane—a big one!"

Morgan glanced out the starboard windows as the 707 taxied toward the terminal building. He saw a red star on the tailfin of an Ilyushin-76 supersonic jet transport, which meant it was flown by the Soviet air force and not the civilian airline. The plane was parked well away from the terminal and was under guard, probably by the KGB. It was obvious that someone of importance in the Politburo had arrived in East Africa: another old friend, persuaded to join Jumbe for a quiet weekend in the country?

Ron Burgess swiveled his seat around to face Morgan. He was scowling.

"What the hell is Jumbe up to?"

"Maybe they're here on safari."

"Is something wrong, Dad?"

"No, Len. Unexpected company, that's all."

Morgan was happy that no reporters had tagged along on his "vacation." Since he'd become secretary of defense he'd had a recurring dream. In the dream he would be in the press briefing room at the Pentagon for his weekly conference, facing a hostile audience. At some time during the conference he would become painfully aware that he'd forgotten to put on his pants. His interrogators were never reporters with whom he was familiar; they varied from dream to dream. The questions he heard were always bizarre, unanswerable, despite his best efforts to be prepared. Once he had been questioned by a group of garden-club ladies; they had cursed him most fouly when he displayed an abysmal ignorance of horticulture. Another time he was confronted by chimpanzees who demanded a learned refutation of the tenets of Darwinism while they jumped up and down on their chairs and jabbered insults.

Morgan again felt as if he were about to appear in public without his pants. He went back over his recent conversation with Jumbe, looking for insight, some clue as to what he might expect. Maybe the rumors he'd been hearing were correct. Jumbe, it was said, had gone slowly mad from grief following the death of his sons at the hands of white mercenaries. Morgan anticipated some painful exchanges with his old friend, but he hoped that the weekend could be salvaged, at least for Len's sake.

The male flight attendant hurried through the compartment to spring the forward door open. Colonel Brick McMillen, the pilot of the Air Force backup crew that had flown to Tanzania with Morgan, came yawning out of the cockpit. He was fluent in Mandarin and had been in the right-hand seat much of the way down. The rest of the crew, and the two Defense Department security officers assigned to Morgan, had watched Woody Allen movies in the main cabin.

"That Ilyushin touched down about half an hour ago," he said to Morgan. "Party of ten, the tower says."

"Any idea who?"

"No, sir. Could find out for you. Go over and strike up a conversation with the Soviets."

"I don't think it's too important, Colonel. Thanks for a good flight."

"Captain Lan flew 707s for Singapore Airlines. The Chinese run the air wing here—you don't have to worry about how the aircraft are maintained."

Ron Burgess was standing by the open door as a ground crew pushed a stairway into place. There was a warm dry wind blowing across the Sanya Juu plains; to the west were the green foothills of Mount Meru, the abrupt and broken cinder cone standing clear against the gossamer sunset sky. A small welcoming party, exclusively Americans, was waiting on the tarmac. They were attired informally, in bush greens and khaki.

Ron said in Morgan's ear, "Ambassador and Mrs. Chalmers Lyman. Chalmers' nickname is Buddy. He's thirty-eight, career FSO, M.A. in law and diplomacy from Tufts. He wrote his thesis on bicameralism in the modern Islamic state. They've been out here a year and a half. Her name is Wendy; the family's well fixed. She took a degree in sociology at Barnard, and she has Swahili down cold. The children are Sharan with an 'a' and Justin."

"Ron, you're unconscious," Morgan said, his most lavish compliment.

He went slowly down the shaky steps with Len. Introductions; protocol. In addition to his kids the ambassador had brought along his deputy chief of mission and some staffers. Buddy Lyman had a corrugated shock of blond hair that hung off one side of his head, a gangling, amiable, pop-eyed ugliness that was somehow endearing. Morgan took him aside.

"What's going on at Jumbe's?"

"I don't know, sir; he has about thirty houseguests."

"I thought he'd become reclusive. Are they all politicians?"

"Sort of a mixed bag, I'd say. From scientists to jetsetters."

"What do you know about the Russians who flew in?"

"Wendy and I were already here when the plane arrived, but Dr. Kumenyere kept us all waiting in the terminal while he went out to meet them. They drove off right away in three Mercedes sedans, with a military escort. I didn't get a good look at any of the Russians. By the way, security is very tight in the area, particularly over at Momela Lakes, in the park. Soldiers, roadblocks, checkpoints."

"What do you make of it?"

"My sources aren't doing me much good there, sir. Of course there's a war on, but it's at the other end of the country. There are rumors that because Jumbe has been rattling sabers, the Afrikaners will try to assassinate him."

"Another fly in their butter isn't enough to worry them."

"People seem to think an invasion is imminent. Jumbe has everyone on edge, wondering what comes next."

Morgan scanned the sky; the jet fighters had disappeared.

"How's the war going?"

"Zaire's been rumbling over a gunboat that was shot up on Lake Tanganyika last week; they've flown sorties across the border and threatened to give the Zambians, who have lost most of their fighters, some striking power. Personally I think a few good rains would cool everybody off."

"Who's Dr. Kumenyere?"

"He's head of the Kialamahindi Hospital in Dar,

which is probably the best health care facility in East Africa. Kumenyere is Jumbe's personal physician, closest friend, and his only remaining advisor. No one in government speaks to Jumbe anymore unless Dr. Kumenyere okays it."

Buddy Lyman looked over Morgan's shoulder at an oncoming caravan of automobiles and military vehicles.

"Kumenyere's back."

Morgan glanced around. "What's he like?"

"In the U.S. he'd be landed gentry. His father is a planter in the Moshi area, wealthy even for a Chagga, and they're the most prosperous, ambitious people in the country. There's a strain of Masai in the family; Kumenyere has all the arrogance and emotional insularity of that tribe. One day he'll be impossible to deal with, the next he's warm and chatty and the best friend you'll ever have. I never know what's on his mind. He's well educated, polyglot, sophisticated. He gets around: New York, Monaco, Gstaad, depending on what's doing. He's wrung a fortune for his hospital out of some very rich people. Wendy says he also has quite a reputation as a lover. One of his mistresses was the actress, distinguished theatrical family, you know the one, that dingbat Marxist, there are rumors she's had a child by him."

The three cars slowed as they came nearer; the party of American diplomats closed ranks and Morgan turned to face his reception committee. A black chauffeur stopped the lead Mercedes with a little grab of the brakes and shot out from behind the wheel to open the rear door.

Dr. Robeson Kumenyere was sitting back crosswise on the seat of the air-conditioned car, talking on a mobile telephone, long legs overlapping at the ankles; an index finger tapped the receiver of the white telephone as he murmured in a voice too low to be overheard. He gave no sign that he was observed, anticipated. He wore French sunglasses, a medium-gray Savile Row suit, black Bally loafers.

The chauffeur reached into his pocket for a handkerchief and rubbed a still-moist bird dropping from the roof. The men in the other cars, apparently bodyguards, didn't budge. Morgan, treated to cool air from the interior, waited for the better part of three minutes with nothing to dwell on but the doctor's profile: the graceful neck; high, Nilotic cheekbones; and a straight-bridged nose which gave him an air of noble distinction.

Kumenyere finished his conversation with a rich chuckle and hung up. He unwound from the car and took off his expensive sunglasses, hanging them by an earpiece from the breast pocket of his jacket.

He stood tall and relaxed in front of the Americans, a slight, amiable smile on his face. He was one of those lithe and physically savvy men whose every move seems choreographed. He had a tendency to look aslant at everyone, an attitude of lazy hauteur that had its charms because his sable eyes seemed incapable of hard focus or harsh judgment; they looked instead perversely enchanted.

Lyman presented Morgan; he and Kumenyere exchanged an elaborate African greeting, handshakes doubled by wristlocks. There was power in the doctor's grip; his hands were almost as long as cricket bats.

"Jumbe is so pleased you could join him," Kumenyere concluded. He mumbled his English as if he were unsure of the language, or not fond of speaking it. He bent graciously to take Len's hand, composed a welcome in Swahili.

"Mr. Secretary! Mr. Ambassador!"

Morgan looked around. A tall young Englishman

with a petite blond girl in hand was bearing down on them across an empty stretch of tarmac, the girl jogging to keep up with his long strides. He looked grim and anxious. The girl was frightened. Kumenyere glanced up at the approaching pair, frowned, looked over his shoulder at one of the cars filled with bodyguards. Immediately there were black men with impressive guns all over the place.

The English boy stopped, intimidated, and looked imploringly at Morgan.

"You're Mr. Atterbury, aren't you? I'm Tobias Chapman and this is Sunni Babcock."

"My father is Blitz Babcock," the girl said in a high strained voice. "I know you've met him in Washington."

"Oh, yes," Morgan said, and Chalmers Lyman nodded. At least the name was familiar. The family had money. Babcock was a horseman or yachtsman or something, and he'd held a minor post in the previous administration.

Kumenyere spoke, angrily, in a low voice to one of the bodyguards.

"No, just a moment," Morgan said firmly. "It's all right." He smiled at Sunni Babcock, who was very pretty and probably still in her teens, young enough to have a trace of acne around her nose. She and the boy leaned against each other, breathing hard. "Can I help you?"

"It concerns my father," the boy said quickly. "Chips Chapman. He's been missing for quite a long time, and I've been trying to find him, you see. But it's very difficult, there's almost no official cooperation—"

"I know what this about," Kumenyere said to Morgan. He was no longer angry, and he gestured nonchalantly at his guards for a less conspicuous show of weapons. "But I regret that we haven't the time.

Jumbe will be very annoyed if we're late. Let me have a word with them, Mr. Secretary."

He approached Toby Chapman and Sunni Babcock and spoke to them in tones too low for Morgan to overhear. He was pleasant and diplomatic. Toby Chapman was rigid, the girl near tears. They both tried to catch Morgan's eye again, but Kumenyere put his arms around them and smoothly walked them away from the official party, toward the terminal building.

"What's going on?" Morgan asked Lyman.

The ambassador seemed embarrassed not to know. "Chapman, Chapman," he muttered. "I just can't recall the name offhand."

"Those kids are pretty upset. Try to find out what the story is, and see if there's anything we can do."

Kumenyere returned within five minutes, smiled apologetically, and gestured to indicate that the situation was under control. But he offered no explanations.

Almost immediately they were on the road to Chanvai, flashing through those moments when the day is precisely divided into dark and light, earth and sky. They passed villages where the markets were closing down for the night. Domestic fowl, goats, pigs, and children fled from the scream of sirens. But the open road seemed miraculously empty of all other traffic, including motor scooters and bicycles, which might have slowed them down.

Len, his face to the window in the backseat of the Mercedes, identified the nubby tall heads of giraffes communing in a circle of sky, upthrust as if to drink from the dwindling lake of light. In the front seat Kumenyere smiled at the boy's enthusiasm and straightened his impeccable shirt cuffs.

"Jumbe tells me he hasn't been feeling well," Morgan said.

Kumenyere allowed the possibility with a little nod.

"He's still a sorrowing man. Heartsick. His own blood runs thin and cold because of the wanton slaughter of his sons. I do what I can."

"But apparently Jumbe's in a mood for company."

"It's his birthday," Kumenyere said, as if he were surprised that this hadn't been mentioned. But there was a glint of sly humor in his eyes.

"I thought Jumbe wasn't sure what day he was born."

"The anniversary of his coming into this world is of no significance. Rather we observe, in this season of renewal, an important passage to an advanced age grade—a cultural milestone in Jumbe's evolution, in this life and beyond."

Len looked away from the window. "I read about rites of passage in *Facing Mount Kenya.*"

Kumenyere smiled approvingly. It was obvious that he liked Len, and was sensitive to the courage that had enabled him to ignore depressing handicaps.

"Jomo Kenyatta wrote about the Kikuyu, with which many tribes, including my own, have a blood relationship. Among the people of the Umba, Jumbe's tribe, to learn the lessons of life is to be reborn each time. When one joins the ranks of the most respected elders, he must teach the hard and often punishing lessons of life to the less enlightened, so that after earthly death he may justify, before the tribunal of his ancestors, the continuing existence of his soul."

Morgan said, "Jumbe long ago put the ways of the tribe behind him. And he was raised a Christian."

"As a leader of government he is most sensibly opposed to tribal factionalism, an evil which in its worst form can result in another Biafra. As for Christianity— Jumbe will always acknowledge his small debt to the White Fathers. But his roots are deep in this earth, African earth, which the gangsters of the Transvaal defile by their continuing presence here."

"His grief over his sons and over the war is understandable. But nothing good can come of escalating the war by attempting to beat his few plowshares into spears."

"It would depend on the size of the spear, would it not?" Kumenyere said, with a slight rolling of the eyes and a glint of megalomania. Morgan wished he knew more about the intimate relationship of Jumbe and the doctor.

"I came mainly for the fishing and not polemics; if there's going to be a celebration, then tonight I hope I'll be able to toast Jumbe's statesmanship as well as his wisdom. Of course I couldn't help noticing that other eminent guests have arrived."

"Yes," Kumenyere said, too carelessly. "Marshal Nikolaiev concluded a round of talks with our Libyan friends and allies in time to be with us on this splendid occasion. Do you know him?"

"Not personally," Morgan replied, containing his astonishment. What lure had Jumbe used to coax this aging Russian hawk to a perch on his wrist? Victor Kirillovich Nikolaiev was a much older man than Morgan, and the Soviet Minister of Defense. He was not given to lingering unnecessarily beyond the borders of his own country. "I didn't know Jumbe was acquainted with Marshal Nikolaiev. His ministry doesn't have anything to do with the Third World nations."

The driver of the Mercedes braked hard and swerved to miss a striped gazelle bounding out of wilted grass beside the tarmac road. Kumenyere gave him a loud tongue-lashing, conveniently forgetting what he and Morgan had been talking about. He then began a conversation with Len about the wildlife of Tanzania. Like many of his countrymen, he thought there were too many protected animals in a nation that could not raise enough food for its people. Len argued spiritedly for even more conservation.

Morgan settled back to do some thinking. He felt sad, because Jumbe had compromised their friendship to get him here; apparently he no longer cared what Morgan thought. What was Jumbe after? Weapons, obviously, to implement his obsession. He wanted rockets, in a year when three quarters of a million of his people were on famine relief, and the world was in a deepening recession which had everyone anxious. Morgan assumed that Jumbe's traditional allies, the Chinese, who had already pumped nearly a billion dollars into East Africa, refused to dig any deeper.

The only thing Morgan didn't understand was why someone of Victor Kirillovich Nikolaiev's status would spend even five minutes humoring Jumbe. It made him more than a little uneasy.

They came to a crossroads, where Morgan observed soldiers and armored vehicles. Cars and trucks were backed up in a long line, parking lights like the low amber eyes of supplicants, waiting for them to pass. The caravan entered Arusha National Park and proceeded around the misty wetlands of Momela Lakes, a prime bird sanctuary now much reduced in size in a dry year. Morgan regretted that it was too dark for more than a glimpse of ponds—so shallow they were little more than floating gardens—which served as havens for hippos and moonlighting elephants. They drove slowly past a clifflike herd standing very near the road in a glade of papyrus, and even Kumenyere fell silent out of respect for their power. But the beasts seemed indifferent to the motorcade; their ears were flared like antennae to trap the brilliant chatter of the stars.

The road became a narrow track into the foothills beneath Meru, a region of pale-green ghost forests.

The windless air held the scents of wild orange and pepper trees, then pesticide—a tank truck operated by the Mosquito Control had just finished spraying.

In a clearing between hills the lights of the Chanvai estate blazed. There was a stout gate and more soldiers, about half of them (Kumenyere said) Somali and Asian mercenaries. A big sixteen-passenger Sikorsky helicopter in Tanzania's colors sat on a landing pad.

Well behind the main house there were a dozen modern bungalows, like the cottage colony of a luxury hotel, each secluded by plantings: bougainvillaea, flame trees, and frangipani. All of the paths were well lighted. At the bungalow assigned to Morgan three Sikh houseboys were waiting. So was a curious mongoose, taking time off from viper patrol. The animal chittered ecstatically when Len spoke to it in Swahili. They heard music in the main house, exuberant calypso rhythms, and laughter. It was now too cool for shirt sleeves.

While Morgan and Len were changing clothes, Ron Burgess glided up to the bungalow in an electric cart. He'd brought a handsomely bound program for the evening, and a guest list.

"Any press on hand?" Morgan asked.

"No, Jumbe's secretary was adamant about that. Here's a plan of the property Laki gave me. The Russians are billeted in this bungalow, the largest one, behind the north wing of the house. There's a lot of loud talk and some arguing going on."

"They must not know any more than we do."

"We have a radio link with the communications room at the embassy. The radio's in my quarters, and one of the embassy staffers is monitoring for me. Speaking of communications—" Ron laughed. "Laki told me that telephone in Kumenyere's Mercedes isn't hooked up to anything. He was just chatting to himself, putting on a show for us."

"Are we going to get anything to eat?" Len said with a sigh.

"Dinner's promptly at nine, East African-Indian cuisine. It'll be followed by various entertainments, including a trip to a hide in the park for a look at leopards feeding."

"Leopards! Can *I* go, Dad?"

"Sure. We'll all go."

Ron shook his head. "Sorry, sir. Jumbe's scheduled a colloquium at eleven for the VIPs."

"Attendance required, I assume. Well, it's his party."

"Most of the men have their wives with them. Laki says they've been here a week. They appear to be having a terrific time. But Jumbe's made himself scarce. There's one peculiar thing: No one from the Tanzanian parliament is here. And Jumbe didn't invite representatives from other African governments. But these days he's not getting along with many of them."

Ron went over the list with Morgan; he had already made copious notations in the margins.

"Damon Paul. He's the Fifth Avenue jeweler, and one of the world's authorities on gemstones. Lukas Zollner. Swiss mathematician and Nobel prize winner. Maurizio Ambetti, Italian physicist and Nobel prize winner. There are three other mathematicians, almost as eminent as Zollner, on the list. Dr. Saul Markey is a crystallographer. Alex Kachurdian is an epigrapher and etymologist—"

"What?" Len said, laughing.

"Epigraphy is the study of ancient inscriptions; I don't know what the other means, but it may have something to do with dead languages." Ron made a circle on the list, isolating a name. "I'm really curious about this man's presence. Henry Landreth, British theoretical physicist."

"I seem to be in fast company," Morgan said. "Does he have a Nobel too?"

"He should own one by now. But he's lucky he doesn't have a prison record instead."

"How's that?"

"I checked him out with the press officer at the British Embassy. Landreth was Britain's top nuclear theoretician after World War Two. He worked at Harwell on some top-secret research involving neutron beams. He was a protégé of Klaus Fuchs and Dr. Bruno Pontecorvo, both of whom were spies. They gave the Russians secrets that put them in the nuclear club years before they would have made it on their own. Fuchs went to prison; Pontecorvo defected to Moscow. Landreth was in his mid-thirties then, approaching the height of his powers. He was accused of helping Fuchs feed information to the NKVD officer who was running Fuchs. Landreth claimed he was unaware that he was being used as a go-between, or that he was handing over vital information to a foreign national. Fuchs backed his story and there wasn't enough evidence to convict. But Landreth had a muddled history of Communist sympathies during his post-grad career at London University in the thirties. The U.K. press tarred him with the Commie brush. He was banned forever from working at sensitive installations, which effectively ended his career. He's living in Tanzania now, but he doesn't teach. He has some connection with the government, a minor post in the Department of Antiquities."

"Okay," Morgan said. "Let's go mingle."

The main house consisted of two one-story wings with a large kitchen in the rear and a screened verandah with the best view of the seven lakes. Most of the guests, wearing tropical resort clothes and light sweaters, were on the verandah. The Russians hadn't shown up yet. The furnishings ran to bamboo and floral prints, sisal mats on the concrete floors. There were vivid paintings by East African artists, some Makonde sculptures, but there was not much of Jumbe in evidence, except for a small carved wood bust.

Dr. Kumenyere was acting as host in Jumbe's absence. He had two women with him, a tawny Eurasian bombshell named Nicola, who licked her lips as if she were masturbating, and a satin-finish Masai country girl who wore an exquisite *shuka* and heavy gold plugs in her enlarged earlobes. She was so ill at ease she seemed brittle; her remote eyes were on a level above everyone else's.

Morgan was introduced. The few Americans there looked delighted, as if the party, pleasant enough before, had become a major event in their lives. The European scientists looked him over carefully, and not without suspicion. He was a warlord, overseer of the Pentagon billions, the arms machine they roundly condemned. The Italian Nobel laureate jumped on Morgan right away about some matter of U.S. foreign policy that had offended him.

Morgan easily outmaneuvered Signor Ambetti and took a reading on the mood of the guests, something he had become very good at during his three years in Washington, where the ambience of the "better" parties accurately reflected what was happening in government circles: crisis, scandal, a major policy as yet unannounced, choice backstairs gossip. Someone always knew a secret but was free only to drop hints; inevitably there was more suppressed excitement than in children the night before Christmas.

And this was the tone of Jumbe's party. They were all waiting for the best Christmas ever. But if anyone talked about what he knew, even to another initiate,

Santa Claus would pop back up the chimney in a twinkling.

Morgan accepted a gin and tonic from a houseboy and tried to find out why certain guests were enjoying Jumbe's hospitality.

Damon Paul was a dapper man with crisped blond hair and a high color from his week of exposure to the African sun. He was a guest, he said, of Tanzania's Gemstone Council. The country was a consistent but not high-volume producer of diamonds. It was all a matter of Kimberlite formations, or pipes, he explained. These fossil volcanoes were the principal source of natural diamonds. South Africa was particularly well endowed with large and economically important pipes. Was Jumbe interested in gemstones? Damon Paul's color deepened, as if from a sudden pleasurable surge of blood pressure. His eyes grew softly introspective. He smiled and shook his head. Jumbe, he said, knew a great deal about geology, but he had very little interest in personal ornamentation.

Henry Landreth, physicist and traitor, occupied a basket chair with a young and lovely black girl in a flowered *kanga*. From time to time she stroked the back of his wrist with an insinuating finger. Landreth appeared to be in his mid-sixties. He drank pink gin, like an old colonialist. He had no commerce with his fellow scientists; no one dropped by his corner to talk shop. His was a deadpan face with eyes like drops of tar, too much hair growing wild in the wrong places: above his eyes, in the ears. He smoked a cigarette fiercely, eyes narrowing to slits, as if this pleasure had been forbidden and he was making the most of his defiance.

He talked to Morgan with reluctance. He had not done any work in his field for many years. Retired. Yes, he *had* kept up with developments. But he was rather more interested in archaeology nowadays.

Were there any significant ruins in Tanzania?

"Well, if you're fascinated by digs, you must pop over to Engaruka for the day. Nyshuri, dear girl, would you mind terribly freshening my gin for me? There's a love."

And still Jumbe was missing.

Dinner was served, buffet style, at which point Marshal Victor Kirillovich Nikolaiev and his party arrived en masse, creating the kind of circusy stir all Russians take delight in. Kumenyere's relief at seeing them was evident.

The Soviet Minister of Defense, who was wearing a business suit too heavy for the climate, surveyed the dining room and caught Morgan's eye. He seemed to care about no one else who might be there. He brushed Kumenyere aside, walked over to Morgan and, with a sudden happy smile, embraced him. He was a Georgian, short, but with a weight lifter's torso and strength. He had to reach up to get an arm around Morgan's shoulders.

"Mr. Secretary, no one is tell me about you until I'm here. What unexpected pleasure!"

Morgan replied in kind; they shook hands and embraced again. They had never met; but the dossiers, with photographs, which each man had on the other were detailed and up-to-date. They could have chatted for hours on a quasi-intimate basis. Morgan observed that Nikolaiev continued to dye his hair black. His health seemed generally good, although he was a heavy breather and had lost an eye to diabetes three years ago. He still drank and smoked Turkish cigarettes and was fond of startling strangers at private functions by suddenly shrieking with laughter and stubbing out a lighted cigarette on the surface of the glass eye. Aside from his social idiosyncrasies he was a shrewd, dangerous man, the highest-ranking Stalinist in a country where many people still yearned for a return to the good old days. He was known in some circles as the Dracula of Katyn, for certain infamous acts of butchery committed during World War Two.

Nikolaiev waved his interpreter away from them; he had learned his English, heavily laced with G.I. scatology, in Berlin in 'forty-five and 'forty-six, and he could cope with six other languages. The calypso music had stopped. From outside came the nerve-prickling squall of an animal. Morgan and the Russian exchanged looks of mutual perplexity. Nikolaiev seemed uneasy in the equatorial environment. He squeezed Morgan's arm and drew him closer, spoke confidentially.

"What do you think of that man?" he said, referring to Kumenyere.

"I hardly know him."

"But you're of the same color, like two coons."

Morgan cleared his throat. "We're black," he explained with a tactful smile. "That doesn't make us lodge brothers, like the Benevolent and Protective Order of Elks. To call someone of our race a 'coon' is a form of insult."

Nikolaiev nodded. "Okay. That's not coon, it's *black*. I want to remember that. But let's get serious. What's the reason you're doing here?"

"I came for reasons of friendship. Jumbe invited me for the weekend, and it's been a long time since I've seen him. How well do you know Jumbe?"

"So-so. Meeting him on a state visit to Moscow. Two, three years ago. That's all." He slipped his arm around Morgan's waist and walked him toward the buffet. "Okay, my friend," he said, loudly enough for all to hear. "This looks good chow from smelling it. But not for me. Special diet I'm eating, my own chef daily. We will see each others. Later. For very big and important talk." He chuckled at the absurdity of this impromptu summit. "I'm telling you all my bullshit and you're telling me yours."

There was a total silence. Out of the corner of his eye Morgan saw the expression of horror on the face of Nikolaiev's interpreter.

Morgan laughed. Everyone else laughed too. Nikolaiev roared the loudest, until tears ran from his good eye.

At a few minutes before eleven o'clock Morgan, Nikolaiev, his interpreter, whose name was Boris, and eight other men gathered in the conference room at Chanvai.

A stone hearth with a crackling fire took up one end of the room. There was an area like a conversation pit, ringed with metal patio chairs cushioned and draped with zebra skins. In the center of the ring stood a table, a six-foot oval of solid onyx with veins of orange and rust and white on a massive, beautifully gnarled mahogany stump polished and artificially petrified to resist the borer beetles. The louvered windows in one wall were open; the night droned and screeched outside. Rhinoceros beetles whacked against the screens. The flag of Tanzania was displayed on the wall opposite the windows, a yellow-edged black bar dividing diagonally a field of sea blue and light green.

Each chair had a name on it. Houseboys served drinks to those men who were still in the mood, or cups of the strong, locally grown coffee. The lights in the room had been dimmed to the approximate number of footcandles afforded by the firelight. After a full evening of social discourse none of the men were very talkative, and a few seemed edgy with nerves. They tried to get comfortable, listened to the bats stirring under the roof and glanced expectantly at the pair of doors to the room.

Dr. Kumenyere entered, carrying an attaché case and two gold, leather-bound notebooks under his arm. He stood aside for Jumbe Kinyati, who followed him with his great old head bent at what seemed to Morgan an alarming angle. He had a black wood staff in one hand. He was wearing a plain red-ochre *skuka* and a strip of leopard or cheetah pelt that was bound around his forehead like a sweatband. Morgan had never seen Jumbe when he wasn't wearing a western-style business suit, usually with a white shirt open at the throat; frequently he had also effected a tarboosh, as a gesture of solidarity with the Muslims of Zanzibar.

His feet were in sandals that softly slapped the concrete floor. He took his place at the head of the table, where there was no chair, and stood contemplatively with his fingertips pressing down on the onyx. He didn't look at the assembly. Kumenyere placed the two fat loose-leaf notebooks and the case near Jumbe, and went to close the windows. Jumbe seemed to tremble as the louvers snapped shut.

"Good evening," Jumbe said. His voice gained strength as he drew a deep breath and raised his head slowly. In Africa the buffalo, *nyati*, and not the lion, is the most respected of all the animals, for its speed and power and unpredictability. Jumbe's head was, unmistakably, the head of a buffalo, with even the suggestion of horns in the way his hair grew back over his ears from a kind of tough, wiry gray pompadour. For an African he had small eyes. They were yellow as egg yolk, and widely spaced. His face was angular, narrowing to a clump of gray beard. His massive shoulders were rounded, and there was a hump between them that had grown more prominent with the years. Even in illness—it was obvious Jumbe was not well—he continued to be impressive.

"To my friends Morgan Atterbury and Victor Kirillovich Nikolaiev, welcome. I regret I haven't had the opportunity to be with you before." Now he looked at the other faces around the table. "Much of what I am about to relate is already known to the majority, but I would like to bring our visitors from America and the U.S.S.R. up to date."

Kumenyere took a chair beside Jumbe and sat back, folding his hands, surveying the company with his beautiful, imperturbable eyes. The president stood gazing at the fire for a few moments, then continued softly, "Nearly a year ago the Chapman Institute of the University of London applied to our government for the necessary permits to conduct an archaeological investigation along the eastern shore of Lake Tanganyika, where some evidence of a prehistoric burial ground had been found. Permission was granted. An expedition funded by the Institute was mounted, with the famous archaeologists and explorers Chips Chapman and Erika Weller as field directors."

At mention of Chapman's name Morgan glanced at Robeson Kumenyere, recalling the scene at the airport, the impassioned young man who had said he was Chips Chapman's son. His eyes went unacknowledged.

"Their expedition," Jumbe continued, "established a base camp near the designated site in one of the more remote and least accessible areas of Tanzania. There are no roads and few villages in a mountain fastness of some eighteen hundred square miles.

"Shortly after they began their explorations, all radio contact with the camp ceased. After several weeks of silence, government troops were sent into the district to search for the explorers. Remains of the camp were found, but they had all disappeared. We believed that they had set out along the lake in rubber boats to reach otherwise isolated cliffs, and were drowned in one of the frequent storms that strike without warning during the northeast monsoons. Needless to say, areas of Lake Tanganyika teem with crocodile, so the prospect of recovering bodies was dim."

Jumbe paused, to allow Boris the opportunity to catch up in his translation. He apparently wanted to be sure that Marshal Nikolaiev understood him perfectly.

"How large was the party of explorers?" Morgan asked.

"More than thirty, and a score of Tanzanian laborers and service staff."

"Surely some of them would have remained in camp."

"As it turned out," Jumbe said, smiling at Morgan, "our assumptions concerning the fate of the explorers were wrong. They had seemingly vanished from the earth, but they were alive and well. Just six weeks ago, following months of silence, we learned what had happened to them."

"I don't remember reading about any of this," Morgan said. "An expedition of that size, out of touch with the world for several months? Every bureau chief in East Africa must have been nodding off on the job."

"The expedition was conceived and conducted with utmost care, to guard against unwanted advance publicity. For reasons I think will be evident. The Chapman/Weller discovery is of awesome proportions, unprecedented. They have found the burial place, or Catacombs, of the elders of an advanced civilization that flourished on this continent ten thousand years ago, a civilization that left a complete record of its one-thousand-year history for modern man to study."

"Fascinating," Morgan murmured, looking at the faces of the other men.

Most of them were rapt, already true believers.

Henry Landreth's black eyes reflected firelight, his face was impassive, but his foot nervously tapped the floor. Nikolaiev sat back with his arms folded, wheezing. Morgan was familiar with his expression, a glazed stoicism common to all Russians who think they are in for a healthy dose of *vranyo*, or snake oil.

Kumenyere had left his chair to lower the already dim lights in the room. Jumbe complacently absorbed the skepticism of Morgan and Nikolaiev. Then he pulled the attaché case slowly toward him and unlocked it with shaking fingers.

"Here is a part of that record," he said.

The case was opened; two spotlights in the rafters lanced down.

The case contained a two-inch-thick block of Lucite. Mounted in the Lucite were twenty-four gemstones, egg shaped, red as rubys, each cut into what seemed to be a hundred dazzling facets, like those of a geodesic dome.

The beauty of their combined fire stunned everyone. Morgan's throat dried up; he couldn't look anywhere else. Jumbe moved the case inchwise, turning it to the left and then to the right. Within the icy redness blazed other colors, equally intense: lavender; pink; a shade of gorgeous, lethal blue, like a poisoned sea. Jumbe selected one of the stones and held it between yellow-horned fingers in the dark, where it had its own brilliance, the distant violence of an exploding star.

"They are red diamonds," Jumbe said, looking at Morgan and then at Nikolaiev. "The rarest of the precious stones known to man. Those few previously discovered are far inferior to the stones you see here. Each of the bloodstones, as we have come to call them, weighs approximately fifty carats. The odds against more than one turning up in the course of centuries is astronomical. Yet the bloodstones you see are part of a store of hundreds, preserved in the Catacombs, along with the crystal tombs of ancient men. A priestly caste of yellow men, with straight eyes, who were known as the Lords of the Storm."

He selected another of the bloodstones, passed one to Morgan and one to Nikolaiev. Two more spotlights shone down for their benefit as they examined the stones.

"Damon Paul will vouch for their authenticity," Jumbe said.

On close inspection Morgan discovered that the facets had been etched, almost microscopically, with some kind of writing.

Damon Paul got up and stood beside Jumbe.

"In association with Dr. Markey," he said, nodding in the direction of the crystallographer, "I've studied the bloodstones for several days, and run some tests. They're diamonds, absolutely authentic. Some of the stones are less than perfect, but those minor flaws only enhance their beauty. Any one of them, on today's market, is worth in the neighborhood of two and a half million dollars. Even if they were marketed in this quantity, they would be snapped up at extraordinary prices."

"Don't the etchings detract from their value?" Morgan asked.

"Not in the slightest. By the way, it would take a skilled man working for several months to cut and polish a single stone."

"How long would it take to complete the etchings?"

"I can't imagine. I'm sure there's no way to accomplish the work mechanically. One thing you should bear in mind: Only a diamond can cut a diamond."

"What about a laser?"

"There's a possibility. But technically not within *our* means at this time."

"Has anyone deciphered the etchings?"

"Yes," Jumbe said. "The Chapman/Weller expedition spent nearly six months in the Catacombs, sustained in rooms of crystal that were as bright as a meadow beneath a full moon. With the aid of computers they were able to translate the language and interpret the mathematics of the vanished civilization, known as Zan. The stones we have assembled here are etched with hundreds of equations, some of which indicate that their physicists were successful in unifying the forces of electromagnetism and gravity. Dr. Zollner; Dr. Ambetti; their distinguished colleagues—all agree that the ancient people achieved a sophisticated technology, based on quantum mechanics, solid state, and high-energy physics. And their greatest feat, recorded on another cache of diamonds secure in the Catacombs, was FIREKILL."

A few moments of silence; Dr. Zollner looked up from the pipe he was stoking.

"FIREKILL, Jumbe? What is 'FIREKILL'?"

"Forgive me, Dr. Zollner. You and your colleagues were shown only selected bloodstones, for purposes of attribution and to compare certain models by the physicists of Zan with current research. Someday I hope you will have the opportunity to study the full range of achievements recorded on the bloodstones. For now I would like to keep explanations as brief as possible. Let me say that the country of Zan included most of what today is East and Central Africa. Many great cities were built, of which only the ruins of Engaruka and Zimbabwe are extant; other ruins remain to be excavated in the dense forests of Zaire and Mozambique.

"Nearly one hundred centuries ago, the people of Zan were endangered by 'fires from space,' which might have been a periodic meteor shower of great intensity, or the explosion of the large planet that existed where the asteroids now circle the sun. To prevent certain devastation, they devised a shield called FIREKILL, a spatial distortion achieved by combining the forces of electromagnetism and gravity to create unusually strong gravitational fields. A force field, if you will. It was one-hundred-percent effective. This shield, if erected today over an area as large as, let us say, the city of Moscow, U.S.S.R., would serve as a foolproof antimissile, antinuclear device. No explosion that modern man can create will disturb it. The cost is moderate in terms of expenditures necessary to maintain present defensive postures, the technology available. The necessary knowledge—" Jumbe spread his hands like a conjurer over the array of bloodstones.

Zollner chuckled edgily. "Force field! Jumbe, the concept is a total absurdity. Mathematically, the major problem with gauge theory has always been one of infinities . . ."

Almost instantly the physicists were quarreling.

"Not according to the Zurhellen-Dzaluk models, which predict . . ."

"No, no, the interaction cannot be assumed to be manifestations of the same effect . . ."

"But my work in photon stability . . ."

". . . Supergravity . . ."

". . . Acceleration phenomenon . . ."

Only Henry Landreth, Morgan observed, was silent, sitting back aloofly. Morgan glanced from the red diamond in the palm of his hand (which was sweating, although the bloodstone seemed cold) to Nikolaiev. He now had a good idea of the attraction that had been offered to persuade the old soldier to come to Chanvai. Nikolaiev was impatiently trying to follow the arguments of the physicists.

Jumbe had the floor again. "Although I have no background in the physical sciences, I know that much of your work is based on speculation, and is necessarily incomplete. A lifetime of intellectual drudgery may result in two minutes of truly creative insight. The physicists of Zan, whose genius you have acknowledged, had a thousand years in which to develop their theories."

"If they did contrive a viable force field," Morgan said, "we should all be speaking dialects of Zan today."

"The story of the annihilation of the people of Zan is frightening and fascinating; it will be told, in the course of time, but tonight I must hurry on."

"One more question, Jumbe?"

"Yes, Morgan."

"The discovery of these stones, apart from what may or may not be engraved on them, would seem to be an archaeological triumph. The credit, apparently, belongs to Chips Chapman and Erika Weller. Why aren't they with us tonight?"

"The answer is quite obvious," Jumbe said with a placating smile. "The members of the expedition were exhausted from their work in the Catacombs, where they knew no division between day and night. They are now recovering, as honored guests of the Tanzanian government, in a location that must remain undisclosed for now. At their request they will be incommunicado, untroubled by representatives of the media, until they have had time to recover their strength and put all of their valuable data into an acceptable form for presentation to the world's scientific communities."

Almost before he finished speaking, the doors to the conference room burst open, startling the men inside. Somalis and Sikhs in uniforms of pale green and blue filled the hall. They were heavily armed. Their commander, who was carrying a submachine gun, walked in. His finger was on the trigger. With a swagger stick he turned the lights in the room all the way up. His

eyes glittered. He had pox-scarred cheeks and shav-
ings of curly white in his full beard. He crossed the
room to Jumbe and Kumenyere and spoke urgently to
them.

Everyone else was trying to talk at once. Jumbe
turned gravely to his guests, signaling for silence.

"Gentlemen! I deeply regret to tell you that the government of Kenya, in support of the despot Manchere
of Zambia, has declared war on our nation. Their
fighter planes have crossed the border to the north
and inflicted damage on the airport at Sanya Juu.
Chanvai is a likely and immediate target. In order to
insure your protection in this crisis, I must ask you to
accompany my elite guard to a retreat that has been
well fortified for just such an emergency. Your wives
are already on the way." A howl of protest. *"There is
no time to lose,* and your co-operation is very much
appreciated."

The soldiers didn't wait for volunteers. They
seemed well rehearsed. They came in quickly and
cleared the room. They were patient, but firm.

As Morgan rose he felt a hand on his shoulder, and
looked around at Dr. Kumenyere.

"Please be seated, Mr. Secretary," Kumenyere said
softly, pushing him back into the chair. He was strong
enough to make it seem easy. Morgan, thinking of
Len, swallowed the anger that had risen in his throat
and tried to relax.

Nikolaiev was in a fulminating rage as he confronted the commander of the guard. He kept throwing his interpreter aside. His face was the color of
beet soup. He shrieked oaths in Russian as the doors
of the conference room were closed again.

Jumbe said harshly to Boris, "Tell him to take his
seat, or General Timbaroo will shoot out his other
eye."

Timbaroo laughed and, from a distance of seven

feet, pointed the nine-millimeter Ingram machine gun, equipped with a Sionics noise suppressor, with one steady hand at Nikolaiev's face.

Boris didn't have to say another word. Nikolaiev stopped screaming. He looked incredulous. He allowed himself to be gentled back into his chair by Boris. He sat there, chest heaving, sweat pouring down his face. He spoke, quietly and at length, to his interpreter, not taking his eyes off Jumbe.

Boris turned to Jumbe. "Marshal Nikolaiev informs you that if we are all not immediately released and afforded safe conduct to the airport, there will be severe reprisals by the Supreme Soviet."

Jumbe wearily waved his objections aside.

"Tell him that within the hour you will all be safely on your way home.—And you, Morgan, with your son. There is, of course, no war declared or undeclared with Kenya, and no danger to anyone here. I've placed our eminent scientists in protective custody only as a precaution, to keep the great secret of the Catacombs from leaking out until you, representatives of the world's superpowers, have had a chance to act. Now then. Would either of you care for a glass of our excellent Dodoma wine to moisten your palates and settle your nerves?"

Morgan felt the dangerous pulse in his temple slowing down. He opened the hand he had clenched around the bloodstone, and set the stone on the table. He gave it a little spin. It skittered off the onyx and hit the concrete floor. He was more than a little surprised, and apprehensive, when it didn't shatter.

Jumbe understood. He smiled.

"None of this is fancy, Morgan. You are not dreaming. The bloodstone is real, just as Damon Paul said it was. Virtually indestructible. The Lords of the Storm meant to leave records that would endure, in a timeless place. The Catacombs exist. FIREKILL can be a reality too, if you wish it to be."

"You seem to have caught your distinguished guests by surprise, Jumbe. And you aren't a physicist. If FIREKILL exists, who told you about it?"

"Dr. Henry Landreth, who was my official liaison with the Chapman/Weller expedition. As you must know, Dr. Landreth was discredited in his profession for certain indiscretions considered treasonous by the British. But his brilliance was in no way diminished by his poor judgment. On another set of bloodstones, secure in the Catacombs at this moment, is the complete formula for FIREKILL, which Dr. Landreth has translated."

Morgan accepted a glass of wine from Kumenyere. Jumbe faltered and grasped the edge of the table. The doctor hurried to his side, but Jumbe spoke to him harshly in Swahili, turning him away.

He looked again at Morgan, then at Nikolaiev. His eyes were so far back in his head it seemed he might faint. But his voice was strong.

"Must I elaborate on the importance of FIREKILL? It can guarantee invulnerability from nuclear attack. The nation that has this guarantee will surely be preeminent in world affairs for a few years—until the desperate loser devises new and more terrible weapons to circumvent even FIREKILL.

"I offer one of you an opportunity. I care nothing about the ultimate ambitions of superpowers. Africa will endure, as it always has. For the black man. It makes little difference to me which of your nations is the first to build FIREKILL. According to Dr. Landreth, both American and Russian scientists have been at work on a comprehensive nuclear defense. Charged-particle or hydrogen-atom beams are costly and impractical. Other ABM systems have failed. FIREKILL will not fail."

"What price you asking?" the Russian said with a skeptical smile.

"I am not interested in selling the secrets of FIRE-KILL to the highest bidder. In exchange for the formula bloodstones I want mobile nuclear weapons and the men to employ them. Either the Russian Scoundrel or the American Whippersnapper. Ground-launched cruise missiles with terrain-contour-matching guidance systems will also be acceptable, despite their lesser range. You have thirty days from this hour to begin delivery. The FIREKILL bloodstones will be released a few at a time as the weapons systems arrive by air. The key stones, already selected by Dr. Landreth, will be paid when the systems are fully operational. Needless to say, the weapons you give me could not successfully be turned against your own countries, even if I had a motive for doing so."

"Instead you intend to destroy the white government of South Africa," Morgan said.

"Yes, Morgan."

"The result will be a catastrophic loss of human life. Black lives, Jumbe. Have you thought of that?"

"The first shot will be directed into a remote area of the Transvaal—Mount Blouberg would do. The Afrikaner government will have the opportunity to empty Durban before the second shot destroys it. The government of South Africa will then surrender to a coalition government composed of political prisoners from Robben Island and other black leaders now in exile."

"I think you underestimate them."

"You underestimate the panic which the threat of nuclear devastation will cause. Afrikaners will clamor for surrender. But this is not a concern of either of your countries, whose official policies regarding those racists are very well known."

Nikolaiev spoke to his interpreter, who replied: "So

are our policies regarding the dissemination of nuclear weapons."

"What do you have to say, Morgan?" Jumbe asked.

Morgan had another sip of wine. The Sikorsky helicopter was taking off almost directly overhead, and he waited for the noise to fade.

"I think," he said regretfully, "that FIREKILL is a figment of your imagination. And all of this is a hoax—on an unprecedented scale; obviously you've taken infinite pains and invested a great deal of money. But a hoax nonetheless."

Jumbe smiled and serenely picked up a double handful of the brilliant bloodstones. His dark face swarmed in their fabulous light; his eyes turned red as hellfire.

"Can either of you afford to be wrong?"

Morgan, gazing at the stones, felt, as Jumbe intended him to feel, a trickle of doubt. He glanced at Nikolaiev, who sat sweating and grimacing, staring at the hoard of bloodstones.

"The stones may well be an archaeological treasure," Morgan concluded. "As for the rest of it—why not take us to the Catacombs?"

"Yes, we must see Catacombs," the Russian said quickly. "Then we know with our own eyes what you are telling is the truth."

Jumbe shook his head. "A difficult and dangerous trip, even for those who know where they are going. Unfortunately, I have not been able to go myself." He paused in midbreath, as if speared by pain; Kumenyere glanced at his pocket watch and looked concerned. Jumbe lowered his cupped hands and, trembling, replaced the bloodstones one by one in the block of Lucite.

"If you doubt the experts you've heard, or think that their testimony is part of a conspiracy, then choose a sample for your own experts to analyze.

Choose any one stone. But remember: I want the weapons in thirty days."

Jumbe picked up his staff and shuffled slowly out of the room, not looking back. General Timbaroo closed the doors behind Jumbe, then stood with his back to the doors, his submachine gun across his chest.

Kumenyere opened a cabinet, slid out a drawer in which were mounted identical cassette tape recorders. He removed the cassettes and placed them in pockets on the inside covers of the gold leather notebooks. He presented a notebook each to Morgan and Nikolaiev. Morgan found his notebook quite heavy.

"The book contains a complete computerized translation of the language of Zan," he said. "The tape will help your intelligence agencies to conduct voiceprint analyses of our other guests, should you have questions about their identities. When you're ready to leave, you'll be driven directly to the airport by General Timbaroo's men. But take your time, please. Stay as long as you like. Have another glass of wine while you ponder your choice of bloodstones."

Kumenyere smiled indulgently at them and took his leave. Nikolaiev chuckled, mopping his face with a handkerchief.

"Madmen," he said, leaning toward Morgan, tapping his forehead with a blunt finger. "So much craziness we're hearing. Mad, mad! What a situation for meeting you first time, my dear friend." The Russian held out both hands to the glittering bloodstones, an infatuated gesture partly redeemed by the curling of his lip. "What you think, who makes these writings? Ten thousand years ago? Civilizations, like ours? Such lies!"

"There are strong occult and primitive traditions."

This was translated for Nikolaiev. He chuckled again.

"Fairy tales." He heaved himself up from his chair and hovered over the attaché case on the table, touching one of the bloodstones, then another. He put back the one which Jumbe had given him. Suddenly he scooped up a stone at random and turned. He tossed it casually to Morgan, who was startled as he snatched the stone out of the air.

"Taking it. Why not? Some, what's the right word, suckers we are. Little reward for our long travels." He took a jeweler's cloth from the case, selected a diamond for himself, wrapped and stuffed it carelessly into a pocket of his coat. Then he picked up an untouched glass of wine, drank some, made a disbelieving face, and said, pointing to the glass, "Another hoax!"

He came over to pump Morgan's hand. Outside an animal screamed in the night.

"Terrible country," Nikolaiev complained. "Too much sweat. We should both go home before these *chernomazy* shooting and eating us."

Morgan could still hear the Russian's laughter as he went outside with his interpreter to the car that waited to drive them to Kilimanjaro airport.

And then Morgan was alone, faintly warmed by the dying fire, thinking about the diamond in his hand, with a market value (Damon Paul claimed) in the millions of dollars. He wondered if there actually had been a Chapman/Weller expedition. Easy to check it out. He wondered what Marshal V. K. Nikolaiev was really thinking when he pocketed the irresistible bloodstone.

Jumbe's story of FIREKILL was too fantastic to believe, but . . .

Morgan was disturbed by a chill of premonition, of despair, as if some vital exchange had taken place between the bloodstone and his own flesh. He was feeling, not thinking, with the innate arrogance of modern man.

As recently as sixty years ago no one had believed the atom could be split, or that men would reach the moon. Or that the bones of humanlike creatures, three million years old, would be discovered in a gorge called Olduvai, located only a short distance from where he was sitting. Africa yielded its mysteries with numbing slowness. On the banks of the Nile the great pyramids crumbled, riddled by the sandy winds of two thousand years. Once the desert of Egypt had been rich farmland. Was theirs the highest civilization to evolve before Christ? Or could Egypt have been a colony, a satellite state that faltered and died when it lost touch with an even more advanced civilization? If the Hawaiian Islands were abruptly cut off from the rest of the world, their society would disintegrate, in an astonishingly short time, into a primitive archetype. Within two centuries there would be only vague race memories of television, airplanes, neon lights.

He recalled other phenomena he had read about or seen: cave paintings of remote peoples in surprisingly contemporary modes of dress, dry cell batteries resurrected from the furnace-lands of ancient Mesopotamia, the interiors of Egyptian pyramids untainted by the smoke of torches: Either the builders had been able to see perfectly in pitch darkness, or they'd had some source of artificial light.

Morgan went out under the stars to catch his breath, clear his head, scratch an itch of indecision. General Timbaroo was a silent, shadowy presence nearby. The darkness seethed with unseen life, primordial violence was all around. Morgan could make out Kilimanjaro surprisingly well, as a distant snow-field beneath the transiting moon.

Perhaps it was all nonsense. But he was fascinated with the concept of a civilization whose leaders had

built their memorials in the earth and not on it, to
endure for a hundred centuries and then a hundred
more.

*Catacombs.*

Rubbing his fingertips lightly over the facets of the
bloodstone, Morgan could just feel the tiny pictographs etched there. He was overcome with a sense of
imminent danger, the folly of disbelief.

"General Timbaroo?"

The mercenary came briskly forward, three paces,
and clicked his bootheels together.

"Yes, sir!"

"If a car is ready for me, I'd like to start for home
now."

# KINGDOM MISSION

Ivututu, Tanzania
April 29

In the mission hospital Erika Weller worked with a mind-numbing intensity until well after sunset, trying to keep up with the needs of critically ill men and women. She was certain it would not be long before she heard the boots of Colonel Ukumtara's *askari* on the stairs outside. No doubt her punishment for plotting an escape would be mild: an elaborate, scornful dressing down from the colonel himself, then close house arrest during those hours when she couldn't be at the hospital. No community meals. Perhaps she would also be deprived of morning Mass.

Raymond Poincarré had returned just before dusk from the airstrip with many cartons of supplies that had to be unpacked and put away; he'd been busy in the hospital storeroom and hadn't come upstairs for his evening rounds. Her only company, aside from a couple of nurses who were virtually sleep-walking, was Father Varnhalt, who had arrived dutifully after vespers with communion wafers for those patients able to accept them. At least his phonograph had been silent for a while. But the mourning drums of the neighborhood villages had begun, along with the yaps and chortles and bloody howls of jackal and dog baboon in the rocky hills and ravines behind the mission.

The only sound she had been listening for, and hadn't heard, was the engine of the Bonanza as it took off for the return hop over the mountains to Mbeya town.

That was significant. It could mean that Bob Connetta had succeeded in temporarily disabling the plane before Dr. Poincarré arrived. Bob was a twenty-three-year-old graduate student in archaeology, the son of an American colleague of Chips'. The Chapman/Weller expedition had been Bobby's first major venture into the field, and one that would make him famous out of all proportion to his experience. That is, if he lived. She couldn't condemn Chips for having delegated him to sabotage the Bonanza—no one else had the opportunity. But she was worried.

Chips had been fitfully asleep for more than an hour. She replaced his IV bottle, a five-percent dextrose solution in water, and tried to rouse him; but when she spoke he replied deliriously, replaying some yacht race or other he'd been involved in years ago. Erika couldn't cool him down and was worried about his breathing. She wondered if she should insert an endotracheal tube.

Father Varnhalt, wearing a purple-and-white surplice over dust-smudged khakis, was down on one knee, mumbling in Latin at the bedside of another patient. When she turned around, tears squeezing from her eyes, she saw Raymond Poincarré at the door, watching her.

"He's worse," Erika groaned. "It's just consuming him, like a fire in a hollow tree."

"Sometimes it happens that way. Then there's a remission. We'll try more procaine penicillin."

"Useless! Nothing . . . bloody . . . *works*, only the grace of God is going to save the lot of them."

"Erika!"

She struggled to control herself. "Yes. All right. Nothing good's going to come of carrying on, is it?

I'll . . . prepare an injection, or do you want to drip it?"

"Injection," he told her.

Erika opened the pharmaceuticals cabinet and took out the little bottle of penicillin, broke the cellophane pack of a fresh disposable syringe. While Raymond looked at Chips' chart, Erika administered the drug.

The doctor said quietly, not looking at her, "The pilot had a slight mishap on landing."

Erika felt a cold flash of fear. "I hope he wasn't hurt."

"No, it's nothing, really. Flat tire. Of course he hasn't a spare."

"Couldn't he take off with a flat tire?"

"Any competent bush pilot could manage that, even in the dark. The problem seems to be in coming down again. Rather than run the risk of crumping a new airplane and having the government sack him, the pilot has decided to remain until a new tire can be dropped to him in the morning."

"That's . . . sensible."

"I think so. He prefers, naturally, to stay with his aircraft. I let him know there was rather much risk of contracting the fever if he put up at the mission. He'll be uncomfortable, but we'll send supper and a bottle of wine later."

Erika stared at Raymond, wondering just what he was trying to tell her. Apparently he'd arrived too late to prevent Bob Connetta from slashing the Bonanza's tire. Was he now letting her know how hopeless it would be to attempt to steal the plane with the pilot, who was undoubtedly armed, watching over it?

Raymond finished taking Chips' pulse, and made a notation on the chart.

"By the way, Colonel Ukumtara has requested that you take supper with us this evening, at nine o'clock."

"Tell him how genuinely delighted I am, but I'm afraid—"

Raymond glanced up, frowning. "Erika, it isn't a request you can reasonably refuse."

She was about to protest again but another nurse, one of those assigned to the temporary ward in the school building, had come hurriedly upstairs.

"Doctor, can you come? There's a woman they've brought in with a snakebite, she bleeds from the nose already."

Raymond whirled. "Get me antivenin from the storeroom." He hesitated a few moments, looking back at Erika with an unexpected expression: exasperation, helplessness.

"It's vital that you be there," he said, and was gone; Erika heard him running almost heedlessly down the unsafe stairway outside.

Around eight o'clock Erika came to a curious standstill, as if her vital machinery had frozen. Her mind was a void; the simplest task required excruciating concentration. She had pains in her chest and her mouth quivered uncontrollably. Her best friend among the nurses, Alice Sinoyi, dropped by and noticed her distress. Alice led her home and drew a precious hot bath for her, laced with aloe juice and some kind of stinging botanical that made Erika's blood race. Alice spent a half hour soaping Erika, rubbing her down with a sponge, crooning the Sonjo songs of her childhood.

The treatment worked; Erika was revived. After her bath she had an additional mild tonic for the nerves, some Scotch and Fiuggi water, and realized that she could face the coming ordeal with patience if not spirit. She felt clean, lonely, bereft, abstracted. She put on a freshly ironed bush outfit and desert boots, another surgical mask, and went along at a quarter past nine to Colonel Ukumtara's bungalow, still feeling half a step beyond reality.

A woman who had died of fever was being removed from the school building by silent relatives. The body had been rolled in a straw mat, which was covered with black cloths and baobab leaves. A *muganga*, splendid in a stifling, vintage military greatcoat which he wore only on important occasions, walked alongside sprinking herbal medicine on the cloths, an antiseptic barrier between the dead and the living. The faces of the pallbearers, all men, were smeared with clay. They staggered uncertainly with their burden, as if they had drunk a great deal of *pombe*, the hot thick homemade beer of the bush, to steel themselves for this task. In the distance drums and melancholy, high-pitched improvisational songs signaled another wake in progress. There was an odor of burning in the air, fires of purification everywhere. But against all opposition the fever continued to thrive.

Colonel Ukumtara was one of a rare breed, a Masai tamed and assimilated into the contemporary East African culture. Most of the decimated tribe, who in their prime had been aristocratic nomads with cattle, fierce spearmen and hunters of lions, had failed to make even the slightest adjustments to changes in their environment. Ukumtara seemed to have prospered. He enjoyed French wines and disco music on his powerful transoceanic Grundig radio. He was tall, with a rocklike shaved head, but lighter in color than most Masai; a Hamitic, caucasoid strain was apparent in his bloodlines. His habitual expression was one of gaping good humor, but that could be deceptive.

He wore two rows of medals on his blue uniform blouse and a pearl-handled automatic in a sweat-blackened shoulder holster. He had avoided the fever by staying indoors, burning incense, not bathing, and having a daily dose of Sloan's liniment, which he took internally with a bowl of *pombe*.

The atmosphere in his closed-up bungalow, despite the cool temperatures outside, almost knocked Erika over. But the colonel scowled when he saw she was wearing a surgical mask and insisted that she remove it. No one in the house could become infected; to think so was to invite a malignant fate.

She was late, and they had not waited supper. House-boys served Erika goat curry, eland steak, and peas cooked in groundnut oil, along with a glass of a good Bordeaux that had just arrived from Mbeya. Father Varnhalt was also on hand. He was nearly seventy and suffering from bush fever; he had been a long time at the mission. His hands trembled so badly he was forced to eat with his mouth only inches from his plate.

At some point he had surrendered his faith to the unremitting hostility of the natural world—drought, storm, plague, the evil spirits of the forests. He depended now on ritual, the sterile intonations and responses of a dead language, to get him through the day. He reinforced a precarious hold on reality by talking matter-of-factly about the horrors that had driven fellow priests and white sisters mad in their isolated circumstances.

"One day at Mass Father Sylvanus saw his entire congregation turn to animals before his eyes—creatures with long snouts, tufted ears, and the fiery eyes of dragons. They gnashed their teeth at him, and farted obscenely when he tried to speak. This is true. Mother Celeste was bathing in a pool when she looked up and saw the devil sitting on the limb of a fig tree playing with his penis. He ejaculated demon seed into her water; his seed turned into thousands of little biting creatures which tried to tear the chaste white flesh from her bones. Father Xavier Antonio was walking along a path in the Loita when he encountered a giant. One side was hair, the other stone. The giant, whose name was Enenauner, beat on a tree with his club until Father Xavier went deaf from the noise. I know this to be a fact."

Colonel Ukumtara ate heavily, washing down his meal with copious wine. He had gained at least twenty pounds during his idle weeks at the mission, most of it in his belly.

"Your religion is foolish," he said, pointing his bread knife at Father Varnhalt. "The Masai know this. The Bible is too long. There is too much to read. Why should we pray to a man? Men die, and are no longer real. We know this by looking around and seeing that they are not there. The moon and the sun endure. They are real. We see them, every day, in the sky. Evil spirits are real; with our own eyes we see the evil they do. Then pray to the evil spirits who would harm you, so you will not be harmed. Pray for the sun to come up in the morning and cast away the dark where evil hides. This is sensible; this is good. *Your* religion will have us all crazy like you."

"The sun will always rise; it is God's law."

"What if it doesn't? What if there's no light tomorrow, and tomorrow after? Don't you think the evil spirits will be all over us then? Who will you pray to when that happens?"

Father Varnhalt tried to smile at this nonsense, but his emotional and theological resources failed him again. Some horror residing in his head caused a rearrangement of his features. He spilled wine on himself.

Raymond Poincarré sat with his hands in his lap, eyes glazed, his own meal largely untouched. Erika put a steadying hand on Father Varnhalt's arm and glared at Ukumtara, who was too busy eating to take notice of her displeasure. She wondered what would happen if the colonel could have a glimpse of what lay inside the Catacombs, a look at the cat people of Zan with their watchful, mesmerizing eyes. If he didn't faint dead away he might be transformed, temporarily, into a jackal, which was about what he deserved.

Ukumtara suddenly pushed his plate aside, frowning, and poured more wine for himself.

"I don't like eating with you," he said to Father Varnhalt. "You put me in a bad mood. Go along to your own house now."

Father Varnhalt's throat lightened; his eyes swam with tears.

"Will you go with me," he asked Erika, "and see that there's nothing under my bed?"

Ukumtara roared, but his laughter ended in a coughing fit. He got up to change the frequency on his radio, finding Cuban *salsa* on a station in Maputo, Mozambique.

As he was listening he braced himself against the top of the low bookshelf where the radio was, a look of intense concentration in his eyes. He pressed his right hand against his chest. He seemed short of breath. He strained to release a belch. Then his eyes rolled up in his head and he sat down heavily in a chair. He was beaded with sweat.

Raymond looked around at him.

"Is something the matter, Colonel?"

"I'm not feeling well. Indigestion."

"I've told you often, it's no good bolting your food the way you do."

Ukumtara's face was contorted. "Pain . . . here," he panted, still holding his chest.

Raymond raised his eyebrows and got up from the table.

"What sort of pain? As if your chest is being crushed?"

Colonel Ukumtara, now very short of breath, stared at him.

"Yes . . . that's it."

Raymond examined him. The colonel's skin felt clammy.

"Does the pain seem to radiate from your chest? Is there numbness in either arm?"

"What happening . . . I'm sick . . . the fever . . ."

"Erika, would you fetch my medical bag for me? It's just there, in the bedroom—now, Colonel, you must lie down. On the floor. Let me loosen the strap of this shoulder holster. Also I want these boots off."

When he had Ukumtara prostrate with a small pillow under his head, Raymond took his blood pressure and listened to the chambers of his heart. He looked bleakly at Erika. The colonel was moaning with fear.

"You mustn't excite yourself. Your blood pressure is low, your pulse rapid. No, it's not the fever. I suspect you've had a heart attack, how severe I can't say."

"Aieeeeee!"

Raymond held him firmly. "I'm sure we can save you. But you have to do what I tell you and keep calm. Erika, I need from the hospital storeroom sodium bicarbonate, epinephrine, dopamine, and five hundred milligrams of calcium chloride. Also an oxygen supply, enough to last until we reach Mbeya hospital. Father Varnhalt, see if you can get the Peugeot station wagon started, and send at once for Sergeant Mchanga."

By the time Erika returned at a jog from the storeroom, there were soldiers on the veranda of the bungalow and Father Varnhalt had brought the mission's station wagon around. Three hundred thousand miles old, it stood rattling and shaking in a cloud of noxious carbonized smoke, one headlight blinking amber with every faulty stroke of the pistons. Inside, cockroaches had consumed everything edible.

Erika knew they could never hope to cross the Mbeya Range in the pathetic rusted wagon, but the colonel was just too long to transport lying down in a Land-Rover.

Colonel Ukumtara was semiconscious; he had vomited up much of his dinner. Raymond pumped drugs into him and clapped an oxygen mask on his face. Four soldiers carried the colonel outside to the Peugeot and placed him inside. His feet stuck out past the tailgate. Raymond motioned for Erika to get behind the wheel. He crouched in the back with his patient. There was no room for anyone else in the wagon.

"Where are you taking him?" Sergeant Mchanga asked.

"To the airplane."

"But—"

"Yes, I know, there's a risk; it's also the fastest way. This man is very ill. Don't just stand there, open the gates, Sergeant. Erika, get going!"

Sergeant Mchanga issued orders at the top of his voice; the gates were unlocked. Erika coaxed the balky wagon across the mission yard to the track outside, which in the light of the scimitar moon was a pale-red slash through sparse *miombo*.

"How is he?"

"Fair," Raymond muttered. He looked back at the lights of the mission as she negotiated the bumps and ruts down to the landing strip. The blue-and-white Beechcraft Bonanza was sitting at the near end, at a slight tilt over the port wheel. Erika pulled up a few feet from the right wingtip and lay on the Peugeot's horn, which wasn't as loud as the noise the engine was making. She couldn't see the pilot, a former Rhodesian tea planter named Weed, in the cabin, and apparently he hadn't heard them approaching.

Erika got out, stepped up on the wing of the Bonanza, and opened the door.

Weed, a small man, was slumped in the right-hand seat, the remains of a sandwich on the seat beside him. There was a nearly empty bottle of the '62 Bordeaux in his lap. He had drunk some of it, because he was out cold and snoring. The rest of the wine had soaked into his clothes.

The plane settled as Raymond added his weight to the wing and looked over her shoulder.

"Move aside," he said to Erika. He dragged the pilot from the cabin. On the ground he shook Weed vigorously, but saw only the cloudy whites of his eyes and heard a few protesting groans.

"What'll we do?" Erika said.

"Get in and start the engine, Erika, there's no time to lose."

Erika threw out the garbage and settled herself in the reeking cabin while Raymond made Weed comfortable in the front seat of the Peugeot. She flipped on inside lights, consulted the manual for basic information about the plane and ran through a preflight check. It looked like a dream to fly, once she had it off the ground. The tanks were three-quarters full. She turned the engine over.

Raymond reappeared on her right, leaning into the cabin.

"Can you do it?" he said loudly.

"Yes! But we'll have to pull out the seats to make room for—"

"Colonel Ukumtara isn't going. Good-bye, Erika. Good luck."

"What?"

"Take off. Now. Get us the help we need, Erika. I can't manage anymore, not by myself."

"Raymond, what about the colonel? Won't he die?"

She realized with a slight shock that she had never seen Raymond smile before; she had thought he couldn't.

"There's nothing wrong with his heart. I put something in his food—a mild bush poison to produce the symptoms you observed. The rest was suggestion: simple witchcraft. Never underestimate its power. Because the colonel may have convinced himself that it's his time to die, I could have my hands full trying to pull him through."

"You've been *planning* this? What about Weed?"

"I also doctored the wine."

"Raymond, my God, I thought—"

"You couldn't have done it yourself; they wouldn't let you past the gates." He grasped her shoulder reassuringly. "I know you wanted to take Bobby; but there was no way to work it out without arousing suspicion. He understands. Now you're free. But hurry."

"What will happen to you?"

"Nothing. I responded properly to a genuine emergency. You stole the plane while my back was turned."

He smiled again and closed the cabin door, jumped from the wing, and stood clear. For a few moments Erika was too stunned to make a move.

*Free.*

Her heart began to pound. She fastened the harness and tried to recall what she knew about taking off in a single-engine plane with a main tire pancaked.

Erika carefully pivoted the Bonanza, wincing at the heaviness she felt to port. She pointed the nose at the tight thicket of trees at the end of the eighteen-hundred-foot salt-pan strip and turned on the lights. She needed full power before the roll. The plane began to tremble in place as the tach needle crept up the dial to 3000 rpm. Then she eased off the brakes and built up speed, gripping the yoke too hard in her anxiety; it had been almost a year since she'd logged any flying time.

She applied hard right rudder to get the weight off the deteriorating tire, added fifteen degrees flaps for additional lift, moved the nose trim up with her left thumb, felt the handling smooth out—and then she was airborne, clearing, with not much room to spare, the trees and a small flock of roosting ivututu birds spooked from thorny heights by the noise of the plane.

One of the ungainly birds, big as a goose, shot up against the undercarriage behind the nose gear. There was a considerable impact and the Bonanza shuddered, but then it climbed steadily higher and there seemed to be no harm done. Except to the hapless bird.

Erika looked back through wide windows at the banked lights of Kingdom Mission, and said a prayer that those who were alive tonight would still be living when she returned. She climbed to five thousand feet, leaving the landing gear down: The reduction in air speed was at least twenty knots, but she was afraid that the shredded tire might damage the gear door, leaving her with no options when it came time to land in Nairobi. She could either balance on two wheels on a concrete runway or attempt a gear-up landing on grass; but if the Bonanza's gear became stuck halfway, then any landing would end in a potentially fatal crash.

Erika came right to zero four zero. Ahead of her, beyond the rash of lights that identified Chunya town, an outpost on the road to the soda works at Lake Rukwa, was an earthly void, part of the great central plain of Tanzania: an area of torrent courses, virgin bush, and semiarid savanna the size of Belgium. Nearly all of it was infested with tsetse fly, and seldom visited by man.

A peak was rising up out of the range of hills beneath the airplane. Erika detoured around it and got out the charts, made contact with the radio beacon in Mbeya. She plotted a heading that would take her parallel to the eastern branch of the Great Rift Valley all the way to Nairobi. At 65 percent power the flight would last a little less than four hours, leaving her with ample fuel reserves.

Erika put the Bonanza on automatic pilot. Then she let herself drift, focusing on jet magnitude, stars in her eyes, a vision of the heavens ceaselessly busy, as colorful as bees in a hive.

About twenty minutes later, when she made a routine instrument check, Erika saw that she was in trouble.

Oil pressure had dropped and there was a corresponding rise in the cylinder-head temperature. She immediately lowered the speed to 150 knots.

Erika remembered the ivututu she had collided with. Father Varnhalt had told her that the rare birds had a talismanic reputation in the Rukwa Valley: the power of life and death over human beings. Her mouth was dry from the altitude. She watched the gauges. Half her oil was gone. There was no chance that she could reach Nairobi without repairs. She had, at best, fifteen minutes to put the Bonanza down before the cylinder head cracked.

Erika consulted the charts. She was just over the Rungwa Game Reserve and at the western edge of Ruaha National Park, a vast and virtually unpopulated tract. The nearest airport was at Iringa, a plantation town about 120 miles east of her present position. Even if she trimmed for slow flight, she had little hope that she could make it. But ahead of her lay nothing but darkness and certain disaster. Erika's teeth chattered in the thin cold air as she made the course correction.

She saw, to the east, a long pulse of yellow light,

like a crooked tube of decaying neon. At first she thought it was heat lightning low on the horizon. But it didn't fade away after a second or two. As she flew closer, she realized she was looking at a bush fire.

The fire, burning between the forks of a sand river that must have been spring fed in this dry area, had consumed several hundred acres of savanna. Trees were exploding in its path. There seemed to be hundreds of animals in panic flight along the wide, flame-orange channels of the river. Rhino, waterbuck, zebra, buffalo; sleek and desperate cats of all kinds. Some had fallen; they lay motionless in shallow pools of water.

A light plane had appeared, cutting across the advancing wave of animals. It circled in front of the fire, avoiding dangerous drafts generated by the heat, and flew downstream at near-stall speed, about fifty feet above the left-hand channel.

Erika thought, *If there's a plane there's a camp of some kind, a landing strip.*

She came around to the right in a 360-degree turn of her own, at an altitude of a thousand feet. Then she saw what was happening, and turned sick with outrage.

They were poachers. There was a man braced in the open doorway of the Piper Super Cub, firing an automatic weapon. He seemed to be after rhino this time. The carcasses of elephants and big cats already littered the intermittent watercourse, out of reach of the billowing fire. On this pass three of the ponderously swift rhinos, raked and slaughtered, went down in blood-spattered waves.

Then the Piper's pilot pulled up sharply, and flew directly at Erika.

She took evasive action. He was either stupid or half blind. It hadn't occurred to him that there might be another plane in the vicinity this time of the night.

Erika flew low across the river channels and the hordes of animals and saw how much killing had already taken place. By daybreak the skinners would be busy along the edges of the blackened, cooling savanna, taking pelts and tusks and the valuable "horns" of the rhinoceros, which were ground up and sold as an aphrodisiac in Asian countries.

She sensed, rather than saw, the other plane. Turned her head quickly. The Piper was closing in, to the left and a little above her. They couldn't have missed the fact that it was government property she was flying. Maybe they thought she was a warden.

Against the firelit sky she had a glimpse of the tall man in the doorway, long black hair streaming rakishly away from his forehead. His expression was intense. As if he had brought her magic, he held in his hands a marvel of live flame, replica of the holocaust below.

Bullets beat shockingly against the fuselage, they smudged windows on either side of the cabin with punctuated frost. Erika flung herself sidelong and hauled back on the yoke, heading for the stars. Her breath was like a block of granite in her chest, pinning her to the seat. Forgetting about the threatened cylinder head, she flew at full speed, climbing at over nine hundred feet per minute, outdistancing, even with a dirty plane, the slower Cub.

There was no more gunfire. But things started going wrong, too fast.

Erika leveled off and looked around at the receding fire, now a crawl of ochre in the blooming bush. Her field of vision was restricted by the crazy-cracked windows and she couldn't locate the other plane. Then she thought she saw the running lights, at a much lower altitude, back by the river. With so little time to waste they had returned to their slaughter, having decided that she was in distress and would

have a long walk home from the bush—if she survived
the inevitable forced landing.

Erika took inventory. The cylinder head was now
seriously overheating; she could smell the hot metal.
She had only about twenty percent right rudder and
the plane was vibrating alarmingly at 170 knots, as if
one of the bullets had hit the propeller. Her speed
was dropping, she was losing the engine, she couldn't
stay aloft much longer. She had to attempt a landing
while she still had some control.

She spiraled the Bonanza down to a thousand feet,
looking for a level, treeless space. Six hundred feet.
The air close to the ground was warmer, it was more
difficult to handle the plane, and she was close to
stall speed.

*Oh dear God*, Erika thought.

There was nothing around her but low hills, woodland, thick bush—and, off to her right, a glimmer of
water, what she hoped was swampland or a riverbed.

She raised the landing gear, and was overjoyed
when it thumped solidly home. She heard the gear
door shut tightly. The odds were a little better now,
she thought.

Moments later the engine quit.

Erika pushed the Bonanza toward what appeared to
be a glade, saw spiked black trees coming up too fast
toward the gliding, faltering plane, was jolted by the
impact with the uppermost branches. There were
screeching, cracking sounds. Erika fought to keep the
wings level, the nose up.

She went in, the Bonanza rebounding from a resil-
ient mat of tangled brush like a flat stone skipped
across the surface of water. But a fire blazed up from
beneath the engine cowling and she screamed in terror, averting her face instinctively.

There was another, harder jolt that chipped two of
her front teeth and left her with an aftertaste of

sparks. She felt a sharp pain in her kidneys. Then the plane stopped as if it had hit a wall and her head snapped forward against the yoke. A few moments later the engine fire sizzled out as the nose of the plane sank into a gruel of water and vegetation in the midst of tall bulrushes and papyrus and thorn trees aglow with lichen silver.

Blood trickled down her face as Erika sat back, groaning. She fumbled with the release of her belt and harness. Then her hands went slack and she slumped forward again, unconscious.

Within half a minute the dead stillness of the glade was broken by the sounds of insects and wildlife in dense proliferation. Nocturnal life in the glade resumed as if the intrusion had never happened: as if the twisted airplane and the woman always had been, and always would be, a part of that small plot in an immense, untracked wilderness.

## SANGRE DE CRISTO
## MOUNTAINS

**Colorado, U.S.A.**
**May 6**

As Matthew Jade reached eight thousand feet the color of the sky was changing, to a sapphire blue observed cleanly between stands of ponderosa pine, with no veils of dust or moisture to dim its burning brilliance. He put on his shades and, with the sun now at an angle to make its heat felt through the rarefied atmosphere, he unbuttoned his shearling coat as he rode along, scarcely handling the reins. There was a breeze at his back as the slowly heating air rose and was replaced by cooler valley air. The spring flies came in droves to the wrapped dead calf tied to the packhorse. In the deep sunless places of the mountain, snowpack was gradually melting down to cloud ice.

Up by Cave Lake, a tarn accidental as a tear in the unbroken forest of spruce and fir, there was some activity at the digs which the University people had been working on and off for a couple of years. Jade stopped to have coffee and pass the time of morning. One of the girls, an undergraduate hooked on paleontology, had sprained an ankle and was soaking it in ice water. She was a classmate of Sam Gault's girl, and knew Jade's name and ranch when he mentioned them.

"The Warshield? Over by Silverpeak?"

"That's right."

She looked indignant. "The strip miners have really been creeping up on you."

"If it's not them, it's the condominium builders. But the bad times have put an end to all the construction."

"I hope you don't plan to sell out to the coal companies. Before you know it, everything west of the Rockies will be a wasteland." She winced at a shooting pain in her ankle, but seemed proud of the injury nonetheless. "Last year I was working in an eight-foot trench and part of it collapsed on me."

"You ought to get out of old bones and into something safer."

"I'm used to being bunged up. I started barrel racing when I was ten. I like your old bald-face horse there. He's practically straight, isn't he?" she said, referring to his Thoroughbred bloodlines.

"He's seven-eighths pure."

"Good mountain feet?" Jade nodded. "Bet you'd take five thousand for him," she said roguishly.

"Bet I wouldn't."

The horse trader's gleam left her eye. "Where are you going with all that calf meat?"

"I'm after a cougar."

"Tracking him?" the girl asked, probing her tender ankle and wincing again.

Jade smiled. "I'm not that good. I did track him awhile last fall with dogs, so I know approximately where to find him."

"You're not going to kill him, are you?"

"I have to, or risk losing seed stock."

The girl pouted, looking at one of the rifles he had with him.

"I don't like the idea of you shooting him. They're all disappearing, you know. They'll be extinct before long."

"I'm in business. And this cougar's hurting me."

She tried to flex her foot. "You wouldn't happen to have some Epsom salts with you? Bigeliol? Traileze? I'll try anything to bring this ankle down." She looked from Jade to the diggers, who were probing layers of marl for ancient femurs and toe bones. "Oh, well. We're all going the way of the dinosaur anyway. It's gobble and chew and swallow and shit, and to hell with who gets shit on."

"Miss, you just hang in there," Jade told her, and remounted his bald-face horse, Rimfire out of Fire's Fancy.

The girl looked up at Jade, and into his eyes.

"Maybe I could come around and visit you and your horse sometime."

"You just better do that," he said, not concealing his admiration for her. She was pretty and discontented and at loose ends—and less than half his age, which was why he didn't tell her he would pick her up on his way back down. He wondered if he should have. He was another quarter mile up the mountain before it occurred to him that he hadn't asked her name.

He drank some brandy from his pocket flask and thought about the cougar he had seen only once, months ago, moving cannily but without great speed a few hundred yards ahead of some untrained and eager dogs. The cougar lost them easily, left them bugling in runabout circles at the base of a shale cliff. Through binoculars Jade had observed something conservative, perhaps arthritic about his movements.

Even after a mild long summer of what should have been easy pickings, he looked shrunken, a derelict mooching around in thrift-shop fur. Undoubtedly he lacked the flash and pounce to pick off small game, pike and pocket gopher and yellow-bellied marmot, and with his instincts compromised by old age, his wind unsound, the long watchful stalk after roving herds of mule deer was beyond his abilities.

Jade reasoned that the cougar had survived the winter only because of some strange, chinook-dominated January weather. Thawing and quick refreezing mired many of Jade's winter range cows, so the cougar had feasted and grown fat on these helpless animals. Now in balmier months he probably spent a great deal of his time draped dozing in sunlit trees, descending from his subalpine retreat to score the welfare beef in the lowlands, gumming it if he had to, returning home with a drunkard's belch and a pleasant opinion of life.

The calf Jade had with him was more than a day ripe, and though it was still sound enough, it was meat which an aggressive young predator wouldn't touch. He dragged it for almost a mile behind his horse, hoping he was close enough to the cougar's lair to attract him. He left the carcass near a trickling creek that would be roaring with meltwater in another week. Here he found cougar tracks everywhere, some only a few days old.

He rode to higher ground, to a cirque from which he had a downwind view of the creek and the dead calf lying open in the sun a few yards below some dense juniper. Farther on he found a small meadow with spring grass and wild flowers pushing through the worn-out snow cover and left his horses there. He went back to the cirque with his rifle, a Winchester M70, improvised a bench rest, and settled down to wait, hoping that the buzzards, already visible in their slow steely wanderings above the next peak, would leave something for the cougar to be curious about.

Jade waited three and a half hours, scarcely making a move.

When the cougar finally appeared, he came lazily and without caution, scattering the half dozen buzzards who had long since occupied the carcass.

Jade took plenty of time identifying him through the eight-power scope mounted on his rifle. With a shift of the wind he thought he heard a helicopter puttering around somewhere to the southeast, but it was a long way off and no threat to his concentration. The cougar sat down near the calf. He looked to the left and to the right and yawned. Then he leaped straight up off the ground as the flat crack of the ought-six echoed through the canyon and eddied away with the wind.

Coming back down, Jade paused to have another ounce of brandy, chased with a purifying mouthful of mountain water, and studied the shale ridge he'd seen on the way up. It was a long, unstable descent bare of vegetation, virtually nothing more than a loose rockpile, held together in places with rotten ice, another considerable hazard. The ridge would save him half an hour or so, not a critical savings since he had half the afternoon left to get back to the ranch.

But having so easily taken a life, even the life of a predator far past his prime, Jade felt a familiar, pressing need to buy back into the game, to generate some velocity away from the limbo he'd drifted toward these past few months.

He freed the packhorse to follow or not follow depending on his mood and got up on Rimfire, turned him toward the ridgeback. The slightest clumsiness there, or lack of communication, would mean a tumble of about three hundred grinding, skull-popping feet. And then what was left of horse and man would free fall for several seconds in the swiftly darkening air of a blue mountain canyon.

Jade heard the helicopter again but shut out all distractions, devoting his mental energy to the exercise, turning them into a single creature working, thinking together, instantly responsive to the dangers of the treacherous descent. The packhorse, carrying the slung-over cougar that Jade was taking to the appropriate authorities in Silverpeak, followed well behind

them, all but sliding downhill. Loose rock skittered
ahead of the horse and rider. Gusts of wind froze
them delicately in place, like high-wire performers, for
seconds at a time. Halfway down Rimfire began to
grow tired; his aching knees shook. Jade felt a rising
fear, an impulse toward panic. He absorbed the
horse's fear and redirected it into the broad air around
them, then projected to Rimfire strong images of pasture, good grass, shelter from the seething wind.

Rimfire found new strength, and the descent was
completed without incident. But they were both soaking wet when they reached bottom. Jade stopped in a
protected cove to change his shirt and give his horse a
rubdown.

They were crossing a boulder-filled creek when the
wind again brought the sound of a helicopter to Jade.

This time it was nearer. The *whap-whap-whap* of
the rotor blades cracked off the canyon cliffs like an
avalanche. Jade turned for a look as his horse went ear
shy and quirky in troublesome water. The packhorse
showed teeth and a panicky eye and also balked; Jade
had his hands full getting both to dry ground. As he
did so the helicopter, a Jetranger, flew steeply down
at them and landed fifty yards away in a streak of
meadow.

Jade noticed a Forest Service decal. He kept riding,
but slowly. There were four men in the helicopter.
One of them opened a door and got out before the
blades stopped turning. He was wearing a business
suit. Jade recognized him immediately. His name was
John Guy Gibson, and he was Deputy Director of Operations for the CIA. He supervised what remained of
the agency's covert activities and the few good men
who lasted through a decade of debacles, inept lead-
ership at the top, poor morale, and the heat from Con-
gressional brimstone.

Gibby was a tall, ramshackle man with rimless glasses and thinning hair. There was a wine-colored birthmark on his high forehead, near the right temple, which Jade had always fancied as a blot on the escutcheon. His suit didn't fit too well, as if he'd had some luck with one of the crash diets he was always trying.

Gibby showed his long teeth in a grimace of annoyance, waiting for Jade . . . who approached him slowly, thinking of a cardinal rule of The Company, from which he had retired after a blot or two of his own: *We never explain and we never apologize.*

In addition to the pilot there were two other men in the helicopter. One had to be a security officer assigned to Gibson. The other was wearing a ranger uniform. Jade took a deep breath and let half of it out.

"Rimmy, hold!" he hollered. His left hand closed on the butt of the saddle gun holstered behind his left leg, and as Rimfire stood his ground steady as a courthouse monument, muscles clenched, Jade drew and jumped and somersaulted neatly in the meadow grass, flipping himself over the Marlin .44 magnum rifle. He came up lever cocking it, aiming at John Guy Gibson's stomach.

Gibby looked pasty behind his birthmark. He took a fast step back, stepped on a round rock, and almost fell.

"Matthew, God's sake! What do you think you're *doing?*"

"Takes a lot to get you out from behind your desk, Gibby. How long were you rattling around up there looking for me? It may be that I won't like your reasons."

"I told them. *Told* them you were impossible! I'm already on record I'm totally against this!"

"Against what?"

Gibby pointed a shaking finger at the shale ridge.

"We saw you come down that hill. The pilot told us how reckless it was. You're still taking wild chances, trying to get yourself killed at every opportunity."

"You calling me a misfit again, Gibby?" Jade said with a thin-lipped smile. He had the pleasure of seeing Gibby's complexion turn a shade paler in the slanting sun. But he wasn't particularly in the mood for comedy. He glanced at the men in the helicopter. They looked worried, and should have been.

Jade straightened, pointed the rifle away from the CIA man.

"I've always known what I was doing, Gibby. If I hadn't, I wouldn't be standing here now scaring the shit out of you."

Gibby looked irritably at his watch. "Never mind. This is no time for old grievances—"

"I kind of thought that's why you're up here."

"I'm here," Gibby said unhappily, running a hand through his windblown hair, "because the president wants to see you."

"This must be my lucky day," Jade said. "Except I know damn well it isn't. What about?"

"He'll explain. But there's no time—"

"Where is Boomer? In Washington?"

"No, the Coast. He—"

"Uh-uh. Forget it."

Gibby shaded his eyes and stared, perplexed, at Jade.

"He told me you'd say that."

"Did he tell you I get seasick on a waterbed?"

"*Everybody* knows that," Gibby said impatiently. "It's part of your jacket." He couldn't resist a sneer. "I thought you would have licked that problem by now, with your devotion to Eastern disciplines."

"I had Hopi shaman teachers. But we all need our weaknesses to remind us we're human, Gibby."

"The president told me if you were going to be stubborn, then I should remind you he carries an overdue bill in his pocket. He wants you to remember—" Gibby's tongue pressed between his teeth as he tried to get the message straight. " 'Many long legs.' "

For a few moments, Jade looked puzzled. Then he sat down cross-legged in the grass, holding his rifle by the barrel. He laughed and laughed.

"Okay," he said, wiping a tear trickle from one eye. "Have that spare ranger you brought along take my horses down to the ranch. And let's go see what Boomer has on his mind."

# THE MARITIME WHITE HOUSE

Channel Islands National
Monument, California
May 6

The sea off the cliffs of Anacapa was placid, as a Navy helicopter carrying Jade, John Guy Gibson, and his security man circled a schooner in a small cove on the channel side of the rocky island. From a height of four hundred feet Jade could see, without binoculars, a school of Pacific gray whales migrating north in the gold caldron of sunset. The Navy destroyer that accompanied the president on his frequent holidays under sail had anchored outside the reef, and an antisubmarine helicopter was on picket duty above the Santa Barbara Channel.

The pilot set the pontoon-equipped helicopter down close to the president's seventy-six-foot, outrageously expensive, teak-and-mahogany schooner, called the *Hondo*. The three men went aboard.

A tape deck programmed with Herbie Mann and Chuck Mangione competed with the din of a rookery: The shoreline teemed with seals. There were cormorants and sea gulls overhead, and a tame brown pelican on the mizzen spreader. The shadowed water was clear enough for Jade to see, a dozen feet down, greenish-brown kelp forests slowly stirred by some current undetectable on the surface. Wet suits and scuba gear were drying on the decks, along with a basket of pink and orange sea anemones.

The president was yelling something: a greeting, an

insult. Boomer looked thin and hectic in a golf shirt and raspberry slacks. Jade noted the other two men taking their ease under a Bimini awning in the stern. Familiar faces. He temporarily forgot his uneasiness at being afloat.

"Matt, how you feel today, buddy?" Boomer waved a hand at the cove. "Like glass, huh? But I've got a bucket ready for you. Gibby, you want to get in on the pool? My money says Matt lasts ten minutes before he whups his guts." Boomer looked Jade over with a faint insolent grin. He didn't bother to get up to shake hands; they had known each other too long for even that much formality.

"Janey and the kids okay?" Jade asked.

"Yeah. They ask about you. I tell them you're still holed up licking wounds. What do you want to drink?"

"Nothing. I just want to get off your damn boat."

Boomer grinned again. He was forty-seven, a year and a half older than Jade. At a glance Boomer looked very fit. He was baked the color of a clay flower pot. His eyes were still a bright and fulminating blue, but his hair was down to a thinning half inch of fuzz, burned by aggravation, by the internal volcano that powered him. Jade also noticed the slight bitter twist to his mouth, becoming more pronounced the longer he served a wobbling and demoralized nation as its Chief Executive.

Boomer introduced him to the other men: Morgan Atterbury, the secretary of defense, and Stephen Gage, the president's national-security advisor. Jade hadn't followed the Washington scene too closely since his friend's election, but he knew that Atterbury, formerly CEO for a major West Coast electronics firm, had been doing a good job in the world's toughest bureaucracy. Gage was a Rhodes scholar and award-winning author. He was a big, overweight, bearded man with cold eyes and a barely civil manner. Boomer said that two thirds of his body was ego, and the rest was very thin skin. He had muscled nearly everyone else aside to sit at Boomer's right hand when the tough decisions were made. Apparently Gage had a lot to offer; Boomer was on the defensive these days, but he was no dummy.

Boomer had come out of nowhere with plenty of the family's oil money behind him but only the governorship of Oklahoma as a political base, to win his party's nomination as a compromise candidate. Then he nabbed a close election, which the incumbent president managed to kick away through overconfidence. Boomer, deficient in vital areas of political expertise, had learned fast in three years. He was brash, scrappy, tireless. He knew how to use the media to advantage, and he was increasingly well liked overseas. His best efforts to pull the country out of a disastrous slump probably would not show results for another two years. In the meantime he was catching hell for the mismanagement of previous administrations.

"I suppose," Boomer said, taking in Gibson's long-suffering expression, "that you and Gibby had the chance to get reacquainted on the way out."

"Like old times," Jade agreed. They had stayed as far away from each other as they could in the Gulf-stream jet, which belonged to The Company; Gibby, a collector of Chinese porcelains, had spent most of his time leafing through auction catalogues.

The CIA man cleared his throat and smiled gamely. "May I know about 'many long legs'?" he asked.

Boomer frowned at Jade. "Should we tell him?"

"I hate to think of the man-hours he'll waste trying to find out."

"My family and Matt's go way back," Boomer explained. "Before we got oil rich and started putting on airs, our respective granddaddies swapped worthless mineral rights and wind-broke horses and good-time ladies. Their drinking was a scandal and they raised all sorts of hell together. When Matt and I got acquanted, we resolved to carry on in the glorious tradition. We saw each other during the summer, when my folks shipped me out to the Colorado ranch for seasoning. Well, boys go through definite stages of development. The first pony, the first bare-knuckle fight, first trophy head; by age sixteen I was a certified cocksman at Choate. But Matt, he was younger and hadn't had any yet. So that summer when we got together I promised to fix him up."

"For a certified cocksman, you should have been able to do better than Minnie Long Legs," Jade complained.

"She was a part-Paiute Indian girl," Boomer said to Gibby. "So skinny you could shave with one of her shinbones. But Minnie could get it on; and she'd come at the top of her voice."

"She also had a husband. But you didn't tell me about him."

"I figured all I had to do was keep a lookout. Then I got sort of involved with that little horse bum from Colorado Springs: Daisy, or Jonquil, or something like that. So Minnie's old man, he was about thirty, I think, his name was Pinky Bob Steers, he came home pissed from the Crudup Cafe and heard Minnie go off like a cyclone siren: Matt had generous proportions, even when he was a kid. Pinky Bob didn't need to inquire as to why she was screeching thataway. He got his ax from the woodshed and went charging in and came back out dragging Matt by the hair. All Matt had on was his shirt. Minnie lit out for the tall timber while Pinky Bob stood at the grinding wheel making the sparks fly from his ax. Matt was kind of an interesting pale-green color. Since Pinky Bob was taking all that time to make his ax good and sharp, I figured I had a chance to negotiate. Hey, Matt, should I tell Gibby what your balls cost me?"

"Why not? A little more humiliation won't make any difference."

"Let's see. I gave Pinky Bob five dollars cash, my car radio, a pretty good spare tire, two cans of Marvel Mystery Oil, the Pendleton shirt off my back, and what was left of that quart of Southern Comfort we'd been nipping at for three days."

"Too bad we can't buy the Russians that cheap," Gage said with a rumble of laughter.

"It's not a bad analogy. Pinky Bob knew just what his wife and his dignity were worth. He had a sense of proportion. But we've lost ours. I think we've spent about three hundred fifty billion dollars since I came into office and God knows what the Russians have spent, and what do we have to show for it? For the last twenty years we've been sliding downhill into a depression trying to support an unproductive bureaucracy that can wage war but can't do one damn thing to protect the country." Boomer grimaced and finished his gin and lime. He stared at Jade. "Well, maybe we have a chance to do something about that now."

Gibby looked at his watch and said with a stiff smile, "Because we're running so late at this point, and time apparently is a critical factor in our planning, shouldn't we get to work?"

Boomer nodded, and got up to lead the way below.

"We'd better have this conversation in the main salon, so the goddam Russians can't hear every word."

"They around?" Jade said.

Boomer made a motion of submarines gliding beneath the waves.

Morgan said, "One of ours has been playing tag with one of theirs all day." He pointed toward the ocean. "And their trawlers have ears that can hear the coins drop in a pay phone in Wichita."

"Maybe you should confine your weekend vacations to Camp David," Jade said to Boomer as they went below. The midships salon had seven feet of headroom, practical, built-in furnishings, carpeting, indirect lighting on the red-toned mahogany, and oil paintings by Boomer's eighty-one-year-old mother, an authentic American primitive. There was a good-sized galley and dining room abaft.

"The hell with that. The Big Bear can't scare me off my own boat. Anyway, we're secure here. Grab a seat, Matt. Gibby, show him the goody."

Jade had a glimpse of extensive communications equipment in a forward compartment before the salon was closed off by one of the Secret Service men who made up the *Hondo*'s crew. Gibby unlocked a cabinet. He took out a plush jeweler's case and a high-powered magnifying glass and handed both to Jade.

Inside the case was the bloodstone which Morgan Atterbury had brought back from Tanzania. Jade pondered it impassively for a few moments, then lifted the stone to see what it looked like beneath the full-spectrum light angled over his shoulder. Finally he held the bloodstone beneath the magnifying glass to bring out the inscriptions. There seemed to be hundreds.

He smiled in bewilderment and looked up. The others were watching with the mesmerized expressions of men in the presence of something of immense value. Gibby broke the silence by leafing through the pages of a thick loose-leaf notebook, bound in gold leather, on a table in front of him.

"How much does it weigh?" Jade asked.

"Forty-eight point six carats," Gibby said, having looked it up. "And it's very nearly flawless. We have an appraisal, a GIA certificate of authenticity."

Jade looked through the magnifying glass again and studied the etchings on one facet.

"What language is this? Arabic?"

"No. It's a complete system of writing predating, and entirely unrelated to, the earliest ideograms and numerals of Sumeria." Gibson tapped the notebook. "A full translation of the pictographs—and there are thousands of them—is in this book."

"Where did the diamond come from?"

"Morgan brought it to us," Boomer said.

The defense secretary smiled. "It was a party favor, actually."

"See if you can get me invited next time."

"Tell him about it, Morgan."

Morgan explained the events leading up to the remarkable Chanvai conference.

"I brought back a tape of the . . . proceedings, which Jumbe provided. Why don't you listen to it, and then I'll try to answer your questions."

Gibby took a cassette from an inside pocket of the notebook cover and slipped it into Boomer's stereo receiver.

"*Good evening. . . . To my friends Morgan Atterbury and Victor Kirillovich Nikolaiev, welcome.*"

At the mention of the Soviet minister of defense, Jade shot a look at Boomer, who looked grimly back at him but said nothing. Jade concentrated on the voice of Jumbe Kinyati. The tape was of excellent quality; even minor background noises like the sharp cries of animals outside the room came through clearly.

"*The Chapman/Weller discovery is of awesome*

*proportions. . . . Catacombs . . . a civilization that left a complete record of its one-thousand-year history for modern man to study. . . . Their greatest feat . . .* was FIREKILL."

Finally the tape ended. The *Hondo* had begun to rock gently at anchor. Jade felt a sharp distress, not entirely due to the motion of the boat.

He said to Morgan, "Kinyati's been a moderate for years. What changed him?"

"Many things. He's old, and frustrated by the slow progress of economic and education reforms in his own country. Tanzania is still among the poorest nations on earth. CCM policies of collectivization—*ujamaa*—haven't been successful in the rural areas. I suspect he's very ill. The death of his sons in Rhodesia several years ago continues to weigh heavily. Apparently he's developed a fanatic's will to stay alive long enough to drive the Afrikaners from South Africa. I think he views the potential holocaust as a memorial to his dead sons."

Gibson got up to illuminate a map of Africa on a viewing screen.

"As you can see, the southern border of Tanzania is about twelve hundred miles from Pretoria. Almost all of South Africa is within reach of intermediate-range tactical nuclear weapons. Ours, or the Soviets'."

Jade scrutinized the bloodstone again. "Are the Russians taking this seriously?" he asked the CIA man.

"Yes, from what little we've been able to learn. Naturally it's very difficult to know what they're thinking. But they've always been nutty on the subject of flying saucers. Some key members of their scientific establishment devoutly believe that we've received periodic visits from extraterrestrials, so it shouldn't be too much of a reach for them to accept an ancient buried civilization, or whatever."

"When was the meeting in Tanzania?"

"A week ago," Morgan replied. "I came back immediately, via Torrejon."

"Do you still think this is a hoax?"

"If it is, Jumbe's taken in quite a few people, including some respected, hard-headed scientists."

Morgan glanced at Gibby, who continued, "We have voiceprint comparisons of nearly everyone who spoke on the tape you just heard. They are who they were represented to be—including Marshal V. K. Nikolaiev. Voice-stress analysis tends to confirm that all of them, including Jumbe, devoutly believed in what they were talking about."

"But voice-stress analysis isn't very reliable."

Gage said, "It only means that otherwise sensible men may have convinced themselves of the unbelievable and the impossible."

"Jumbe's forcibly detained his eminent guests for a full week. There should have been an uproar from family, friends, colleagues."

"Tanzania's on a war footing," Morgan explained. "There's not much shooting, but Jumbe has closed the borders pending the outcome of what he calls 'a national emergency.' No one can enter or leave the country. Travel is restricted. The press has been muzzled. There's no way to learn exactly what's going on."

Boomer had been silent for an unusually long time, his face closed in glum contemplation. Now he said, "But the South African Department of National Security knew right away that you and Nikolaiev had paid a visit to Jumbe. And left in the middle of the night. With all those warmongering broadsides from Jumbe, they're getting a little paranoid."

"How much have you found out about the Chapman/Weller expedition?" Jade asked Gibson.

"Members of the expedition assembled in Dar es

Salaam over a ten-day period beginning the eighteenth of September of last year. They left Dar for Lake Tanganyika on the twenty-ninth and established a base camp in the Makari Mountains. Almost immediately after that, as you heard on the tape, there was no further contact with them."

"They were looking for a prehistoric burial ground. How did they know it might be there? Have other explorers covered the same territory?"

"As far as we know, only one. Dr. Macdonald Hardie."

"Who's he?"

"I should have said the late Dr. Hardie; he died in a flash flood in Africa sixteen years ago. He was a paleoanthropologist who had a bit of money laid by, enough to give him independence from the university and foundation cliques. He was determinedly anti-establishment, always challenging the accepted theories of evolution. In a thirty-five-year career he made some significant discoveries, particularly in East Africa and the Afar region of Ethiopia. His most famous find was the bone clusters of approximately fifty Ethiopians, who lived a communal existence some three million years ago; these individuals were strikingly human in form. He was accused of misinterpreting the fossil form as a direct link with modern man, and it was rumored he had perpetrated some post-Piltdown trickery, although other anthropologists stopped short of calling him a fraud."

"Was this the burial ground Chapman/Weller hoped to find?"

"No. Apparently he was very secretive about his Tanganyika discovery, which he made before he died. If Hardie did stumble across the Catacombs, he had to realize it was one of the most significant scientific discoveries of all time, demanding rigid silence and many years of painstaking exploration with a few archaeologists he trusted completely. Chips Chapman, for one."

"If Hardie confided in Chapman, why would he wait thirteen years to investigate?"

"It's just a guess that Chapman knew what he would find. Assuming that Hardie made notes of his discovery, they're missing from the archives at Edinburgh University, and no one we've talked to in the academic community knows anything about them."

"But his daughter may know about the Catacombs," Boomer said. "She may even have seen them."

"Sounds like a good break. What's the matter, can't you locate her?" The *Hondo* was creaking and rocking as a collision of twilight air masses in the little cove created a thermal. Jade went pale. "Jesus," he muttered. "What's the matter with this tub? Throw out another anchor."

Boomer laughed and got up to rummage for Dramamine, which he gave to Jade.

"Right now Hardie's girl is almost a neighbor of yours—she's about a hundred miles away from the war shield, at Talon Mountain Federal Correctional Facility."

Jade swallowed his Dramamine and looked up in disbelief.

"*Raun* Hardie?"

Boomer nodded. "That's ironic, isn't it? The FBI wasted three years and fifty thousand man-hours trying to track her down. Justice spent six months on her case, and the trial lasted three months. Raun Hardie didn't whimper, she didn't cry, she never backed down. She was a common criminal, legitimately accused of a Federal crime, maybe an inch away from being a murderer, but somehow *we* came out of it looking like the bad guys. Now we need her, badly, and I wonder how far we'll get."

"Have you talked to Hardie yet?"

"Basically it's a matter of finding the right approach," Boomer said optimistically.

"Good luck," Jade said through clenched teeth. He was holding his stomach.

"Are you going to heave?"

"Don't know yet, Boomer."

"You're making a hell of an impression. Here I was telling everybody how tough you are. Your body is a marvel of science, capable of incredible feats."

Jade sighed and looked at Morgan, who smiled sympathetically; Boomer was a notorious needler.

"Marvel of science?"

"Yeah, I look it, don't I? I make the most of what I have, physically and mentally. Most people get ten percent out of themselves and think they're overachievers. On the tape I heard you tell Jumbe you thought his entire presentation was a hoax. What do you think now?"

"It's still a lot to swallow," Morgan admitted. "But there are facts that can't be disputed. The red diamond I brought back is the real thing. And it would be a tremendous labor to make up a new language consisting of thousands of pictographs, which fill over five hundred pages of translation, just to perpetrate a hoax. Not saying it couldn't be done, but the etymologists we've consulted have been impressed—in some instances dazzled. Then there's the matter of a 'lost civilization,' or race of people. Now, that's wonderful stuff for adventure stories, but there's little evidence except for some unexplained ruins. In place of real evidence that a highly technological society could have existed on the edge of the last ice age, all we have is a great number of 'out-of-place artifacts,' curiosities turned up in the course of routine field work by investigators during the last hundred years. A couple of examples should do.

"In the Museum of Natural History in London there is the skull of a Neanderthal-type man which was found in the vicinity of Broken Hill, Rhodesia, in 1921. Neanderthal man goes back to the Upper Pleistocene age. The skull came equipped with a perfectly round hole on the left side. If an arrow or spear had penetrated the bone, there would be radial cracks. The hole had to be made by a projectile traveling at a velocity of nearly three thousand feet per second."

"In other words," Jade said, "a bullet. With a hell of a hot load behind it."

"Exactly. The skull opposite the hole was broken, blown out from the inside. A typical wound resulting from a gunshot. The skull was found in the ground at a depth of about sixty feet, so it's almost a certainty that the owner was shot many thousands of years ago. No other explanation comes close. Another example: Many models of workable airplanes have been discovered in such places as a tomb in Egypt. A fragment of a Chaldean book called the *Sifr'ala* is almost a hundred pages long in its English translation; basically it's a construction manual for an aircraft, with reference to vibrating spheres, graphite rods, and copper coils. The *Sifr'ala* also contains a nearly complete lesson in aerodynamics: wind resistance, gliding, and stability. Back then they may have known as much about flying as we do now. I could go on for a couple of hours about ancient aerial surveys, spark plugs found in rocks half a million years old, accounts of atomic warfare in Hindu records, electroplated gold jewelry from the tombs of the pharaohs, platinum and aluminum smelters that require extremely high temperatures—but you get the idea."

"I think you're sold," Jade observed. "But even if the Catacombs exist, the real hoax could be FIREKILL. Only Dr. Landreth knows for sure. He convinced

Jumbe that he alone has the key to this formula. But as a source he's highly questionable."

"There is a theoretical basis for the concept of a force field," Morgan said. "Going back to ancient sources, we know that the Egyptians did some significant research in electromagnetics. They used variations of a Van de Graaff generator and Crookes tubes to negatively charge electron beams, which then negatively charged small objects. If they were able to experiment on a large scale, they may well have constructed the pyramids by floating those huge blocks of stone into place. If FIREKILL is authentic, it could consist of simple machines that produce, using solar energy, enormously powerful electromagnetic waves, either to repel missiles in trajectory or pull them apart, turning them into harmless fragments in space."

The *Hondo* settled down into a gentle rocking-chair rhythm. Jade held his head for a few moments, breathing deeply.

Boomer said, after a long silence, "We wouldn't want to be the last superpower on the block to acquire FIREKILL. Because of the waiver provision in the Arms Export Control Act, I have the authority to send weapons and advisors anywhere I damn please without informing Congress, as long as I think there's a qualifying emergency. But even if I have incontrovertible proof that FIREKILL exists, giving nukes to Jumbe is out of the question."

"What Jumbe doesn't realize," Gage said, "or chooses to overlook, is the fact that the economy of South Africa continues to support the entire continent. There are fifty-one black states in Africa, and most of them are in terrible shape economically. The O.A.U. is bitterly antiapartheid; its leaders clamor for economic sanctions in the UN—but without the billion dollars in illegal trade that goes on each year with the Afrikaners, most of black Africa would face starvation and political chaos."

"Quite a dilemma you have there," Jade said helpfully. "I wonder what this conversation sounded like at the Kremlin."

"Politically the Soviets are as conservative as they've ever been," Gibby replied. "The Politburo doesn't take risks with the motherland. But when they see something developing that looks like a sure thing, they'll bet heavily. Afghanistan, for instance."

"If they can't steal FIREKILL," Boomer said, "I'm reasonably sure that on twenty-nine May they'll pay the asking price just to take a hard look at the concept of an electromagnetic umbrella over their heads. And they'll absorb the moral indignation of the rest of the world with their customary indifference."

"But they're not going to steal the FIREKILL stones from the Catacombs. I am."

"Aside from the fact that you're a better man than anyone the KGB has in Cobra Dance, we have another advantage. We have Raun Hardie."

Jade took another long look at the bloodstone.

He had never been particularly enamored of gems, even expensive ones, but the bloodstone exerted an attraction that went beyond the venal. It was, perhaps, many millions of years old, exposed to the artistry of man only in the last ten thousand years or so. The discovery of even one red diamond was a freak of chance. It was difficult for him to conceive of others, of nearly uniform size and excellence. They could have been collected only through arduous effort, by people who had a vast knowledge of the interior of the earth, and who were skilled in advanced deep-mining techniques.

He wanted to know more about these exceptional people of Zan, despite the barrier of a hundred centuries. How they had lived, why they had perished. He held in his hand a fraction of their history, which he couldn't interpret. The bloodstone seemed infinite in its depths. Observing it, he felt observed himself: with skepticism and, perhaps, defiance.

*Come if you dare.*

Jade looked up.

"The twenty-ninth of May," he said to Boomer. "It isn't a hell of a lot of time. And I don't know who I'll be up against it, if the Russians decide to play it the way we will."

"We're working on that," Gibby told him. "Even at the risk of compromising one of our assets within the KGB."

"And they're working on us," Jade said, thinking of the submarine that had been prowling in the vicinity of the *Hondo* all day. But Gibby chose to interpret his statement as a rap against the internal security procedures of The Company. His face darkened almost enough to eclipse the hot gel of birthmark.

Boomer got up, forestalling a scene.

"Gentlemen, if you don't mind, Matt and I have some personal matters to discuss before he leaves."

When they were alone, Boomer said with his bitter smile, "How's your tummy?"

"I'll live."

"Do you want a drink now?"

"A little brandy and water."

Boomer took a couple of bottles from the bar cabinet.

"What kind of shape are you in? Do you still have the body of a thirty-year-old?"

"Twenty-nine," Jade said. "I'll never turn thirty."

"One day you'll just go quietly from the peak of your youth to advanced old age," Boomer said admiringly, handing Jade his brandy. He fixed another gin and lime for himself; they clinked glasses together. "From my mouth, et cetera. The exceptional thing about you is that you don't look exceptional. When I tell people you once ran three hundred fifty miles in three and a half days to win a five-dollar bet, they think I'm a blowhard. You're what, five ten, a hundred and fifty pounds soaking wet?"

"One fifty-two."

"No visible muscles. Just that rawhide cowpoke look. You up to this one, Matt? It's a tough proposition."

"You wouldn't have bothered me if it wasn't."

"The usual business arrangements, then," Boomer said. "You'll be under contract to the Windward Corporation. Special consultant, twenty years at seventy-five thousand a year—or a lump-sum insurance payment to your estate, if it comes to that. Windward will provide all necessary services, and you have a blank-check expense account. Gibby has the contract with him—sign it on your way out. You report directly to me."

"Fine," Jade said, nodding, thinking of other things. "Does Gibby have you spooked about me?"

"Nothing new. He brought out that psychoanalytic profile they did before you . . . chose to retire. Goddam thing runs to a hundred and twenty pages. But it didn't tell me anything I haven't known about you since you were ten years old. Of course there's a lot of shrink-tank jargon abstracted from your basic Freud: stress models, predictability factors, and so on. Conclusion: Nothing can ever equal the risk you took to get out of Lefortovo prison. Now you can't be trusted under game conditions because you may have become so infatuated with overcoming risks that subconsciously you continue to pile them on, just to find out what it takes to break you. According to the shrinkers, either you think you can't die, or you're afraid you won't."

Jade whistled softly, tunelessly, and failed to smile.

He sipped a little of his brandy and water, staring mildly at Boomer.

"What do you think?"

"I don't buy it," Boomer said aggressively. "Our esteemed social scientists always get a little edgy when they're confronted with a throwback. Some men are born mechanics. You're a born adventurer. You like to tinker with situations and make them work, and the more complex the better. I've wanted to put you to work since Nell died, but we haven't had a scram worthy of your talents. As for Gibby . . . we know what's troubling him. He looked pretty bad when Haydeen turned up in that well behind his house with a concrete block wired around his neck. You were the scapegoat. If I'd been in office then, I would have stopped his play."

"Maybe he doesn't count himself out even yet."

"Now you're questioning Gibby's loyalties. I won't have that." Boomer's eyes were hard. He started to pour himself another big splash of gin, thought better of it. He put the bottle down. "The governors of six Western states will be aboard in an hour. Better get yourself home. And stay there, if you're concerned about Gibby failing to cover your ass. On a personal level I don't care for him either, but I can depend on Gibby because his loyalties are easy to define. He loves his country. I wish I knew ten more men just like him. And you."

Jade reached for his hat. "Okay, Boomer."

"Anything you need before you go?"

"A copy of the tape, and everything pertaining to the bloodstones. Landsat and SLAR reconnaissance photos of the area in question. Weather forecasts through twenty-nine May. I'll submit a shopping list in the morning. Tomorrow I want to see Raun Hardie at the prison, ten o'clock my time. You'd better go ahead and have that drink. It's the sea air."

Boomer didn't waste any time. He swallowed the gin straight, without his usual twist.

"You laughing, Matt?" he asked, still looking vexed.

"Not yet."

"I didn't sleep last night, thinking about the possibilities. Because there's no other way, my friend. Disarmament? You can't talk sanely about an insane predicament. Two great nations squander their heritage, too much of their future resources, and an inexcusable amount of raw brainpower to perpetuate the military myths of the past, for the sake of a balance of terror. Nuclear stalemate. The words curdle on the tongue. I hope like hell Jumbe is right. I'm praying FIREKILL exists. The Lords of the Storm. They sound like gods. Think of that, Matthew. They have looked upon mankind and seen that we are assholes. From their infinite wisdom and compassion is distilled a drop of pity. A bloodred drop. Maybe FIREKILL is a gift from the gods."

"On the other hand," Jade said, "they may have a godlike sense of humor we won't appreciate at all."

## ZANZIBAR ISLAND, TANZANIA

### May 7

The estate of the merchant Akim Koshar, situated a hundred feet above the Indian Ocean on a coral cliff, looked from the air like the remains of a party cake served at a Polynesian restaurant. The estate had been expanded many times during the century, gaining a labyrinthine border of walls, some of which were broken and crumbling; the outermost wall was ten feet high and six feet thick but it had no hard edges and seemed to be melting down in the brutal sun. The stucco was painted in shades of pastel orange and banana yellow. Koshar's estate was ringed with clove groves, dark conical evergreen trees that grew to heights of fifty feet. Inside there were parasols of coconut palm, which created splash patterns of light and shade, their yellowed fronds intersecting over tile roofs colored in loud mixed purples and reds. A private mosque, with a minaret like an unlit candle, was as blue as the sea.

Koshar, refreshed by his midday prayers, walked out onto the broad terrace that overlooked the water and glanced at the agent Moscow had sent to him. His initial reaction was one of approval. Despite the heat and the island's high humidity, which was not noticeably diminished by a mild offshore breeze, the man known as Ket Lundgren looked like vacationing royalty—penniless, minor royalty, but with the assurance of his bloodlines apparent in every understated gesture as he stood talking to Daniel Mkassu, Koshar's most valued aide.

But the visitor was neither Swedish by birth, nor royalty: His real name, unknown to Koshar, was Michael Belov, and he was a high-ranking officer with the KGB. For seventeen years he had been one of the three or four top operatives for an ultraclandestine directorate, Department CD, which the CIA and other national intelligence groups referred to as Cobra Dance. Belov, as Lundgren, had impeccable credentials as a journalist. He published a magazine of opinion in Stockholm that was read by influential politicians around the world and which lost a substantial sum of money for the KGB every year. His wife was a prima ballerina with the Royal Ballet; they were an intellectual-artistic couple with a host of powerful friends, in demand for prestigious parties everywhere.

Belov was tall, standing head and shoulders above the diminutive Koshar. He wore faded jeans and sandals without socks and an unpressed white linen jacket over a half-buttoned blue shirt. He was troubled by thinning hair, which he parted on the left, but otherwise he appeared disconcertingly flawless. He maintained a blazing tan and his durable body looked accustomed to hard knocks.

Koshar noted the amphibious plane tied up at the dock of the mangrove-lined bay below the main house, and the medium-sized, obviously expensive bag Belov kept close to hand, and concluded that he traveled very light or had something irreplaceable in the bag. Koshar wet his lips surreptitiously, wishing he knew more about the sudden keen interest of the U.S.S.R. in certain recent activities by the Tanzanian government. But he accepted their pay and provided information or services as required, and avoided asking even the most harmless-seeming questions. His major flaw, an insatiable curiosity, was well balanced by untiring patience. In good time he would discover why the British scientist and turncoat named Henry Landreth was of critical importance; he might even learn, to his ultimate profit, what the visitor was carrying in the guarded bag. For now, despite the urgency of the business at hand, the courtesies had to be observed: His guest, familiar with Muslim customs, understood.

They were served lunch on another part of the terrace, in a gazebo made of ant-proof mangrove poles with bamboo sunshades; they were closely watched but not disturbed by the red colobus monkeys and motley parrots in a windbreak of mango trees that stood between the house and the sea. Michael Belov spoke English and French with equal facility, and he had a flair for amusing anecdote . . . although, as in the case of some polished public speakers, his humor seemed learned and not native to him. Koshar, who seldom traveled farther than to the mainland of Tanzania and depended on the handful of foreign consuls and their occasional guests for intellectual stimulation, was delighted by Belov's presence.

But gradually his delight was tempered by a chilly feeling of being at bay. Koshar, skilled at intrigue and intimidation, observed that Belov was never off guard, even in this peaceful, isolated setting. Charmed as he was, Koshar felt that he was being studied as if he were potentially an opponent. Even in repose Belov revealed a hint of the predator who would become terrifying and lethal in a moment of crisis. The merchant suspected his visitor was that rarity, a man of intellect and sensibility who could kill another man with passionless objectivity. He was intrigued by the prospect of introducing Below to an animal of similar stripes, to see how they would respond to each other.

After lunch the two men settled into the back of Koshar's antique, armored Daimler-Benz, a car that had belonged to a Nazi official in Poland during World War Two. In accord with the merchant's love of vivid color, the car had been refurbished with nine coats of hand-rubbed, high-gloss, gold-flake pistachio green. Mr. Mkassu drove, and two cars filled with bodyguards accompanied them.

Koshar handed Belov his Swedish passport, other documents, and letters of reference.

"Your passport has been stamped to show that you entered Tanzania two weeks ago, before the borders were closed. You have been staying at the Oberoi Bwawani on Zanzibar and Kilipamwambu in Chake Chake since your arrival. These letters will secure for you respectful and instant cooperation from our frequently corrupt and inefficient public servants. You may travel without restriction anywhere in the country, even to the so-called war zones."

Belov nodded and filed the papers away.

"Have you located Henry Landreth for me?"

"Unfortunately, no. We can be reasonably certain that he was among the group of scientists and other eminent persons removed from Chanvai by helicopter on the night of April twenty-ninth."

"What about friends of Landreth? Was he keeping someone, a man or a woman? He might have confided in a lover before he was sequestered."

"From all reports he was a solitary and secretive man. His sexual preferences are not a matter of gossip; if there was anything bizarre about his appetites I would have heard. He owns a small house in Oyster Bay, but has been absent from that house for almost a year. He was often seen at Chanvai during the month of April."

"Then I need access to Chanvai. Will I be allowed to call on Jumbe?"

"Apparently he was quite dissatisfied with his last encounter with the press, and is seeing no journalists at present. Also he has been in ill health, and on his doctor's orders has not left Chanvai for several weeks."

"His doctor would be Robeson Kumenyere. Can I get to him?"

"For a purely social occasion."

"I may want to consult him, privately, about the matters that concern me."

"He's a shrewd and careful man, as he has reason to be. And a good pistol shot. But you could take him forcibly, with expert assistance. Is that wise?" Koshar concluded, with a heavy-lidded glance at the Russian.

"Not yet. You have no idea of where Jumbe is holding his house guests?"

"Inquiries must be made with the greatest discretion. Members of the Elite Guard are handsomely paid, and loyal. General Timbaroo has a unique method of dealing with those who do not fully grasp the seriousness of their responsibilities. In the nineteen fifties a troupe of baboons was brought into a secluded area near Chanvai for naturalists to study. They are fierce and inhospitable animals with a rigid sense of territory; protected, they flourished. Even leopards are frightened of them. You can imagine the fate of a lone soldier, securely tethered by the wrists to a stake in the ground, when the baboons discover him."

"Interesting," Belov said, but he looked faintly annoyed by the digression. "I suppose you have no news about the Chapman/Weller expedition."

Koshar shrugged apologetically.

"Why not?"

"It's a very large country, Mr. Lundgren. Despite the new microwave relay systems, communications in many areas are nonexistent. Where you find telephone exchanges, they are controlled by the government. There are many old missions and hunting lodges in forest districts that nearly defy penetration. This is why we need a man like Tiernan Clarke."

Belov gazed at Koshar for several seconds.

"I work alone."

"As you wish; it is my obligation only to furnish you with the information you urgently need. Clarke is an associate of mine, a former game hunter and now an animal catcher, under government licenses which I obtained. He has a ranch at Lake Manyara. I've provided him with an excellent living in those times when the catching and exporting of game animals from Tanzania is forbidden."

"He poaches for you?"

"Yes. There's a steady demand, despite stringent export bans, for pelts and horns and tusks. Almost a risk-free endeavor, compared, say, to the smuggling of cloves from Zanzibar, which is still punishable by death. But let me tell you about Clarke. He has a rather colorful background. He was an expert in the construction and employment of two-stage bombs for the IRA's Provo wing until greed prompted him to steal a war chest of several thousand pounds. He was overtaken by his fellows and left for dead with a bullet in his head which, obviously, failed to kill him. As a result of the gunshot he has a few less ounces of brains than the average man and certain physical defects which he's managed to overcome; he's a charming hoodlum, a hard worker, a ruthless opportunist, and slightly mad. In the past fourteen years he's flown over or walked through nearly every square mile of Tanzania. He has native poachers working for him in all the game preserves, a crew of eyes and ears I sometimes envy. He may already know where these explorers are being detained. If not, I believe he will soon find out."

"Can you trust Clarke?"

"With what little information I choose to give him."

They were driving now through the slovenly outskirts of Zanzibar Town in a haze of dust, past markets and lurching minibuses and a herd of skinny humpbacked cattle strolling along the road. Teenage herders, their heads wrapped in threadbare jackets as protection against the sun, flicked the cattle with ropes to keep them from wandering into the paths of vehicles. Along the channel the tide was out, exposing broad mud flats and beached dhows, a type of seagoing ship little changed from those that had sailed to Red Sea and Indian ports almost two thousand years ago.

Near the Zanzibar Hotel they turned down a sunless street only a little wider than the car itself, driving past old Arab houses, their windows covered with intricate wooden latticework. The street opened into a broad square with open shops and stalls. Several whitewashed buildings with balconies and brassbound, arched teak doors dominated the west side of the square. This complex housed the offices and stores of Akim Koshar.

Belov followed Koshar through room after room crowded with curios for the meager tourist trade. In another back room several ivory carvers were at work under bright lights with their dentist's drills, turning chunks of elephant tusk worth more than thirty dollars a pound into obscene *objets d'art*. The floor was white with ivory chips and dust.

"Tusks are very expensive now," Koshar said, "but still there is a good profit to be made. I have a standing order from France for all the ivory porno I can produce."

They continued through passageways with small barred windows which let in an odor of tidal wrack and stenchy mud. At high tide the waters would be lapping at the stained green seawall only a few feet outside. They came to a locked and guarded storeroom in the depths of one of the buildings.

Inside, Tiernan Clarke was sorting through bloodflecked leopard and cheetah pelts piled high on a table; he was arguing in Swahili with one of Koshar's clerks. Nearby there was a wired bundle of elephant tusks, some weighing close to eighty pounds, which had been cut off the fallen elephants with a power saw. Each bore a prominent inked brand. Clarke had also brought in rhinoceros horns worth double their weight in gold.

It was hot in the room and sweat flew from the hunter's brow when he shook his head. He wore shorts and a sleeveless bush shirt that needed laundering. He was a big man, with high squared-off shoulders and skinny dark legs displaying a polkadot collection of old scars from ulcer and claw. He had long swept-back hair the texture of a lion's mane and one eyebrow permanently out of kilter from a bullet crease. It gave a droll look to his ready smile when he turned and saw Koshar.

Koshar nodded but didn't say anything. He approached the table and examined a couple of skins. Clarke plucked a mangled cheroot from his shirt pocket and stood back chewing on it, head down, grinning with an intimate ferocity. From time to time he lifted his head to study Belov with his coal-black stare.

"Carelessly killed," Koshar said, letting go of a glossy fur with claws attached.

"It was shoot fast or forget the whole thing. And we had a flying warden butt in, at just the wrong moment."

Koshar looked displeased. "Where?"

"Along the Little Simkiapi, in Ruaha. I dusted his

tail feathers with a few rounds, enough to cause him to set down long before he reached home base. He should just now be walking out of the bush, if he can walk at all.—Or perhaps," Clarke added, rolling the cheroot to the other side of his mouth, "the warden was a she. That's been on my mind. I had only a glimpse, but there was something womanly in the bones of the pilot's face."

He returned his attention to the table to defend his wares, pulling out a magnificent black leopard pelt.

"Now this one is as near-perfect as the potentates could hope to find. It's a *gahr-jus* fur. Worth the price of the lot, in my estimation. But the others are only slightly less desirable, and with skill can be sewn into many a fine coat or slipcover."

"Hmm," Koshar murmured, stroking the leopard, working his fingers deeply into the fur while trying not to admire it.

"Not a bullet wound anywhere," Clarke insisted, pressing his advantage. "Instead the animal's chest was crushed, as if by a kick from an elephant during the furious stampede." He glanced around at Belov again. "Are you interested in hunting, boy-o?"

"Not the way you do it."

Clarke lowered his head again, a mannerism that seemed compounded of shyness and a sense of inferiority; but Belov guessed that it was a deliberate contrivance to conceal murderous impulses from the unwary. Tiernan Clarke may or may not have been unbalanced, but he would be dangerous to anyone who didn't understand the type. Clarke came toward him with a cringing show of teeth like a dog that wants to be petted and forgiven, but Belov recognized the sham and shifted his weight cautiously, hoping Clarke wouldn't be fool enough to work off his wretched pique by initiating a brawl.

Koshar looked around, frowning, and said in Swahili, "I wouldn't touch him. He will kill you."

Clarke stopped a few feet short of Belov and mulled this new idea while obsessively wiping his big and lumpy hands on his shirt until he had smoothed away the momentary rage. He looked up, grinning resentfully.

"You haven't made the gentleman's name and business known to me."

"He wishes not to be known."

"Oh, well." Clarke picked his teeth with a fingernail and continued to size up Belov. He seemed to find him wanting, but was not in the mood to pursue an apology for the insult that had inflamed him before.

"He must be a very dear friend or perhaps a partner, as you've so casually introduced him to *my* private business."

"He is not interested in your business. Only in incidental services which you may be able to provide." Koshar beckoned to his clerk and whispered to him, rapidly counting off sums on his fingers. Clarke, eager to hear how his account was being settled, walked away from Belov.

"The usual for this lot," Koshar said, with a careless sweeping gesture across the table. Clarke looked stunned, and ready to choke.

Koshar lifted a cautionary finger in his direction. "And," he said, casting a swift reappraising eye over the richest pelt, "three thousand shillings more for the leopard." Clarke settled back on his heels, chomping down on the cheroot, momentarily silenced but not pacified by this bonus.

"Three thousand! With that I'll barely make expenses for the month. The cost of avgas alone—"

"I know too well. But perhaps you can earn another ten thousand shillings by noon of the twelfth of May."

Clarke looked at Belov and, more closely this time,

at the bag he was carrying. It made him tense. He spoke in Swahili, a language he had decided Belov didn't know.

"For backing up the gent? What's his game, assassination? I tried that line of work." With a toss of his head his long hair flew back from the roots, exposing some serious scars. "It didn't agree with me."

"Let's speak English," Belov said.

"A party of explorers is being held, somewhere in Tanzania, by the government," Koshar explained. "We want to know where. Ten thousand and your expenses if we find out by the deadline. For each additional day it takes you to come up with the information, your fee will be reduced by a thousand shillings."

Clarke laughed, but he looked preoccupied trying to comprehend the importance of their request.

"Explorers?"

"Archaeologists," Belov elaborated.

"Oh, yes." Clarke shrugged. "Bloody country's full of *them*. There are digs everywhere. You have no more to go on than that?"

Belov shook his head.

"Well, man—unless I have some names. How many explorers? What were they looking for? Did they have the proper licenses, or were they caught out of bounds? All this will have to do with my success, or lack of it."

Koshar looked at Belov, who said, "He's right. Tell him."

"The expedition was an important one, led by Chips Chapman and Erika Weller. They were looking for an ancient burial ground near Lake Tanganyika; for the last six weeks they have been unwilling guests of the government, in an undisclosed location. I know only that they are somewhere on the mainland, and not in prison. Their numbers are between thirty and forty."

"That many? It would require a considerable effort just to feed them. Have you considered the possibility that they're all enjoying the hospitality of a shallow grave?"

"Yes," Belov said.

"But it seems unlikely," Koshar objected. "Despite his recent attempts to overextend his authority, Jumbe is neither a despot nor a murderer."

"I should have heard something already," Clarke said doubtfully. "What did they do, stumble across King Solomon's mines?" He beamed at the other two men, who made no reply. "All right, then. You'll have your explorers, if they're still alive. And in five days. But for five thousand a day."

"The fee is not subject to negotiation—" Koshar began, coldly. Clarke cut him off.

"Not subject to negotiation, is it? Well, now, you're not the one who's likely to get his head shot open again, for being in the wrong place at the wrong time perhaps, or asking too many questions. If this job's to be on the economy plan, then bloody find them yourself."

There was silence in the room, except for a buzz of flies around the table, the hoot of a freighter's horn in the channel. Koshar took out a platinum tin of snuff and placed a pinch of it in one cheek. Only a slightly accelerated pulse at one brown temple betrayed his fury.

"Pay him," Belov said.

Clarke, pleased with himself, turned and looked Belov in the eye.

"It's that big, is it?" he said, this time in reasonably good Russian.

Belov cocked his head a little to one side, and smiled noncommittally.

"For the work I did with the Provos," Clarke told him, "I went to school in Moscow. And as you can tell,

I have an ear for language. It's the KGB, is it not? I've had some practice in identifying you gents."

"Mr. Clarke," Belov said, his smile now indicating a certain amount of favor, "there's no doubt in my mind that you're a man of rare ability."

"That's the truth," Tiernan Clarke said earnestly. He spat particles of tobacco from the tip of his tongue, then threw the soggy cheroot on the floor of the store-room. "How about buying me a decent smoke to seal the bargain? This one's had it."

# VON KREUTZEN'S
# SHOOTING PALACE

**Bekele Big Springs, Tanzania**
**May 7**

Alone in a great bronze bed-ship, with dirty clouds of sail luffing around her, rocking gently and sometimes sickeningly whenever she moved a muscle, Erika Weller felt as if she were adrift on the blinding tide of the incoming sun, about to leave the confines of smoke-scarred walls and float through the windows.

But she sensed there was something different about the windows since she had last been conscious of them, as ragged frames for stars; they were no longer just empty space in the walls which admitted everything with wings, from tsetse flies to bats. Opaque glass had been installed, or something like glass, but her eyes were too vulnerable, it made her head ache to look directly at the windows.

Usually about this time, after a few minutes of growing awareness of herself and her surroundings, of lucidity and the desire to think, Erika would lose consciousness or sink back into that agreeably gray state of mind where pain seldom intruded. But this morning—or was it morning?—as she began to dim out, she writhed and gasped for air, then whined at the impact which these small efforts made on her tortured body. She realized that she was urinating, uncontrollably, in the bed.

It happened without discomfort and, despite the fact that she had no reliable sense of her own muscles,

Erika felt a certain satisfaction in knowing that she was functioning humanly, normally, although in a most primitive way. Afterward she couldn't feel the wet. She clenched her thighs, flexed, and was aware of soft binding cloth.

She lifted her head and was dizzy almost at once. She bit down on her crusted, dry underlip and finally felt the pain, tasted fresh blood. The spell passed. Erika saw that she was covered to just above the knees with a drab but neatly folded blanket, then swaddled, in some wide strips of a clean absorbent material, like an infant. Her hollowed belly was bare. From what she could tell she had on nothing else but a torn white football shirt with grass stains. When she tried to touch her face she was shocked to find that she was securely tied to the frame of the bed.

She moved her body again, experimentally: The bed swayed beneath her. She rested her head, on some sort of improvised pillow, and scratched with her fingers at the surface she was lying on. Loose cloth; beneath that, a rubbery plumpness, like a raft-size air mattress.

Erika breathed deeply and raised up, head and shoulders off the bed. Springs creaked loudly. The light swarmed; her heart began to pound frighteningly. But she took a determined look around.

Not much to see. Her point of view was obscured by mosquito netting, the sails of her dreams of freedom. Sunlight speared down, as if from small chinks in the roof. The netting was splattered with guano. The bed itself was a monstrous curiosity, a bronze replica of a sailing ship, with tall masts fore and aft.

*Where was she, and how had she come to be here?*

Erika felt suddenly demented, ablaze with the unreality of her predicament. She cried out; it was the weak petulant voice of a starving bird. Her eyes filled with tears.

When she blinked to clear her vision, turning her head again, she saw the black man beside her bed, nodding ecstatically, grinning, as if he were overjoyed to find her conscious. She was startled, but not afraid.

He was tall and standing on one foot, the other foot braced against the inside of his locked knee, a nomad's untiring stance. Her first impression was that he had scarcely enough skin to cover his bones—they seemed about to pop out everywhere. He had a pet mongoose on one shoulder and wore a Scottish tam and a tarnished old stethoscope around his neck. His face was kind. There was a lump or wen near the center of his forehead, like a mound of intuition, or an unrealized third eye.

He held up the stethoscope and waved it while hopping around in a storklike circle. The mongoose went sinuously from one shoulder to the other, pausing to stare at Erika with its glittering eyes.

Abruptly the black man ceased celebrating, put his other foot on the floor, and padded over to the bed. He spread the netting and put four fingers on her forehead lightly, as if he were testing the heat of a griddle. He grinned to find her cool. This close she noticed how scarred he was, and how dusty. There was fine dust everywhere in his hair, on his nondescript clothes. But his hands were clean.

"No more fever," he announced. "I making you better. Me."

"Doctor?"

"I? No. At the Jo'burg mines, helping doctor." He showed the stethoscope again, shy and proud. "Many accidents. Good helper, I."

"Must—get up."

"No, no. Wait. Coming back, I." He turned and disappeared from her view.

Erika drew a tremulous breath. From outside she heard the emphatic, derisive blare of a bull elephant.

She closed her eyes and saw herself, in a panic, fighting to keep the single-engine airplane in the air over dark *miombo* woodland. *Piece of cake*, she heard Chips Chapman say. In her ringing ears his voice sounded so close, and comforting, that she looked up, expecting to see him in the room with her. Then despair grabbed her like a wave of the ocean and thrust her deep down into some rolling, suffocating depths. No, he wasn't here. He was *there*. Way back there and dying, with all of the others.

Erika smelled something hot and savory and opened her eyes again.

The black man had reappeared, minus his mongoose, and was busy by the side of the bed. Looking at his face, she made another, fever-distorted memory connection, seeing him hopping around like a maniac, a lighted torch in one hand, smoking up the walls and ceiling as he drove the bats away. The memory was so small and flickering it might have come from a month ago, or childhood.

Fear licked through her like a rasping tongue. She tried to sit up and almost knocked the bowl from her benefactor's hand.

"How—long?" she groaned, still unable to clearly speak her mind, to articulate more than a few words at a time.

"No, no."

"I was— Plane crashed. Did it?"

Nodding, he held her head up with one big hand so hardened by calluses it seemed armored, and made her drink a slightly bitter but not unappetizing broth.

"Each day I think, tonight digging hole for her. Me. But you fooling me. You want to live, so bad. Okay. Drinking more, now you be better."

"I—"

"Drink, mum. You no strong yet."

"What's—?"

"Oh, digging some roots, I. Boiling them. Killing the *houma*, before it kill you."

"No more."

He put her gently down. He had brought more strips of clean cotton batting. He undid the soiled cloths between her legs, bathed her with a courteous professionalism and changed her. Erika kept her eyes closed.

"Let me up now," she said, when he had finished.

"Oh, no. Rest yourself. Two or three steps, that is all, then you falling down." His knees quaked realistically. "Same this house. She shake like anything." He chuckled.

"What is—whose house—?"

He pantomimed the aiming and shooting of a rifle. "Very old. Safaris, they coming here."

"A hunting lodge."

"Tomorrow, the next day, you will see. Getting up then."

"But I—my friends need *help*." She tried to plead with him, and was made aware again of her tied hands, the wrists cushioned to prevent chafing with collars of sponge rubber so old it crumbled easily.

Erika began to sob. "You don't understand. Please. Why do you have me tied like this? Untie me."

He looked wary, as if there were a threat in this request. He came back to test the bindings.

"No, mum. Not safe yet. You falling out of bed, hurting yourself."

Erika didn't believe him. She wondered, fleetingly, if she was a prisoner again, if he was other than the benefactor he seemed. But she was beginning to float, warmed and lulled by the swallows of strong broth. She saw him fading away, toward a door.

"Wait—tell me. Your name."

"Ijumaa," he said. "Oliver. Me."

"Oliver. And I—I'm Erika. *Merci. Mon ami Oliver.*"

He grinned at the unfamiliar pronunciation of his name, dancing a little in place, delighted. Erika remembered then that *Ijumaa* was the Swahili word for Friday. She smiled wanly at him and went to sleep.

In her dream time she crawled through one of the Swiss-cheese walls of the Catacombs and encountered Oliver again, in a moony chamber of preserved priests. He was like a long splinter of ebony within the crystal tomb, but he looked different, forbidding, enchanted by status. She wondered again how the ancient people had achieved such a purity of preservation, without a single patchy flaw of decay—they all looked ready to breathe upon resurrection.

The wen between his eyes had enlarged and reddened. Dream time flickered and she was back in the hunting lodge, bound in the huge floating boat-bed as he came through the doorway. His third eye was a bloodstone. It seethed brilliantly as his body froze, lifelessly, upright. Within the red diamond she saw movement, like the blur of a tornado. The bloodstone flew apart and from Oliver's forehead gushed a full-sized cheetah, leaping down to join her on the bed, the journey.

They were on a river now, a river flowing backward, leaving the giant-sized icon of Oliver behind. She felt the terror of immobility. The cheetah sat in profile at her feet, weightlessly, and its jaws parted in a licking yawn. Then the head turned and the eyes, a riled orange, appraised her. She stared back in fascination and dread. Why was he displeased? And where was she going?

Her vision blurred; the face of the cheetah was enshadowed, simplified to tones of light and dark. A straitened mask, then a barred gate, then the strokes of a pictograph; a language she had labored to learn.

But now her knowledge failed her. Was it a warning, or a summons?

Her heartbeat awakened Erika. She was aware of odors, earth sounds at night, the faint husking intonation of a big cat prowling in the near dark of her room. The spoor of the animal was unmistakable, frightening. She turned her head in time to see him, high in the haunch and with dappled nape, the glowing orb of an eye as he strode through the doorway on his way out. She opened her mouth to scream but had no voice. She lay then in the chilly night of the veld with nothing closer to listen to than her heart, racked by tremors, wondering if, when she closed her eyes again, the cheetah would return and do something terrible while she slept.

# CHANVAI,

## Momela Lakes, Tanzania
### May 7

In the early afternoon Jumbe, discreetly supervised by Dr. Robeson Kumenyere, devoted an hour and a half to affairs of state. He spent much of this time on the telephone cajoling or lashing nervous members of Chama Cha Mapin-duzi, Tanzania's ruling party, and his military high command, who had allowed a section of the Tazara railroad near the southern border to be slightly damaged in an air raid. He spoke soothingly to certain other heads of African states, and to the British foreign secretary, a long-time admirer. He was, repeatedly, reassuring about the state of his health.

When the telephone link between Chanvai and the seat of parliament in Dodoma failed, almost a daily occurrence, Jumbe dictated a memo rejecting a "strongly worded protest" from Pretoria in response to an affirmation of hostility and call to arms quoted in the *Tanzania Daily Mail* and subsequently picked up by the world news services. The remainder of his time he alloted to a delegation of Scandinavian bankers who had waited at Chanvai for two days to see him. Jumbe had begun to tremble from exertion, but he calmly told the bankers that Tanzania would rebound from the effects of the long drought and the expensive military "police action," and would resume interest payments on existing loans within a year's time. He used this piece of projected good news to extract a pledge for additional millions to bolster the trouble-

plagued highway and port facility construction programs.

"A good day's work," Kumenyere said, when the
bankers had left for the airport. He gave added support to Jumbe's hand as the president held a match to
his meerschaum pipe.

"It's thievery," the old man said sadly.

"But they're so eager to give us credit—the World
Bank regularly comes begging to bury us in dollars."

"In the end we are only robbing ourselves. We can't
hope to repay the debt we have now, although I've
tried to keep it within a few zeros of reality. And as
long as our economy is subordinate to international
capitalism, we will always be an indentured nation."
Jumbe coughed raspingly. "Another failure to leave
behind me."

"I don't want to hear any more talk like that today,"
Kumenyere told him, a hand at Jumbe's wrist as he
clocked his pulse. "Your prognosis—"

"My prognosis, I should hope, is in the pouch that's
just arrived from the airport."

"Nothing ever escapes you," the doctor said admiringly.

"Let's see what your colleagues in Houston had to
say," Jumbe said, his smile overcast by dread.

"I feel that I ought to have time to—"

"We'll study the medical report together. My
pulse?"

"Altogether unsatisfactory. I've cautioned you be-
fore, anxiety can be more of a danger at this stage
than the aneurysm itself. Now I'm going to give you
Valium, and I want you to rest quietly for two hours.
Then you may read the conclusions which the doctors
Tustin and Grunewald have reached. You know that
I'll keep nothing from you, Jumbe."

The old man grasped his arm, an affirmation of
friendship, of dependence.

"Just keep me alive—until South Africans are free. Then nothing can matter."

"I promise you."

Jumbe took the tablet of Valium, twenty-five milligrams, with a small glass of wine.

"And no one must find out—how ill I really am."

"Trust me, Jumbe. You know how much I love you."

"Remember. We need time tonight to prepare my speech. I want you to read it over several times. You'll be standing in for me before parliament, and the world."

Kumenyere smiled diffidently. "I'm willing to die for you. But a speech—I'm no politician. I'm afraid I'll make a fool of myself."

After leaving Jumbe's guarded bedroom he collected the sealed diplomatic pouch, courier delivered from the Houston Medical Center in Texas, and took it to his bungalow. There he mixed a drink and examined the contents of the pouch.

The world-famous heart specialists in Houston, Tustin and Grunewald, had returned the X rays which he had personally made, in great secrecy, at the Kialamahindi Hospital in Dar. They showed a dilation the size of a peach pit on the wall of one of the great arteries feeding the heart in question; death would occur almost instantaneously following a rupture. He leafed through the long evaluation by the surgeons, who were prepared to fly to Tanzania to perform the operation that would save the patient's life. In his precarious condition, they concluded, Jumbe could not safely be brought to them.

A knock on the door. Kumenyere left the papers and X rays on his desk and went to open it.

Henry Landreth stood outside in the stinging heat, his face twitching unhappily beneath a wide-brimmed bush hat. He had a glass of pink gin in one hand.

"There are problems," he said. "We must have a chat."

"Come in," Kumenyere said impatiently, and went back to his studies.

Henry wandered into the bungalow behind him, wincing at the drafty chill from the air conditioner. He picked up one of the X rays. In its black-and-white simplicity, it looked like a brooding thunderstorm.

"Devastating," he said. "Even a layman like myself can tell that's no good. Can it be fixed?"

"Bypass operation." Kumenyere gave him a look at the doctors' letterhead. "Almost routine for these chaps. But they're the best."

"What was Jumbe's reaction?"

"He hasn't seen the X rays yet. I've gradually prepared him for the worst."

"What about the poor bugger who actually needs the operation?"

"Ah, but he no longer needs it. He died ten days ago, in hospital."

"Unattended and unmourned?"

"I made it easy for him. After all, he did me a good turn. By presenting me with just the symptoms I needed, at the right time."

Henry studied the doctor's smoothly handsome, pious face.

"As long as we're talking about murder—"

"Are we?"

Henry shuddered. "Let's continue our conversation outdoors. The bloody cold in here will have me croaking like a frog."

Kumenyere picked up a heavy rifle and they walked down a rough track toward Big Momela, where islands of pink flamingos shimmered in the sun. All around them, for several square miles, was the Chanvai Game Sanctuary. A warden in a Land-Rover went bumping across a stretch of short grass-

land still wet in low places; the meadow was populated with buffalo and kongoni, a type of antelope
with a sloping back like a giraffe's, and curly horns.
Directly behind the crater lake, and fifty miles away,
Kilimanjaro was slightly beclouded in an otherwise
perfect sky.

Even as they walked in the humdrum noon of sun
and insects, Henry slipped into a state of meditation,
his mind filled with a vision of bloodstones. He had
spent weeks in the Repository deep in the throat of
Kilimanjaro, studying the stones for twenty hours a
day. He had come to think of them as living entities,
with intelligence, will, even the power of life and
death over those who came into contact with them.
His fellow explorers had faded to unimportant shadows in the radiance of the stones, and after a while
they ceased to exist for Henry. When he decided to
remove some of the stones and reveal what he had
learned about FIREKILL to Kumenyere, he experienced
no difficulty in murdering Jack Portline, who attempted to stop him from leaving the Repository with
the diamonds.

But now, when he was in the doldrums, a sink of
anxiety, Henry was frequently concerned that he'd
made a mistake in taking away even a necessary handful of the bloodstones. He was neither superstitious
nor inclined to occult explanations for the mysteries
and paradoxes of existence, but he felt that if the
stones had not been missing, the mountain would be
quiet. He had experienced the power of the long-dead
cat people, the Lords of the Storm, from the unimaginable distances of their tombs. While in the Catacombs he had been susceptible to the flood of im-
agery and perceptions that followed unwise eye
contact with the creatures. *Transformation*, Erika had
called it. One did not actually change shape or sprout
catlike whiskers; but one became, for moments or

even hours at a time, more animal than human. He'd been away from the Catacombs for several weeks, but he felt the haunting pressure of their eyes in his mind, their fierce disapproval. If he could put the blood-stones back, then perhaps— But that was idiotic. And not at all possible; things had gone too far, the stolen bloodstones were hostage to implacable ambitions: his own, and Robeson Kumenyere's.

"The mountain's heating up," Henry said forebodingly. "And the Kibo glaciers are already melting. Seismic activity is stronger than it's been at any time since 'sixty-six."

Kumenyere was gently incredulous. "You're worried that Kilimanjaro will erupt?"

"It won't take a major eruption. With the ice retreating, a million tons of rock could be loosened by the continuing jolts and come tumbling down from the rim. And the entrance to the Catacombs will be buried forever."

"I think Kilimanjaro has been in this state many times during the last ten thousand years. Yet the entrance was there to be found, by the clever Dr. Hardie."

"It was pure luck on his part," Henry snapped. "He had very little to go on. Some rock paintings above Nyangoro that seemed to be the faces of cheetahs, but were language, a schematic drawing, symbols he had the wit or inspiration to interpret as ultrasonic frequencies. A bright child with the proper sonar equipment could then have found his way to the Catacombs."

"He was the first. But you'll have the credit."

"Even if the Catacombs could survive a really serious upheaval, we ought to remove the FIREKILL bloodstones from the Repository. Without delay. There's too much at stake."

"You shouldn't be a worrier, Henry. It gives you no

opportunity to enjoy life. You're going to be a very rich man, your past dishonor willingly forgiven."

"Forgiven! I was misjudged, falsely accused, shamed, *ruined!* You have no conception of the work I was capable of doing, the discoveries I might have made if they'd left me alone. England has despised me for thirty years. But someday they'll appreciate how deeply I loathe them all!"

"I'll personally supervise the erection of monuments to you all over the East African Federation; perhaps there'll even be one back home in Trafalgar Square, ha-ha. Now I have some good news. The fever at Ivututu has claimed more victims. Two are dead, two more in a condition that might be described as hopeless idiocy, their minds burned up."

"Chapman?" Henry said, too eagerly. "Is he dead?"

"Not yet. But it's only a matter of time for all of them. It was certainly worth the great risk I took to introduce the virus; we've learned a great deal about it, and we may well develop an antivirus that will save countless black lives in future. So your friends will have been sacrificed in the service of two causes—oh, Henry, now look what you've done! All of your expensive cigarettes are in the dirt."

Kumenyere, rifle in the crook of one arm, bent gracefully to help the Englishman replace the unsoiled Dunhills in his gold case. He observed Henry's trembling hands. "Do you know what it is they say in the States? 'You're climbing the walls, man.' Ha!"

Henry straightened, and screwed a gritty cigarette into his ebony holder.

"Does Jumbe know about the epidemic?"

"I've kept it from him. He would bear the responsibility for all those lives much too heavily."

"Yet he'd willingly blast half a million white South Africans into radioactive moonbeams, given the chance." Henry shook his head, dismissing the incongruity. "It doesn't help us if *all* the fever victims die. Not if Erika Weller is roaming around free."

"I rather doubt that she is. She took off in a crippled aircraft in the middle of the night, and nothing has been heard from her since."

"Sheer incompetence, letting her get away like that!"

"An unfortunate combination of circumstances. We had no idea she could fly an airplane. Obviously she couldn't fly very well."

They broke through a living curtain of small dotted butterflies dancing in their path; the track took them downhill, past groundwater forest thick with tamarind and wild orange trees. A big green monitor lizard, bulbous with jowls, squinted at them from atop a termite-infested log. Henry stumbled over a root in the track, and Kumenyere put out a hand to keep him from falling.

"I think, Henry, that you should return to seclusion in Dar and let Nyshuri amuse you during these long days. The waiting *is* difficult. Even for me, and I have a great deal of preparation to do before I assume the presidency. Let the Russians and the Americans conduct their frantic investigations. They'll waste their energies looking six hundred miles in the wrong direction for the Catacombs. It's safe to presume that Erika Weller is dead. At your insistence, I passed on instructions concerning Raun Hardie to some capable friends of mine in America."

"There's only a possibility," Henry brooded, "that she knows where the Catacombs are. Hardie doesn't mention her in his account of the discovery. But it's common knowledge that she was raised and educated by her father; she accompanied him nearly everywhere until the day he was killed. I have this feeling in my bones—it's better to do away with the girl, before the Americans have a chance to interrogate her."

"So there are no more 'flies in the ointment.' Who else can find the Catacombs? Just you and I."

As they rounded a bend near the lakeshore, Kumenyere paused in a patch of shade and suddenly shouldered his high-powered rifle, throwing back the bolt, seating a cartridge designed to blow the heads off most game animals. Henry looked around in astonishment, then fear.

Kumenyere grimaced and waved him aside. "Get behind me. But move slowly and then keep still."

Henry Landreth looked back over his shoulder, seeing for the first time the old female elephant blocking the track ahead of them. She was chocolate colored from mudbaths, with a pitted raspy forehead and huge tusks turning gunmetal gray. She stood in a shifting pattern of light and shadow in a threat display, her trunk raised, one foot swinging. In Africa elephants are sized according to their estimated tusk weight: The matriarch might have been carrying a hundred and eighty pounds in matching ivories.

"*Huyu mbaya sana,*" Kumenyere murmured. That one is very bad.

"Why don't we just go back now?" Henry said timidly, unnerved by the size of the elephant, knowing how fast she could charge if provoked.

"No. She's in *my* path. And I don't stand aside for elephants."

Kumenyere took aim with his .470 rifle. "They tramped my brother, and they nearly ruined my father's farm. They can be hunted to extinction, and I wouldn't care."

He fired. Henry cringed.

The old elephant roared and turned away, a foot and a half of her left tusk shot off, the pulp and nerve exposed. In her agony she reared up on her back legs, to a height of fifteen feet, and lost sight of them. She went crashing off into the swampy brush beside the track, sending flocks of rails and black-winged stilts into the air.

"She'll remember me," Kumenyere said with satisfaction, ejecting the brass cartridge from his smoking rifle. "She'll have that toothache until she dies." He smiled. "Well, Henry. What else is on your mind?"

"I did hope to spend a few minutes with Jumbe."

"Yes, you should." Kumenyere put an arm around the Englishman. "Try to be cheerful and reassuring. Convince him, again, of the rightness of the course we've chosen for him."

Henry Landreth turned his head toward the fabulous mountain, a look of yearning, of obsession in his eyes. He said passionately, "We should use the excuse of possible eruptions and landslides to evacuate everyone from the base of the mountain. It's a one-in-a-million chance that thrill seekers or amateur volcanologists might stumble on the Catacombs. But we can't afford even those odds. No one must be allowed to go near Kilimanjaro until we're done."

"Jumbe will certainly approve of that." Kumenyere tightened his grip on him, knowing how distasteful Landreth found it to be embraced by a black man. "Don't worry, Henry. Nothing will happen to Kilimanjaro. The Lords of the Storm knew that it will endure as long as the continent. Kilimanjaro stands for everything that once was great, and will be great again, about Africa."

"I have a feeling in my bones," Henry said, still gazing into the distance. "I think I should go back. I *know* I should go back, and wait for whatever comes."

Suddenly his eyes opened wider; he gasped in Kumenyere's fierce, bone-grating embrace.

"You should do," the doctor said softly in his ear, "only what I tell you, and when I tell you. Make no mistake about that."

# FEDERAL CORRECTIONAL
# FACILITY

## Talon Mountain, Colorado
## May 7

A spring snowstorm, powered by tricky winds gusting
to fifty miles an hour, swept down out of Wyoming
just before dawn and created nearly impossible conditions for the takeoff of a helicopter. The storm was
predicted to clear the area by noon, leaving four
inches of wet snow on the ground. Jade figured they
could drive the hundred miles from his ranch in two
hours, and he was impatient to find out what Raun
Hardie might have to tell him about the Catacombs.

John Guy Gibson reluctantly agreed not to wait for
flying weather; he and the security officer assigned to
him, a man named Parcher, piled into Jade's big
black-and-chrome, four-wheel-drive Custom Bronco,
which was equipped to plow through drifts that
would smother most automobiles.

Jade handed over to the CIA deputy a microfilm
file he'd studied for two hours the night before.

"Do you feel you know any more about Raun
Hardie than you knew before?" Gibby asked Jade as
they headed west. Three pairs of quartz-halogen headlights blazed through a flying mush of snow.

"Only that prison life doesn't agree with her. That
could be something."

Jade mumbled his reply. He wasn't in a talking
mood. He'd had a disturbed, sleepless night. About
four he'd finally gone into Nell's room, needing solace,

a sympathetic hearing. But she'd been missing more often of late. The window that had remained cracked on a view of eternity was shut, despite his proficiency, his techniques of recall: He found that he was as blind as if he were gazing into a mirror at his own grieving face. There was a stillness he hadn't noticed before. Nell's room seemed abandoned for good, despite his determined efforts: the daily hothouse flowers, her personal effects scrupulously kept. Jade was shocked.

It was as if Nell no longer existed—or rather, desired to exist for him. He sensed, somewhere, her faint and poignant smile. He was left to himself to solve the enigma of Raun Hardie.

After the death of her father, when she was fifteen, Raun had settled in the states, in suburban Washington, D.C., with guardians, including a motherly, sensible woman who smoothed the rough edges. Despite a lack of formal schooling during the years she globe-trotted with her father, Raun had little difficulty settling in with her peer group and adjusting to the academic routine at a good private school. She was *summa cum laude* at George Washington University, then an editor of the law review at the University of Virginia.

In her college yearbook photo, taken eleven years ago, she seemed to be thinking, not posing, her face turned a little away from the camera, the fingers of one long hand pressed against her temple. She was about to smile, or laugh; she was, rather than conventionally beautiful, fresh, engaging, original. And her face, with its heavy cheekbones and wealth of lashes, coronet of braids and dark husky hair, did appeal to the camera. It was a face that invited contemplation, and might easily inspire devotion.

Raun Hardie was spirited, inquisitive, and quickly impatient with the evolutionary pace of good works in bureaucratic Washington. She lasted two years in a promising job at HEW, then quit to form a consumer advocate group called Gray Cells, which published a monthly newsletter to inform the average American about the greed and incompetence of big business and big government. Despite the contrary opinions of disgruntled bureaucrats and post-trial autopsies in the press, there was never a taint of subversive intent or unlawful militancy about Gray Cells. The organization had numerous well-connected supporters, but it survived largely through the efforts of volunteers, and kept its accounts in good order. Raun became an accomplished public speaker and debater, skillful at prying open closed minds without making enemies; not surprisingly, by the time she met Andrew Harkness she was one of the best-known women in America.

Harkness, at the age of thirty-seven, had distinguished himself as a young man with exceptional promise in government. He was a foreign-policy specialist, already the number two man on the National Security Council staff: brainy, aggressive, and a favorite in high places, which allowed him to exercise a considerable talent for head knocking, imposing his will and viewpoint in matters of strategic policy. He first encountered Raun Hardie on an otherwise social occasion; before the evening was an hour old they were locked in a bitter debate that provided a fund of gossip in the capital for days afterward.

Apparently neither relished the opinion that the debate had been a draw; they resumed a few days later, privately, and after that, despite her anti-Establishment bias and his primary role as a champion of official White House policy, it was evident that they had commenced an unlikely but passionate affair.

In his public life Harkness seemed little changed by Raun's influence, if she tried to influence him at all;

his prospects were untarnished by the liaison. So it came as a shock, a little more than a year later, when Harkness resigned his post, citing insoluble conflicts with his superiors, including the president. Thus he ended a career he had begun as a graduate student in foreign affairs at Princeton.

At the time of his press conference he was prematurely gray, subdued, grim, and thoughtful, in contrast to the abrasive ebullience he had demonstrated during his quick rise with the administration. Immediately after his resignation he went into seclusion. Three months later an edition of *Gray Cells* was entirely devoted to an article written by Harkness, setting forth in convincing detail secret plans of a cooperative effort by the Department of Defense and the CIA to sponsor armed revolution in Warsaw Pact countries. His information was distilled from nearly twelve hundred pages of reports removed from top-secret government files unavailable under the Freedom of Information Act.

When he was arrested, in a mountain hacienda in New Mexico, Harkness freely admitted he had taken the material, because "At no time in our history has the shadow business of government so unconscionably jeopardized the future of its people." He exonerated Raun Hardie of complicity in the theft, and stood trial in the Federal District Court in Albuquerque. The trial was long, and complex, and most of the citizens Harkness had sought to protect paid little or no attention. But no verdict was reached. Several weeks after the trial began, Raun Hardie joined forces with an underground militant group called the '66 Strike Command. They invaded the courtroom and removed Andrew Harkness at gunpoint, touching off an explosive drama that was still flickering on the pages of the world's press four and a half years later.

All of the eight young men and women who collaborated on Harkness' escape were heavily armed, with automatic weapons, including Raun herself. In the courtroom the elderly jurist hearing the case suffered a stroke from which he never recovered. Outside the courthouse the militants and their hostages split into three teams and went in different directions. In the van with Raun and Harkness was a girl named Bonnie McBride, daughter of a Wall Street lawyer, and an ex-Marine and car thief from Louisiana, Bobaloo Blanchard. They had one hostage, a court reporter, who was released unharmed within minutes.

Subsequently Raun's team split again, and took advantage of a great deal of confusion involving an identical van and two couples who closely resembled the fugitives to get far away from Albuquerque. The authorities could never prove that this coincidence was part of a master escape plan.

Other members of '66SC weren't so lucky. Two of them, and a policeman, died in a shootout at a roadblock on the interstate near Truth or Consequences, New Mexico.

Raun and the rest of the group disappeared. Bonnie McBride later was identified as a lay missionary working in a Central American republic with which the U.S. had no extradition agreements. The FBI immediately put Raun Hardie and Andrew Harkness at the top of their most-wanted list.

Almost three years to the day she spectacularly changed her stripes, Raun Hardie walked into a police station in Waterloo, Iowa, and gave herself up.

She'd been working at a farm cooperative in the next county, but she seemed to have suffered from her lonely life as a fugitive. Her hair was shorter and lighter. Otherwise she'd made no attempt to disguise herself. She claimed full responsibility for plotting Harkness' escape. She knew where he was, but would not tell. She wanted only to have a speedy trial, receive her sentence, and be left alone.

The heat of pretrial publicity was enough to fry the brains of everyone involved. Raun chose as chief counsel of her defense team a man whose sober dignity was no substitute for his lack of experience in court, and she stranded him without a viable way to defend her. She had done it, she said, because Andrew Harkness was a courageous man who had chosen to serve only his conscience, and she could not idly watch him subjected to the prolonged injustice of a government inquisition. Only the young and incurably idealistic found this a persuasive argument; the liberal community was inclined to dismiss Raun Hardie as an embarrasment because of her involvement with a muddled, murderous group of self-styled revolutionaries.

When she commented, infrequently, on her predicament, Raun seemed to be involved in a kind of mental torture that passed for philosophical insight. Her affair with Harkness was analyzed at length, to her detriment, embellished with speculation and gossip. Because she wouldn't speak to reporters and was indifferent to the public's appetite for the notorious and lubricious, the press did not treat her kindly. She also refused to cop a plea.

The government prosecutors, all of them highly ambitious, took this refusal as an invitation to turn the courtroom into an arena, with the tacit approval of the presiding judge, the honorable Harry Stokes Wanda. They pressed their open-and-shut case vigorously, condemning Raun as a gangster, a symbol of everything evil that could be expected to evolve from open dissent and civil disobedience. She was found guilty on all counts.

Judge Wanda, before sentencing, delivered a lengthy citation, including her culpability in the deaths of a fellow jurist and a young policeman, and her failure to cooperate with the law by revealing the whereabouts of Harkness; above all, he took her to task for her unwillingness to repent. He then gave her fourteen years.

There was, as she began serving her time, a backlash of sympathy, a "Free Raun Hardie" movement, but it came too late to be of much use. In prison she frequently had been ill or depressed, and very bitter about the length of her sentence. A book analyzing her character and exploits had been the top nonfiction best seller in the country for several weeks, but some serious questions about her motives remained unanswered.

It was commonly believed, in the Justice Department, that despite the vital issues in contention at Andrew Harkness' trial, he would have served, at most, two years in a minimum-security prison. Why then had Raun Hardie taken such desperate risks, thrown so much of her life away, to spare him a mildly punitive sentence? And why, with both of them at large, had she abruptly decided to give herself up? Had she still been living with him at the time she walked into the Iowa police station? If not, where was Andrew Harkness today, and what had happened to their relationship? Harkness must have known that by surrendering himself as well she would have benefited from a greatly reduced sentence.

Instead Raun was stoically paying for them all. And the mysteries persisted.

Fifty miles from Talon Mountain, John Guy Gibson was jolted from a doze and looked fuzzily around. The sky had lightened, the snow was burning to rain. They were on the ragged western edge of the storm.

"Where are we now?" he asked, peering at the steep, white-capped evergreen forests above them.

"Black Alder Canyon."

Gibby blinked, and tried to recall why that sounded familiar. The heavy tires whined on a tight wet curve.

"Isn't this where your wife died?"

"That's right," Jade said, with no change of expression; but he seemed to be in a hurry to leave the canyon behind. In front of them, on the road, a heavily hung aspen dropped part of its load of snow. Gibby tried to envision hurtling tons of it, piling deeply from wall to wall, enough snow to bury Nell Jade in her car for more than two days of subzero temperatures. Jade had been traveling only a few minutes behind her, in the Custom Bronco. And he had been here, waiting at three in the morning, when the plow blade scraped down to metal and broke open the glass. Gibby had seen snowbound soldiers in Korea, pale blue, welded to their weapons. Nell Jade, he imagined, had been a piece of ice sculpture in a brittle parka, in an eerie white cocoon spun from her freezing breath.

Gibby glanced at Jade and wanted to say something graceful, to muster a tribute. But he was more than a year late. Instead he tried to divine the effect which Nell's terrible fate continued to have on Jade's suspect psyche; how damaging, in the long run, it might prove to be. Outwardly Jade hadn't changed. He was terse, pragmatic, and observant. And preternaturally quick, a sleight-of-hand artist with gun or knife. Though Jade was only average in size, there was about him an epic quality: He threw the shadow of a king. One expected from him deeds, dynasties, legends.

The legends existed, all right, but the times had changed. In the pursuit of the bloodstones there could be no margin for error. Was Matthew Jade slower, softer than he had been? If he was faced with a difficult choice in a crisis, and made the wrong decision, then they would all know. Too late.

"There's one thing about the whole case that keeps

coming back to me," Jade said, after another long silence.

"What's that?"

"Andrew Harkness' grandfather and father died of an identical form of cancer. His father was only 41 years old."

"So what?"

"I just said it keeps coming back to me. I don't know why."

Raun's stomach was hurting so bad that by the time she reported to the dispensary, she thought she was going to throw up.

The charge nurse, whose name was Madsden, looked sympathetically at her.

"Not the flu again?"

"I don't know. Cramps," Raun complained; she was unable to straighten up.

Madsden glanced at the clock in her brightly lit, glass-front cubicle. The time was twenty minutes to ten.

"Dr. Murtaugh's running late this morning, but I expect her just *any* minute. And there aren't too many ahead of you."

Raun glanced to her right, into the fluorescent-green waiting room of the dispensary. She saw two black women wearing the institutional denim jumpers. They sat on opposite sides of the big room. One was tall and gnarled and twisted, like a tree rooted on a windy hillside. She leaned forward tensely on her cushioned bench staring at *Seasame Street* on the black-and-white TV. The other, who was short and plump, with a hairdo like Nancy in the funny papers, held a handkerchief to her face, sniffling disconsolately. Her eyes, like the eyes of a soft animal in a burrow, stared at Raun.

Raun turned back to the nurse.

"I'm really nauseated."

Madsden got up briskly from her creaking swivel chair and pressed a buzzer releasing the door to the treatment area. It sprang open a couple of inches.

"Come right on back with me, dear."

Raun followed her, past cubbyhole offices, unoccupied, on the right, rows of gray metal file cabinets on the left. They made a couple of turns, Madsden pausing before the doors of rooms which she then rejected for undisclosed reasons. Finally she put Raun at the very back of the warren, in a tight room with a single misted window from the overproductive radiator. The window, like all others in the prison, was covered with a grid of heavy wire the thickness of a chain-link fence.

"Ought to be warm enough for you here," she said cheerfully. "Just strip and put the gown on, and if you feel like you're going to faint or anything, buzz me. I'll send the doctor as soon as she comes."

"Thank you," Raun whispered, as she was hit by another cramp.

She leaned against the treatment table until it passed. The door closed behind Madsden. Raun sat down and wearily unbuttoned the straps of her jumper, took off the blue-checkered shirt. A hard rain rattled against the window. After taking off her underwear, she fumbled with the ties of the coarse cotton gown, knotted one of them and crept onto the table. She lay on her side, drawing her knees up. This afforded some relief. She'd had very little for breakfast: coffee, grapefruit juice, a few bites of toast, she didn't know what could have hit her so hard. Maybe it was all in her head. Maybe she was just unlucky. She felt very tired. She had begun to perspire in the hot room.

The lights went out.

Power failures happened frequently in this lonely

prison. Usually the lights began to glow again after only a few seconds. Raun lay listening to the perk of steam in the radiator and wondered if a drink of water would ease her discomfort. After a while she sat up on the edge of the padded table. Through the foggy window she could make out lights in another wing of the prison.

So the failure was confined to her area—the dispensary and hospital ward next door. It was well into the morning, there was nothing to worry about. But this day, like so many of them lately, seemed to have been born dead. Her nipples puckered hard beneath the gown.

To amuse herself while waiting, and give her nerves a break, Raun conjured a familiar scene: a south Pacific beach, enormous warp of sun through the slats of palm trees, trade winds. The sea on a reef, booming distantly. She placed herself there, bare browned feet toeing out just above the surge line, where the sand was firm but wet enough to accept and hold, for minutes at a time, sculpted footprints.

She made a lot of aimless footprints, fine tuning her sense impressions to include the tang of oiled heated skin, the feel of her hair whiplashing across her face, the slight grit of sand between her thighs as she strolled along. It was seductive, absorbing; and the part of her mind that remained like a mushroom in the darkness of her prison sentence reacted with alarm. Because she was getting too good at these excursions, removing herself from the horrors of tedium. Raun realized that once she achieved her beach and full stature in that pleasant dream country, she might spend an entire day, then a week, perfecting just one footprint. Turning slowly, thoughtlessly, like a goddess on a spit of sun. There she could be immortal . . . while the imprisoned self burst and perished, drooling away intelligence.

Raun slid painfully off the table, clutching her belly, and farted, which helped a little. She had another, doleful inspiration: She was developing colitis. She was about to take a drink from the sink when she heard voices outside. She paused to listen. The voices stopped. Raun couldn't be sure, but she didn't think it was Madsden. Or Dr. Murtaugh, whose broguean English was instantly recognizable.

If the lights had been on she wouldn't have been uneasy. But she'd been waiting in the stuffy room for, she couldn't tell, maybe twenty minutes. Sick as she was, Raun craved human contact.

She opened the door. The hall outside was darker than she had anticipated. It gave her pause.

The voices again. Just whispers this time. Raun thought she heard another door opening, closing.

In an office at the front of the dispensary a phone began to ring.

Between rings Raun discerned the faint squeaks of nurse Madsden's swivel chair. The phone rang seven, eight, nine times. But Madsden didn't pick up. Why? Her chair was agitated, it bumped against something. A desk, a wall. For no good reason the nape of Raun's neck crawled like a caterpillar.

Looking cautiously out, she saw at the other end of the hall a faint light from a window on the yard as another treatment-room door was opened.

Opened slowly, by someone standing at arm's length in the hall.

Raun had an impression of a very long, almost emaciated arm, of hunchback tallness, a watchful face illuminated in profile, like a rind of a Stygian moon. Of an upraised hand with something pearly, or silver, lethally angled in it. She remembered the black woman who had been so enthralled by *Sesame Street* in the dispensary's waiting room. And the other one, staring at Raun, a touch of fever in the round and childlike eyes.

The phone stopped ringing. Its persistence had been comforting, its absence inspired terror. The chair continued to squeak. Raun stepped back and closed the door silently, not allowing the latch to click into place. Her heart was trying to break through the bones of her chest.

Someone, she thought, was going to be killed.

It was a grim aspect of prison life she'd only heard about. Who were they looking for, and what could she do? Raun forced herself to open the door again. She had to know where the women were. She strained to hear them.

*That the dentist office, fool. Thought you said you knowed where you was.*

*She back here someplace, that all we need to know. Just you look around and keep shut.*

*Fool! Shoulda made that nurse tell us.*

A soft giggle.

*Why don't you go ask her now, see if you can lip-read. Ha!*

Their words became indistinct, as if they'd teamed up and were now whispering with their heads together. Raun fought a strong cramp, and tried to remember how to get from the treatment room she now occupied to the front of the dispensary. A few steps down the hall, right turn into the next hall, right, no, *left* at the file cabinets to—

"Raun Hardie!"

She was shocked to hear her name spoken. With no doubt remaining of the intended victim's identity, her impulse was to run, screaming, for help. Now she knew it was no accident that she'd become so sick right after breakfast, that the only lights to go off were in the dispensary.

*Dear God,* Raun thought, *don't let it happen. Don't let this happen to me!*

Her ability to think rationally even under great stress saved her, at least for the moment. If the women stalking her were taking such pains with the job, and had the wit and confidence to call her, expecting her to blunder innocently into their hands, then undoubtedly they had secured the outside doors as well, so no one could get in or out. And one of the doors was electrically controlled, from Madsden's office.

The phone was ringing again. Stunned, then hopeful, Raun listened to it.

All she had to do was reach Madsden's phone and get through to the prison administrative offices, then try to stay alive for another ninety seconds or so until the guards came with their shotguns. She could crawl under the desk, or—

*Just get moving!*

Raun stepped out into the hall and the loose gown caught rippingly on the doorknob. She reached behind and undid the single tie that held it in place, stepped away naked. She would, she hoped, be more difficult to make out in the gloom of the dispensary without the white gown. Raun could see very little herself. Her assassins might be behind a door just a few feet away, or about to turn the corner.

She was so frightened she knew she would be hopelessly clumsy if she tried to hurry. She forced herself to think, to listen, at almost every step.

The phone quit. She'd been using it as a kind of beacon, a homing device in the dark. Without it Raun felt stranded, miles from safety. But she kept going, trying to keep her breathing under control so she wouldn't break into giveaway sobs.

The file cabinets. Now she knew where she was.

With her fingertips she made light contact with the

opposite wall and came to the first of the small door-less offices, used by physicians who did part-time work at the prison. In Madsden's office, barely twenty feet away and on the opposite side of the hall, a cube of red light was glowing: the *hold* button on the telephone. The small light was powerful enough to illuminate an area of sandwich glass in front of the nurse's desk. From the angle at which she was stand-ing Raun could make out the telephone itself. And the middle drawer of the desk seemed to be hanging open. Except for the hum of a refrigeration unit some-where, the dispensary was very quiet. It was as if the women searching for her had given up, faded into thin air.

Raun focused all her attention on the waiting tele-phone. She moved toward it, more quickly.

Just as she reached the doorway, the swivel chair, with Madsden bound and dying in it, came shooting out of the darkness from the other side of the hall, striking her painfully.

Raun screamed. Madsden's hands were tied behind her and her throat was open from ear to ear; there was a considerable pool of blood in her lap. In a panic Raun shoved the chair away. Horrified, she saw it tilt. Madsden's eyes were open; they stayed open even when her head hit the floor and came to rest at almost a ninety-degree angle to the chaired body.

"There you be."

One of the assassins was coming at her, following the chair she had thrust into Raun's path. Raun glimpsed something long and sharp in a pudgy hand. Giggle, giggle. She smelled the distinctive peppermint odor of angel dust. Raun backed into Madsden's of-fice, slipped on the bloody floor, banged her naked hip and then her elbow against the sticking-out drawer and fell down, the drawer coming free in her hands. In the feeble red light she glanced at the re-

volver that had slid forward with all of the junk which
Madsden had kept in the back of the drawer, then
looked at the black girl filling the doorway of the office, hesitating, incorrigibly giggling.

From somewhere farther along the hall the gaunt
one spoke sharply.

"Fool! Do her. *Provide!*"

The chubby assassin stepped cautiously into the office, quivering with stifled merriment. She raised the
knife and reached down to pull the desk drawer off
Raun. She hesitated again, not quite believing the
small revolver she saw raised up at her in Raun's two
hands.

"Oh shit," the black girl said crossly. "Zola? She—"

A little too late she lunged, awkwardly, with the
knife.

As they drove into the prison, John Guy Gibson
glanced at the small band of sodden young people
huddled beneath umbrellas and pieces of tarp, the
legends nearly rain-washed from their hand-painted
signs demanding clemency for Raun Hardie.

He said sourly to Jade, "She does have her admir-
ers."

Jade was looking elsewhere, at armed guards con-
verging on a long two-story building on the other side
of the recreational grounds, playing fields and courts.
He ignored the sign pointing the way to the administration building and gunned his Custom Bronco toward the scene of the disturbance.

"There's a scram," he murmured. "Better get out
your ID, Gibby."

"All the talk in the world won't do no good now,"
said the gaunt black woman named Zola.

She was crouched in the hall of the dispensary a
few feet shy of the door to the nurse's office. But she

spoke softly, unhurriedly, as if they were neighbors passing a boring summer's day on a front porch somewhere. In her right hand she held a straight razor. Behind her was the body of nurse Madsden, which she ignored. From her position she could see a muddy double image of Raun in the glass above the desk.

Inside, Raun sat trembling with her back against a wall, bleeding (she didn't know how seriously) from a knife slash low on her right side. The revolver she had used to blow apart the fat assassin's head was still clutched in her two hands. The corpse lay between her and the door. Either there was one bullet left in the revolver or there was none. Neither she nor Zola was sure of that, which was all that had kept her alive this long.

Zola, by her account, had already resigned from this life; she knew she was a goner no matter what happened in the next five minutes or so. She claimed to be at peace. Her only concern was that Raun might kill her with that single remaining bullet before she had the chance to cleanly cut Raun's throat, and so Provide.

During the precious minutes she had stood the woman off, and gained hope from the commotion of guards and prison officials outside, and lost hope when they seemed reluctant to shoot their ways in and take a chance on accidentally killing her, Raun had tried to put the two of them on a first-name basis, desperately postponing that inevitable moment when Zola would rush in wildly and try to do the job her companion had bungled.

"Zola, I still don't understand what you 'Provide' by killing me. Who do you Provide for? How can you sacrifice your own life this way? I guess I'm just confused. I know you don't hate me, I've never done anything to you."

"Of course not, girl."

"*Raun Hardie? Can you hear me in there? Let me know you're all right.*"

Zola sighed, and sounded annoyed when she spoke again to Raun.

"Fools. Better tell them, Miss Hardie, it come down to just you and me, and no kind of trickery, like that tear gas, make a difference. I'm no big talker. Quiet all my life, just a handmaiden, I just do and Provide, according to the will of the Messengers, the holiest beings ever lived on this earth. To Provide is to be Elect in the coming life. Crucify and testify. Allah-la-la-la! I come chaste to my Election, weeping tears of joy. This life stinks of sin. They say to me in this place, Zola, eat the flesh of swine. Fools. Water don't wash away your sins neither. And another thing, this life is filled with beasts who walk and talk like men. Shed blood! Blood is the righteous way to Election. No way do I walk out of here alive. Tell them, Fools. Make it plain."

"What Messengers? Is this some kind of religious—"

"Shut them up out there! Or I get too fussed to talk. Wesley, I put up with his drinking ways. His blows and meanness. But the child, the child, don't you see, went under the bus. Three years old. Wesley sprawled out drunk upstairs. I melted down all the brown sugar 'til it was bubbling in the pot. Threw it in his demon's face. Now I *told* you already, don't want to hear them mens no more!"

"Okay, I'm okay!" Raun shouted. "Just leave us alone, you're upsetting Zola!"

"Better," Zola muttered. "I truly don't mind to talk with you awhile longer, now I gets to know you. What you should understand, it don't hurt 'specially, not if the razor's plenty sharp and that first cut be deep. No pain to speak of. You just black out in a minute or two, drift off to sleep. Peaceful. 'Stead of you puts up a fight and gets butchered real bad."

"Zola, Zola, *please* listen to me! I don't want to die. I don't want to shoot you, either. But I can do it. My father taught me to handle a pistol a long time ago. If you try to come in here then I'll kill you."

"I don't hold that 'gainst you," Zola said generously. "Course you gone do your best." She pondered their dilemma again. "What it come down to, if you got a little bitty purse-type gun, which it sounded to me, then you needs to be lucky *and* good, 'cause one shot won't serve to knock me down, 'less it catchin' me smack in the head. Now what I think, it get to be just a little too quiet around here to suit me, and that's bad, so maybe—"

"Stay put," Matthew Jade said, as Zola began slowly to rise.

Zola stiffened and looked around with extreme caution. She could just make him out, standing barefoot twenty feet behind her, in the center of the hall.

"Where you come from? Nobody else in here, I made sure."

"We pried off a window grate out back."

"So. Where the rest of you? Machine guns, shoot me down like a mongrel dog. Huh?"

"The more troops, the more noise. I came in alone."

"Shoot me yourself then, Mr. Big."

"What the hell, I forgot to bring a gun."

"Lyen fool. How do you think to stop me then?"

"I'll stop you, Mama."

Zola showed a savage grin.

"No you ain't. I got Miss Raun Hardie, right in there, closer to my razor than you is to me. You do any sudden moves, reckon I slice you both, thin off the bone."

"Who *is* that, Zola?" Raun cried anxiously. "Who're you talking to?"

"Just a *man*," Zola said contemptuously. "Sneak in here behind my back. Got him a cowboy hat, looks like." Zola resumed her rise, still watching Jade, who stood relaxed with his hands at his sides. "All right, hat man."

"You'll never make it."

"Zola! No!" Raun Hardie screamed.

"Allah-la-la-la!" Zola cried ecstatically, and she flung herself at the doorway, razor held high.

A split second before she moved, Jade's left arm described a full circle; he pitched in an eccentric but powerful three-quarter sidearm motion a double-edge throwing knife of his own design. It traveled the twenty feet between Zola and himself at nearly ninety miles an hour and chunked solidly into her right ear just as she appeared before Raun.

The impact knocked Zola off balance and against the jamb. Raun pulled the trigger of the small revolver, and the hammer fell on an empty chamber. She continued to point the revolver high, sighting, earnestly snapping the trigger again and again, as Zola took a staggered step into the room and collapsed, skewered, her head tilting forward decisively at the last moment as if from the weight of the cold steel embedded behind her eyes.

# 49 COURTEMANCHE STREET

### Johannesburg, South Africa
### May 8

On a cold smoggy fall evening Lourens Todt observed, from a second-story window of his home in Hillbrow, the prompt arrival of the young man he had come to think of as his son.

While Jan-Nic Pretorius was giving his hat and coat to one of the servants, Todt came halfway down the mahogany staircase to greet him. As usual only an austere handshake passed between them; but Todt unexpectedly allowed himself the indulgence of a quick cheek pat of approval with his left hand. Jan-Nic could not have been more astonished if the tough, dour old man had kissed him.

"Extraordinary planning, Nico," Todt murmured.

"Thank you, sir."

"If Ndzotyana had slipped away from us again, I hesitate to think of the effect this escape would have had on these militant Bantu, so soon after the Ikwezi disturbances."

"The PNF is pretty well demoralized today."

"I'll go further than that; we've smashed them. There's only Solomon Mkhize to consider now, and he can't be effective in exile."

They walked up the stairs together, Todt holding tightly to the railing, his eyes betraying no sign of the pain he felt in his arthritic, all-but-immobile left knee.

He was too proud to install an elevator within the mansion, or to walk with the aid of a cane. On his worst days he now stayed home, and conducted the affairs of the Department of National Security from two small, windowless, maximum-security offices reconstructed from unused bedrooms at the rear of the second floor.

They settled down with tea served by one of the special officers on duty. Todt, a full elder of the Dutch Reformed Church, neither drank nor smoked, nor allowed anyone else to do so in his home.

Jan-Nic was red around the eyes and his hands trembled slightly, but otherwise he did not betray the fact that he'd done without sleep for nearly seventy hours. He'd had his suit pressed and was still operating on his abundant nervous energy, further exhilarated by the triumph of his career.

At the age of thirty-seven Jan-Nic Pretorius was already acknowledged to be the man who would succeed his father-in-law; even his enemies, who called him the Golden Greyhound and found him too social, too aggressively self-serving, conceded that he would someday have a cabinet post. Jan-Nic had conceived and was in charge of the OB branch of the Department, named in tribute to the original Ossewa Brandwag, a rabidly anti-British, pro-Nazi group which his father and Lourens Todt had helped establish before World War Two. The covert OB branch, composed entirely of *Broederbond* zealots within the department, was the instrument of apartheid most feared, because of its apparent omniscience and total ruthlessness, by South Africa's blacks. For three years OB branch had concentrated on eliminating the insurrectionists of the Patriotic National Front; with the capture of Robert Ndzotyana, the PNF's best organizer and most articulate spokesman, Jan-Nic had fully justified Todt's confidence in him.

"What's the latest word?" Jan-Nic asked. "Will Ndzotyana recover?"

"He was severely burned over fifty percent of his body. But he's a strong young man, who can tell?"

"While he lingers, he's dangerous. A living martyr is more of an incitement than a dead one. I should have shot him when he came out of the shafts."

"We aren't savages or sadists, Nico, no matter what the rest of the world wishes to believe."

They drank their tea in silence for a few moments. Robert Ndzotyana, the lone survivor when his meeting place in an abandoned shaft in the Witwatersrand gold-mining district was invaded by OB agents equipped with flamethrowers, had been taken to the nearby Baragwanath General Hospital, a two-thousand-bed facility for blacks in Soweto. Neither man mentioned that the hospital had no intensive-care unit for burn victims, thereby lowering Ndzotyana's chances for survival to the minimum.

"Well, Nico, I realize you haven't been inside your own home for nearly a week, and I shan't keep you long. Unfortunately, fragments of the letter which Ndzotyana was carrying on his person have caused some anxiety. I've been in touch with the prime minister, who believes an investigation should be conducted, and at once."

Jan-Nic shook off the fatigue that was stealthily tugging at his eyelids in the overheated office.

"How much of the letter was readable?"

"Nearly two full paragraphs. And all of the signature."

"You're convinced it's authentic? Jumbe Kinyati wrote it?"

"*Ja.* We have numerous samples of his handwriting for comparison. The laboratory did an excellent job of reconstructing the charred portions. If Ndzotyana hadn't folded the letter into rather a small packet and pushed it deep into his trousers, I doubt that any of it would have survived."

Jan-Nic nodded, recalling the smoking, screaming, nearly naked man who had tumbled, weaponless, from a flame-seared passage of the honeycomb mine. He wondered again why he hadn't automatically pulled the trigger of his own weapon. But he knew the answer. He hadn't wanted to be there in the first place. He lacked a certain essential coldness, a willingness to come to grips with the realities which his meticulous planning produced. He was simply not a killer. Physical violence dismayed him. He had channeled his youthful athletic ability into solitary sports and forced himself to excel to overcome the pain of a poor self-image. He had always been a skilled emulator, first of his dashing father, then of the pragmatic, stolidly courageous Todt, whose exceptionally plain daughter he had married in a demonstration of devotion to the old man. He was strongly sexual, unresponsive to Anna-Marie, and terrified of extramarital involvements; one slip could ruin him, in this archconservative society where he strove to make of himself a monument no man could pass by without tipping his hat.

Todt summoned the officer on duty, who brought a Xerox copy of the letter now fragilely preserved between sheets of glass in a laboratory vault.

The letter was addressed to *My Dear Friend and Suffering Compatriot Solomon* (Solomon Mkhize, the other leader of the PNF, who was currently in hiding in Angola). Jan-Nic read slowly, pausing often to try to fill in the puzzling gaps caused by fire. In essence the letter was an exhortation, almost Biblical in the grandiosity of its language, pledging the full faith and might of the government of Tanzania (Jan-Nic smiled at that) in helping the beleaguered PNF to fulfill its goals. Jumbe declared

> We will be        st of our na
> to acq      nucle    weap
> Trust in the pow          deliver ce!
> A mult      of warhe
> each with the explo      for    to
> equ    ten Hiroshim    Pretoria
> shall peris in the brightn
> our noon! The time is alm    upon
> us, the reck      our impat
> gods a matter of d

Jan-Nic put the photocopied letter aside, and for a time didn't meet his father-in-law's demanding gaze. He helped himself to more tea.

"Well, sir . . . it seems like aimless chest-thumping to me. The impotent ravings of a man we know to be ill."

"Presumably not mentally ill."

"Our intelligence has not been able to establish that. Of course it isn't my department. My own suspicions . . ." Jan-Nic shrugged.

"Nonetheless we will take this . . . disagreeable piece of correspondence as a serious threat to our well-being."

Jan-Nic blew across his cup to cool the tea. His nerves tingled.

"May I ask why?"

"It's an undeniable fact that a little over a week ago the defense ministers of both the United States and Soviet Russia made simultaneous unpublicized visits to Chanvai. After a conference lasting for several hours both men abruptly left Tanzania. The Russians, true to form, will tell us nothing about the travels of Victor K. Nikolaiev; they deny he was ever south of Tripoli. The American government to date has not provided a satisfactory explanation for the sudden departure from his itinerary by Morgan Atterbury. He is, of course, a long-time supporter of and apologist for Kinyati. That letter to Solomon Mkhize, hand delivered we can assume, is dated April 30, *the day after* Jumbe's secret meeting with the world's superpowers. Whose lack of interest in our continuing survival is not a matter for conjecture."

Jan-Nic decided that he was more tired than he had thought; his father-in-law's concern just didn't make an impression.

"I think," Todt continued, "something was said at the Chanvai conference that has encouraged Jumbe Kinyati to believe he will soon have in his possession nuclear weapons capable of being launched from his own country and destroying ours. Highly mobile, medium-range ballistic missiles, to be specific."

"But—what kind of fools would give missiles to Jumbe? Can the buggers all have gone totally daft? *Ach*, I can't take any of this seriously! It's like a nightmare film comedy—superpowers skulking about, meetings in the bush in the middle of the night, all the parts played by Peter Sellers. Jumbe's country is of *no* strategic importance. He has nothing rare or valuable to trade. That coon and all of his kind aren't worth a crate of rusted sabers!"

"Unbelievable as it seems, Nico, that may not be true. I know you're badly in need of leave, you've counted on having some time with Anna-Marie and the children. But the prime minister wants immediate action, and I want my best man on the job. It's a deadly serious game that's being played, make no mistake. If we can move quickly we'll snatch the ball away from the Americans and the Russians. And put an end to Jumbe's schemes."

"What is it, though? What does Jumbe have that can be measured against the death of our country?"

"Diamonds, Nico. Perfect red diamonds each nearly as large as a pigeon's egg, from a storehouse more an-

cient than recorded time. There are symbols etched
on these bloodstones, symbols that somehow are a key
to the holocaust we must prevent."

Todt paused, anticipating Jan-Nic's next question.
"I'm sorry, my son, I do wish I could tell you I've
seen one of the diamonds." His thin lips, usually as
expressive as scar tissue, parted in a rare smile. "But I
know where we may get our hands on one . . . and
the man who can take us to the rest of this treasure."

# VON KREUTZEN'S
# SHOOTING PALACE

**Bekele Big Springs, Tanzania
May 8**

"Oliver," Erika said, pretending to relish the stew he'd prepared for her, "I'm better today. You know I'm much better."

Oliver Ijumaa nodded his dusty head. He sat cross-legged on the floor of the room with the great bronze bed-ship in it, and grinned with pride. His pet mongoose was perched on his knee, eating a candy bar that Erika had found in a flight bag salvaged from the wrecked airplane. A sunset rain of hardshell beetles fell on the quilted plastic packing material that Oliver had tacked over the window frames. A paraffin lantern lit the room.

Oliver had brought, in addition to the pilot's flight bag, a seat cushion from the plane for Erika to sit on, and a small steel barrel full of Tuborg beer. Erika gave Oliver most of Weed's personal effects, including a stainless-steel razor, keeping for herself clean socks, shorts, and a tattered but wearable bush shirt; a mirror she hadn't had the heart to look into; a comb she dragged through her unwashed hair with difficulty; a tube of cortisone hemorrhoid ointment already providing relief from bedsores; and a package of Rough Rider ribbed condoms, from which she fashioned two serviceable *botas*.

She was a little concerned about giving Oliver beer,

not knowing what the consequences would be if he got drunk. But she was nearly dehydrated, dying of thirst and afraid of the water that was available. And she felt it would be wrong, a blow to his manhood, if she drank in front of Oliver without inviting him to help himself. As it turned out he was fascinated with the improvised *bota* but absorbed very little beer: Instead, he had an uproarious good time spraying his face and shirt and mongoose while trying to direct a stream of the warm beer into his mouth.

Erika drank more than was good for her, partially quenching her great thirst. She became intoxicated, which gave her a false sense of well-being.

"What I must do then," she said through her chewing (it was some kind of brawny meat, none too fresh and heavily seasoned), "is to strike out tomorrow as soon as the sun rises. We're in a park of some kind, aren't we? A game reserve. By the way, how far is the plane from here?"

"Heaven knows, mum. Walking and walking, I. Long time walking."

"How did you ever find me, Oliver? Did you hear the plane crash?"

He shook his head. "No. Smelling it."

"You *smelled* the plane? Well, there may have been some fire, I don't remember—can't remember anything, after the poachers." She put down the dented pewter plate of stew. "But if the plane is so far away, how could you possibly—"

Oliver laid a long finger against the side of his nose.

"Smelling it," he insisted. "Very good smeller, I." He had another squirt of beer, which ran down his chin. The mongoose, his own nose quivering with delight, put his paws on Oliver's chest and licked the drops away.

"And you carried me back? Oliver, how long have you been here at the lodge?"

He shied away from the question, and shrugged. "Few days," he said. Erika knew he was lying, but she didn't press him. What mattered was that he had saved her life, and now would help her save a great many others.

"So there's no one around at all? You have no family or friends in the vicinity? You're very much on your own, then. But there must be some sort of settlement, Oliver, or at least a ranger post—with a radio—"

He was aroused, alarmed, by this line of thought. He looked uneasily at the plate beside her, a lid of cooling grease on top. He made eating motions with his hands.

"More. Then resting, few days. Or the fever come again."

"That's ridiculous; you've cured me, I'm well, Oliver, I mean it." Erika was surprised by tears, the fragility of her emotions. "Haven't I proved—"

He sprang up, the mongoose clinging to a forearm by all four paws, and did one of his pantomimes, striding toward the door with vigor, then weakening, collapsing to his knees, panting for breath.

"Well, just let me *show* you what I can accomplish. I'm really my old self again."

Erika got off the airplane seat stiffly, finding it an effort not to tremble. In the red light of dusk her face was a mummer's mask of concentration, slotted eyes glowing deep in her head. The intemperate swigging of beer had resulted in an alcoholic haze; distances were distorted. Now that she intended to leave the room, the door looked very far away. She walked toward Oliver as if she were trying to keep her balance in a swirling, knee-deep tide at the seashore.

Oliver got up slowly and stood aside, frowning at her. The mongoose ran down his leg and out the door, chittering madly. By the time Erika reached the doorway she had broken out in blisters of perspiration.

She hesitated, then bit down on her lip and walked out of the bedchamber in which she had passed the numberless days of her convalescence. One shoulder grazed the jamb in passing. She took a deep breath and sighed with relief. Then she looked around.

In the fading light she was able to measure the vastness, the baronial scale of the hunting lodge. Obviously someone of great wealth—a captain of industry, a titled sportsman—had constructed it during the heyday of colonial domination of East Africa. Overhead, bats flew in and out of the ruined dome, which had been constructed of wood and stained glass. There was a curving mural above the front doors of the lodge, the bright colors of safari scenes dimmed by time. In one panel Erika thought she recognized the stalwart Kaiser Bill, in full uniform, bringing a bull elephant to its knees with a well-placed shot while nearly naked natives danced with glee around him. Before World War One the Germans had controlled most of what was then called German East Africa through force of arms and sheer terror.

Oliver's mongoose nipped down the fat rail of a balustrade to the rotunda floor. Erika followed him. The mahogany staircase had marble inlays. A lantern, placed by Oliver, glowed on a pedestal by the entrance. There were pieces of classical statuary around the rotunda, implausibly robust Teutonic gods and goddesses. Someone, many years ago, had used them for target practice, chipping off ears, fingers, folds of drapery.

The main floor and support columns of the lodge were stone, but enough mahogany had been used in construction to make the lodge a prime firetrap. A lamp dropped in the wrong place would turn the rotunda into a furnace. Erika envisioned the bronze bed-vessel overheating, taking on an other-worldly glow, then slowly sinking into a tumultuous sea of sparks. She licked her dry lips, ignored the painful hammering of her heart, and crossed the rotunda to the entrance. There one ten-foot cast-bronze door, as ambitious a work of art as anything she'd seen in a Renaissance church, stood open a couple of feet.

She went outside, passing from a gloomily baroque vision of man to the starkly primeval.

Before her, from the modest heights on which the lodge was set, was a vista of a thousand square miles, parched savanna and bush, flights of birds in a yellow sky, dark trees like thorny low clouds along a seeping stream. And animals quietly on the move everywhere to the scarce water: baboons, blue monkeys, the inordinately shy bushbuck. Within a hundred feet of the dooryard she saw a twitchy herd of golden impala, passing through what had once been a formal garden.

The red-eyed mongoose settled down to capturing a meal of flickering grasshoppers. Erika ventured farther into the yard and looked behind the great lodge, at an unexpected escarpment of naked rock three hundred feet high, an offshoot from the Great Rift Valley; it cast a premature darkness over them. She saw why the abandoned lodge might well have gone undetected for many years. Its stone exterior had the precise coloration of the rugged rise behind it.

This escarpment accounted for the abundance of game; even without rain some water and minerals would trickle into the lowlands the year round. Erika saw where elephants had demolished an acre of yellow acacia, leaving fragments, splinters, the beginnings of a desert. She was breathing through her mouth and knew she must rest. She sagged down on the rim of a fountain. Masonry, and bronze figures, discolored, dark as ink. From a cherub's blissful mouth a sinister lizard dripped. She heard the ominous hum of tsetse flies; but they hadn't found her yet. She panted. She knew she could not proceed another dozen steps. Her body trembled. In all this openness she was trapped by infirmity, as solidly as if she were anchored in concrete.

Among the stones ringing the fountain there was a larger oblong, as large as the roof of a crypt. She went down on one knee to examine a metal marker. She used her fingertips to decipher the Gothic letters. It was the final resting place of Admiral Von Kreutzen. Whoever he was. Another voyager, far from the mainstream, asleep, in bedrock. She batted away a bloodsucking tsetse, and winced.

Oliver trudged toward her, looking concerned.

"Coming in now. Flies very bad sometimes here."

Erika braced herself, raised her head, and smiled.

"Well, Oliver. As you can see, I'm not exactly going places. Give me—another day or two. In the meantime I know—I can depend on you to carry on, you've done splendidly so far. It's imperative that you get to a radio, a telephone, and notify—let me think now, who would it be best to—never mind, I'll give you names. You call, use my name, they'll pay. Tell them—an emergency exists. Kingdom Mission, Ivututu, Tanzania. Everyone dying. Help must be sent immediately. There must be—official inquiries, the UN, I don't care. They'll know what to do. Oliver, are you listening? With your—capable assistance, I know we can pull this off."

He did a little scuffling dance of uneasiness, grinning. At this level, eyes at his knees, the fraying edges of cutoff trousers, she was made aware of what a load of testicles he carried, they hung down almost a foot, big fistlike bulges that caused him to walk with a slight bowlegged stride. He was almost inhumanly endowed, balls enough to burst through the always dusty, glittering khakis he wore.

Erika raised her eyes to the escarpment behind the lodge.

"All the dust," she said. "You're always—so dusty. You told me you'd been a miner, near Joey's. That's what you're doing here, isn't it? Looking for gold. I'll wager you've found it. That escarpment. You know a gold-bearing hill when you see one, don't you?"

His wide smile pleaded innocence even as he backed away in fear.

"Oh, mum. Tanzania very poor. No gold. No gold."

"What about the Lupa gold field near Mbeya? I heard you downstairs last night—all night. Pick, pick, pick. Chinking away at some rocks. It's all right, Oliver. Please don't misunderstand. I'm happy for you."

"Coming in now. Bad flies."

"Is it that you're afraid to help me? Afraid the authorities will somehow get after you for prospecting on government land? You needn't be. I'll see to it that you're amply rewarded. Trust me, Oliver. My friends—are *dying*. I must get word out."

Oliver looked around unhappily. He clapped his hands to his head.

"Oh, heavens," he moaned.

"Oliver, I'm sort of a prospector, like you. I'm an archaeologist, do you know what— Never mind. I look for treasures, the remains of old civilizations. Tribes that lived a long time ago. Right here in Tanzania, my associates and I discovered the most astounding treasure anyone has ever seen. More valuable than all the gold of the Witwatersrand, I promise you."

He was staring solemnly at her, still holding his head in commiseration, listening. But not, Erika was certain, comprehending what she had to say.

"You've heard of Kilimanjaro, haven't you?"

"Oh, yes. Big mountain. But not seeing it ever."

"In Kilimanjaro, I mean *inside* the mountain, there

are—there are—I don't know how to make you understand—there are *rooms*. And each of these rooms is
larger than all of Admiral Von Kreutzen's lodge. One
of the rooms is a Repository, a—a storehouse, containing hundreds of red diamonds. Immensely valuable in
themselves, but they're etched with a complete record
of a long-vanished race of men. Well, it's a long story,
what happened to us, but we were betrayed, I think.
By Henry Landreth. Yes, it had to be that bloody bastard H-Henry. And removed to this *pitiful* little mission near Ivututu. Either we contracted a fever in
the—the Catacombs, the big rooms I was telling you
about, or else we picked it up at the mission where
they forced us to— But the tragic thing is, I thought I
was free, I'd escaped. Now I'm no better off than I
was before! And so much time has been lost. Oliver, if
I can just get proper medical attention for my colleagues— But you have to do it. Help me. And I
swear—I'll take you to the Catacombs. You can have
one of the red diamonds! In a hundred years you
won't dig enough gold in this godforsaken place to
equal the value of a red diamond. You could own a
house, and a Land-Rover to drive."

Erika was sobbing. She knew that Oliver thought
she'd gone round the bend.

"Oliver!"

He jumped and then nodded, too eagerly.

"Yes. Helping, I." His head continued to bob up
and down; his hands flailed at the swarming tsetses
attracted by their body heat. "Coming in now, dark.
Flies."

He was a good and tenderhearted man, but a loner,
perhaps a fugitive like herself. He had learned the
hard way that it was wise to have nothing to do with
governments, their petit officials, their brutal soldiers
and police. He would continue to take very good care
of her, and listen earnestly to her pleas. Tomorrow,

and the next day, he would find plausible excuses for not making the trek to the nearest radio. He would procrastinate until it was too late for her to do Chips any good—if indeed he was still alive.

Goaded by the vicious bite of a fly on the back of her neck, Erika screamed and lunged toward Oliver, taking him by surprise. She seized the prominent bulges between his strong thighs and dug her fingers into them.

Instead of testicles there were nuggets. She had found his small hoard of compressed gold, carried in pouches in the safest place he could imagine.

"You're lying! This is all you care about! You won't help me, you're too afraid!"

Erika was overwhelmed by attacking flies and her own emotions. She curled up on the ground, trying to protect her face and neck, yelping each time a tsetse nipped flesh. She felt Oliver's hands on her. He picked her up as if she had no more heft than a market basket and carried her at a jog into the lodge. He put her down on the lowest step of the staircase and went to slam the big bronze door.

The rotunda reverberated, like the inside of a bell. Erika sat with her head in her hands, trembling.

Oliver came back. "Blood on your face," he said. "Bad, such flies. Maybe catching the sleeping sickness, you."

"Oh, don't worry," Erika said irritably, barely able to breathe.

She pulled herself to her feet and started up the stairs. She had to rest, every third step, and for longer intervals each time. A bat went whispering past, up and out through the broken dome.

"I'm going to bed. Tomorrow—I'm leaving." Her declaration had a slight ringing echo. "You hear? Walking—out of here on my own. And I'll make it."

From the top of the stairs she looked back at Oliver, at his impassive face in the shadowy rotunda.

He looked different somehow. She wasn't used to seeing him absolutely, powerfully still—not smiling, nodding, dancing, doing one of his shy pantomimes. His long fingers were slowly curling, uncurling. There was about him an aspect of loosely controlled violence; and she was unexpectedly, irrationally afraid of him.

"No, mum," Oliver said. "No leaving here, you. If you do that, you will surely die."

# FEDERAL CORRECTIONAL
# FACILITY

## Talon Mountain, Colorado
## May 8

"Miss Hardie, I'd like to introduce Matthew Jade. He saved your life."

Raun looked from John Guy Gibson to Jade, moving her eyes but not her head. She still felt a little sleepy from the sedative given her hours ago. She was lying nearly flat in a narrow hospital bed. They had cleared the entire infirmary ward, which was now locked and heavily guarded. Several CIA agents, protection specialists, had been flown in to ensure her safety.

"Did you have to kill Zola?" she said crossly. "Wasn't there some other way? That poor demented woman."

"She didn't leave any options."

"Take off your hat so I can see your face."

Jade removed his Stetson and took a step closer to the bedside light.

Raun studied him. Curly, brassy hair grizzling at the temples, a high forehead, a formidable wedge of jaw, a slightly bemused, inquisitive expression. Small secluded eyes, just a hint of blue.

"How could you do that? With the knife. It was dark and she was moving, wasn't she? My father used to throw a knife—for fun. But he said you couldn't hit a moving target very well."

"It takes practice. About twenty hours a week, for twenty years. You get to where you can hit a tomato seed in a shit storm."

"Oh, I see. What an interesting way to spend your time. You must be the star of one of the CIA's traveling horror shows. A program of old favorites, by request. Subversion, assassination, the politics of torture."

"I'm just a local rancher," Jade said affably. "By the way, that was good shooting. Or I wouldn't have been in time to do you any good."

Raun looked as if she was going to be sick.

"Oh, God. I didn't want to think about that." She licked her lips, wincing, and dropped a hand to her right side.

Dr. Murtaugh, a freckled plump woman with a severe hairdo, appeared at the side of the bed.

"Raun, it was a superficial cut, I didn't have to take stitches. But it'll be painful for a couple of days."

Raun caught her breath and relaxed, closing her eyes for a few moments. Then she tensed again, as if she were reliving her ordeal in the dispensary. She asked for a sip of water and focused on Gibson.

"I suppose you're in charge here. Are you going to tell me what it's about? Why were Zola and—that girl trying to kill me? Or don't you know?"

Gibby glanced at the doctor, who smiled and nodded and excused herself. When the door of the ward closed behind her there were only three men around the bed, including Gibson's bodyguard, Parcher; he was operating a Nagra tape recorder.

"We can be reasonably certain that the attempted assassination has to do with an important archaeological discovery that your father made many years ago, near Lake Tanganyika."

Raun looked perplexed. "I grew up in Africa.

Kenya, Tanzania. But—Dad's major discovery came before I was born, in Ethiopia. The Afar communities. He's famous for—"

"We know. We're talking about the Catacombs, a huge burial ground for an ancient civilization which he found just a few weeks before he died. We thought you might have been with him at the time."

They were all watching her closely. Raun looked deep in thought, unenlightened.

"We have reason to believe that President Kinyati of Tanzania ordered this attempt on your life, because he's afraid you can supply us with detailed information about the Catacombs, and pinpoint their location."

"Catacombs? Lake Tanganyika? You mean—"

She was suddenly silent, watchful, guarded.

"I may know what you're talking about. But why should I tell the government anything? Look what the government's done to me."

"All I can say now is that something found recently in the Catacombs by other explorers has a direct, vital bearing on the national security, and we must verify—"

"Oh, hey. Try again. I mean, that's just not where I'm coming from, all right?"

"Miss Hardie, you were within a few seconds of dying this morning, and if you aren't willing to take that seriously—"

"Gibby?" Jade said. "You're not making much of a presentation." He smiled warmly at Raun. "She has a right to be skeptical. I think I ought to assure Raun that the government is charged with responsibility for her well-being, so she'll have airtight protection from now on."

"Thanks."

"But you'll be living a little differently—in max security, observed around the clock. Lights on twenty-four hours a day. Until you're eligible for parole, that's what—?"

."Three and a half years from now," Raun said grimly. "You've made your point. Are you sure you're just a rancher?"

"Cowflop between my toes."

"I'll bet. Okay, you do the talking. If I want to be really loyal, patriotic, and sincere, could I get out of jail? Now?"

"What can you do for us?"

"Well—suppose I tell you that you're totally wasting your time, that someone is putting you on? That'll save you a lot of trouble, and maybe it's worth a commutation."

"Do you know where the Catacombs are?"

"If we're talking about the same thing. Dad stumbled onto this—burial place while he was looking for something else. But this is the part I don't think you'll like." She looked somewhat anxiously at the faces around the bed. "Believe me—there's nothing inside worth a second look. Ancient civilization? That's a reach. It's a roomlike cave with a low ceiling. Some well-preserved mummies, potsherds, primitive artifacts. There are a few pictographs scratched on the walls, I didn't get a very good look at them. But nothing that could possibly be of significance to any government. Nothing that's worth my life. I'm telling you the truth! I'll take sodium pentothal or a lie-detector test if you want me to."

Gibby, after a few moments, sighed bleakly and glanced at Jade, who seemed unperturbed as he stared at the woman in the bed.

"How much time did your father spend exploring the Catacombs?"

'Two days. He would have stayed longer, but I twisted my ankle the first day and it swelled up badly. It could have been broken, and he wanted to get me to a doctor. You know what a problem that can be, we were in the back of beyond. He made a lot of notes in one of his green books—"

"What kind of book?"

"Like a diary, dateless but with lined pages; they were all covered with dark green cloth. He bought a case of them at one time, and never used anything else for his observations. It was a trademark, almost, everyone in the profession made jokes about Dr. Hardie's little green books. Anyway, he was anxious about me so we broke up camp. He said he'd probably come back and finish the job one day, but he wasn't really excited about the find."

"What happened to that notebook?"

"Oh, Lord, there were so many! It's probably at the University of Edinburgh, with the rest of his papers. That's where I shipped his files when I cleaned out the villa in Dar. I also sold most of his library to a second-hand dealer, but none of the notebooks was included. I don't think. But there were boxes and boxes."

"So the green book with a description of the Catacombs could have slipped through accidentally, and turned up in the bookshop. Remember the dealer's name?"

"Sure. Mr. Ganges. I guess he's still doing business there. On Maktaba Street, near the New Africa."

"Did your father go into the Catacombs without you?" Jade asked.

"The second day, after I twisted my ankle. I couldn't even stand up. We thought it would get better, so he went ahead with his exploration. I didn't see him until past sundown. By then I was in such pain I was almost delirious. I was running a fever."

"Is it possible that Dr. Hardie made a second discovery at the site, that there was a lot more to the Catacombs than a chamber filled with mummies?"

"A major archaeological discovery? My father wasn't the type to get excited about anything, but I would have known."

"Maybe what he saw in the other Catacombs was so amazing that he was afraid to say a word, until he'd had a chance to thoroughly explore the find on his own."

"He trusted me," Raun insisted. "He would have dropped a hint, given it away. Whenever I had a birthday due and he'd planned something special, his mouth would twitch at the corners and he'd try not to smile when he looked at me. Then I'd go to work on him, and get him to spill the beans."

Her head turned restlessly on the pillow. She looked around the dreary prison ward, falling into a visible depression, bluntly reminded that the joy and freedom she'd had as a girl might be irrecoverable.

"He must have been concerned about your condition when he came back," Jade said. "You were feverish—you might not have been fully aware of what was happening, what he had to tell you."

"I don't know. I just don't remember. The pain was bad. He had to carry me. He must have walked all night. The next thing I knew I was in a flying medic's plane, on the way to Dar."

"Do you remember the location of the Catacombs?" Gibson asked.

"Yes. By that I mean I couldn't locate it on a map. But I could find the place again. I'm bush trained. I have a photgraphic memory for terrain."

"You're not going," Jade said.

Raun stared at him. Her voice, when she spoke again, was low but fierce.

"Then you won't either."

"Miss Hardie," Gibson said, "there's a great deal we can do for you. But you have to try to be reasonable—"

"I don't think I have to talk to either of you again if I don't want to! Go ahead. Put me in deaklock. Bright lights, I can't use the john without somebody watching. The way I've been feeling lately, I'll go berserk in about a week. What good will that do any of us? Reasonable. Huh. First I was posioned this morning, then I nearly had my throat slashed. I was lying naked in a pool of blood with about sixteen men milling around staring at me. They told me this was an easy place to do time. Friendly white-collar criminals. Your choice of wallpaper in your room. Just like a Howard Johnson's. I've done one year and it went down like thirty. We've been snowbound for seven goddam m-months."

Raun began to cry. She was one of the rare women for whom tears were an enhancement. Her eyes looked larger, softer, her pasty skin took on a compensating glow.

"I want a presidential pardon. Then I'll lead you to the—the Catacombs, if that's what you call it. You'd better decide in a hurry. One hour. Then I'll never say another word, never!"

She looked stubborn; she looked as if she meant it. Jade thought of the long trial she'd endured, stoical months under intense examination. In different circumstances he would have admired her toughness of spirit. Now he took pains not to show his exasperation.

"Boomer available this afternoon?" he said, turning to Gibby.

"He can be reached."

"Let's you and I have some conversation," Jade said, and he smiled at Raun Hardie as they left.

The rain had abated; they walked across the rec grounds, Gibby backing against the wind as he tried to light a cigarette.

"Maybe it's a hoax after all."

"No," Jade said. "Hardie made his discovery. But he didn't let his daughter in on it. He might have been afraid to."

"Why?"

"Archaeologists don't lead such dull lives. They're prey for certain types of entrepreneurs, those who deal in black-market artifacts. Some of them could be depraved enough to grab a fifteen-year-old kid who wasn't discreet and set fire to her toes until she spilled what she knew about daddy's latest discovery."

"So Hardie was protecting her. But he jotted down a few notes. What's your gut reaction?"

"Everything Raun was telling us is true. But she's careful about what she says."

"Meaning?"

Jade kicked apart a waterlogged clump of snow.

"I get the feeling that somehow I'm being used. I don't like that feeling."

"She offered to take a lie-detector test."

"Sure—we'll hook her up to a polygraph, and also run her by a couple of your best interrogation teams. She'll make out just fine. No inconsistencies. The work she used to do was close to that of an investigative reporter; and she spent three months in the dock handling some very tough cross-examination. She's had the course."

"Do you want to take her with you?"

"Do I want two left feet? This must be my lucky day. Except I know damn well it isn't. Will Boomer give her that pardon?"

"On your say-so."

Jade stood staring at a line of blue sky near the horizon. A muscle in his jaw was working hard.

"Let's do it then."

## DAR ES SALAAM

Miss Sunni Babcock, of Basking Ridge, New Jersey, awoke shortly after daybreak in the suite at the Kivukoni Five-Star Hotel suffering from what she would have described as a "bad body" had anyone been there to listen to her complaints. She had a low-grade fever, an upset stomach, a feeling of having been insistently pounded on, like a badly dented fender, with a rubber mallet. Being alone again—Toby had left her alone much too often lately, she thought—gave her a touch of homesickness and dark, dark melancholia. She was crazy about Toby Chapman and would follow him to the ends of the earth, but she missed her mother and father and little brother and her championship jumper Moody's Gate, and when she finally got home she was going to *kill* Ernie if he had let the horse go to pot.

So it was the middle of May, springtime in Basking Ridge, and she lay there naked in the tangled bed that was damp from night sweats, thinking about the cool green lawns around the Japanese-style ranch house on Loring Lane, the collie dogs and the cats, the lilacs and fruit trees coming into bloom. In Dar es Salaam (which she thought of as "Turd Town" in her grimmer moments) it was dust and heat and socialists who couldn't say enough bad things about America, even your high-type socialists at the embassies, where you just had to put up with the badmouthing because they had the only decent food and parties available.

Could they really have been here for six weeks? And when was Toby going to give up?

Sunni sniveled and tried to get comfortable, but almost immediately she was sorry for the thought: How would she feel if it was *her* father who hadn't turned up for months and months, and no one was willing to give her a straight answer about what could have happened to him? Beside herself with anxiety, that's how she would feel. Worried sick.

It was really amazing that Toby could hang in there, day after day, waiting hours to see the minister of this or that, spending a fortune on bribes, and not lose his temper and bash somebody. Well, he'd come close a time or two: It was interesting to see him getting red from the neck up, like a thermometer with all the hot mercury shooting into the bulb. But he'd never taken his frustrations out on her. That was the really beautiful thing about Patrick Tobias Chapman. He was as considerate, mannerly, and loving as he'd been from the day they'd spotted each other on the Quai d'Orsay—and just sort of drifted together through the Sunday strollers, irresistibly attracted, smiling at each other. When they were still two or three feet apart (hadn't spoken, eye contact only), she'd felt exactly as she had once upon a time in physics lab, doing the experiment with a high-voltage Tesla coil, her skin tingling wildly and every hair on her body quivering upright. It was as lush as any orgasm she'd experienced to date. Talk about *turned on*. They'd scarcely skipped a night of lovemaking since October, and right now, queasy as she felt, she could get a ripple going in her groin thinking about those bashful chestnut eyes and his crazy English cowlick. It was real. *It was meant to be.*

But where was he so early, and why hadn't he told her he was going out? She quickly gave Toby the benefit of the doubt. He was depressed and scarcely slept anymore; probably he'd gone for an early walk around the brassy, scum-edged harbor that lay across from the hotel.

Sunni felt a threatening dry tickle in the back of her throat; her compact body was slicked all over, as if greased, and sooner or later she was going to upchuck. Might as well get it over with. She eased out of bed and went into the bathroom and knelt, then erupted with more violence than she'd anticipated, and at both ends, which made her feel nasty and childish and disconsolate. Her bowels had been nothing but water for days. When she had cleaned up as best she could she crept into a tepid shower and bawled her heart out.

Toby was sitting on the side of the bed when she came out of the bathroom, cleaner but a little wobbly and short of breath. Her neat round tummy still looked bloated. His large hands were knotted between his knees; he was staring in a funk at the brown tile floor. Sunni slipped an arm around his waist and rested her head against him.

"I'm not feeling so great, Tobe."

"You're rather warm."

"I know it. Maybe I picked up a *dudu* at that Pakistani restaurant last night."

"Why don't I ring the hotel doc?"

She made a face. "His clothes aren't very clean and his breath smells bad, like, I don't know, chickenshit. Maybe I'll get better after I have some coffee, you think?"

"I hope so."

"Where'd you disappear to so early?"

"Airport. Trying to find that bush pilot, Dodds. You know, the one that the other pilot said might have seen something down Mbeya way." He sighed. "No luck."

"Oh well." Sunni tightened her grip on him and tried to sound cheerful. "Something's going to break for you. Any day now. I feel it in my bones."

"Yes. Must keep plugging away, that's all. It's what Dad would do." His smile was the saddest thing she'd ever seen. There were lines of strain in his twenty-year-old face, a heaviness of self-doubt in the sunken eyes. No appetite, little sleep, he was getting too skinny for his six-foot three-inch frame. Sunni was smaller, almost petite, but her arms would easily go all the way around him.

Breakfast didn't help. As usual they waited three quarters of an hour to be served. During their first week at the Kivukoni Five-Star Hotel, Sunni had been infuriated to the point of tears by the staff, all of whom were so vague and distant and inefficient they seemed to be sleepwalking. But she and Toby had learned that most of the blacks in Dar were like that, and it had nothing to do with your stereotyped lazy black African. Too many of the people in this pock-marked paradise were half starved: Famine, kwashiorkor, and intestinal parasites had been facts of life for generations, and as a result their brains didn't work very well.

Once they had their food, Sunni couldn't choke anything down; but she did sip a little tea. Toby was so preoccupied he didn't notice her own lack of appetite. He was analyzing a fistful of messages from strangers responding to the offer of a reward he had posted in public places around Dar.

The English-language *Daily Mail* and the Swahili weeklies had refused to run his ad, for rather hazy reasons. It was the official position of the government of Tanzania that the explorers were missing in a largely unexplored, inhospitable region of the country, and despite the fact that the government had more urgent problems to deal with, reasonable efforts were being made to locate them. The attempts of individuals to find the explorers could be interpreted as criticism of the government, which was always met with stringent censorship.

Toby had become expert at sorting out the sly cranks and con artists from possibly legitimate sources of information. This morning there were no possibles to follow up on.

And it had lately occurred to Toby that the police were sifting through his mail and messages before he received them. From time to time he was rather obviously followed by plainclothesmen. They could have chucked him out of the country at any time. But he sensed that the *polisi* preferred to have him here, severely restricted like all other foreign nationals from travel to outlying districts, than in England or the States broadcasting his suspicions that the government of Tanzania was implicated in the disappearance of his father.

After breakfast Toby grimly stuck to his routine, driving a rented Fiat with valve problems and almost no shocks left; the streets, even in the best areas, were in wretched condition. First they visited the British embassy to see if there had been any replies to Her Majesty's Government's latest official inquiries. They were in the midst of a move to the new capital in Dodoma, but the embassy staffers were sympathetic and helpful. Still, they were at an impasse. The first secretary told Toby and Sunni that there was nothing new on the cocktail-party circuit, just the same stale speculative gossip: The explorers had drowned in Lake Tanganyika; they had inadvertently strayed across one border or another to be slaughtered by soldiers and piled in a mass grave; they had perished in a cave-in or earthslide.

From the embassy they drove to the National Museum, to an office of the Antiquities Division of the Ministry of Education, where Toby had long since worn out his welcome. Today no one cared to see him. They called on a few correspondents and stringers for the news magazines and dailies of six countries, none of whom were anxious to become too inquisitive about the Chapman/Weller mystery.

Two of the correspondents had attempted to send cables to their publishers, suggesting that there was a story here worthy of the talents of important journalists; but the cables had been returned to them by the police, with the advice that they keep in touch with Jumbe Kinyati's press secretary for the latest word on the search for the explorers.

"I thought journalists were supposed to have guts," Toby complained as they drove down Independence Avenue toward Barclay's Bank. "If we could break just one major story in the world's press, that might prompt some action by the UN. Then the government here would have to change its tune."

"Tobe, don't you think—I mean, couldn't you accomplish more if you were back home? Honestly."

He braked hard to avoid a clerk in shirt sleeves cutting blithely into traffic on his Vespa.

"No. I'm staying here. Because my father is here, and I know he's in trouble. It's just a matter of—of finding someone who's willing to stick his neck out, and not worry about the consequences."

"I wonder," Sunni said abstractedly, staring out the window at a glimpse of rainless clouds and Russian freighters in the harbor a block away. "I wonder if— *now* I wish you'd gone with me to the reception for the Indonesian dance troupe yesterday. I met a man there—he knew Daddy when Daddy was chief of protocol in Washington. His name is Lundgren, and somebody told me he owns a magazine in Sweden, or was it Denmark? Anyway he's very impressive. The women flock around him."

"Really?" Toby said, with a slight curling of his lip. "If he owns a magazine, it might be worth talking to him."

"All right, luv."

Toby wedged the Fiat into a space near the bank. They got out. Sunni took two steps on the crumbling sidewalk and paused. The festering bazaar of the port city, the fumes, the humid salty air, seemed to have stagnated into something quite unbreathable. She touched her chilly forehead, watching an unexpected fog blight downtown Dar, and let her fingers trail down one side of her face. She smiled when Toby turned to see what was keeping her, a dear foolish smile. And keeled over against him as he hastened back, falling out from under her woven hat with the big lazy brim. Toby, with the aid of a passerby, carried Sunni into the cool silence of the bank, where the manager, Mr. Mukome, waved them into his office. Sunni came around lying on a settee with a cold cloth on her forehead.

"What happened?" she said.

When she was sufficiently revived, Toby drove her to the Kialamahindi Hospital in the Upanga District of Dar. Sunni didn't protest too much. The fact of fainting scared her. She'd only done that once before in her whole life. And she was still feeling woozy.

Sunni was routed to a treatment room by a nurse who requested that Toby wait elsewhere. He wandered outside, remembering that he had left his camera bag in the trunk of the Fiat, which was too easy to pry open. He retrieved it and walked around the palm-shaded grounds. The hospital, recently built, consisted of half a dozen white coral block-and-concrete buildings in the Moorish style. It was set amid pools and gardens which had remained pleasantly green despite the prolonged absence of the monsoon. Everything was neat and well maintained, which in Tanzania usually meant Chinese funds and administration.

A shell path took him past one-story offices, the kitchen and a cafeteria, a helicopter landing pad, and a massive building out of character with the rest of the architectural scheme. It was modern, windowless, an inverted flat-top pyramid with a moat around it. Some sort of laboratory. Beyond this large building there was a small private area, secluded behind a screen of thriving croton plants and with a wire fence and locked gate. Above the tops of the green-and-red plants he glimpsed the tiles of two bungalow roofs.

Toby yawned; he was bored and depressed and fidgety about Sunni's fainting spell. He went to the creeper-covered gate and peered into the compound. He heard low voices, one of them English. A man's voice.

The bungalows were on opposite sides of a courtyard; the verandah of the nearest bungalow was set at an angle to the gate and there was some kind of flowering vine growing around the mangrove posts, so he could see unobstructedly only a small part of the verandah. A wicker basket swing made slow quarter turns on a squeaking chain.

As it turned toward him Toby had tantalizing glimpses of a slim black nurse in a hospital uniform, curled up shoeless in the deep scoop of shade afforded by the basket. She had unbuttoned the dress and her youthful breasts were exposed. She played with one of them, like a tired puppy with a favorite ball. She spoke in Swahili, which Toby didn't understand, her statement ending in a pealing laugh.

A man came momentarily into view. Sixty-five or
so, wearing unpressed drill shorts, his legs hairless, his
kneecaps shocking as snow in the wavering heat. He
placed a cold glass between her breasts and she shuddered deliciously.

Toby held his breath, squinting a little. Lately he'd
become just nearsighted enough to know he should
consider glasses. The gray-haired man turned his head
sharply toward Toby, as if to avoid a darting insect,
and his face was cast into the sunlight.

Toby recognized him immediately. He could not be
mistaken. It was Dr. Henry Landreth, late of the
Chapman/Weller expedition, obviously in decent
health and well accommodated.

More than a year and a half ago Toby, down from
Cambridge for the weekend, had been introduced to
the notorious physicist aboard his father's yacht in
Fowey harbor. Landreth was shaky, threadbare, seething with secrets. He clutched a sort of diary, covered in soiled green cloth, which he had unearthed in
a used-book shop in Dar. It was the key, he claimed,
to the most fabulous archaeological discovery of the
ages.

Toby stepped away from the gate, his heart giving
a sudden lurch of happiness. But caution overtook
him like a swiftly moving shadow.

If Dr. Landreth was alive and apparently flourishing, what had happened to the others? Why not a
word from this man in more than six months? What
did anyone really know about him, except that he'd
once betrayed England—a fact his father had been
able to stomach only with the greatest difficulty, even
though Landreth had come to him with an apparently
dazzling proposition, potentially the most daring adventure in a career of celebrated achievements.

Toby took several deep breaths to contain his excitement and belatedly looked around to see if he was

observed, although earlier he hadn't noticed any bored plainclothesmen keeping tabs on him. This corner of the hospital grounds appeared to be seldom visited.

Satisfied, he unzipped his camera bag and took out the Minolta XG-1 with autowind, slipped a 250-millimeter zoom lens from its case, and mounted it. He moved cautiously back to the gate. The black nurse was still turning in her swing, drinking from the tall glass. Landreth had disappeared, although Toby could hear the sporadic rumble of his voice from inside the bungalow.

Toby waited, the sun on his head, sweat trickling, in a state that veered from nervous exhilaration to barely suppressed fury to tears of frustration.

Finally Henry Landreth reappeared, but he was hidden by the black girl. There was nothing for Toby to photograph. Landreth seemed to be doing most of the talking. His words were inaudible, but clearly he was on edge about something. His shoulders hunched up and down, his hands sawed the air. She replied in monosyllables. He took a cigarette case from his shirt pocket, lit up, turned his head after a deep drag to expel the smoke away from her face. Toby snapped a picture. Waited. The gray head came around again, idly, eyes unfocused. Toby took a second picture, hastily packed his camera gear, slung the bag over his shoulder where it wouldn't be in the way, grabbed the fence and scaled it, jumped down into the yard. He strode quickly to the verandah.

"Dr. Landreth!"

Henry Landreth looked as startled as if someone had fired a pistol in his direction. The head of the black girl popped out of the basket swing at a wry angle; she stared at Toby with her mouth open, then quickly withdrew. The basket rocked a little as she hurriedly buttoned her dress.

Landreth's hands were poised in the air as if he'd been caught in the act of opening a safe that wasn't his. Sweat glistened on his face. His expression prompted an unexpected laugh from Toby. He paused near the steps to the verandah, glancing from Landreth to the black girl and back.

"It's Tobias Chapman," he said. "We met in England, when my father was putting the expedition together. How *is* he, anyway? I've been looking everywhere for him."

Landreth recovered from his surprise; eyes narrowing, he put the cigarette to his lips.

"My dear fellow, whoever you are, you have no business being here."

Toby bit his lip in anger.

"I told you who I was. Chips Chapman is my father."

Landreth had regained most of his composure. His eyes were brackish, hostile; his lips twisted rudely.

"I'm afraid that means nothing to me. I've never heard of him. Nor do I know you. Please leave at once. This hospital has a private police patrol. You can be beaten for trespassing here."

The black girl got out of the swing. Landreth glanced at her meaningfully. She went into the bungalow.

Toby's neck was red; his face swelled with malignant humor. He leaned toward the verandah as if he were about to dash up the three steps and seize Landreth by the throat. Landreth licked his lips and leaned back; Toby's righteous force was irresistible.

"Don't you dare threaten me with a beating, you miserable treasonous *bastard*! I've spent six weeks in this godforsaken country waiting for some word about my father. You were with him. You must know where he is. Tell me!"

"I *am* sorry, but you've made a mistake. I'm not—

who you take me for. Now be a good chap; really, I mustn't be disturbed like this. I'm—a very sick man. I'm here for rest and treatment. I simply cannot tolerate—"

"What? Are you denying that you're Dr. Henry Landreth?"

"Deny it? Of course I do." He had a coughing fit that bent him like a question mark and seemed to leave him bloodless as a snail.

Toby's hands fell to his sides. He stared in astonishment and dismay at the unkempt, feral scholar. All of his worst fears about his father's fate crystallized at the level of his heart. Something evil and disastrous had taken place. This man, contemptuous of loyalties, so casual in his betrayals, was obviously hiding here. Hiding from the world. Toby felt a shock of caution, but he couldn't be silent.

"That's a fucking lie; and you'll pay for it. I know very well who you are." His voice broke. "I can *prove* what I know."

The black girl reappeared. She looked down at Toby with an expression of innocent wonder.

To Landreth she said in English, "They're coming."

"Very well. Thank you, Nyshuri." His lackluster gaze passed over Toby, dismissing him. "You can avoid a great deal of unpleasantness by leaving at once, however you came. I'd say you have a minute at most." He turned and went into the bungalow and shut the door. Toby was left alone with the black girl.

Nyshuri shrugged her comely shoulders and said with a sympathetic smile, "Go on now; when he gets in one of his moods he can cause quite a row."

"Bugger him," Toby said under his breath, but he backed away from the verandah, glancing at the gate he had scaled.

Nyshuri pointed to a path along the hedges.

"The other way. To the street. That gate isn't guarded during the day."

She seemed truly anxious to avoid trouble. Toby nodded and went off at a jog beside the hedges, which snaked through the grounds. He was soon out of sight of the bungalows. He came to the gate Nyshuri had told him about, and clambered over it without difficulty.

As he walked back to the main entrance of the hospital, he was breathing hard, unable to concentrate his thoughts, to bridle his panic. He kept his eyes open for the hospital guards as he returned to the clinic for Sunni.

Her examination was over. She greeted him with a pretty, downcast smile.

"Feeling better?"

"They gave me some pills for the—the nausea."

"Let's hop it, then."

"Tobe, you look as if you were running. What's the matter?"

He tried, but couldn't find his voice right away. He'd begun to doubt himself. Perhaps he'd just been overexcited, carried away by a striking resemblance. At the same time he was frightened. He did have photos. If he *was* right, if he *had* found Landreth, then there had to be serious reasons behind the man's strong denials.

Toby had a bitter lump in his throat he couldn't swallow. For the first time he faced the dreadful prospect that his father might be dead.

Sunni sat close in the Fiat on the way back to the hotel. She was in a very loving mood. She didn't take her eyes off Toby, but she didn't pressure him. Gradually he choked out his story.

"No wonder you're so upset! My Lord! What are you going to *do?*"

"I just don't know. You're looking pale again, luv, are you going to be ill?"

"I'm not sick at all, actually. I'm—two months pregnant."

"Oh, that's good. I'm glad it's nothing serious."

"Toby!"

Toby shot another look at her, then veered to the curb, stalling the engine. He put his arms around Sunni and held her tightly.

"I won't be twenty until next month," she sobbed. "I haven't done my junior year yet. I was going to ride in the Penn National this fall!"

"Oh, you'll have loads of time for all that after the baby comes," he said soothingly.

"You mean you really want it?"

"Don't be absurd; not want *our* baby?"

"But we're not even married yet, Tobe. You know, that's not a big deal for me, I'll be happy just being with you, but my mother, wow, I wouldn't know where to put my face if—"

"Not to worry. How long before you, I mean, when it's obvious and all that?"

"Oh, another couple of months, I guess."

"Loads of time, then," Toby said, and kissed her. But he was looking grim again. "Time for Dad to be at the wedding."

"And he *will* be there, Toby," she said fervently. "I just know he will."

# RUAHA NATIONAL PARK

When Erika was certain that Oliver had left for the day to pursue his primitive mining activities on the escarpment, she packed in the flight bag what few provisions she could carry and left the lodge, heading along the dry bed of the sand river in what she thought was a northeasterly direction.

For several days, for Oliver's benefit, she had languished, complaining of aches and pains and keeping to her bronze bed-ship in the empty, echoing upstairs. She seemed too weary or despondent to lift her head when he came with the meals, which he continued painstakingly to prepare. Oliver's solicitude was further enhanced by the fact that she no longer spoke of sending him for help, or of leaving herself. Erika ate, because every scrap of food he brought was essential for building strength, and when Oliver had the confidence to return to his work, she labored at exercises, knowing that she couldn't fail again.

No matter how long it took she had to stay on her feet, keep walking until she reached a settlement and transportation to the outside.

As she began seriously to work on her endurance, she was just able to walk up and down the mahogany staircase without palpitations and rubber knees; within two days she could jog down the stairs, around the rotunda and up again. She rejoiced and doubled her efforts, ignoring the sharp pains in her sides, persistent leg cramps, and nausea.

Five days: Erika felt that she couldn't delay any longer and tried to assess her chances realistically. Her training might carry her, at best, across four to six miles of moderately difficult terrain per day, with a long rest at midday and shorter intervals after that, until nightfall. She thought she could survive, with minimum precautions, at least three nights in the bush.

She felt guilty about raiding Oliver's meager stores. He had set up his own quarters in the kitchen of Von Kreutzen's palace, a vast shadowy two-story room equipped with a couple of squat tons of rusted woodburning stoves, stone barbecue pits with flues, a deep well beneath the tarred but badly deteriorated floorboards. Oliver had sealed off, with more of the quilted packing material from the storage compartment of the wrecked airplane, a dark recess in the kitchen that had once been a pantry.

There he lounged, nightly or during those infrequent hours when he didn't feel like working, on a camp cot, his kerosene lantern lit. He smoked his pipe and listened attentively to a cheap transistor radio that received little more than faint strains of music through gusts of static. Over his cot was a fading color photo in a plastic frame of some tall grinning soccer players, each with a ball under one arm. He kept his valued possessions in a metal footlocker: well-oiled tools and guns and a razor-sharp *panga*. Most of the food was here with him—tinned goods on a shelf; unidentifiable haunches of black and purple meat, smoke cured and hanging from the ceiling. The atmosphere, with or without Oliver's own finely powdered pungency, was stifling.

Erika used Oliver's *panga* to slice a dozen strips of

jerky from the hams, which she rolled in plastic. She helped herself to three small tins of condensed milk, some tea bags, biscuits, sugar cubes, salt; after a brief grapple with her conscience, she also appropriated a Swiss Army officer's knife that was loaded with handy cutting and boring tools in miniature. Right now she needed it more than Oliver did.

Rummaging through the rest of his belongings, she also came across a little tin of yellow grease, like Vaseline, which she knew would help keep the biting flies off. Matches, a metal cup, an enameled saucepan, his best blanket, an eight-inch square of metal grill, a soiled green ranger's cap, and she was ready to go. Her clothing and shoes were just adequate for a long tramp. Even in a dry year, by keeping to the riverbed she would find water when she required it and, just as important, shade much of the way. If she ran out of food, she could eat termite grubs or grasshoppers; she'd done it before.

Erika didn't give a second thought to the prospect of spending a night in the wilderness. She had learned long ago just how to make a smokeless slow burning fire in the earth, and sit cross-legged with the blanket thrown over her from head to toe, warmed and dozing.

At first, exhilarated by a sense of escape, of purpose nearing fulfillment, she was inspired to go quickly: and the going was relatively easy. The riverbed in most places was about thirty yards wide, with a few pools of water linked by slow moving trickles that glittered in the golden light of early morning. There were modest boulders and a couple of fallen trees and steaming clumps of dung from visitors earlier than she.

For a time Erika followed a well-beaten elephant walk that meandered through the drying-out vegetation and acacia trees denuded of bark and lower branches by elephant or impala. Soon she came across a family of a dozen elephants digging wells, plastering themselves with mud at the riverbank; they would follow this mudpack with a dry coating of blown dust or sand, then rub ponderously against a handy rock or termite hill to rid themselves of skin parasites. Erika moved slowly and cautiously downwind of the herd and soon left them behind.

After a while the river ran narrowly between hills, often sinking beneath the surface. In these places the high sagebrush was thicker, dust covered. Erika paused on a flat, tipped rock to catch her breath and smear her wet exposed skin with a thin coating of grease. There was life all around her, but little that was visible to the untrained eye. A bateleur eagle in the sky, a vulture, some blacksmith plovers. In the massed trees overhead blue monkeys chattered. She had picked up a piece of solid straight limb from a rotting tree to use as a staff, to probe likely thickets for snakes before passing through. But she knew the snake menace in Africa sometimes was exaggerated. They were everywhere—cobras, vipers—and deadly; they were also among the most timid of creatures and would slither away from the swishing sound of a staff in tall grass or bush. She avoided altogether tall dense brush where animals might be sleeping. This was also lion country, leopard country. She hadn't seen one, and didn't wish to.

By noon the droning heat had sapped some of her confidence. She had expended too much energy and was trembling. She had no firm idea of how far she had traveled; at times the river twisted and turned and all but doubled back on itself.

Erika stopped near running water, inspected the weeds carefully for snails that could carry bilharzia. She made a twig fire in a circle of stones, set water to boil, stripped, and bathed. She dried naked in the sun while drinking several cups of tea with milk and lots of sugar.

The will to push on was strong again, but Erika forced herself to rest, in the shade of the blanket suspended from three makeshift posts. The rock on which she lay was far from comfortable, but the flight bag made an adequate pillow. She went soundly to sleep. When she awoke, she estimated an hour had passed.

Groaning, stiff in every joint, she crept to her feet, packed, and resumed her journey.

On the scarp behind Von Kreutzen's shooting palace, Oliver had labored day after day for several weeks in a narrow rift, chiseling out a speckled vein of gold-bearing ore. In an area where the lode was most prominently exposed, it was also nearly inaccessible. The rift ran diagonally across a broad facing at an angle of thirty degrees. It was only about four feet wide at the surface, tapering to inches at the bottom. He was forced to work head down, clinging to the sun-struck facing by his toes and the fingers of one hand, swinging his miner's hammer in short awkward strokes, pausing to work partly dislodged ore chunks free with his skinned and bleeding fingers.

Under these conditions some sort of accident was inevitable. A sliver of rock flew from his hammer and lodged in a corner of his left eye. The pain was excruciating. If he hadn't tied the hammer to his wrist with a strip of leather he would have dropped in into the cleft of the rock face. Oliver withdrew and sat up, the left eye closed. With a copious flow of tears the pain was lessened, but not much.

Oliver wearily gathered his tools and dropped them into a rush basket, on top of thirty pounds of ore he had found worth collecting. He made his way down to the lodge, hoping that Erika would be able to locate the bit of rock piercing his eyeball and remove it for him.

The sun was in the west, the shadows of afternoon lengthening. His pet mongoose, roused from a nap inside a stone urn at the entrance to the lodge, slipped between Oliver's legs and bounded up the stairs to Erika's room. Oliver followed at a slower pace, hurting, a hand over his eye, and discovered that she was gone.

He looked around and saw that the flight bag and all of her clothing was missing. He squealed in dismay and ran back down the stairs to the kitchen. A fast inventory of stores and personal belongings convinced Oliver that she had a trek in mind.

Tears ran down his cheek; he trembled. The mongoose stood on the edge of the cot, fur ruffled, distressed by Oliver's continuing, anguished squeals and erratic behavior. Oliver snatched up the *panga,* then put it down and searched for a pad of cotton, which he soaked in a medicinal oil from a vial he kept in a leatherette case at the bottom of the footlocker. He fastened the pad over his suppurating eye with strips of soiled adhesive tape he'd been saving. Then he tested the edge of his *panga* by whacking off a sizable hunk of a tough hanging haunch. The mongoose pounced on the strip of dried meat, sank his teeth into it, and shook it as if he had a viper by the throat.

Oliver left him behind and bolted outside. He had no trouble picking up Erika's trail. He set off along the riverbed at a steady bowlegged jog, wearing only his thong sandals, his good eye searching out her track. She couldn't have been easier to follow if she'd been riding in a big red bus.

By late afternoon Erika was resting after every thirty steps, though the river channel had become broad and flat.

She resisted sitting while she tried to get her breath, afraid she wouldn't have the power to force herself to her feet again. She had abrupt, fascinating hallucinations. She heard a railroad train. She saw a lawn filled with people playing croquet. She smelled her father's favorite pipe tobacco. Hugo, her first great love, looked up from the hood of a 1937 V-12 Hispano-Suiza he was waxing, smiled, and waved. When she moved she felt curiously dazzled, out of contact with the earth and her surroundings.

Erika knew she should have stopped for good long ago; but an image in her mind of almost limitless distances to overcome caused her heart to constrict in fright. She hoped for a second wind, an elemental push, enough strength to maintain her for a final mile before dusk. Tomorrow . . . but she was too dispirited to make plans, to think beyond the next short bend of the river.

Dispirited, and addled. At some point, after one of her frequent pauses, she had simply walked off without the flight bag, leaving everything vital to survival but the blanket, which earlier she had rolled up and wore suspended across her back by a string of tough creeper vine.

The loss was devastating, yet she could not make up her mind to backtrack and retrieve the bag. Erika was unreasonably afraid of what lay behind her: the dark, lost time, some incomprehensible evil like a blot on her trail, which she had felt for the last hour or so.

She stood swaying between mirrorlike pools of water, the sun glaring down on her from a prison house of trees; she cried wretchedly, one hand shaking out of control. She heard a chattery crackle of semiautomatic rifle fire, a shout. She imagined it was Chips Chapman, calling for help . . . then she heard her mother crooning lullabies. And another, unmistakably British voice, calling, if not to her, to someone nearby.

Heedless of the likelihood that she was being deceived by a fresh hallucination, Erika plunged ahead, through water, shifting sand, low scrub, demanding of her punished body reserves of energy and nerve. Black spots swarmed before her eyes, formed a curtain of premature night through which she continued to fight her way, stumbling, dragging her feet, falling.

She got up twice and struggled on but couldn't rise the third time. She lay spent, hearing again the voices, so distant it was impossible to distinguish words. They were bearing away from her. She lay on her side, semiconscious, patiently waiting for the blackness to disintegrate into familiar spots, for the spots to dance and fade away.

Before Erika could see clearly she smelled the animal nearby, and sensed its power.

The animal announced itself with a doughty grunting, and desperate whistling sounds of effort. Erika cautiously eased herself to a sitting position in the scratchy dry grass and looked around. A dozen yards away a rhinoceros, almost to pieces, was down on its front knees but trying to rise. In the beaten grass behind it there were blood slicks where it had gone down before. If the rhino had managed to stagger just a little farther the last time it might have stepped on her.

One violent petite eye studied Erika as the rhino tried to heave itself onto all four feet. Its horn was missing, hacked off as it had lain helpless. Erika got to her feet and leaned against a low limb of a sausage tree. She smelled the animal's keen blood and was humbled by its passion to live. And she knew if it got underway again it was capable of anything, including a last blind charge to destroy whatever lay in its path.

Weak as she was, Erika made tracks.

Above a group of mature baobob trees on the plain

in front of her, a strand of grayish smoke hung in the evening air. The trees looked to be half a mile away. As she walked slowly toward them, dazed and sore, eyes fixed on the smoke as if it were a signal of deliverance, she heard men and the sounds of a camp. She smelled their food, and lusted.

There was a Land-Rover, muddied, a battered derelict. A tent had been pitched. Two men wearing bush shirts and shorts and high stockings with their shoes were hunched on campstools by the fire, eating roasted meat off the bone. They were white. A third member of the party, black and overweight, with tribal scars on his face like worry beads, was cleaning guns. Erika crunched her way through brush to the inner circle. All eyes turned her way. Astonishment. She was, obviously, a novel sight.

But the two white men, nondescript, quintessentially British, in their forties or early fifties, also seemed out of place. They were like a pair of clerks, decent hardworking civil servants who had scrimped all their lives to pay for an adventure. And this was it, a cheap and sleazy safari. They seemed morose by their crackling campfire, eking out what glamour remained in this disillusioning situation.

"How extraordinary," one of them said, breathily. He sucked grease from between his fingers, not taking his eyes off Erika.

"Manners, Timothy," the other reminded him gently.

Timothy rose. "Good evening, missus. What a pleasure. Would you care for a bite to eat? Then there's tea, of course."

"Or perhaps a whiskey. She does look a bit knackered, don't you think?"

Timothy smiled. "She does at that, Lex."

"Albert," Lex called to the black man, "why don't you leave off polishing the bloody arsenal long enough to bring us that bottle of Cutty Sark we've tucked away for special observances."

Albert seemed to groan as he turned his head away and got up from the fallen tree on which he'd been sitting. He plodded toward the Land-Rover, which was parked a few feet beyond the fire, nose on.

Timothy stepped away from his campstool, casually dropping a gnawed bone into the flames.

"Well, well. I'm Timothy Wardrop. And this geezer is Lex Pynchon."

"Get stuffed. Pleased to meet yer, Miss—"

"Erik . . . a."

"Sit down; do sit down, Erika. Afraid we haven't much to offer in the way of accommodations, rather roughing it as you can see."

Albert was groaning again as he yanked cartons and duffels from the back of the Land-Rover. He seemed to be suffering from some deep psychic pain. The other men ignored him.

"But where in heaven's name did you come from?" Lex asked Erika. "Can there be a tour group nearby?"

Erika shook her head, her eyes thick with tears of thanksgiving. She found her voice.

"I'm alone. I was—in an accident, some time ago. My plane crashed."

"*What?*" Lex said.

Timothy narrowed his eyes. "That is a rather nasty patch on your forehead—you must have been struck quite a blow. Inconceivable you've managed to survive in this poxy place. Was anyone with you?"

"No."

He took her by the elbow and lowered her to the campstool. Closer to the fire, Erika saw how ragged they both were. Timothy had gone without shaving for a couple of days; his hair was twiggy and he had a rank odor. There were dark spatters on his shirt that might have been grease, or blood, and she thought fleetingly of the rhinoceros, seemingly used for wanton target practice. She swallowed and shuddered and stared at a drooling hunk of steak which Lex was turning on a spit.

Timothy continued to hold her by the elbow, twisting to shout at the black man, "Albert! The whiskey, man, and I don't mean the day after tomorrow."

"Well, I don't know where you *put* it," Albert whined.

"Don't go sarky on us, I'm warning you. Lex, would you have a look, there's a good chap."

Lex got up scratching. The sun didn't agree with him; his lips were scabbed and he had an ulcer on one cheekbone, another on his right forearm.

"Whatever you say, Timothy."

Albert let out another shrill, despairing cry. Lex glanced at Timothy across the fire, smiling bleakly, and shrugged. Timothy hunkered beside Erika, his hand sliding from her elbow to her wrist, almost a caress. It was not a clerk's ninny hand; she felt a rasp of callus that gave her goosebumps.

Erika moved her head a little away from the fire, which was making her skin smart. She turned to look at him. They were almost at eye level. He was mouse brown and anonymous, his face without character. Both he and Lex seemed like overage waifs, not legitimized by ordinary human emotions.

The confidence in his grip was almost worrisome. She tried to smile, to be grateful.

"Can you—help me?"

"Not to worry, Erika. No more tramping about. A dollop of whiskey, a good feed, you'll feel a hundred percent in no time."

"The others—"

"Oh? Thought you said no one was with you in the aircraft."

"I mean— It's a long story."

"Well. Take your time, dear girl." Timothy turned to lift a stoneware coffeepot from a grill over a circle of coals. He poured scalding coffee into a mug. Lex came back, jauntily brandishing the bottle of Cutty Sark. Albert trailed him sulkily.

"Albert, mind the meat don't char. Now then." He broke the seal on the bottle and offered it. "Sorry, Erika, we've come away without the Baccarat goblets. Should hit the right spot all the same."

She nodded, took the bottle with her free hand, sipped cautiously. It was better than she could have imagined. Lex, whistling tunelessly, began slicing pieces of medium-rare steak into a plate for her.

"Erika's got quite a story to tell, she says," Timothy remarked idly. He was stroking her wrist.

"I'm dying to hear. But we must let her eat. Biscuit, Erika?"

"Yes." She put the bottle to her lips again. As she did so she heard a pitiful moan that stirred the hairs on her nape. It was human, not animal. She glanced quickly at Albert, but the moan hadn't come from him.

"What was that?"

"One of the prisoners, most likely," Lex said, sounding bored.

Somewhere on the darkening plain there was a piercing shriek from a feline predator, the parrotlike, raucous cries of jackals. Erika felt the night closing them all in; they were pledged, magically, to the circle of fire, each other's humanity, the unstable mood of the moment.

"Prisoners?"

Timothy jerked his head toward the Land-Rover.

"Just there. Nothing for you to be concerned about, they can't harm you."

"They've had a very trying day," Lex said with a solemn wink.

"What did they do?"

"Poachers," Timothy explained.

"Oh. Oh, I see. Then you—you're with the government."

Lex sliced a bit of tenderloin for himself and popped it into his mouth.

"Warden? Us?"

"We're of the Guv, not the government," Timothy said cryptically.

Lex liked the joke. He rocked on his heels, laughing.

Erika got up suddenly, her eyes wide, and twisted away from Timothy's grasp. A piece of wood on the fire snapped like a shot. With her blood running cold she turned and walked to the Land-Rover.

The two men remained where they were, craning casually, keeping her in view. She still had the fire in her eyes and couldn't see well by the silvering light of the sky. There was some baggage scattered on the ground behind the Rover. She heard a dismal sigh, saw movement, looked again.

They were two black men, lying a foot apart, naked, wounded, horridly acrawl with flies, lashed hand and foot, tied to the back of the vehicle by their ankles. One of the prisoners moved his head in slow anguish. The other was breathlessly still. Erika dropped to her knees in shock, her face inches from a putrifying eye, from the buzz of flies. She bolted up with a scream.

"Oh, no. No, no, no!"

Lex and Timothy came on the double.

"What's the matter?" Lex said. "We told you they was a bad lot. *Poachers.* Tried to skimp on the Guv, go into business for themselves. Wouldn't pay their tithes. The Guv don't take kindly to such actions."

"Jawbony tonight, aren't we?" Timothy cautioned. "Natter, natter, natter."

"What's the beef? She's never going to tell a living soul."

"You can't—you mustn't do this. It's monstrous. *Look* at them."

"Calm yourself," Lex said uneasily, scratching and shifting his weight from one foot to the other. "We was all getting along swell, wasn't we? Here's how to look at it. These coons are tougher than you think. Dragged them a couple of kilometers, that's all. Wore the arse and goolies off them. They'll recover, but damn if they'll cheat on the Guv again."

"I *demand* you release these men while there's still a chance—but this one's not breathing! What's the matter with you, how could you be so unspeakably vicious—"

Timothy sauntered over, coffee mug in hand. "Dead, is he? That's news." With a flick of his wrist he doused the head of the silent one with the steaming coffee. Flies filled the air, the unfortunate victim bucked and gave off a hissing scream.

"You bastard! How dare you treat another human being this way!"

"What's that? They're just wogs."

"Now she don't like us," Lex said, his shoulders drooping.

"Shut up, sod."

"Whatever you say, Timothy. But couldn't we get on with it, like? Seeing as how she's not going to go for a little bit of sugar?"

They both looked at Erika, as they had looked at the suffering black men on the ground. With a chill-provoking ingenuousness.

"She's not what I'd call flaming great tit."

"But she's had her share of hard knocks, don't you see. Still she must have some juice in her yet."

"I don't reckon we're in a position to be choosy."

"That's it exactly."

"Now just a moment," Erika said, although her throat felt as if it were clogged with quick-drying cement.

"Can't see the harm in a little sport," Timothy said.

"As we both have a touch of the clap, I don't suppose it matters which of us goes first," Lex said, a hand on his belt buckle.

Erika began to back away from them.

Somewhere in the thicket beneath the score of trees that made up the stand there was a ripping crash, a series of grunts and snorts. Albert reared up, his carved face a sheen of fear.

"Rhino!"

"That old brute?" Timothy said. "He must be three-quarters dead by now. Well, don't stand there, take the Rigby and go finish him."

"Not me!"

"Do what you're told, you fucking imbecile, if you don't want to wind up joining these two behind the Rover!"

Erika turned and ran, but was shoved hard from behind and pitched over on one shoulder. She rolled to the edge of the campfire. Sparks bit her cheeks, glowed in her hair. Timothy snatched her up and dusted her before she could burst into flame. Then her clothes disappeared in tatters, as if the men were two callous children plucking the wings off a fly. She lost, in moments, everything but her sturdy shoes. They were adept at rape, it was a professional collaboration, she hadn't the strength to resist.

Fortunately a numbness crept through Erika; she was anesthetized by despair, an acknowledgment of total defeat. All feeling was reduced to a sullen heartthrob, a struggle for breathing room. The jolting, humiliating attack couldn't concern her. She was free to move only her head, but that at least was a blessing. She didn't have to look at Lex, whose scabrous face was only a foot or so from hers, or Timothy, who stood staring vacantly over Lex's shoulder as he wrestled his unwieldy peggo out of his pants.

Behind the Land-Rover she glimpsed a startling resurrection: a dark angelic figure rising slowly from his knees with one widespread, lethal wing poised and glittering in the moony light. A prisoner, she thought, miraculously made whole and freed from his bonds. His face turned toward the scene of this new atrocity but she could see nothing but a single huge, clotted white eye. He looked away, one hand on the ground for balance, head forward like a sprinter's, pointing toward Albert, who was oblivious of everything but the rape while he loaded his rifle in slow motion.

Erika realized that he could only be another hallucination, this avenging angel; yet he seemed more real than the cutthroat now rompering her, laboring with a monotonous broadside of balls against her exposed nates to achieve his mean little spasm.

She watched in fascination as the angel seemed to fly, low to the ground, arriving in a frenzy at the shoulder of the startled Albert, who barely sounded his cry before he was whacked solidly across the chest by the sharp edge of the angel's wing. Erika gasped in admiration; there was no immediate evidence of injury but the black man's arms fell helplessly. The muscles which enabled him to raise his arms had been cut in two. The rifle dropped but before it touched the ground the angel was off again, heading her way in a series of powerful leaps and bounds, and she observed that he had no wings, only a *panga* with a blade some two feet in length.

In the background Albert was running in agonized circles, weeping, his useless hands flapping at his sides. And behind him, the wounded hornless rhino, survivor of enough gunshots to kill half a dozen men, burst into the clearing.

The angel, with a drawn-out cry of retribution, flew again, over Erika and the hunched back of Lex Pynchon. Timothy reeled away from a savage backhanded blow with the flat of the *panga,* and for two seconds, at most, all their business was in suspension. Erika looked up at the bandaged but familiarly dusty face of Oliver. His good eye was distorted with rage and Erika quailed, certain that he was more angry at her than her attackers, that his next blow would be aimed at her throat.

Instead he glanced at the rhinoceros, which had come to a momentary halt while sniffing out its victims in the clearing. The rhino rounded on the unfortunate Albert, who had fallen and was awkwardly trying to get to his feet.

Oliver snatched Lex up by the back of his shirt. Lex dangled a few inches above the ground, his penis, like a plucked chicken's neck, at a twitching right angle to the rest of him.

Oliver pointed with his *panga.*

"Get up!" he shouted at Erika. "Run!"

Then he turned and sized up the squirming man he held. He brought the *panga* down in a smart chop, discarded Lex with a contemptuous heave and returned his attention to Timothy.

Erika rose shakily to her feet, hearing a ghastly trampled scream from Albert. She looked around as the beast trotted a few feet beyond its victim and stood snorting bloodily, trying to distinguish with its poor eyes the shapes milling near the fire.

Timothy had picked up a glowing brand with which to defend himself. Oliver, demonstrating the adroitness of a Russian dancer, sprang at him in a stylish crouch and circled, feinting, weaving, his *panga* swishing too fast for the eye to follow. The befuddled Timothy began falling to pieces like a badly made clay statue.

Lex was up and running, half cocked, toward the Land-Rover. Oliver leaped to intercept him, then heard the rhinoceros coming; he changed direction to snatch Erika out of the way. The rhino, for all its wounds, was almost as quick on its feet as the black man.

Oliver, shouting, tried to distract the animal, to draw its second charge away from Erika; but it was Erika, naked, her pale backside gleaming, who received all of the rhino's attention. She ran straight for the woods in a panic, not the best strategy for eluding a charging rhino.

If this one had been healthy and of sound wind, it would have overrun her. The best it could manage, as she plunged into barbed brush, was a blunt toss of its hornless head that caught her in the buttocks and hurled her against a tree.

Her arms absorbed most of the impact. Erika fell in a heap, the bones in her right wrist cracked, the breath knocked out of her, and lay still.

When she disappeared from its path, the rhino promptly forgot about her, took a few drunken stagger steps to one side, then continued to bull its way between the trees, growling in rage, terrifying what was left of the resident night life, until it reached the plain again.

Dimly Erika heard the sound of the Land-Rover's engine at high speed. Moments later there were shots, but the Rover kept going.

"Erika!" Oliver called, a little after that.

She tried to rise. The pain in her back wouldn't permit it. Her back muscles wouldn't work at all. She nearly fainted and lay still once more, panting, bleeding, utterly helpless, as Oliver continued to call and beat the brush in his search for her.

# WARSHIELD RANCH

Raun Hardie had been moved from the hospital at
Talon Mountain several days after her run-in with the
fanatical Zola and her hopped-up confederate, and the
next morning at five fifteen Jade was at the side of
her bed in one of the guest rooms at the ranch, his
blue eyes gleaming in the faint light of dawn; he was
all business.

"Time to get started."

"Wha?"

"Dress warm. Sweater and jacket. I'll see you outside in five minutes. Don't disappoint me."

Raun pushed the hair out of her eyes and focused
on him, but by that time he was on his way to the
door. She looked at the windows, at a thick rime of
frost on the glass, shuddered, and thought about
ducking under the covers again. But then she remembered, with a twinge of exhilaration, that because of
Matthew Jade she was alive and free. And, more than
anything else, she wanted to remain free. So she
thought she'd better humor him, go along with his
plans. Something he'd said about getting into shape . . .

Just five minutes later she was on the long roofed
front porch of the log ranch house, yawning hard
enough to crack her jaws, struggling to run the zipper
of her too-tight jeans all the way up. If the jeans had
belonged to his wife then she'd been a petite woman,

with the bones of a fledgling. The sun was just coming up, there were patches of snow everywhere, it
couldn't have been more than thirty-five degrees out.
She tried a smile (might as well be friends), and then,
looking more closely at Jade, she saw that he was
barefoot. It was her first intimation that he was more
than just an eccentric, he was a little crazy.

"Where are we going?"

"Little hike. That way." He pointed toward the
mountain peaks to the west, now tipped with morning
gold.

"Oh. Well, couldn't we have some coffee first? I'm
f-freezing."

"Later," Jade promised. He smiled slightly. "You'll
warm up on the trail."

He started off at a pace that was just short of a jog,
went about a hundred yards, then looked back at
Raun as if he couldn't believe she wasn't keeping up
with him. She was still standing on the porch but, determined to be a good sport, she hastened to join him.

"How much later?" she asked, already breathless.

Five miles later, almost all of it uphill. When they
reached the high grove of aspen where Lem Meztizo
was cooking breakfast over a fire, Raun was half
frozen, nursing blisters and a black curse in her heart.

Jade had walked her and Jade had run her, over
short stretches, and he had waited patiently, without
expression, his silver-gray bulldogger's Stetson tipped
forward almost over his eyes, while she picked herself
up several times after collapsing from exhaustion. His
apparent indifference to her suffering was bad
enough, but he came to seem inhuman: He had feet
like horseshoes and the tireless lope of a wolf.

Often he would become bored with her slow progress and go off and leave her; at least she would lose
sight of him through the sapling forests and, feeling

discouraged and abandoned, limping, her lungs like a furnace, she would fall down, unable to move. But the power of his steady gaze always aroused her; she would look around until she located him, sometimes in a tree, sometimes mounted on a stack of leaning rocks like the prow of an old schooner, and with only a slight upward tilt of his chin he would have her, witlessly, on her feet and staggering forward.

Lem fetched a blanket for Raun; she wrapped herself tightly and huddled by the fire. The purity of the air she was breathing had given her a fierce headache. She was trembling so badly she couldn't hold the cup of coffee which Lem offered. He had to hold it for her while she sipped. He said nothing, but she felt his kindness and concern and was grateful.

Lem Meztizo the Third was a mixed breed of cowpuncher and, apparently, Matthew Jade's only confidant. In contrast to the other two hands who worked the Warshield's five thousand acres and were typical of their kind—the squint watery gaze, the scuffed-to-the-bone look—Lem Meztizo had a certain brilliance, the style of an eccentric grandee. He was big enough to match the wild elegance of his Arabian gelding. His teeth were lined with gold and he had long peroxided hair, gathered into a ponytail by a mummified tarantula partly entombed in precious stones. Though he carried a paunch he was not a soft-looking man, and he was as light on his feet as a roller-skating bear.

Raun drank more of the coffee and through her stuffed nose sorted out the odors of a range breakfast steaming over the fire: wheat cakes and eggs and sausage and spicy scrapple. She came slowly alive to the undeniable charm of a wilderness at seven thirty in the morning, sighed in appreciation when Lem placed a heaping plate in her lap.

She was astounded at her appetite; she couldn't pack the food in fast enough. But her feet were still sore and the curse remained, intensifying whenever she glanced at the obvious Jade, who was attending to a bump he'd found on a fetlock of one of the cow ponies Lem had brought with him to the high country.

Raun knew, or thought she knew, what she was in for. She'd blackmailed Jade and of course he resented it, so out of simple malice he would try to break her, make her quit. She stared at the fire and thought that the Irishman who had said "Don't get mad; get even" was her kind of philosopher. She felt a weak stirring of the pride that had been all but forgotten during her months in prison.

No, she wouldn't quit. Her revenge would be all the richer for this unnecessary torture—and for those desperate years in hiding, the demeaning trial and sentence by the government of the United States. She could handle anything Matthew Jade decided to throw at her.

"You want me to do *what*?"

Raun looked up in shock from the second breakfast she'd been enjoying; across the fire Jade was hunkered down intent on his own meal, eyes on his plate. He didn't look at her.

"I said we need to work on your legs, build them up. From the photos I've seen we'll be parachuting onto rocky ground."

"From a plane? Are you *crazy*? I don't even like to fly!"

Jade cleaned his metal plate with half a biscuit, popped it into his cheek, and shrugged.

"It's the only way. But if you have some training, the odds are more in your favor. We'll try to get in half a dozen practice jumps before we leave here."

Raun put her plate aside and got slowly to her feet. Her knees wanted to buckle. Her lips were white. She looked at Lem, who was frowning, obviously sympathetic to her plight. It was also obvious he was not in a mood to contradict his friend Jade.

"My father and I didn't get there by parachute. Now look. You'll just have to be reasonable. I'm game for almost anything, but jumping out of airplanes? There has to be another way!"

There wasn't.

At five o'clock that evening, the end of a day which to Raun already seemed two weeks long, she and Lem Meztizo met with Jade in his pine-paneled study.

Raun collapsed into a chair covered with sheepskin while Lem pulled the drapes and Jade put a cassette into the Betamax. On the screen, Landsat images from the EROS Data Center of the U.S. Geological Survey appeared. They formed a mosaic of that part of Tanzania called the Makari Peninsula, a mountainous area jutting into Lake Tanganyika.

The western slopes were heavily forested, teeming with animal life, but the summits of the mountains were barren. Along the landward approaches to the peninsula there was almost nothing: no roads, no trees, no signs of human habitation except for a small military post that must have been there for punishment duty. With regard for the difference in temperature, the Makari was Tanzania's Siberia.

"The easy approach is from Kalemie, in Zaïre," Jade explained. "That's just across the lake, by helicopter or boat. But we can't use Zaïre as a staging area because of the current regime."

"A Land-Rover can make it easily," Raun pointed out. She was too tired to sulk.

"Even if the three of us could pass ourselves off as tourists in Tanzania—which we can't; the borders are closed—we'd never be able to justify our presence in a restricted area. As it is we'll have to dodge patrols most of the day. The Tanzanian Air Force has helicopters and light planes overflying the peninsula."

"Why? What's so *important* about the Catacombs? And what's the hurry getting there?"

"The rates go up after the rainy season," Jade said.

Raun lapsed into an unfriendly silence, but her mind was busy.

She didn't like Jade but she knew the man was no fool; and the U.S. government would not have acted so quickly to have her released if they were not vitally interested in something that was to be found in or near the Catacombs. Urgent plans had been formulated based on meager and (apparently she was the only one who knew this) false information. It was a farce, a comedy of errors—but parachuting onto African hardpan, risking a broken leg or worse, would be no joke.

She had tried to tell them part of the truth, that the Catacombs were like a dusty corner in a dull museum, worth the labor of only the most painstaking archaeologists. *She remembered very well what she had seen there.* No one was paying the slightest attention. What would Jade think now if she told him the true location of the Catacombs? And if she was believed, would she then be expendable? Raun had awakened that morning feeling free, but her freedom, she realized, was conditional. What the government had granted could be snatched away. No, she needed to find a way to put the brakes to their scheme without jeopardizing her pardon. And that might take some time.

"When are we going?" she asked Jade.

"We need to be in and out of the Catacombs before the twenty-ninth of May."

"That's only two weeks!" Raun looked in dismay at the repetitive views of bleak plateau and dry mountain range—hundreds of square miles. *The rates go up after the rainy season.* She wondered what just one night in that hell would cost her, and swallowed hard.

"Look, I won't jump. That's final. If you can't get a helicopter to set us down, then—I want to forget the whole thing."

Jade turned off the Betamax and turned on a lamp. He sat down and packed a corncob pipe with hairy-looking tobacco and got the pipe going. Lem Meztizo stood by the lamp minutely examining a twenty-dollar double-eagle gold piece on a gold chain he wore with a polished leather vest. Away from the range he wore his wealth with fancy pants and silk shirts: bejeweled charms and amulets and magic rings and lucky twenty-dollar gold pieces. After the coin he took out an antique railroader's pocket watch and listened to it chime. He killed time with the attentiveness of a surgeon.

Raun sensed channels of communication open between the waiting men that she was deaf and blind to. And the waiting grew on her soul like a callus.

"This isn't a matter of simple cowardice," Raun explained with a tightly drawn smile. "It goes deeper than that. It's—sheer terror, and it's in the bone."

Jade said mildly, "Nobody's missed you back at the clink. And your lookalike is probably getting bored in deadlock."

"I see. So that's how you handled it."

"Our safest bet is a twilight drop from a C-130 overflight. All the equipment we'll need—trail bikes, extra gasoline—can be parachuted in once you've picked our spot."

"I can't do it."

Jade whistled between his teeth. "Must be my lucky day," he said. "Except I know—"

He got up without another word and went to the telephone on his desk, a bulkier instrument than most she'd seen. She had no way of knowing that this was a secure line from the ranch to the NORAD communications center in Cheyenne Mountain, seventy-five miles away. Jade dialed a series of numbers, and hung up.

Thirty seconds later the phone rang, just once. He picked up the receiver and said, "We have a cancellation."

"Wait," Raun said.

Jade glanced at her. She had thought she was going to be okay, stiff upper lip, carry on regardless. But when she tried to smile, her face felt as if it might crack; then the tears came in a flood. She put a hand beside her nose and pressed her cheek hard, and the tears ran between her fingers.

"Give me—more time."

"Omit," Jade said over the phone, and hung up again.

Raun couldn't stop crying.

"I'm really tired. You wrecked me today. I ache all over, and I—I just can't think anymore."

His habitually intent expression seemed to soften, or maybe it was the blurring effect of her tears.

"You could use a good soak," Jade said. He looked almost cheerful. "If you just want to relax after your bath, I'll have dinner sent to your room. Then we'll see you bright and early."

The use of Jade's hot tub went a long way toward easing the soreness in Raun's body, too long unexercised: He seemed to have a therapist's knowledge of her anatomy, and throughout a day that had been torturous but (in retrospect) carefully planned, not one muscle had escaped his attention. Lem had taken care of the blisters earlier and, once she was out of the tub, he produced a small miracle named Lee, a Vietnamese woman skilled at massage. Then, in quick order,

came a second miracle: a perfect dry martini which
Raun enjoyed in small sips while Lee trod with diminutive feet the length of her bare back and legs. At
first the massage hurt like fury and then it began to
be enjoyable; then she passed into a state of bliss.

Lee and her husband Ken, who had Americanized
his name from Kien, were from the time of the boats.
Two of her children had died on the South China Sea,
during a long starvation drift southward to Singapore;
two others were now in college in the States, their tuition paid by Jade. It was a side of him Raun wouldn't
have suspected.

Ken did the cooking on the ranch. He had been the
*sous chef* at a fashionable Saigon restaurant before
the Americans arrived. He had acquired a magical
touch with the plain food of the American West:
chicken, beef ribs and chili, a thickly textured bread.
Stuffed but revived, Raun took her ease on the porch
with Lem as the sun was setting, staining the sky the
color of iodine. Jade had not appeared for dinner; she
wondered where he was.

Up to a point Lem wasn't reluctant to talk about his
employer. He confirmed what Raun already was convinced of: Jade had operated on the dark side of the
CIA. Then, as a result of some crucial but unauthorized action he'd taken, a top CIA official had been
murdered and another had disappeared. Lem wasn't
sure, but apparently they'd been "moles," or Russian
plants within The Company. Jade had resigned and
returned home to the ranch.

"I hadn't seen him for, maybe it was eighteen
months," Lem reflected. "Didn't hear a word. He'd
been gone long stretches before, but I just began to
think, maybe this time he's dead. Then he showed up.
Matt's an initiate of the Black Wolf Society, that's an
Indian thing, and I always have thought of him as half
wolf anyway. But that half was near dead; burned

out. He told me there'd been some trouble, and he looked to be expecting more, so I got ready for it but nothing ever happened. Later on he said he'd been in Russia, where he went to get himself arrested on purpose. He had to get next to a prisoner in one of those jails nobody ever gets out of alive. This one was called Lefortovo, I think, run by the KGB. He found out what he needed to know. Then he broke out of there and made his way to Finland all by himself. Soon as he got home, shitfire, the roof fell in at the CIA."

Raun gazed at the risen, nearly full moon. "How did he escape from an escape-proof prison?"

Lem said with a gold-edged smile, "You know that old expression, 'been there and back'? Matt's the only man I ever met it truly applied to."

"I don't understand."

Lem seemed on the verge of elaborating, but a luxury pickup truck with a lot of chrome on it and a loud radio was driving up to the house. He pushed off from the porch rail he'd been sitting on and sauntered over to greet the visitor, a runty Hopi Indian with a handsome haughty head and curly shoulderlength graying hair. He wore a buckskin jacket and baggy trousers, carried a large carpetbag with him.

"Hello, John Tovókinpi."

"Hello, Lem Meztizo."

"New set of wheels?"

"The truck belongs to my nephew, Ephraim Rohona. He said that I could borrow it as long as I used the low gear only, turned on all the flashing lights, and drove on the shoulder of the highway, not the highway itself. Then everyone would realize it was me, and stay far away. Have you seen Múte? He has sent for me."

"He's at the home pasture, updating the herd ledgers. He'll be along. This is Raun Hardie, a friend of ours."

John Tovókinpi looked closely at Raun for almost a full minute, without a trace of expression. Then he turned and said to Lem, as if he'd forgotten Raun was there, "She is better-looking than Taláwasohu, who I also admired for the purity of her voice. Do you suppose I could have my dinner now?"

"Right on in, John, Ken will fix you up."

"Who was that?" Raun asked, when the Indian was out of earshot.

"John's a Bow Clan sorcerer, one of three or four left among the Hopis, and there are only about five thousand Hopis left anymore. Too easy to push around, I guess, and they've always been fatalists, Matt says, not realists."

"What's he doing here?"

"Matt has his own way of preparing for things," Lem said evasively.

"He called Matt 'Múte.' What does it mean?"

"Swift runner."

"And who is Taláwasohu?"

"That was Nell's Indian name. Matt gave it to her. Means 'Star before the light of morning.'"

"That's beautiful," Raun said wistfully. "It's hard to believe he's ever led a normal life."

"He has here."

"And he was married."

"Well, that happened after he left The Company. Then he figured he could take on the responsibility. He was crazy about Nell. And I mean, she pitched in around here in spite of her background."

"What was that?"

"Family had money. Never worked up a sweat with their hands. Nell was a professional singer, concert type, had a good career going. Came out here and in no time she learned veterinary medicine. She was as good as if she had a degree. One of those with an instinct for it. She could spot a sick horse in the remuda before any of the hands knew something was wrong."

"She died in an avalanche? That's horrible."

"Matt's still taking it hard."

"Yet he gave me her clothes to wear."

"He grew up practical about things like that." Lem took out a pocketknife and sheared off a spot of ragged leather on one of his bootheels. "Well, I'm going on into town, haven't drunk the last three beers on my six-beer diet. You want to go along?"

"I'm having a very hard time keeping my chin off my chest. Bed for me."

"Night then."

"Lem, why does Matt want you to go along with us?"

Lem balanced a gold toothpick on the end of a fore-finger, then put it in a corner of his mouth.

"Needs somebody he can depend on; knows his mind without him having to say a word. That's useful in a tight spot."

"And of course he doesn't trust me. Have you done any parachute jumping, Lem?"

"Nope," Lem admitted, with a doleful tilt of his rock-star-blond head.

"I don't think you like the idea any better than I do."

"I go where Matt wants me to go."

"Why?"

"John Tovókinpi says we used to be brothers in an-other life, and I sort of have to look after him this time around. Don't know if I believe that, but what I do know is that I have a lot of love for him."

With a casual wave of his hand, Lem swung down off the porch and left Raun to reflect upon another aspect of Matthew Jade: his ability to inspire the de-votion of those few people who were close to him.

\* \* \*

Down by the home pasture, a quarter of a mile from the ranch house, Jade met with one of his hands, a towheaded twenty-six-year-old native of Pagosa Springs named Andy von Boecklin. Jade raised seed stock on his range, not market beef, and the home pasture was filling up with the heavies, pregnant cows who would remain in relative seclusion until they dropped their calves through the remainder of the spring and into summer.

Andy got down from Shoo-Bob, his venerable cutting horse, and took off his gloves.

"There's a couple of cases of hydrocele on the south range. Not too bad yet." From a distance, on the rapidly chilling night air, came the sounds of voices raised in hymn.

"Tell Lem. See anything of interest today?"

"Just those pilgrims camped on Red Cloud Mesa. Most of them white, but I saw a couple of black faces too. I don't see how they can go around dressed in burlap that way—I'd itch myself to death. And that food they're always cooking, I wouldn't want to put any of it in *my* mouth. What do they call themselves again?"

"Vassals of the Immaculate Light. They're okay. What else?"

"Trout fisherman. All by himself down along the Picket Wire in a camper truck. Ford. Arkansas plates."

"What's he like?"

"On the heavy side. Going bald. Kind of a droopy mustache. A real greenhorn."

"Why? What kind of fishing equipment does he have with him?"

"Lots of hefty-looking plugs. Gang hooks. More like he's after tuna than trout. Retired. Says he spends all of his time nowadays fishing. Didn't see any good fly rods. I told him, you won't catch none of our mountain trout with those Arkansas spincasters of yours. Hatchery trout, that's about all they got down that way, hell, they'll grab anything you throw in the water. Garbage. But he didn't believe me."

"Uh-huh. Better get up to the house and help yourself to ribs and some of that two-alarm chili before it's all gone."

"Now you're talkin'," Andy said.


Raun went to her room but found herself in the predicament of being too tired to sleep soundly. The best she could manage was a restless doze.

At a quarter after one in the morning she was awakened by the sound of drumming from Matthew Jade's bedroom, an accompanying Indian chant. She sat on the side of her bed listening for several minutes, until curiosity got the best of her. Then she slipped on a flannel robe—it was cold outside and chilly in the house—and went down the hall to his bedroom.

The door was open a few inches. The drumming and the toneless chant continued. The room seemed to be filled with blue smoke. She looked in and saw John Tovókinpi stripped to the waist and seated cross-legged on a ceremonial robe, a bowl of water on one side of him, a bowl that held a long, elaborately carved, smoking pipe on the other side. Various religious articles or fetishes had been arranged in a semicircle around him. He had the small drum between his knees. The head, of taut animal skin, was filthy; the drum looked very old.

All the furniture in the bedroom had been pushed against one wall. Matthew Jade lay on his back near the opposite wall. At first she didn't recognize him. He was stretched out rigidly, hands at his sides. He wore a Hopi kirtle made of fox skin and pelt and a white buckskin robe. An open eye was painted on his forehead, a white hand on his chest. The smoke escap-

ing from the room was acrid and stung her eyes; she
suppressed a cough.

It seemed to Raun, as she stared at the prostrate
Jade, that he wasn't exactly resting on the floor. He
seemed rather to be levitated two or three inches
above it. The smoke was so heavy there she found it
difficult to ascertain just what she was seeing. She
was a little dizzy, as if the smoke were a mild hallu-
cinogen. But suddenly her heart palpitated; she was
frightened. The painted eye on Jade's forehead
seemed to be observing her.

Raun backed away from the door and went quickly
to her own room. She was a long time lying in the
dark, uneasy, trying to keep the drumming from af-
fecting her pulse rate. Hairs were prickling on her
arms.

*You know that old expression, "been there and
back"? Matt's the only man I ever met it truly applied
to.*

The Russian agent whose American name was Bill
Sawyer spent a second miserable night on the woodsy
knoll that overlooked the home pasture of the Warshield ranch. The May afternoon had been warm
enough, with a nice easterly breeze riffling through
the glowing aspen, but shortly before dusk the temperature in the valley, hard by the Sangre de Cristos
at seven thousand feet, began dropping, and by moon-
rise it was down to thirty-seven degrees. Around mid-
night the moon was obscured and the east wind
brought a fine steady rain. His shearling coat leaked
and his ungloved hands froze. Sawyer, a city kid from
Leningrad, was no outdoorsman. To make matters
worse, he'd picked up a bladder infection and was
constantly unzipping his pants and waiting intermina-
bly to produce a few drops of urine.

When he started sneezing he abandoned his post (at

the ranch they'd long since bedded down for the night) and climbed into the camper, which had been hurriedly requisitioned for his assignment. The camper was well stocked with food and fishing gear, but he couldn't get the propane-fired heater to work. There were only two blankets aboard, an inexcusable oversight, both of them thin enough to read newsprint through.

He changed his socks, opened a can of corned beef, and ate while, just for something to do, he listened to the playback of several scrambled telephone conversations that had been transmitted over Jade's secure line. The rain quit and he went outside to try to pee again. He observed some mule deer down by the shallow river and heard what he thought was a mountain lion's screech, which got on his nerves. Then he turned in for a couple of hours' sleep.

Reinforcements arrived about four A.M. Sawyer put the coffee on and went outside to greet the newcomers.

"Hi. Bill Sawyer."

Even though it was the middle of the wilderness at an ungodly hour the other two men shook his hand, just as Americans meeting casually would do. Their impersonations were, had to be, impeccable.

"Steve Roper."

"I'm Ted Clemons."

Sawyer marveled that these men, among the elite of Cobra Dance, undoubtedly had been in Moscow just seventy-two hours ago. They drove a camper similiar to his: a few dents, a little honest prairie dirt. They were bigger, younger, more fit than he was, but nothing about them would attract more than passing notice. Roper wore a red-and-black checkerboard coat and a slightly tacky rancher's straw. Clemons wore steel-trimmed glasses, a California Angels baseball cap, and a camouflage jacket with NRA patches on it.

"How's the fishin'?" Roper asked, with an unmistakable Kansas twang.

"Not bad." Sawyer's teeth chattered. "Come on in, fellas, have some coffee."

The three men crowded into his camper. Clemons began to tinker with the balky heater and soon had it working.

"So what've we got?" Roper asked after sipping some of his coffee.

"Besides Jade there's three ranch hands, an Oriental couple and a girl."

"Girl friend?"

"I don't think so. He spent the day trying to get her into shape. Long hikes, calisthenics. She looked to be hating every minute of it. Then about eight o'clock two more men drove up in a Subaru Brat. They brought a lot of gear. Hard to tell from this distance, but I'd say they had at least half a dozen parachute packs with them."

"That's interesting," Clemons said.

"Maybe they're skydivers."

"The big question is, who's the girl?" Roper said, not expecting an answer.

"Anyone checking up on you?" Clemons asked Sawyer.

"A cowboy rode by today. Looking for strays, I suppose. We shot the breeze. He was wearing a button pinned to his shirt with THE BIG PISTOLERO written on it. All hick and a yard wide."

"Maybe."

"Then I guess I ought to mention the Jesus freaks."

"How's that again?" Roper said.

"That's what they call them over there. They're a religious commune camped a couple of miles west of here. Men, women, kids, they look like leftovers from a cheap Bible flick. Harmless zealots. I went down to chat with them but the smells and the homilies drove me away."

"Don't blame you."

"Where'd you fellas drive in from?"

"Denver," Roper said. He looked at his Timex wristwatch. "Better get some shuteye while we can. Get up early, go fishin'. That's what we're here for. To get a few fish on the line."

"Excuse me, will you?" Sawyer said. "Nature calls, goddammit."

# THE KIVUKONI FIVE-STAR HOTEL

**Dar es Salaam, Tanzania**
**May 15**

Michael Belov, Cobra Dance's man in Tanzania, had lunch on the awning-shaded terrace of the Kivukoni with Sunni Babcock and an irate Toby Chapman.

Sunni had spent most of the previous day tracking him down through the good offices of the Swedish embassy and had promised, when she finally had him on the phone, "a really earthshaking story." Belov, amused by her breathless earnestness, readily recalled meeting Sunni at a party or reception, recalled being charmed by her good looks and ingenuously accurate impressions of Dar es Salaam. He accepted her invitation to lunch because, at worst, it would be a painless two hours. And he wasn't doing much but hanging around this down-at-heels place waiting for Akim Koshar's network of informants to provide him with a lead that would point the way to the FIREKILL diamonds. Waiting edgily, he was too aware of the steady drain of time and the risky choice he might be forced to make if Koshar failed him. He would then have to kidnap Robeson Kumenyere, and squeeze the location of the Catacombs out of him.

"There's this man named Henry Landreth," Toby began.

Belov, a highly disciplined agent trained to be prepared for the unexpected during all of his waking moments, nevertheless nearly dropped the razor-point pen he'd taken from his pocket to dutifully record details of the "earthshaking" story he'd been promised. And if the earth didn't literally move at that instant, because of the way his heart palpitated he did feel as if he'd been standing a little too close to a bombshell.

Nevertheless he had himself quickly under control and smiled casually at the tall English boy, who was having difficulty deciding what to say next.

"What about him?" Belov prompted.

The story then came out in a pent-up jumble, with Sunni trying to help by throwing in her two cents' worth; Belov had to keep interrupting to get Toby to slow down and straighten out his chronology, supply missing pieces of the background. Fortunately their drinks arrived after only a twenty-minute wait. Toby drank half a *konyagi* and lime in a hurry; this calmed him somewhat. He finished crisply his recital of the events of the day before: Landreth's surprise at being recognized, his clumsy attempts to deny his identity, the presence of the black girl named Nyshuri.

"This is serious," Belov said, when Toby finally ran out of gas and sat staring at his clenched hands on the table. "Very serious. I want to get to the bottom of it immediately."

"Thank God!" Sunni said. "You don't know how hard it's been trying to get someone to listen—"

"I've talked to newspaper johnnies before," Toby said with a challenging look at Belov, "but in the end they've all been intimidated by the Tanzanian government."

"I assure you that I can't be intimidated, Toby. I'll move heaven and earth to document the truth, and see that it's released to all the news services without delay."

"Bless you," Sunni said fervently. Her eyes filled with tears. "We've been *out of our m-minds*—"

Belov held her hand for a few seconds. "Now, now.

Leave this to me. Toby, did you say something about photographs—?"

Toby nodded. "I took two or three shots of him. Haven't had the chance to develop them. The film is still in the camera in our suite."

"Why don't I take the film with me? The embassy will have the photos for me tonight."

"I'll run up and get the camera," Sunni said.

She was gone about ten minutes. When she returned she came toward them slowly, rubbing her elbow, her face screwed up as if she were going to cry.

"Toby," she said in a squeaky voice.

Toby jumped up.

"Luv? What's the matter?"

"There was a man in our room—a black man. He was *stealing* your camera. I caught him at it. He knocked me down when he ran out the door. I was so scared I couldn't even yell."

She had begun to shake. Toby held her tightly.

"Landreth! The rotten bastard." He glanced at Belov. "You see?"

"I'm sure it's no coincidence. I would have liked to have the photos, but they aren't essential. Toby, do you remember the layout of the hospital? Could you sketch the grounds and the location of the cottage where you saw Landreth?"

"I think so."

Toby put Sunni in her chair and she sipped her drink with a queasy expression, still trembling occasionally. Perhaps it had dawned on her what might have happened if the thief had been carrying a knife. Toby applied himself to the sketch that Belov wanted.

"I think the best thing for the two of you is to stay close to the hotel until you hear from me. Give me twenty-four hours, and don't worry."

"Mr. Lund*gren*? Mr. Chet Lund*gren*?"

Belov looked up and beckoned to a tall African in a

striped dashiki carrying a message board with a little tinkling bell atop it.

"I'm Lundgren."

"Ah, yes sar. There is *in*quiry for you, the lobby please."

Belov smiled at Toby and Sunni and excused himself. He followed the messenger to a dim corner of the lobby, where a brown-skinned man in a white suit turning rusty at the creases waited with his hat in one hand and a small package in the other. The man had a dental arch as long and narrow as a paper clip, and donkey teeth. He nodded several times to Belov, almost bowing, as Belov gave the messenger a coin and waited for him to depart.

"I am from Akim Koshar, Mr. Belov. He asked me to deliver this to you."

"Open it," Belov said, making no move to accept the package.

The man looked puzzled, but did as he was asked. Inside a jewel box was a greenish flat stone the size of a thumbnail, intricately carved on both sides. He held it up for Belov to inspect.

"Do you like it? I was told—any piece of jade would do. The message would be clear."

Belov hesitated, then smiled and took the jade, which depicted two feathered serpents locked in celestial combat. He slipped the piece into his jacket pocket. Perhaps, he thought, in some curious way it might bring him luck in their race to the Catacombs.

"The message is clear," he said to Koshar's man.

# VILLA BIB-SHALA

Dar es Salaam, Tanzania
May 15

"I'm very disappointed."

Lady Hecuba ha-Leví de Quattro-Smythe, naked in her boudoir, drew a straight razor from anklebone to kneecap along the smoothly muscled, golden-brown calf of her left leg. She dipped the lathery razor in a crystal bowl of water and gave it a swish to clear the edge, then lifted her eyes to the mirror in front of her. She pouted at the beautiful black girl who stood awkwardly a few feet behind her, twisting a necklace of twenty-four-carat iridescent gold around one fist as if it were a common piece of package twine. As she had expected, Nyshuri looked at the floor and hunched her shoulders in discouragement.

"I was only thinking of you," the black girl mumbled. "It was a very great risk to steal it. The Asian woman who owned it insisted that the hospital be turned upside down. But of course it was her fault she lost the necklace. She was a fool to wear it to the hospital in the first place."

The flashing of the gold links in the light and airy boudoir seemed to agitate a molting Madagascar green tree boa which Lady Hecuba maintained in a large terrarium nearby. It whipsawed around the bare climbing branch in its cage and bumped its head resoundingly against the sliding glass door in front. Hecuba frowned and, with the razor suspended, reached behind her with the other hand.

"Have I said I don't like it?"

Nyshuri, somewhat mollified, stepped forward and dropped the thin but weighty links into the palm of Hecuba's long hand; the necklace was swallowed, covered by inch-long lacquered nails. Hecuba scraped her flawless leg again and removed the few remaining flecks of lather with a soft cloth. Her eyes, always her first concern after her bath, were duskily painted, drawn to points that curved upward to the fragile hollows of her temples. She favored Nyshuri with a concupiscent look.

"You know my appetites almost too well."

Nyshuri began to smile, but Hecuba cut short her approval with yet another pout.

"I have many gold necklaces. I'm not ungrateful, but I feel that the love and affection which I have never denied you has been compromised. Gold is gold, but it is not the red diamond you have so tantalizingly described and promised to bring to me these past two weeks."

Nyshuri looked stricken with guilt. Hecuba rose, chose from her luxurious wardrobe a sand-colored sari, and put it on. Her third-floor apartment in the Villa Bib-Shala, located a few miles north of Dar off the New Bagamoyo Road, was surrounded by a deep terrace with a tile roof. The entire east wall of the apartment was open to the sea fifty yards away, and the rooms were always cool, filled with light but not, due to ingenious methods of screening and shuttering, the direct rays of the sun.

Hecuba left Nyshuri to fret for a while about her failure, poured an ounce of an aromatic Algerian wine from a chilled silver decanter, and enjoyed her commanding view of the Indian Ocean, which in the late afternoon was running blue as blood beneath the skin and littered with the rickety boats of a native fishing fleet. Below her on the terrace, chairs scraped stone as servants went about setting up for one of her thrice-weekly, by-invitation-only parties.

In socialist Tanzania cabarets were decried as deca-dent but not officially banned, although it was now impossible to get a license to operate one, even in the new government-owned hotels that stood, three-quarters empty, along the northern strand near the coast road. The few cabarets in Dar remaining from the old days were poorly patronized and offered little in the way of entertainment. Closings by discouraged owners happened more frequently as the borders of the country continued to be sealed. Only Lady Hecuba ha-Leví de Quattro-Smythe (she had lavished this pedigree on herself, claiming the privilege if not the official status of a few past liaisons) had evolved a way to flourish in straitened circumstances. But she'd had loads of experience at making the needs of others suit her own, enriching herself at the same time.

She was the sole offspring of a forbidden and even-tually fatal affair between a Moroccan princess and a handsome Sephardic Jew in North Africa. Both par-ents had committed suicide; Hecuba subsequently survived a guttersnipe upbringing in the slums of Tangier as the unofficial ward, hashish supplier, and bed partner (at the tender age of eight) of a British expatriate who wrote dense symbolic novels with his right hand and pornography with his left. In the thirty-odd years since his demise she had supported herself with a cunning mind and a supple body, prof-iting handsomely from a total lack of compassion for the human race.

She would always be two-thirds alley cat, and she knew it; lacking the aristocratic touch of the world-class courtesan, she had confined her activities to the fringe fleshpots and second-rate nations of the world, cultivating a rough vibrato singing voice, a polyglot flair for languages, a good business head. Invitations to her parties were always eagerly sought. The Villa Bib-Shala was the one place in all of Tanzania where diplomats from both eastern and western bloc countries mingled freely with government leaders and important businessmen from Tanzania and other African nations. Their gifts to their hostess were offered with discretion. A one-hundred-shilling note was the norm. It was placed inside a well-concealed drawer in the belly of a large bronze buddha in the main bathroom. Somehow Hecuba always knew who was not being generous with her, or not contributing at all. Their phone calls requesting invitations to the villa were not returned by Hecuba's social secretary.

It was a cruel ostracism, particularly for those who had heard about the type of entertainment which Hecuba, when she was in the mood, could provide with the assistance of one or more of her pet snakes, the hypnotic beat of a Congo drum, and some dramatic lighting effects.

Hecuba turned suddenly and went back to Nyshuri. She lifted the black girl's chin on the ball of her thumb and smiled into her eyes. With the index finger of her other hand she dipped into the remaining half ounce of sticky, sweet wine, then pushed the finger gently between Nyshuri's slowly yielding lips. Nyshuri's breasts lifted; she sucked gratefully.

"You see, I don't want to doubt you, Nyshuri. I don't ever want there to be a cause for mistrust between us. I love you very much, but our love can so easily be destroyed if we're not completely honest with each other.

"Now what sort of lark have you got up to?"

She withdrew her finger and wet it again. She stroked Nyshuri's trembling lips lightly, then, deli-

cately, inserted the finger to tickle her palate. Nyshuri's body tautened from the pain and pleasure of
this tease. She gasped, bit gently, released the sweet-
tasting finger. She swallowed hotly, a flush that
plunged straight to her loins.

"I wasn't lying to you," Nyshuri said breathlessly.
"Henry showed the diamond to me. He said it was
very old, and worth more than the crown jewels of
England. He called it a bloodstone."

"And the writings?"

"Yes! Marked all over with the writings. By people
who lived, oh, ten thousand years ago."

"How remarkable."

Nyshuri, quivering a little from excitement, held up
hooked fingers.

"Henry says they were more like big cats than people. Cheetahs. He's seen them himself. I think he is
afraid of them, although they are all dead, in tombs
like glass."

Lady Hecuba dispassionately turned Nyshuri back
to the subject of diamonds.

"Could Henry read the inscriptions on his bloodstone?"

"Oh, yes."

"Did he tell you what they meant?"

"No, he wouldn't tell me."

"And he wouldn't tell you where he found the bloodstone, or saw the creatures."

"No. He only said there were other bloodstones,
many others."

Hecuba put her glass aside and her hands strayed
to the full breasts of the trembling girl. Hecuba undid
the top two buttons of Nyshuri's dress and gently
popped her breasts free of the material, as if she were
squeezing mangoes from a sack.

"Oh, oh," Nyshuri moaned, feeling the slow pressure
of Hecuba's thumbs beside her nipples.

"After all," Hecuba persisted, "I don't wish to have the bloodstone; such rarities are obviously dangerous to possess."

"Henry doesn't sleep well. He paces the floor at night. *Oh, do that again!* I think since the English boy appeared he's afraid he might be found by others, and killed."

Hecuba kissed Nyshuri on the cheek while peeling the dress from her body. "I only want to see it with my own eyes. Then you can take the bloodstone back."

"But I've looked and looked, and I can't find it! Henry is too clever!"

"You'll be clever too, won't you? You'll ask to see the bloodstone again, and this time you'll be watching when he puts it away."

Fifteen minutes later Hecuba rose on her knees from the labor of lovemaking, leaving Nyshuri spread-eagled on the bed and all but gibbering as she waited for completion.

"Which one?" Hecuba asked indulgently. "La Gorda?"

"No," Nyshuri gasped. Reason had deserted her. "The boomslang. But hurry!"

Hecuba padded lithely to another of the terrariums she kept near her bed, slid back the door, reached inside for the dark snake draped sullenly in the crotch of a scale-polished tree branch. The boomslang, one of nature's most lethal creatures, had like the boa in an adjoining cage begun to molt, making it twice as surly as it ordinarily was. The snake turned its head in her grasp, revealing an opaque, sky-blue eye. Hecuba removed the boomslang from the cage and carried it to her bed.

Nyshuri looked at the angrily darting head, at blind death in the blue eye, and shrieked ecstatically. She had no way of knowing that Hecuba recently had pulled the bloomslang's fangs so the snake would be usable in her act.

Nyshuri slowly raised both knees and Hecuba snuggled the boomslang against her belly and mons veneris. When the snake slid hugely down between her legs Nyshuri climaxed and fainted, almost simultaneously. Hecuba came too, although not so powerfully, inspirited not by the pseudomenace of the boomslang, which was old stuff to her, but by her knowledge that their unorthodox tribalism was being closely and secretly observed.

Hecuba put the snake back in its cage, revived Nyshuri with cold astringent cloths and cooing words of adoration, and sent her on her way in a dreaming daze, with one more reminder about the bloodstone.

By then it was nearly dusk. Seabirds cried and the waves hissed on the shore. She let Jan-Nic Pretorius out of the small room next to the boudoir where he'd been cooped up for more than an hour, with nothing to do but stare through the two-way mirror at the women and listen to their conversation.

At a glance she knew just how aroused Jan-Nic had become by the staged lovemaking; he was paler than usual, sweating, almost sick from sexual excitement. He couldn't keep his eyes off the boomslang in its cage.

Hecuba had judged that, like a lot of his puritanical countrymen, he had a deeply seated yen for black women. She had deliberately seduced Nyshuri in front of him when there was no real need for it. And, to keep him edgy now, she found it amusing to flaunt her naked body when she might easily have slipped into a fresh sari. The South African Department of National Security paid her well for information, but she'd always mistrusted zealots. Although she had no taste for fair-skinned blond men, this fellow they had sent to her was undeniably handsome—and a little too self-assured, undoubtedly someone of great importance in their police state. He'd made the vital mistake of condescending to her, as if she were a common whore. She was now quite a bit more than even, and enjoying herself immensely.

"Could you use a drink?" she asked Jan-Nic.

He requested mineral water with lime; Hecuba poured it for him while he stared at the sea and asserted some control over himself and the sexual images branded into his brain. When she came with his teetotaler's cocktail he looked at her in a new way, flatly and with a frigid reserve, as if he had decided her continued nakedness was a deliberate insult to his sensibilities. He didn't have the look of a killer, like some of the Afrikaner agents she'd dealt with. But there was a hint of something else that obscurely threatened her; tormented too long, the sexual beast within him could slip its leash and go into a frenzy, the result of which might be a bloody nightmare.

Having no more to gain, Hecuba draped herself chastely and reclined on a chaise to study her superb skin in a magnifying mirror.

"Now you know all that I know," she said.

"It isn't enough," Jan-Nic brooded. "I must have one of the stones. If they exist. I don't think I trust this girl. She steals for you. She might say anything to please you."

"She lies, of course, she exaggerates, they all do. But she has no imagination. It's beyond her abilities to make up such a story. There are a few facts worth considering. Dr. Henry Landreth was a famous British physicist who fell into disgrace. He now enjoys the protective hospitality of Dr. Robeson Kumenyere. Make no mistake about that one, he's very powerful, and quite close to Kinyati. I am well enough acquainted with Dr. Kumenyere to know that he would not be looking after Landreth unless he stood to profit by his generosity. Furthermore, he assigned Nyshuri to keep Landreth company, to amuse him and take his mind off his troubles. It would seem that Dr. Landreth is supposed to be missing, or dead. Yet he lives in seclusion at the hospital, suspicious of strangers, afraid for his life, while he awaits—his mistress tells me—an event of cataclysmic magnitude."

Her voice was a purr as she lifted her jaw to assay her profile in the mirror; an insolent olive-shaped eye peered hugely at him. "What could that be, and what does it have to do with our strange red diamond?"

Jan-Nic, remembering the conversation he'd had with his father-in-law a week ago, the partially burned letter from Jumbe Kinyati promising black Africans a retributive holocaust (*Pretoria shall perish in the brightness of our noon*), stared in distaste at Hecuba. She greedily took their money, but, being of suspicious blood herself, she had no sympathy for his country. His people were virtually friendless in the world; still it was unthinkable that they would not endure in their chosen land. *They must.* Jan-Nic felt an instant's panic, firmly suppressed. So much depended on him. He couldn't afford a wrong move. But he'd already decided what he had to do.

"I don't think your lover will be of further use to us," he told Hecuba. "I'm going after Landreth myself."

Michael Belov, his left arm in a sling supplied by the Emergency Department of Kialamahindi Hospital, walked through the grounds at nightfall with the air of a man resigned to waiting many hours for his X rays to be developed.

He paused in the center garden to watch the tropical fish in a saline pool. The sun was setting, profusely reflected from the bronzed windows of the inverted pyramid that dominated the upper end of the dogleg hospital grounds. He nodded pleasantly to a bored guard, one of three patrolling with a .22-caliber submachine gun over one shoulder; he knew their patterns well by now. Toby Chapman hadn't reported seeing any guards the day before, so apparently he'd thrown quite a scare into Landreth, who had then complained to the head of the hospital: Dr. Kumenyere. A fourth guard was now permanently stationed by the padlocked gate of the hedge-enclosed compound fifty yards or so beyond the pyramid.

Belov moved on, in the direction of the pyramid and the helicopter landing pad.

He'd spent most of his afternoon at the hospital. An imaginary sprained wrist was his excuse. He had a permanent bump caused by a long-ago but harmless leak of synovial fluid from the wrist joint that lent credence to his complaint of injury. When he wasn't being examined, Belov prowled the grounds until he

knew every path and doorway by heart. Having
looked over the big generator shed, he briefly considered a blackout to cover his anticipated snatch of
Henry Landreth. But to do it properly, while he was
making good use of his time elsewhere, required plastic explosives and a timing device. The tools he had
available were limited: a pair of heavy-duty wire clippers which could be concealed in one of the big cargo
pockets of his bush jacket, a roll of filament tape. Also
it was obvious that any kind of explosion would disturb the drowsy guards, inspire them to take some
sort of furious, impetuous action that would surely be
to his disadvantage even with the lights out. It was
better to know where they were at all times, and work
around them.

Just an hour ago he'd had a good look at his quarry.
Landreth, deep in conversation with Dr. Kumenyere,
had emerged from the pyramidal building and walked
to the compound gates with him. Landreth seemed to
be trying to convince his host of a course of action,
which the doctor rejected with a solid shaking of his
bent head. Landreth then produced from a pocket of
his jacket what looked to be a letter.

Kumenyere glanced at it and shook his head again,
smiling. Then he made an attempt to placate the Englishman. They stood face to face outside the gate, Kumenyere with a hand on Landreth's shoulder. Landreth shouted "We'll let Jumbe decide!" He turned on
his heel and disappeared through the gates, which the
guard promptly locked behind him.

Kumenyere remained in place for several seconds,
stiff and erect as if he'd received a pole up his backside, staring after the departed Landreth. Then he
shook his head wearily and returned to the pyramid,
looking through a sheaf of papers on a clipboard as he
walked.

With the light fast disappearing from the hospital

grounds, Belov took off his sunglasses with the heavy French frames and reconnoitered once again. The guard on the compound gate was accustomed to seeing him by now and didn't rise from his campstool when Belov came within twenty feet of the fence.

He'd already picked his spot, where the fence made an abrupt angle away from the main hospital grounds. There, after dark, he couldn't be seen by guards or anyone else, unless they came around the corner. The fence wire was like cheap baling wire, and rusty. There was an overhead light in a metal shade where the fence made almost a right angle. But jacaranda trees grew in wild profusion along the shell path, the branches arching over the fence, a natural canopy that would all but eliminate the light from the low-wattage bulb.

Beside the path workmen had begun a slit trench for the installation of sewer pipes that were stacked nearby and loosely covered with a tarpaulin. The path, wide enough to accommodate a small sedan, jogged another hundred yards through the deserted, heavily planted back acreage of the hospital to an isolated gate with a guard post that would probably be attended at night. But it didn't matter.

Belov had worked out all the details but one—how to quickly remove the Englishman from the hospital grounds once he pried him out of his bungalow—when a blue Toyota hatchback drove toward him through the lower hospital grounds.

The black girl at the wheel skidded the Toyota to a stop, parked it a few feet to the right of the gate and parallel to the fence. She had her own key to the padlock on the gate, which she opened, chattering in Swahili with the guard.

So this was Nyshuri, Landreth's girl friend. Her presence would be a minor complication. But the hatchback, already headed in the right direction, was like a gift. Now it wouldn't be necessary to leave Landreth in the slit trench with a tarp over him while he brought a car down from the back gate.

There was little he could do until well after dark. He went back and sat for a while in the crowded anteroom of the Emergency Department, where no one paid attention to him. Then he dawdled over a meal in the cafeteria. About nine o'clock he saw Nyshuri in the kitchen of the cafeteria putting together a tray for herself and Henry Landreth. She left by a back door.

Belov had a second cup of coffee and read his horoscope in the *Daily Mail,* which promised him extravagant returns for diligent effort. Just what he wanted to hear. Five minutes before the cafeteria closed he strolled outside again.

The Toyota hatchback was still parked by the fence. The guard on the gate had been changed, from a young man with a ewe neck to a pot-bellied old man enjoying a cigarillo. Belov heard recorded music from Landreth's bungalow which he identified as Brahms' B-flat piano concerto. The dazzling beauty of the *allegro non troppo* flowed through his mind. Obviously, given the grandeur of the technique, the pianist was Russian, but which Russian? Then he had it: who else but Gilels? He hoped Landreth and his mistress were having a relaxing evening together.

To avoid the scrutiny and challenge of the new guard, whom he soon would have to kill, Belov circled around behind the massive inverted pyramid and dropped the sling he no longer needed in a dustbin. The path here was a mix of finely ground shell and dirt, which made for a more quiet approach to the compound fence at the point where he planned to break through.

The cutters were in the big cargo pocket on the

right side of his bush jacket. In the left-hand pocket he had his sunglasses and a familiar-looking, small plastic bottle with a label identifying it as a common type of nasal decongestant spray manufactured in Switzerland. But the bottle contained something altogether different, a spray that removed the fatty acids from the nerve endings of the face (or the genitalia, if one preferred), producing, for about the next thirty minutes, a condition of helpless agony. If the face was sprayed, then the victim also felt as if he were suffocating as the sinuses drained continually into the throat.

As he'd anticipated, Michael Belov had no difficulty reaching the fence unobserved. He paused for a few moments, gently pushing aside the broad leaves of the croton plants that covered the outside of the fence.

The virtuoso piano of Emil Gilels was louder. The bungalow was only about twenty feet away, at an angle. One story, overhanging roof, long front porch or verandah, with a smaller porch that might have been used for servants' quarters attached to the back of the bungalow. Belov heard a toilet flush. Inside a couple of lamps were lit, casting their light from the windows onto ground that was barren except for outbreaks of scrub palmetto, motley bougainvillaea.

There was just enough light filtering down from the pole overhead to assist him in cutting a good-sized opening in the fence. The only trouble was, somebody had been there before him.

Belov suppressed his annoyance and dismay and stood perfectly still looking at the fence, ignoring the nighttime bugs whirling around his head. The wire had been cut to a height of six feet, bent inward, bent back again so that the intrusion wouldn't be readily noticeable. He let his own clippers fall back into the side pocket and took a longer look at the bungalow, at the possible places of concealment around it. There weren't many, so it didn't take him long to find his adversaries.

Two men crouched side by side in a clump of palmetto not far from the steps of the sagging back porch. His first thought was of the Americans, of Matthew Jade, perhaps. They had somehow come across the trail of the enigmatic Englishman. Not that it really mattered who they were. He knew they were up to no good, and had to be prevented from getting their hands on Landreth.

The piano concerto ended, and was too soon replaced by a shrill female vocalist who wanted to be taken to Funky Town. Nyshuri could be seen boogeying by a window. The bathroom light snapped on and Henry Landreth's spindly torso was visible in sections through the opaque glass louvers until he sat down. In the yard there was a tiny gleam of light as one of the waiting men exposed too much of the crystal face of his wristwatch.

*Amateurs,* Belov thought; even so he wasn't anxious to tangle with them. But it had to be done.

One of the men, tall and lean, rose from the ground and moved swiftly to the back porch. He eased the screen door open and crept inside. But the rock music was loud and would have covered any incompetent moves on his part.

Belov slowly bent the cut wire of the fence inward again until there was enough of an opening for him to pass through. He took his large sunglasses from his pocket and disassembled them. One earpiece became a sheathed steel blade about three and a half inches long, thin and sharp. He waited until he was sure the tall man was occupied within the house, then squeezed through the fence and approached the man waiting on the grounds.

When he was just three feet behind the man, Belov cleared his throat softly.

Instead of diving forward out of the palmetto and rolling away in an immediate evasive move, the heavy-set man looked up and around, rising instinctively on the balls of his feet and showing the whites of his startled eyes. He also exposed his throat. Belov could have cut it for him, but it might have taken the man thirty seconds or more to lose consciousness. He had already grunted once, in alarm. Belov thrust the blade through the outside corner of the man's left eye and rammed it into the brain while restraining with a fierce grip the pocketed hand that held an automatic. He let go of the knife and caught the man by the necktie with his free hand, lowered the dead weight silently to the ground. Then he retrieved his knife and went after the other one.

He was halfway to the back porch of the bungalow when a loud bang sounded on the hospital grounds, and the lights went out. The generator had been blown.

*They are doing absolutely everything wrong*, Belov thought with a mixture of fury and impotence. Which meant they weren't Americans, who could be trusted to show some professional competence in these affairs. For an instant he considered retreating before he was swept up in the inevitable chaos that would follow the act of sabotage.

But he'd come too far to quit now, and he couldn't afford to lose Henry Landreth.

Belov entered the house, hearing screams, shouts, the sound of a struggle. He knew what was happening; the man he was after had kicked open the bathroom door and dragged Landreth out.

"Nyshuri! Help!"

The black girl wasn't capable of lending much help. Apparently she was still in the living room of the bungalow, frozen in fear, crying out in Swahili. Belov pictured the guard at the gate fumbling with his keys in the dark, trying to get the padlock open. He heard the solid *thunk* of a blunt instrument against thinly padded bone and the aspirated groan of Henry Landreth lapsing into unconsciousness.

It sounded like too hard a blow. He turned a corner into a hallway and saw a pencil-thin beam of light shining on Landreth's pallid face. There was blood oozing from one nostril. He was slumped against a wall, his trousers down around his knees. His assailant, hunkered beside him, couldn't decide whether to pull them up or yank them all the way off before carrying Landreth down the back steps.

Belov made a neutral sound, neither word nor grunt. The other man turned his blond head and spoke sharply to Belov in Afrikaans, a language he recognized but didn't speak.

"You've got the right string, baby, but the wrong Yo-Yo," Belov said, sounding a lot like John Wayne. He was unsure of the strength of his blade in a close struggle, so he jetted the man with spray from the bottle he was holding in his other hand. But this one was better trained, or a better athlete, than the man he'd killed outside. The spray missed his face as he threw himself over the partially supine body of Henry Landreth and somersaulted through a doorway at the end of the short hall.

Belov was afraid he'd come up out of his tuck-and-roll with a gun in his hand, which would complicate matters. But apparently as he rolled to his feet in the living room he became entangled with Nyshuri, knocking her flat, provoking fresh screams of terror.

To add to the confusion there was a burst of machine-gun fire outside, as if the guard had decided to shoot his way through the gate. Belov glanced once at the dim form of Henry Landreth slumped in the hall. Was he breathing? Nyshuri was still screaming, but he heard the slap of a screen door as the interfering South African escaped from the bungalow.

Belov cursed him and made his own, reluctant decision. His chances of getting Landreth away from there now were nil, even if the blackout continued. The police or soldiers would soon be on hand, shooting or arresting anyone who looked the least suspicious, sealing off the grounds. He couldn't afford to be picked up. Time to call it a night. He was confident that the Catacombs were close, very close. He had only to exercise patience and care. Tomorrow, or the next day, he would have the information he needed and be on his way.

## WARSHIELD RANCH

The instructors brought in to teach Raun Hardie and
Lem Meztizo the Third the rudiments of parachute
jumping had set up a practice area in the largest of
the two barns on Jade's ranch, and for two days, when
she wasn't hiking and doing calisthenics and wind
sprints to build her endurance, Raun learned how to
survive leaping out of an airplane from a mile or so in
the air.

She was determined that she was not going to make
an actual jump. *No power on earth—* But at the same
time it was imperative to give the impression that she
was cooperating, and the techniques which the experts taught were not difficult to learn. Rolling backward and forward on a tumbling mat, keeping feet
and knees together and her chin tucked in. Launching
herself from a small trampoline and rolling forward
over one shoulder. Jumping from a six-, then a ten-
foot-high platform. Learning, after coming up with a
chipped tooth and a bloody lip the first time because
she was too loose and casual, how the shock of impact
is taken up by the strength of the legs and then dis-
tributed along one side of the body by rolling through
thigh and hip to the shoulder.

Raun was fitted for a red-and-yellow jump suit,
boots, and helmet. She learned the theory of canopy
control by hanging from an actual harness and pulling
on the lift webs. She practiced jumping from the plat-

form with a second chute, which, they solemnly told her, was useful in case the first one opened improperly. Admittedly a rare occurrence, but . . . A Roman candle, it was called. From any distance above a thousand feet the body would meet the earth at a speed of one hundred sixty miles an hour.

Uh-huh, Raun said. Her mind was far away. It was a meaningless consequence for thumbing your nose at Fate. She'd already reached her absolute limit, ten feet above the tanbark in the barn. *Wild horses wouldn't drag*— They taught her how to get rid of that first tangled chute in case she needed to open the second. At the end of fifteen hours of instruction and practice she felt quite competent. But it was all for nothing. She was just biding her time.

On the evening of the sixteenth she went for a hike and jog before dinner and was surprised to find that she had been looking forward to this time; Lem Meztizo, claiming that he was feeling the results of months of physical neglect, went with her.

Their course took them down by the Picket Wire, where the three trout fishermen were wading upstream and about thirty yards apart, serenely looking for that last catch of the day. One of them, the portly Bill Sawyer, turned and noticed them and waved. He and Raun had never spoken, but in a sense they were friends: It was one curious effect which the beauty and isolation of the ranch had on people. Raun waved back. From Red Cloud Mesa came the wind-borne tang of cook fires, voices of children playing. The sky was streaked with yellow cloud. They came to a tree with horizontal low branches ideal for chinning.

Raun managed three and a half. Lem astonished her by pumping his heavy body up and down fifteen times before dropping lightly to his feet and sucking wind.

She almost wished Jade were with them. A stray

thought, from nowhere, but it nearly knocked her over. *Of all people.* Raun smiled involuntarily, the smile twisting into a grimace. When he was around she always felt a prickle of animosity. He was too quiet for her, a spooky kind of quiet, she liked people who *talked*, who let you know what they were all about. He could be a boor. His mystical bent dismayed her. Jade had power over her, and although in the end it was she who would win, Raun felt, in the meantime, uncomfortable and resentful. He used his loneliness like a shield—well, she'd been guilty of that a time or two in her life, strike the objection. But why did he keep his dead wife's room untouched, except for a change of greenhouse flowers daily, as if it were a shrine?

Last night he'd spent three hours—and six minutes, to be exact—in there. She could understand what a shock it must have been to lose Nell, to stand helplessly by knowing where she was but unable to reach her as she slowly asphyxiated. When you expected the one you loved to die, knowing for months there was no hope, it was tough enough, but somehow easier to endure. With Andrew . . . But she couldn't think about Andrew Harkness, not now. She had to deal with Matthew Jade. Getting him to open up a little, talk about something personal and human and not about his obsession with the Catacombs, might be a help.

They jogged the last two hundred yards up to the house, accompanied by a couple of the wild-looking collies who lived on the ranch. Raun was puffing hard but determined to make it. Looking over at Lem, she saw that his face had turned the shade of a ripe tomato. But he was keeping pace, his belly moving ponderously with each short stride: He ran like a man trying to avoid breaking eggs.

Lem sneaked a look at Raun and his mouth turned up in a grin. Raun began to laugh and then, totally winded, she tripped on a clump of grass and sprawled. The dogs jumped over and circled around her, and one stuck his long nose into her ear. Raun lay back, nuzzling the collie, looking at the dots of stars that swam in the darkening sky. She felt an emotion she'd been without for so long it seemed foreign to her nature: a flash of happiness and contentment.

Her euphoria, in a milder form, lasted until 5:06 A.M. the next morning, when she was awakened by the sound of a helicopter landing at the ranch only about thirty yards from her bedroom window.

Raun turned her head on the pillow and there was Matthew Jade, in profile, his face turned toward the silver-gray windows in the dark room. The running lights of the helicopter flashed on the window glass. Raun thought she had locked her door the night before, but apparently that didn't mean anything to him.

"MORNING," he said, as if he knew without having to look that she was awake.

"What are you—" Jade cupped a hand to his ear and leaned toward her.

"I SAID, WHAT ARE YOU—"

"TODAY'S THE—" The helicopter pilot cut his engine then, and Jade lowered his voice. "Today's the day."

She sat straight up in bed, tingling from shock.

"It is not. You said Saturday!"

"I lied. You're as ready now as you'll be then, and it's better if you don't have time to think about it too much. Trust me on that, Raun."

"I'm not leaving this room!"

Jade didn't argue. He walked over, stripped the comforter and blanket from her, and left her shivering on the mattress in her snug yellow flannel pajamas.

Too snug. She put her knees down and her hands in her lap.

"You can put your jump suit on, or I'll carry you out of here in your pj's."

"You s-son of a b-bitch!"

"My mother," Jade said, "would grieve to hear you say that. Either you go up in the wild blue yonder today, or I'll bury you back at Talon Mountain."

"No you won't," Raun said, glaring at him.

"Be ready in ten minutes. We have to go all the way to Denver to catch our flight."

He had the courtesy to leave her alone then; Raun frantically studied her options. Today or tomorrow she had planned to twist an ankle or knee just badly enough so that she'd have to stay off it for a few days. Other than deliberately scalding herself in the shower or cutting her wrist with a safety razor, which made her feel even more squeamish than the prospect of leaping from a giant transport plane, there seemed to be no way to avoid climbing aboard the helicopter Jade had ordered for this ungodly hour.

In the end she got off the bed, used the john, brushed her teeth, and zipped up her jump suit over thermal underwear. She packed some clothes and carried her boots outside into the dawn.

The helicopter was a late-model twin-engine Huey with room for sixteen passengers. The parachute instructors were loading the copter. Ken was on hand with fresh doughnuts and coffee.

"I put champagne on ice for tonight," Ken said, grinning at Raun.

"Lovely," she said, and smiled bravely for him.

"You be just fine. Mist' Jade take good care of you. That man is a prince."

Then she was inside the helicopter strapping herself into a bucket seat opposite Lem Meztizo, whose face in the morning light was like wet cardboard. This wasn't so much fun for him either, Raun thought. He offered her a stick of chewing gum in a shaking hand.

"Must have been some bad ice at the Purple Pussy last night," he said.

"We should take a strike vote. Right now."

Jade heard her and turned his head, made a thumbs up gesture as he went forward to join the pilot. They took off, circling slowly above the ranch yard before heading northeast. The interior of the copter filled with blinding sun. Lem put his head down and chewed, his jaw bulging, his face slick with sweat. Raun closed her eyes, heart thumping.

Down among the aspen and flowering cherry on the Picket Wire River, Bill Sawyer put his binoculars in their case and went back inside his camper to pour pancake batter on the hot griddle. Steve Roper and Ted Clemons joined him. Their clothes smelled of fish. Probably his did too.

"Where do you think they're going?" Rope said to Sawyer.

"Not far. They don't have any gear. Just parachutes. Probably scheduled for some practice jumps on one of the airbases hereabout."

"Should be getting some word back today on the girl," Clemons said.

"Let's hope," Roper said. "But maybe we shouldn't wait too long."

"I've got the same feeling," Clemons admitted. "Could be we ought to let her speak for herself."

Sawyer glanced at Roper but didn't ask what he had in mind. He was not cut from the same cloth as the Cobra Dance men, and was glad of it. When they finished with Raun Hardie she would be nearly unrecognizable as a human being. A few hanks of hair, misshapen flesh over the many broken bones. But berore she died they would know everything about her life that was worth knowing.

"Dark or light?" Sawyer said, referring to his pancakes.

"I like mine with blueberries," Clemons told him. "Got any frozen blueberries?"

"Poke around in the freezer there, you'll probably find some."

On Red Cloud Mesa the Vassals of the Immaculate Light, sixteen adults and seven children, had been up and around at their campsite since the first colorless light of dawn. They began their day with a prayer circle: kneeling, heads bowed, hands joined. They wore sackcloth dyed a burgundy color that unfortunately looked like dried blood, and sandals which they cobbled themselves. The men had their heads shaved, except for a hedgelike V of hair on the right side of the scalp. Following sunrise prayers there was breakfast, meager fare boiled in pots or baked in ashes Indian style. To the casual observer they were leaderless, yet well disciplined and never idle. Obviously they supported themselves through crafts: They made baskets and leather goods. The children had school for four hours a day; each adult had something to contribute to their education. The Vassals owned books, junker cars, simple tools, and odd-sounding musical instruments. Bathing was part of an arcane ritual practiced only on solemn and sacred occasions. They welcomed visitors, and bored them to death.

The trained observer might have wondered why all of the children were at least ten years of age, why there were no babies at their mothers' teats. In fact, none of the women were pregnant. All of them seemed a little too healthy for the nomadic life they lived. But, since the Vassals' arrival at the Warshield ranch five days ago, no one had cared enough to pass much time with them, or ask detailed questions. They looked and sounded harmless. They wished to be alone. They had their wish.

At Lowry Air Force Base Jade and the others transferred from the helicopter to a venerable bucket of bolts, a C-130 Hercules built in the fifties. The four-engine plane was painted in camouflage colors. To Raun it was like being in the belly of a whale with steel ribs and a ringbolt-studded floor. She had to keep her teeth locked so they wouldn't chatter. Lem was chewing aspirin and still looked sick.

The C-130 took off, and as soon as they were airborne the instructors kept the novices so busy they had little time to think. They put on their chute packs. The operation of the static line was explained to them. Raun clipped and unclipped her parachute static line to the release cable overhead with stiff gloved hands. There was a warning about the impact of the slipstream that went in one ear and out the other. The parachute straps chafed the insides of her thighs. In the back of her mind a child was screaming. Five years old. She had climbed a tree in the yard of their home in Kenya after a beloved ocelot kit, and couldn't climb down again. Looking at the ground, she felt her heart fall out of her body, dizziness spiral upward to her throbbing head.

*I won't I can't I won't.*

Jade spread some oversized color photos on the floor, which was covered with a nonskid material the texture of sandpaper, and had them kneel opposite him. The four engines made too much noise to permit normal conversation. He spoke to them through their headsets.

"This is where we're going. It's an area of alpine tundra in Rocky Mountain National Park near Fall River. The closest thing I could find to the contours and sparse vegetation of the Makari headland above seven thousand feet. You can see that most of the snow cover is gone, but the ground will still be frozen a couple of inches below the surface, and hard as a sidewalk."

He made a circle with a grease pencil.

"The drop zone is clear of big rocks, but there'll be plenty of small ones. The banks of the river are steep and covered with scree; avoid them. We'll come in at three thousand feet over the DZ, make one pass to take a look. All right?"

A red light flashed beside the door on the left side of the fuselage. The huge plane banked slowly and was depressurized. They went on oxygen. Jade tapped Lem on the shoulder and held up ten fingers.

An instructor, his safety line clipped to a ringbolt on the floor, raised the door. Lem got to his feet. In his Corcoran jump boots and with his sassy blond hair tucked out of sight in his helmet, he looked robbed of his vulgar but cheerful style, out of place and as awkward as an overgrown child. The instructors moved pointedly away from them, as if they had become pariahs. Lem reached up to hook his static line to the release cable, missed, smiled desperately, tried again.

Raun looked at the concave hole in the side of the plane where the door had been. They were flying through clouds at 135 knots. The noise of flight was now deafening. She began to shake her head in agitation. She was down on both knees and she dropped her hands to the floor too, trying to get a secure grip on a couple of ringbolts.

She felt Jade beside her. He had to yell to make himself understood.

"Raun—!"

"No! No! Get me *down,* please! Don't you see I'm scared? Doesn't that mean anything to you?"

He pulled her to her feet, one arm around her, gripping her tightly. Her knees were trying to bend the wrong way. Jade reached up and hooked her static line to the cable.

"Stay here! I'll be back for you!"

Raun lurched and caught a handhold on the fuselage. Her eyes were shut. She couldn't open them. The plane trembled in the turbulent air above the Rocky Mountains. Raun made incoherent noises. She was too close to the open door. *She could fall out!* If only they would close it, give her a chance to breathe again.

She heard something that sounded like a scream. She turned her head slightly.

The green light had come on. One minute to the drop zone. Lem was huddled on the floor in the back of the plane. Amazingly, his nerve had broken too. He just couldn't bring himself to jump. *Good for him.* But Jade was furious. He kicked Lem viciously, not once but several times. Lem screamed again as he tried to claw his way farther back toward the tail. A rope of saliva hung down his chin. His eyes were ghostly in their panic.

Raun's emotions changed suddenly. She was filled to erupting with the most intense anger and hatred she'd ever known.

She forgot where she was, she forgot her fear. She charged at Jade, the release catch at the end of the static line rattling along the overhead cable. She flailed at Jade with her gloved fists.

"Let him. Alone! Don't kick him. Again! Or I'll. Kill you, *you bastard!*"

His hands came up to deflect the blows. He looked no less angry than she. Raun pressed on, swinging wildly, hampered by the bulky parachutes she was wearing. She was dimly aware that they were too near the insubstantial sky, nothing but sky back there and a glimpse of dazzling white mountain peaks in the distance. She didn't care. She only wanted to destroy Matthew Jade. If she could have used her fingers to better advantage, she would have ripped his jugular from his throat.

An instant before he deftly caught her by the wrist and elbow, pivoted, and flung her, like an overstuffed pillow, from the airplane, Raun caught the change of expression in his eyes and realized she'd been tricked.

Then she was tumbling, ass over teakettle, in the slipstream behind the big plane. Muted sun flashed in her eyes. The craggy enormous earth tilted, revolved beneath her as the parafoil streaming out behind her jerked her upright but failed to slow her down very much.

Never having jumped before, Raun wasn't immediately aware, as she fell, that something was wrong with her main chute. A portion of the canopy had blown between the rigging lines and wasn't fully developed. She couldn't maneuver and was falling much too fast: eighty feet per second. She had a little better than twenty seconds to go before hitting the earth with an impact that would shatter her spine.

"She doesn't know anything's wrong!" Jade shouted, all but falling out of the plane himself as he tried to keep Raun in sight over the drop zone.

"She's got her hands on the harness—she's trying to maneuver!"

"No good!" Jade said. "Let it go, Raun, let it go! You know how. Remember!"

They were circling too far away, they couldn't see what sort of effort she was making to release the tangled, all-but-useless canopy.

"Maybe this wasn't such a good idea!" Lem said with a dreadful attempt at a smile.

*"There it goes!"*

Raun had succeeded in releasing the chute pack and canopy but now she was free falling, limply, almost face up, below a thousand feet now. She turned over lazily, arms extended, a euphoric or, perhaps, agonized gesture.

"Five hundred feet!" Lem said. "Mother of Mercy. Grab the big ring, Raunie. *Hit the brakes!*"

The smaller reserve chute uncurled like orange flame in the air and formed a perfect canopy.

"Two hundred feet, maybe," Jade said, his lips white. "She's going in hard! Let's get down there."

They came to earth a quarter of a mile away from where Raun lay, harnessed and unmoving, her bright jump suit muddied from a long pull through a thinning snowfield freckled with brown-and-gold ground cover. Jade dumped his chute and helmet and ran, easily outdistancing Lem.

When he got to Raun she was sitting up, head on her knees. She had released the harness. A boot had been slashed by a sharp rock, there was a raw patch on the end of her nose. But she got up without difficulty, measured Jade, and punched him solidly on the jaw.

He took the blow, although he might have avoided it. Raun stepped back wincing, shaking her hand. She didn't look angry anymore. She looked fulfilled.

"I hate your guts for doing it," she said. "But I understand why you did it. Quits?"

"Must be my lucky day," Jade said, rubbing his jaw.

"Oh, shut up."

"Why'd you wait so long to open your chute? I thought you froze up."

"It's not what I thought it would be. It was so fascinating I forgot how hard it was going to get the moment I ran out of sky."

She hid a smile from Jade, the smile of a woman after her first great orgasm, achieved with the one lover in her life she will remember before all others. They heard the sound of a helicopter coming to pick them up; the parachute instructors were on their ways down and the Hercules was returning to base.

Raun looked wistfully at it.

"When can we do it again?" she asked, smiling.

# VON KREUTZEN'S
# SHOOTING PALACE

Bekele Big Springs, Tanzania
May 18

A little before dark Oliver Ijumaa came down from the escarpment carrying a double load of gold-bearing rocks in handmade baskets suspended on a yoke across his shoulders. He was still shortsighted in one eye from the rock splinter that, fortunately, Erika had been able to help him locate and remove. His other eye was cloudy from dust and bright sun. The load he carried, almost 150 pounds, had him wobbling.

He wondered what could be done tonight to ease the severe spasm in Erika's lower back. For three days she'd been unable to sleep; the pain had her delirious much of the time. No need to tie her down in the bronze bed anymore—she could scarcely move at all. Hot, wet cloths applied to the lower back had given her some relief, but not enough. . . .

Oliver was exhausted and preoccupied, and so missed all the signs that ordinarily would have warned him his territory had been invaded. The absence of his pet mongoose from the dooryard was most significant. Then there were the silent trees, the vacant waterhole below the lodge.

A black man with a shotgun rose slowly from his place of concealment behind the fountain in the front yard. He was pointing the shotgun at Oliver. He wasn't the law; too ragged. Oliver shrugged off his load, staggered, caught himself, stood there dazed, looking slowly around. Two more cutthroats appeared. One of them was a white man wearing an Aussie campaign hat and gold chains on his bared, black-pelted chest. He carried an Ingram M10 submachine gun in one hand. In his other hand dangled the bloody, fly-caked carcass of Oliver's mongoose. He let Oliver have a good look before flicking it away.

"Here's our boy-o now," Tiernan Clarke said. "Fetch him inside, Bulami."

The man with the shotgun approached Oliver, who watched him impassively. The muzzle of the shotgun pressed into Oliver below the angle of his jaw, tilting his head upward. Oliver swallowed and walked dumbly toward the lodge. Tiernan Clarke kept pace on the other side of him, but not where he would be in the way if the shotgun needed to be fired. The other black man jogged ahead to open the door.

"What's your name?"

"Oliver, I."

"Oliver what?"

"Ijumaa."

"Find much gold up on that rock, Oliver?"

Oliver knew it was useless to try to deceive or stall this man, who had humid black dangerous eyes and a deranged twist of a smile. Oliver held up his fists. "This much."

"You'll be kind enough to show us where it is."

"Yes, boss. All keeping in my trousers, I."

Tiernan Clarke looked at the testicular bulges in Oliver's tight torn pants and laughed delightedly.

"There's some style to you, Oliver Friday. I could use a good man like yourself. Unfortunately you had the bad judgment to kill one of my best blokes. I suppose you recall the misdeed. When I've exacted the proper penalties for your rashness, you won't be of much use to anyone. And then there's the pending claim of Mr. Lex Pynchon, also in my employ. Lex is still very angry about the loss of four inches of his precious dingus, rendering him fit for fornication only with pygmies or prepubescent females. He is thirsting after revenge, as they say. I did promise him we'd be back with your own goolies. Too bad they turned out to be solid gold—now I shall have to keep them for myself."

Clarke was still laughing as they entered the rotunda of the lodge. Oliver stopped short, ignoring the shotgun at his throat, and looked up the stairs.

Two more men, both Europeans, were bringing Erika down. Each of the men had an elbow, supporting her. Her bare feet dragged the steps. Her head lolled. Bulami gave Oliver a cruel poke with the shotgun's muzzle but Tiernan Clarke waved him off and studied Oliver's face intently.

When the men with Erika had brought her to the floor of the rotunda, Oliver licked his lips and said her name, twice. The second time she lifted her head slowly and gazed at him. Her eyes were bleary. But she smiled.

"Oliver. 'Swonderful. We have help now, everything's—all right."

Tears appeared in Oliver's eyes and rolled down his dusty cheeks. Clarke nodded to the men holding Erika and said to her, "How's the pain now, darlin'?"

"No pain. What you gave me—a blessing."

"I have a tricky back myself, so I'm never without strong medicine."

Erika yawned. "Could sleep and sleep."

"You will, darlin'. You will. Go with the lads now."

"O . . . kay," Erika said dreamily, and she was taken out the door.

"And you will come with me," Clarke said to Oliver, who had turned his head for a last look at Erika. He had no doubt that he would never see her again, and that he himself was about to be killed in some drawn-out and unspeakable manner.

They took Oliver to his quarters in the old kitchen. He was tied standing up with baling wire to a stout square wooden post while Clarke walked around smoking a cheroot and muttering to himself.

When he had his thoughts collected, he approached the captive and put his face inches from Oliver's own.

"This is all I promise: Some answers to my questions will prolong your life, and ultimately your passing will be less painful than what I had in mind when we came in here. Will you cooperate with me, then?"

"Yes, boss."

"How did you come across Erika?"

"Airplane. Big crash. She hurt."

"Um, yes. Saw the patch on her forehead. Far from here?"

"No, boss." Oliver smiled, showing all of his teeth. "Taking you, I."

"Never mind. I suppose it *could* have been her, that night we were collecting pelts down along the little Simkiapi. Looked to be a woman pilot I was shooting at. Tell me about the aircraft, Oliver. Did it have a tail like this?" Clarke made a broad V with his hands.

Oliver's brow wrinkled as he thought, and then he smiled again. He tried to nod but could barely move his head; there was a tight loop of wire biting into his neck.

"Did she tell you where she had come from?"

"Mission. Many others, her friends. All sick. *Houma.*"

"I haven't heard about an outbreak of fever. What mission?"

Oliver looked perplexed, strained to remember, and panicked. He was sweating profusely, anticipating the displeasure of his interrogator.

"Doesn't matter; it fits," Clarke said, half to himself. "So she made an escape. Government soldiers may be looking for her. That's worth knowing. Now listen carefully, boy-o, you're doing fine. Did Erika mention a place where there might be—hidden treasure of some kind?"

Oliver expressed his delight at the question. "In the big mountain. Kilimanjaro."

"Kilimanjaro, hey? But she was flying from the opposite direction when I encountered her. What kind of treasure, did she tell you?"

"Very big diamonds. *Red* diamonds."

Clarke laughed cynically. "Well, well. That's an impressive story, Oliver."

"True. *Erika* telling me."

"Perhaps I shouldn't doubt you. But I can't imagine the Russkies being anxious about a hoard of diamonds, no matter how valuable they may be. No doubt Erika will confirm everything you've said. In the meantime I'm of a mind to test your truthfulness." He looked back over one shoulder at Bulami. "That big locking spanner of mine in the Rover. Bring it."

Bulami was gone for nearly five minutes. Tiernan Clarke had several nips of whiskey from a stainless flask and talked earnestly to himself while he paced and ignored his prisoner. The sweat continued to pour from the tormented Oliver, whose limbs were cramping from the tightness of his wire bonds and a loss of vital salts from his system.

When he had the wrench, Clarke applied it to a finger pried from Oliver's fist by Bulami and the other black man. He tightened the grooved jaws until blood spurted from beneath the fingernail and bones snapped. Oliver screamed and hung limply against the wires that were cutting into his flesh.

"Red diamonds?"

"Red . . . diamonds, boss," Oliver panted.

"Kilimanjaro?"

"Telling me, big rooms in the mountain."

"Fascinating. But farfetched. Let's just do another finger." He was watching Oliver's eyes, which were glazing. This time he selected the pinky on the same hand. Oliver screamed and sobbed. Blood dripped freely from the mutilated fingers.

"You have told me all the truth that's in you?" Clarke said softly, the heel of his palm under Oliver's chin.

"Yes, boss!"

"Tell me something else. While Erika was lying helpless in that bed upstairs, did you at any time have your way with her?"

"No, boss!"

Clarke snapped his fingers for a knife. He opened the five-inch stiletto blade and squatted in front of Oliver, placed the point against the inside of Oliver's thigh near the groin. He pushed the blade in an eighth of an inch. Oliver gasped. A red spot the size of a quarter appeared on the dirty khaki trousers.

As if he were carving a turkey, Clarke expertly slit the rotting material to rags, exposing the hard sacks of nuggets Oliver wore suspended below his own balls. Two snips and Clarke had the gold in his hands. He got slowly to his feet, pressed a hand against the small of his back, looked around the kitchen, and said, "Burn it."

Bulami went out again and came back with a plastic jerrycan partially filled with gasoline. Obviously they were concerned about their fuel supply, because Clarke ordered him to spread the gas around sparingly. The floorboards still had enough bug-proof pitch in them to burn briskly. A little of the gas slopped on Oliver's sandaled feet and wet the rags of his trouser cuffs. The fumes further irritated his eyes. He strained against the tight wires and got nowhere.

The fight went out of him, perhaps his will to live. His eyes rolled back in his head and he moaned softly.

Bulami fashioned a torch from rags and went around the kitchen, fifteen hundred square feet of it, setting fires. Some of them whoosed up brightly, dislodging bats from the dark beams overhead. They darted frantically through the oily, rising smoke. The heat, within a minute, was almost unbearable. Tiernan Clarke took a last disinterested look at Oliver, who seemed comatose, and left with his men.

Left Oliver with a pinch of hope, and virtually no time to take advantage of the one break Clarke inadvertently had given him.

The quilted packing material with which Oliver had sealed the cave-like pantry, his inner sanctum, was being flamelessly consumed, giving off noxious brown fumes as it melted into the already overburdened air. Oliver held his breath. At least they hadn't wired him to one of the great iron cookstoves, which he wouldn't have been able to budge; he would have cooked to half his size and weight, a charred curling sliver of a man, while the iron at his side turned incandescent and glowed through the night.

The stout post he was wired to might not be so stout after all—in twisting and bracing against it he had felt a fine downsifting of sawdust in his face, a tremor of weakness. Borer-beetles and termites had honeycombed the bolted timbers during years of tenancy. If he could just break the post in two before the flames crawled as far as his feet . . .

Oliver tensed the length of his body, forgetting for the moment the agony of his smashed fingers. His muscles bulged, the veins of his arms and neck stood out shockingly. He grunted and threw himself forward, straining against the wire and the post. He heard a distinct crack and felt another tremor.

Screaming now, he lunged again and broke the post in two just above his head. But it was too hot, too hot— the fire leaped all around him, in moments he would be ablaze himself.

He needed then to rock and twist the length of post to which he was still attached, pry up the long nails that held it to the floor. On his third desperate try, choking from the smoke and the wire at his throat, the base of the post yielded partway; Oliver pitched forward with the weight of it bearing him down. On his knees he wriggled frantically, his neck elongated as he tried to work the throat wire from the post without cutting his throat first. He was dizzy and fainting before the wire slipped from the jagged end of the post.

Rolling over, he worked his hands up inches at a time, freed them, sat up, and untwisted the wire that held him by the ankles.

Flame seared his skin; he hobbled and plunged heedlessly across the burning floor to the circular well covering, a sheet of hot iron with handles. He thrust it aside and dangled, feet down, in the cool cistern, found a narrow ledge of rock, reached up and pulled the cover back into place, cutting off the light, shutting out the heat.

Then he fell, half conscious, eight feet into black still water.

# WARSHIELD RANCH

Silverpeak, Colorado
May 17

The parachute that had failed to open properly for Raun Hardie was recovered and, back at the field, examined carefully; but no good reason for the malfunction was discovered. A one-chance-in-ten-thousand mishap. The instructors responsible for Raun's training and safety were mortified. They opened the other chutes and repacked them meticulously. Shortly after noon the C-130 lifted off for the drop zone some sixty miles away and they did it all over again, this time with wind conditions marginal. Raun went in without a hitch but Jade wound up in the icy river, and decided to call it a day.

Lem explained to Raun that he'd made about thirty jumps in the past two years. His apparent anxiety had been planned from the beginning to help take Raun's mind off her own trauma. Lem was, like Jade, a helicopter pilot: They frequently leased copters for ranch work. He proved his ability by flying the two of them back to the Warshield in a JetRanger while Jade returned to Lowry Air Force Base for conferences with the support team that would be flying them halfway around the world.

"When do you think we'll be going?" Raun asked Lem.

"Tonight, maybe. Early tomorrow morning for sure—Matt's getting that old itch. Better sleep while you can."

Raun nodded; with half the day gone she was already exhausted. When she looked at Lem, she felt a twinge of guilt about what she was doing, leading them totally astray. But she'd made no promises; after a week or so of tramping up and down mountains looking for Catacombs that didn't exist there, probably Jade would be ready to call the whole thing off. Then she would be free to go her own way, that was the deal. How they would get out hadn't been explained to her, but she was sure Matthew Jade had a plan. He was every bit as meticulous as he was ruthless.

At the ranch they flew low over Red Cloud Mesa and some of the Vassals of the Immaculate Light looked up at their passing; a couple of the children shielded their eyes and waved tentatively. Lem circled the yard and set the JetRanger down near the big barn.

"I'll have Ken put a couple of steaks on," Lem said as they walked toward the house.

"You can look me up in the hot tub. And then if Lee will just come through with one of her great massages—"

Lem grinned; his step slowed almost imperceptibly for a few moments. His grin seemed to go on too long. His eyes had turned to slits. She felt his hand on her elbow.

He said quietly, "Keep walking and talking, Raunie. But stay shy of the house."

"Why? What's the matter?"

"Something's wrong here. I don't know what. Smile. I think we're being watched. You just remembered something in the helicopter. Let's go back for it. Make it sound good."

Raun saw nothing, except a piebald horse drifting by itself at the perimeter of the ranch yard. It looked like Andy von Boecklin's cutting horse, Shoo-Bob, but it had no saddle or bridle. Odd to see Shoo-Bob there, in the middle of a working afternoon.

Raun raised her voice. "Lem, we'd better get the trout fillets. Give me a hand with the cooler?"

Lem nodded and they started back to the helicopter. They had a hundred feet to go. His hands were in the pockets of his fringed suede jacket. He had the ignition key ready.

"Not too fast now. Easy. We'll—"

Lem stopped suddenly, arching his back slightly. Raun looked at him in astonishment. She heard nothing but the sound of the wind. He staggered for a couple of steps, lost his balance.

"Shit," he said breathlessly, and sagged to his knees. "In the back! Run, Raunie, get the hell out of—"

Raun saw the stubby frosted dart fastened like a leech to Lem's jacket, pinning it high between his shoulder blades. Lem tried to get at it with a couple of half-hearted swipes of his big hands. Then he fell over in the grass. His lips moved, but his eyes were fading out of sight behind drooping lids.

"Run," he whispered.

She turned in terror and felt the sting of another dart fired into her thigh; the impact was like being kicked with a sharp-pointed shoe. She stared down at the dart, a half-inch projection, tried to pluck it like a strange obscene flower. Suddenly she was reaching down from a remote height with fingers clumsy as bananas. She couldn't keep her balance. She fell, it seemed to her, very slowly, absorbed by the sight of her long shadow swelling, blotting out the lawn. There was no sensation of flesh meeting the ground, she could feel nothing from her toes to the root of her tongue. Her brain still worked, but blandly. Her shadow thickened and enfolded her, crushing her gently to sleep.

\* \* \*

Matthew Jade arrived by helicopter outside the town of Silverpeak, twenty miles from his ranch, a little after four o'clock. He walked half a dozen blocks from the fairgrounds and took a corner table in the restaurant of the Prospect Park Hotel, which featured blue-and-white-checkered tablecloths, lazy Susans on the tables, and a color photo of the president of the United States over the door, taken when Boomer had more hair.

There were only a half dozen other customers, a few idlers in the bar next door, the sounds of electronic game machines. Jade ordered Jack Daniel's and water and a steak sandwich. A couple of local ranchers dropped by to say hello. At four thirty, as he was eating his sandwich, a husky man in his thirties wearing cowboy clothes that were too new stumped across the pegged hardwood floor in his stiff pointy boots and drew up a chair. His name was Duke Wooters; he was Jade's direct liaison with John Guy Gibson in Operations.

"Food any good here?" he asked Jade. "Place I ate last night had Kaopectate on the wine list."

Jade laughed. Duke ordered a Coors from the waitress and sat forward, hands folded on the tablecloth.

"You're going to break something, jumping out of airplanes at your age."

"Linblad didn't have enough time to put together the deluxe tour. What's happening?"

"Cobra Dance is heavily involved in the Tanzania caper. They have a man there now. Someone they think a lot of. He's in deep cover, and coded. There may be three men in the KGB who know his identity. Unfortunately none of them finks for us."

"What about our three fishermen?"

"Sawyer, Roper, Clemons. Sawyer's wife died a few years ago. He has a little place up on Bull Shoals Lake in the Ozarks. Used to work for the power company in

Fort Smith. Twenty years. Retired now. The other two are from the Denver area. Littleton. They have wives, kids, mortgages, insurance programs, the kinds of jobs that allow them to take three or four days off when the mood grips them and enjoy the beauties of the wilderness. We can only check so close without tipping off their wives, and they could be agents in deep cover too, alert for any kind of negative vibrations. The only thing that doesn't look quite right to me is the fact that three days ago Roper was laid up with the flu. He got out of a sickbed to go fishing."

"Maybe it's the best medicine. Or maybe Roper One is holed up in a Holiday Inn while someone from Cobra Dance who looks like him through a telescopic lens is taking his place. The same for the other two. But if Cobra Dance is here, they made me in a hell of a hurry. How?"

Duke scratched a newly sunburned and peeling nose. "Given the circumstances, the fact that you're close to the president, the KGB made an educated guess. And your activities of the past few days confirmed it."

Jade nodded and finished his sandwich. "These sons of bitches just might be a load of trouble for everybody."

"We could get a friend of Roper or Clemons down here for a positive ID."

"Negative vibrations. They'd have a contingency plan which might provoke some wet action. For the same reason, we don't want to take them into custody for the next day or so."

"Couldn't do that anyway. Roper and Clemons have been missing all day. We don't know where they are."

Jade stared at him. "Lem and Raun went back a couple of hours ago. Is my Bronco in the parking lot?"

"One of your hands drove it to town this morning. Want me to go along?"

Jade thought about it. "No. If we're dealing with the trade here, I want to get along home looking dumb and happy."

Five twenty-four in the afternoon. A leaden overcast had stifled the sun when Bill Sawyer put away the binoculars he was using to keep the Warshield ranch buildings and the road under surveillance. No sign of life there except for the corralled remuda horses; nothing had stirred in the spacious yard since ten after three, when he had seen Lem Meztizo the Third, then Raun Hardie, stagger and go down loaded with a potent combination of thiobarbiturate and succinylcholine.

They had subsequently been removed to the house by Roper and Clemons. He couldn't guess what was happening inside now, or how soon it might be over. His head and eyes ached from the continual effort of focusing through the binoculars. And his bladder infection was worse.

Later he would blame eyestrain and his need to pee for his carelessness. The wind was blowing luminous snakelike waves through the grama grass below the rocks where he'd been maintaining his watch. With his binoculars and walkie-talkie in a shoulder bag he climbed down and sought a stand of trees and unzipped his pants to relieve himself. While he was dribbling erratically on a lichen-covered windfall he heard sage grouse explode from cover somewhere to the northeast, behind his back. His camper was parked in that direction. He turned slightly to see what had gotten the birds off and saw Matthew Jade standing about forty feet away, observing him. Jade had one of Sawyer's fishing rods in his right hand. His other hand was free, and empty.

The shock of seeing him gave Sawyer a painful stricture. He tried to smile. A few drops of urine dribbled on his pants.

Jade said in street Russian, "It's too quiet over at my place. No dogs barking. When you've got a dozen dogs around, they're always carrying on over a rabbit or a pika. The business you're in gets pretty crude sometimes, but I hope like hell your buddies didn't kill any of my dogs."

"What?" Sawyer said, looking terribly perplexed. "What was that you said? I don't speak any foreign languages."

"Face me," Jade told him in English. "Full front. Now what about my friends?"

Sawyer was carrying a chrome-plated Smith & Wesson .44 magnum upside down under his partially zippered nylon Windbreaker. As he turned slowly he dropped his leaking weenie, which he'd been holding between the thumb and middle finger of his gun hand, and went for the revolver. It looked like a pretty good deal. Jade was not, apparently, armed. No need to ventilate him, just put him somewhere on ice temporarily until Roper and Clemons decided what to do with him.

Jade's wrist flicked and the reel sang alluringly in a glimmer of sunlight through the lowering overcast and Sawyer, drawing but not drawing fast enough, blinkingly saw the curve and dip of the sinister, multi-hooked thing, saw it coming, flying at the whim of the slickly cast and sizzling filament. But he couldn't stop pissing and draw his weapon and get his feet moving all at the same time and so the plug hit him full on the exposed pecker, dropping its several complicated hooks to the plump underside, biting, as pressure was applied, like a clot of bees.

Sawyer was now willing and eager to blow Jade's

brains out but, free of the upside-down holster under his left arm, the revolver hung up in the teeth of the zipper track just long enough to thwart any advantage his firepower would have given him.

Jade then gave a firmer, no-nonsense-now tug to the line, the tip of the casting rod nodding Sawyer's way, and Sawyer almost screamed, more from fear of potential damage than actual pain.

Mouth open, he brought the revolver all the way out, but slowly and with no steel in his wrist, and deposited it in the grass. He looked down reluctantly at his full-fledged pecker and saw it half erect, held up by the taut line and the articulated, phony-bug lure, dark blue with wavy yellow lines down its back. Blood was oozing at three barb points but happily he was intact, at least for the moment.

Jade began reeling in his catch; Sawyer, wincing, stumbled toward him, still too shocked to feel humiliated.

The interior of Jade's plain-looking log ranch house followed a simple floor plan. There was a large central living area with a fourteen-foot beamed ceiling, a combination kitchen and dining room on one side, and a sleeping wing on the other, with three ample bedrooms and two full baths, one of which contained a sauna and hot tub. There was no attic and no basement. Windows were small and high: The winter winds blew long and fiercely in this part of the country, and snow frequently drifted as high as the eaves outside.

The ranch office and Jade's study were in a separate wing connected to the kitchen by a short entryway, which also contained a mud room-half bath. The kitchen had enough stainless restaurant-size equipment to handle meals for up to thirty men a day. The year-round hands, Andy von Boecklin and Clete

Davis, lived in one bungalow on the eastern perimeter of the fenced garden plot behind the main house; Ken and Lee had a similar bungalow on the west side of the garden, which Ken had just finished composting in anticipation of the new growing season. Two thirty-foot windmills pumped water for irrigation and provided electricity for the ranch.

Steve Roper and Ted Clemons spent a lot of their time after three fifteen in Jade's study, looking at the reconnaissance photos of the Makari Peninsula on Jade's Betamax. There were a lot of them. At intervals Clemons raised Bill Sawyer on the walkie-talkie. Reception was marred by static but everything looked okay down there. Roper and Clemons had a long talk, putting together everything they knew and could deduce about Jade's mission to Tanzania. It was quite a bit, but not enough to satisfy them yet.

Clemons poured coffee from the hot plate and looked at his watch. Five thirty-two.

"Call Sawyer again," Roper said. He was engrossed in a stack of weather projections for East Central Africa, the two-week period commencing May eighteenth.

Clemons tried, but got nothing but static. Then he heard a faint voice, but no words he could distinguish.

"Waste of time. He'll page us when *numero uno* shows up. I'll be back in a little while."

Clemons picked up a cassette recorder and slipped it into a pocket of his camouflage jacket. He walked through the house. Clemons was a virtuoso whistler; he could handle anything—classical, show tunes. As he walked toward the bedroom wing, turning on lamps to brighten the rooms, he worked on the high notes of "Love Is a Many-Splendored Thing." He was almost, but not quite, satisfied with the crystal purity of the sounds he was producing when he looked in on Raun Hardie. He rapped his knuckles on the partly opened door. Her eyelids fluttered. He was encouraged to turn on the overhead light.

"Hello, sleepyhead," he said cheerfully, and approached the bed.

Raun took him in without moving, neither frightened nor very curious. She yawned and brought up a slow hand to rub her face.

"Feeling okay, Raun?"

"I don't know. Who're you?"

Clemons pulled out a folder and showed her some identification. "I'm Ted Clemons. CIA." He sat beside her on the bed. "Thirsty?"

Raun licked her lips. "Uh-huh."

"You would be. You got socked with a helluva load of winky-bye time. Here." He put a hard finger against her left thigh, and she winced. "It'll be swollen and sore for a couple of days."

Clemons turned to the night table and poured water for her from a pitcher.

Raun was thinking about his cryptic explanation. Some of the mist in her head drifted away from an overly sharp picture of Lem Meztizo collapsing on the sod with a dart stuck in his back. Trouble and dismay welled up in her but the tranquilizer in her blood smoothed the emotion away.

"Where's Lem?"

"Taking a longer nap. You managed to jerk that dart out of your leg before you absorbed the full dose. He'll be okay, though, don't worry about that hard-nosed bastard."

"But—what happened? Who—" She tried to sit up. Her movements were awkward, her head drooped. Clemons eased her back down and shook his head regretfully.

"You won't feel so spunky for a little while. Don't try to move around. Want to go to the bathroom?"

". . . No."

He gave her water to sip. "Looks as if the other side got wind of the Tanzanian operation and decided to shut us down. Fortunately we've had the ranch under surveillance, so you didn't come to any harm. But they may have got away with the information they needed."

"What . . . 'other side'? What's going on? Where's Matt?"

"He said to tell you he'd be along in a few minutes. Unfortunately we've had to, uh, scrub the mission."

"Does this . . . could it have anything to do with Zola trying to kill me?"

His blond brows knitted together in a frown.

"Raun, we just don't know yet. Haven't put it all together. But—yes—I *think* it could have something to do with Zola."

Raun handed the water glass back to him, blinked at the ceiling.

"It's off? We're not going?"

"Too risky."

"Now I—I guess I don't have to worry anymore. Funny, you know, it was getting to me, even when I convinced myself—it couldn't possibly make any difference. I mean, not telling them about the real location of the Catacombs." She looked sideways at Clemons. He was smiling.

"Hey, you're full of surprises."

"Will I still get my pardon?"

"Sure. No problem." He took the cassette recorder from his pocket, tested it. "Raun, what we need to do now, with the mission aborted, is debrief you. I just want you to talk through everything that's happened since—well, you might start with Zola."

"At the prison. But I've been over and over that."

"I know, just one more time if you don't mind. Start

with the prison and relate everything up to the moment you were hit by that dart outside today. Keep in mind that something you think is trivial, not worth mentioning, might be a big help—"

There was a sound of a boot scraping floorboards, a convulsive coughing. Raun looked past Clemons, who had turned his head like a shot. Lem Meztizo was collapsing in the bedroom doorway, trying to cling by his fingers to the jamb, his artificially blond hair in a wild thatch around his head, his skin drained of color.

"Raunie . . . wrong guys . . . don't say nothing . . ."

He started to fall, but in the instant before he lost his grip Clemons drew an oddly shaped pistol that fired either tranquilizer darts or explosive pellets loaded with nitrogen mustard gas at a muzzle velocity of seven hundred feet per second. He shot Lem in the side of the head with it. The crash of Lem going down shook the bed.

Raun screamed.

Clemons put the pistol away and turned around. He looked different when he wasn't smiling. Some bitterness had seeped into his eyes. The red in his apple cheeks now looked like wrath.

"We can still do this nicely," he said.

"Who *are* you?"

He reached out and cradled her face in the one hand. Where his fingers pressed—and he didn't have to bear down all that hard—she felt excruciating pain.

"Or not so nice. You decide."

On Red Cloud Mesa the Vassals of the Immaculate Light, partaking of supper by their campfires, turned to look at the Custom Bronco, with only its parking lights on, flying up the rutted road, coming straight at them. The men got up slowly in their burgundy burlap robes, their nearly shaven heads gleaming in the firelight. They gathered around as Matthew Jade climbed down from the cab.

A tall black man with a scar across the bridge of his nose said, "Reason is strength, and strength is peace. The universe is but Light, the perfect Light of our immortal souls in their myriad journeys through Space and Time. Concentrate on the Light, and ye shall find the answers ye earnestly desire."

"Never mind that shit," Jade said. "The rumble's on."

The scarred man turned instantly and said over his shoulder, in a less ethereal voice, "Jacky, Vince, round up the kids and fall back to Point Bravo. The rest of you break out the Sterlings and the XM177s. Stun grenades and full Teflon loads."

Jade stopped as he was taking off his Pendleton shirt and stared at the scarred man.

"Don't get carried away, Starger, it looks like only two guys. Get ready but give me an hour, then come in."

"You're going down there by yourself?"

"They've got Raun and they've got Lem. My house is built like a fort, you can't storm it. I'll try another way." He sat down to pull off his boots and jeans which left him naked except for socks, black nylon briefs, and his hat. "One of the fishermen is tied up in my truck. Bring him out here."

Two of the Vassals of the Immaculate Light opened the Bronco and lifted down Bill Sawyer, who was bound hand and foot and gagged with filament tape. He stood struggling in the light from the fire. His pants were still unzipped. Jade had cut the fishing line but hadn't attempted the delicate job of removing the blue-and-yellow plug from the top of his swollen pecker. It gave Sawyer a decidedly zany appearance. Starger couldn't take his eyes off it.

"Jesus, what did you do to him?"

"Violated all of his civil rights. He says he doesn't understand how a thing like this can happen in a free country, and he wants to call the FBI."

They walked Sawyer away for first aid. Cars were already heading down the long road off the mesa. Those Vassals staying behind were pulling on combat boots and applying black-and-green nightfighter cream to their exposed skin. Jade took his bulldogger Stetson off and placed it on the driver's seat of his Bronco.

"Where'd you get the kids on short notice?"

"Fort Bragg. Army brats. Their daddies are all officers in our antiterrorist units. Let me tell you, those sweet-looking kids are hard as nails. Goddam mad they won't get the chance to shoot a Commie."

Jade nodded. From various compartments of his truck he collected items that he needed for the operation he was planning. He asked for two stun grenades, which, when detonated, created a nonlethal blast, or "thunderflash," that immobilized those exposed to it for up to six seconds.

When Starger came back with them, Jade was tying on a full-length Appaloosa horsehide coat. Laid out at his feet were turtle-shell and deer-hoof rattles, a calabash, and a páho, a Hopi prayer stick. He had darkened his face, hands, chest, and bare feet with oxblood boot polish. He went down on all fours and began tearing up clumps of moss and cinquefoil and applying handfuls of dirt to the sticky polish on his face and in his hair. Within minutes it looked as if he were wearing a beehive. Jade was very nearly unrecognizable as a human being.

Starger watched this makeup job in amazement, thinking of the stories he'd heard about Matthew Jade. Tonight he was convinced they were all true. He was acting like one scary dude.

* * *

Steve Roper was in Jade's office examining the contents of the safe he'd cracked when he heard a horse going crazy outside.

He went to a front window and pulled back one of the shutters for a slant look at the yard. The outside lights had come on automatically at dusk, floods mounted at the corners of the house and barnlot. It wasn't exactly bright out there—about as much illumination as a forty-watt bulb will provide in the average living room. He saw the piebald horse that belonged to Andy von Boecklin race by a couple of feet from the window; it startled him and he drew back, slapping the shutter in place. He'd had just a glimpse and wasn't sure the horse had a rider. There was some kind of hump on its back, like part of the horse itself, a monstrous growth.

Roper took the walkie-talkie from a pocket of his red-and-black wool jacket and summoned Clemons.

Clemons came quickly, trotting Raun Hardie along beside him. He had a nerve grip on her with one hand at the elbow. He put her in a chair and said, "Stay there." Raun sat with her head bowed humbly and gently rubbed the inside of her elbow where he'd pinched her.

They heard a scream like a leaking boiler. Shoo-Bob thudded by again, jumped a porch rail, and bumped against the front door. Clemons couldn't quite get a good look from the office window.

"What the hell?"

"Do you know anything about horses?" Clemons said.

"No. That one's not acting right, though."

"We'd better get rid of him before he kicks the door down."

"How do we do that?"

"Shoot him."

Clemons shook his head wearily and glanced at Raun.

"Bring her along."

He went into the main house through the kitchen to the living room, followed by Roper and Raun Hardie. Through narrow windows on either side of the door they could see Shoo-Bob, or part of him, as he turned around and around and let fly a kick that broke a pane of glass. Then the horse jumped to the yard and moved a little way off.

"He's too much animal to knock out with the darts I have," Clemons said. "I'll have to kill him."

"So what?"

"Fine-looking horse, that's all." Clemons loaded his gas-fired pistol with nitrogen mustard pellets. He opened the front door slightly, looked out. The horse was standing, head knifing up and down, side on to the house and about twenty feet away.

Clemons held the gun out and hit Shoo-Bob in the side of the neck with one of the explosive pellets.

"Good-bye, Old Paint."

Shoo-Bob screamed, reared, came down shakily, took three or four steps, and fell over dead. At the moment of impact the horse seemed to separate into two pieces, or, for want of a better word, entities. Clemons, not quite sure of what he'd seen, stared in fascination.

The horse was stone dead, no doubt about it. But the other—*thing*—a misshappen lump of horsehide, began to quiver. A Hopi death song rose in the chilly night air, beginning like a dry hum of insects. Clemons felt the hairs on the back of his neck tingle.

"What's *that?*" Roper said behind him.

"I don't know."

The lamentation took on new shadings and intonation, growing louder. Something was rising out there in the yard, taking form, assuming stature. Clemons saw an asymmetrical, wattle-and-daub head like a hive, what might have been eyes gleaming deep in the cake of mud and vegetation. A horsehide arm brandished some sort of object decorated with feathers. The rattle of a calabash began as the chant, the prayer, the song, whatever it was, continued ominously.

"Will you look at that?" Clemons said, fascinated. He felt Roper behind him. "What do you make of it?"

"Local character, I suppose."

"Coming this way," Clemons said, as Ahóte, the Hopi spirit bringer of punishment, began to weave and shuffle and stamp the ground, making perceptible progress across the yard.

"Whoever he is, he doesn't like what we did to his horse."

"Get rid of him?"

"Now."

Ahóte was whirling, arms stiffly outthrust. The Appaloosa horsehide shimmered as it caught the light from one of the floods. Clemons raised his gun; a stiff breeze was blowing and it had just changed direction, which worried him, but he pulled the trigger anyway and potted the dancing, wailing figure.

There was a brief flash against the horsehide, a spurt of gas that resolved into a hovering mist. The death song stopped abruptly but otherwise there was no reaction. The calabash shook, Ahóte's jinking dance continued, his sunken enflamed eyes regarded them with implacable hostility.

"Popped right off that horsehide," Clemons observed. "And he must be holding his breath. What makes him so smart?"

"Hit him again!" Roper urged.

"You catch the way the wind's blowing? You want a snootful of that stuff yourself?"

"Let me have a crack at him," Roper said, and

pulled his own weapon, a Colt .38 Super automatic loaded with wadcutters.

But Clemons was just a little slow making room, and Roper had to thrust the door open another foot to take aim. He was at an awkward angle and unable to get a shot off as something popped toward them from beneath the horsehide and the dancing Ahóte collapsed in a protective heap in the dooryard.

The stun grenade went off at their feet, the full force of it expanding into the living room.

Raun was farther back in the room and suffered minimal effects from the shock wave; she was standing and remained in contact with her surroundings. The two Cobra Dance men fell by the doorway and groped, blind and deaf, trying to get their bearings.

Matthew Jade appeared in his horsehide coat and reddish, lumpy, mummy's face. If she hadn't grown up in Africa and witnessed similar grotesqueries at tribal ceremonies, Raun might have fainted. But she was scared. She put her hands to her mouth and retreated, trying not to make a sound.

Jade glanced at her, then collared the two Russians as they were staggering to their feet. He smacked their heads together. They fell down again, dazed but not unconscious. Jade took Roper's Colt away from him and turned to Raun.

"Get away from me!"

"It's Jade."

"Matt! What—what are you doing? Why do you look like that?"

He made a curt gesture with the automatic, shutting her up.

"Any more around?"

Raun shook her head.

"What did you tell them?"

"I didn't know who they were. The blond man, Clemons, had identification. CIA. He said the mission was off. He seemed to know a lot about it. We just talked, that's all, and before I knew what I was doing—"

"Everything?"

"*Yes!* It's not my fault!"

"What about Lem?"

"Oh God. They shot him. I don't know how bad he's hurt. I don't think he's dead."

"Okay. Stay there."

"Where're you going?"

Jade didn't reply. He picked up the groggy Clemons by the back of his camouflage jacket and when Clemons struggled, like a kitten about to be popped into a sack, Jade hit him with the barrel of the gun to quiet him down. The gunsight drew blood. He dragged Clemons into the yard and came back up to the porch for Roper.

Raun followed this time, slowly, and looked out. Jade had propped the two Russians into sitting positions, back to back. Clemons' head lolled, he slumped to his left, Jade patiently reordered him. Roper moaned complainingly and scuffed at the grass with the heel of a boot. The wind blew; those were the only sounds. Roper looked up and squinted at Jade as Jade backed off a few steps. He raised an empty hand to Jade as if to make some kind of offer, as if it were a prelude to conversation. The gun in Jade's hand came up in a no-nonsense attitude, and Raun was drawing a sharp breath when the gun recoiled.

Roper's head flew apart. All she remembered later was an ear somehow perfectly detached and plunking into grass and bugs whizzing in the thin light and a pink smush in the air as if a kid had thrown a watermelon against a wall. There was the report of the pistol, which she felt rather than heard. Then Jade altered the angle of the Colt and killed Clemons too.

Without a thought in her head Raun turned and ran through the living room to the kitchen, out the back door, and around the garden plot into darkness.

Her feet found a trail she remembered; it took her through a pasture rising gradually beneath a dim drizzle of moon. She ran two miles, three, her bones aching, her heels bruised, her lungs on slow bake. Cold air from the mountain crests whispered through waves of tall conifer rising abruptly ahead of her. Sanctuary. She limped into the trees, slowed but determined not to quit until she'd put even more miles between her and the ranch. She was afraid they'd still find her if—*when*—they searched. But she'd get away. She wasn't having any more bloody cold-war games. Let them kill each other. No one was going to get another chance at her.

But it was too dark, she found, to keep on without risking calamity.

After a couple of painful scrapes she realized that the forest floor was littered with fallen trees, each with stubs of branches that could rip her apart if she fell on them. She heard water splashing and cautiously located a cove that had promise: moss ledges, a cold drink, a jumble of boulders that still held some heat from the day. She pressed in between two of them and sat with her knees up, trying not to dwell on what might be coming around, soundlessly, in the dark.

In ten minutes she was fast asleep.

"Come on out, Raun."

Her eyes opened a fraction, squeezed shut involuntarily as the light proved too bright. It was angled down at her, filling the cleft of rock in which she'd hidden. *How?* she thought numbly. Her heart felt

cold and sore. She held up both hands, defensively,
fingers acting as shutters. In front of the light she saw
the clouded breath of Matthew Jade's horse, the prick
of his ears, a big walnut eye. He snorted as if an insect had flown up his nose, and stepped restlessly in
and out of hock-deep water.

"Rimmy, hold." Jade got down and, throwing the
light to one side instead of full in her face, came
closer. Raun got up stiffly. She wouldn't look at him,
though he'd cleaned himself up and put on warm
clothes for night riding. She shook her head in anger.

"You couldn't have found me this fast. Not at night.
It . . . it just isn't *human.*"

He turned on the radio receiver which he wore
on a shoulder strap. It beeped loudly and rapidly.

"Every piece of clothing I gave you has a transpon-
der about the size of a dime sewn into it. The battery
is good for two weeks."

Jade touched the lapel of the sheepskin-and-denim
jacket she was wearing. Raun jerked away from him,
trembling.

"There is nothing I hate about you more than your—
relentless efficiency."

"I just never felt your loyalties were all that consistent, Raun."

"Fine. Fine! I ran away tonight because I saw you
slaughter two helpless men. Yes. *Slaughter.* You're so
proud of your Hopi brothers and teachers. But you're
nothing like them. Hopis are good and gentle—the
People of Peace, Lem called them."

"That's why there aren't many of them left. Don't
waste sympathy on those two I shot. Every one of
their kind is a killer. You were living on borrowed
time when I got there. As soon as they decided you
weren't of any more use to them, they'd have opened
your throat. You might ask about Lem."

Raun held her head, feeling scared again. "Oh dear Jesus. Yes. How is he?"

"He's sleeping off the heavy load of junk they shot into him. Ken and Lee and Andy had lesser doses. They're up and around, but Lem won't be right for another twenty-four hours. Unfortunately we can't wait. I've already wasted enough time tracking you down. We're leaving in an hour."

"Going where?" she asked tonelessly.

"Torrejon, near Madrid. From there to Nigeria. Then southeast to the Makari. To the Catacombs."

She almost screamed at him. She bit her tongue. She bit down on the emotion and tasted blood, cold blood, the proper coldness of her desire to see him, finally, defeated. Raun waited until she was certain her heart was steady, and like a stone. Then she looked up with a thin-lipped smile.

"Did you bring a horse for me?"

"No. Get up on Rimfire, I'll jog along."

"All right," Raun said.

Dr. Robeson Kumenyere, wearing a white hospital smock that might have been tailored by Saint Laurent to go with his striped shirt and red silk tie, stood behind his desk and extended a hand to Michael Belov.

"Good morning, *Bwana* Lundgren. Let me apologize immediately for postponing our interview so often. I have no excuse except for my lack of judgment in budgeting my time."

Belov glanced at the terrace doors, which stood open despite the fact that the air conditioning was turned up high. Exotic birds croaked and trilled in the trees of the small walled garden behind Kumenyere's office. Two tall, heavily armed mercenaries wearing the berets and green-and-blue uniforms of Jumbe Kinyati's Praetorians were on the terrace, their backs to the room.

"One can't help but be aware of the soldiers, Dr. Kumenyere. The tight security. There are rumors in Dar of attempted sabotage at the hospital two nights ago."

Kumenyere shrugged. "A minor incident. Unfortunately our generator was rather severely damaged. It will take weeks to repair, and in the meantime we are now forced to draw power from the not-always-reliable national grid."

"Do you think it was an act of war? Or could the

attack on the hospital have had something to do with your decision to become deeply involved in the politics of Tanzania?"

Kumenyere gestured economically at a comfortable chair in front of his desk, turned, and went to close the terrace doors. He came back and sat down in a swivel chair and passed a hand wearily over his eyes.

"I'm a socialist, of course, but not a politician. I've lately acted on *Ndugu* Jumbe's behalf, at his request; a matter of friendship and love, an attempt on my part to lighten the load on his shoulders. He is not, as we know, getting any younger. But my interests are now, and always will be, humanitarian. I'm a man of medicine. I welcome this opportunity to inform our benefactors and friends in Sweden of the progress we're making in epidemiology and genetic diseases such as xeroderma pigmentosa, almost as much of a scourge as hunger. I had thought *medical research* was to be the subject of this interview. Perhaps I should excuse myself."

"Not at all, Dr. Kumenyere. My apologies. As you know, we've planned to devote much of the winter issue to you and your hospital. And of course your photograph will be on the cover of the magazine."

Kumenyere brightened somewhat and turned to face Belov.

"We have the only arbovirus laboratory in East Africa. It's still primitive by modern standards, but a recent grant has enabled us to order more equipment. I've persuaded some gifted young virologists to join our staff. Perhaps after your questions we'll take a tour, then have lunch at my home."

The telephone intercom on his desk buzzed. Kumenyere picked up the receiver, listened, spoke in Swahili, glanced at his visitor, and hung up.

"Something of a coincidence. Our laboratory has been working on a fever of unknown origin, an isolated outbreak in the bush near Mbeya. A number of the victims have died, and their bodies have been flown to us by helicopter. There's a body on the way now, packed in dry ice. Perhaps you'd like to see how we handle this. I must warn you, despite all of our precautions there is some risk of infection."

"I'm fascinated," Belov said. "May I take photos?"

Kumenyere looked startled. "Of the victim? No. It isn't a pretty sight. The ravages of the fever are quite severe."

"Who is he?"

"A member of a UN geophysical survey team. Belgian, I think."

Belov was given a smock to wear, and a surgical mask. He waited with the team from the virology lab at the helicopter landing pad near the big inverted pyramid in which the morgue was located. Mercenaries carrying Kalashnikov rifles completely ringed the area.

The helicopter, an Alouette II, appeared in the sky, circled the hospital grounds and came in. The body of the fever victim was carried on one of the skids. It had been wrapped securely in polyethylene. Condensation from the vapors of the dry ice gave the polyethylene a milky cocoonlike quality; the body inside could barely be distinguished, but Belov could see that he'd been a tall man, perhaps six and a half feet tall.

The medical team untied the corpse from the helicopter and carried the litter quickly inside the pyramid. Belov followed Kumenyere as the helicopter took off again.

In an isolation room on the ground floor the virologists slit the heavy polyethylene and peeled it back, unpacked some of the dry ice. Kumenyere and Belov watched through a port in one wall. It was a bit of good fortune that the victim's emaciated face was turned toward them long enough for Belov to get a good look.

The victim had a brown beard brittle with granulated vomit, but death had only paled, not disfigured him. Belov easily recognized Chips Chapman from the photos Toby had shown him. He felt a stirring of pity for the tall English boy, whose tenacity and courage he had admired. Now Toby would never see his father again. Belov wished he could break the news to him, but of course that was out of the question. Someday Toby would know; in the meantime he must continue to wait, and suffer, and grow much too bitter for someone of his years.

"No idea what's causing the fever?" Belov asked Kumenyere.

The doctor shook his head. "We've made some progress in isolating and analyzing the virus. Our main hope for the present is to contain the outbreak, so it won't turn into a plague. Always a possibility in such a dry year."

Belov was given a tour of the pyramid, from the morgue to the operating room equipped for laser surgery. It was unused; surgeons with the skill to make use of such instruments were unavailable in Tanzania. He was shown computerized scanning equipment worth half a million dollars, electron microscopes, a big IBM 370 computer idle for lack of experienced programmers.

The arbovirus center on the top floor was busier; Kumenyere currently had a staff of five. There a much smaller computer had been installed to keep track of experiments and procedures running simultaneously in the lab, procedures requiring almost split-second timing for optimum results. A scoreboard with closed-circuit TV monitors advised researchers of their progress.

Kumenyere dimmed the fluorescent ceiling panels until the cold and sterile room was in near darkness. Then he activated all areas of the board.

Twenty-four oval red lights flashed on. They had a surprising depth, brilliance, and luminosity, like the stars as they appear only to those few travelers who have escaped, or almost escaped, the shrouding envelope of earth's atmosphere.

"I thought you said your lab was primitive," Belov remarked, trying to look more closely at the red lights. Each appeared to be microscopically whorled, like a living brain swimming in fire.

Kumenyere put the room lights back on. He tapped his forehead with a finger.

"Technology at best is only a tool. We are poor in brainpower. Inspiration. Genius. But they will come to us, I'm confident of that. We have the machines that will help them achieve breakthroughs in their research and, unfortunately, the plagues at our doorstep."

At one o'clock they were escorted to Dr. Kumenyere's seaside villa by a heavy guard in Land-Rovers.

The chauffeur of Kumenyere's Mercedes had a Skorpion on the seat beside him, a Czech-made 7.62 automatic that fired 850 rounds a minute and was ideal for close-in shooting. Belov also was certain that Kumenyere himself carried a gun. But he made no mention of the armament and the bodyguards, as if he assumed they were a normal part of the doctor's workaday routine. They made small talk about the social whirl in Paris, London, Rome, and all the elegant watering holes in between.

The villa, Moorish in style, was surrounded by an ugly unpainted concrete block wall that looked like a recent addition. There were broken bottles cemented into place along the top of the wall. Kumenyere seemed to have prepared himself for a period of public scrutiny and, perhaps, unpopularity. The driveway gate was just wide enough for one vehicle to squeeze through. Belov had noticed deep scratches on the sides of the Mercedes, and now understood that the chauffeur's depth perception was faulty. This time he made it without mishap, and the car drove up a semicircular drive to the house. The Land-Rovers stayed outside on the sandy road.

There were other guards in the yard, and a scruffy Alsatian that looked as if it had been starved and whipped to a peak of craziness. The dog was on a stout leash.

There were three others cars in the drive, including a blue Toyota hatchback that Belov recognized: He had seen Henry Landreth's mistress drive up in it at the hospital two nights ago.

The captain of Kumenyere's guard came trotting down the steps from the house to open the door for him. He spoke to the doctor in Swahili, but Belov also heard Landreth's name.

Before the captain was halfway through the speech he'd obviously primed himself for, Kumenyere went into a rage. Belov climbed out on the other side of the car and was ignored by everyone but the maddened barking dog. Belov had with him the thousand-dollar gift he'd brought for Kumenyere, which was packed inside a custom-made case.

He studied the scene Kumenyere was making, which he could make no sense of, and looked toward the house. The screen door opened slowly. Nyshuri came out and stood on the verandah in the deep shade twirling a large flower like a parasol in her hands.

Kumenyere became aware of her and broke off his tirade. He started up the steps in a bound, remembered his guest and his manners, swung around to Be-

lov, and flashed a smile, though his brows were
packed with woe.

"Please excuse me, *Bwana* Lundgren—some inexcusable stupidity—I must straighten out this depressing
matter before we—you *do* understand? How kind.
Please wait for me here."

Kumenyere indicated the verandah with a welcoming sweep of one hand, then snapped his fingers at a
houseboy. He pointed to Belov and issued instructions
before turning his attention back to Nyshuri. Then he
nipped up the remaining steps, took her by the elbow—her head came up defiantly at that—and shoved
her into the house.

Belov placed a drink order with the houseboy and
wandered up to the verandah trying to appear that he
was minding his own business.

Through the screen door he glimpsed Nyshuri and
Kumenyere standing halfway down a long hallway,
the blue sea beyond them. Kumenyere raised his voice
again; it was childishly shrill. She answered back,
turned away with a flippant, contemptuous shrug.
Kumenyere grabbed her and spun her into a flat
open-handed smash of one hand to the face; it nearly
took her head off. It cost her a tooth, perhaps: Belov
saw something white and shiny fly out of her mouth.
She sat down in a heap on the floor and held her head
and didn't complain.

Kumenyere yanked her up again and thrust her
through a doorway. The door banged shut. Silence.
Belov sat down in a vinyl sling chair and waited for
his drink.

The houseboy served him from a bar cart he
wheeled from another part of the house. Then from a
pocket of his smock he produced a deck of grimy,
well-thumbed playing cards, which he began to shuffle in midair, demonstrating his dexterity. He did card

tricks for Belov's amusement, smiling ear to ear and revealing blighted gums.

Belov sat back with a haze over his eyes, watching the cards but not seeing them, nodding at appropriate times while he tried to piece together what was happening at the villa.

If Nyshuri was in residence, then it made sense that Henry Landreth had also been here, under Kumenyere's protection. But now, Belov surmised, Henry was gone, a cirumstance that had inflamed the normally tranquil doctor. How had Landreth talked his way past the captain of the guard? A more crucial question: If Landreth was afraid for his life, as he had every reason to be after the aborted abduction attempt by the South Africans, why had he rejected the security which the villa offered? And where was he going?

The girl might know. Getting his hands on her, Belov knew, would not be easy, but he had to try. Finding Henry Landreth seemed his best hope of locating the FIREKILL bloodstones.

After the Russian had cooled his heels for almost twenty minutes, his host reappeared. Dr. Kumenyere had changed clothes. He was now wearing, instead of a tropical-gray Savile Row business suit, a twill lounging outfit with a dark-brown silk shirt unbuttoned over his impressive chest and a neckerchief secured by a gold ring.

Kumenyere made elaborate apologies, had a drink for himself, and escorted Belov to his study, where he exhibited a collection of some forty sporting guns and twice as many photographs of himself with world figures. Belov presented Kumenyere with the gift, a weapon the likes of which he'd never seen. It was a chrome-plated, .22-caliber rifle that fired thirty rounds a second from a 177-round magazine. What made the rifle unique was a telescopic sight that pinpointed targets with a red spot of light projected by a laser.

"The only other rifle just like this one belongs to the king of Spain," Belov said. "And this rifle is accurate up to two hundred yards."

Kumenyere was delighted with his new toy. He immediately closed the shutters, darkening the study. Belov assembled the rifle for the doctor, who tried it without ammunition. The red dot appeared faithfully on each object he aimed at: a piece of Makonde sculpture, the spine of a book on his shelves, a spider spinning a web in one high corner of the room.

But at lunch, which consisted of a chilled seafood salad and an excellent white Bordeaux, Kumenyere was hard put to conceal his lack of interest and his restlessness, and he answered the questions Belov was obliged to put to him in a brusque manner. He ate sparingly, and almost as soon as coffee was served asked to be excused.

"I've taken up quite a lot of your time today," Belov said.

"That's quite all right, but I have so much to do—"

"Perhaps another meeting—"

"Yes, of course, dear fellow, please phone my secretary for an appointment. In a few days' time. My chauffeur will drive you back to Dar when you're ready."

"I could easily call a taxi," Belov protested.

"No, no, you're my guest. I do apologize again for the rush."

Belov didn't want to leave; Nyshuri undoubtedly was still in the house, and he couldn't afford to lose track of her now. But almost as soon as the doctor left the terrace where they'd been served lunch, the chauffeur turned up in the doorway, waiting for him. Belov had another sip of wine and decided there was no point in dawdling.

They were half a mile from the villa in the Mercedes, within sight of the highway to Dar, when Belov asked the driver to pull over.

"Something wrong, sar?"

"I don't know. I'm feeling nauseated. Perhaps if I get out and walk around."

"All right, sar. Take your time. No problem."

Belov took out his handkerchief and coughed retchingly into it as he got out of the car. The chauffeur picked up a folded newspaper from his seat and began reading it. Belov walked along the shoulder of the road for fifty feet or so, bent down for a smooth round stone, and knotted it in his handkerchief. The stone weighed about two pounds. He returned to the Mercedes on the driver's side and tapped on the glass. The chauffeur rolled the window down and turned his head to smile at Belov.

"Better now? Continuing on now, sar?"

Belov popped him on the left temple with the makeshift cosh, and the chauffeur fell forward against the steering wheel. Belov opened the door and dragged him out, pulled the keys to unlock the trunk. Then he went back for the unconscious man. He yanked him erect and propped him against the side of the car as a bus went smokily by on the highway, swerving from side to side to dodge the potholes. The bus was packed with natives and tourists on the cheap. Some of the natives were riding in the luggage racks on top, snoozing, or eating and throwing their garbage along the shoulder.

When the bus disappeared down the road, Belov picked up the chauffeur by his belt and the back of his neck and lugged him to the trunk. Kumenyere had installed a spare diesel tank, and there wasn't much room to pack the chauffeur inside. He reckoned that the rap on the head would be good for a couple of hours, and if he didn't slam the lid tight the chauffeur would have enough air to stay alive.

He got in behind the wheel, backed around, and returned the way they had come.

The Mercedes was easily identifiable as belonging to Kumenyere, and the coastal land was nearly flat, with groves of coconut and banana trees, a scablike salt marsh with clumps of wilting grasses like the fossils of wading birds. Then sand dunes, and above them a glimpse of the roofline of the villa. Belov turned off the track into a camp of some kind, slogans of the defunct TANU party fading on the whitewashed walls of concrete rondevals; most of the windows had been broken out.

He hid the car, taking with him the chauffeur's small Skorpion automatic. Even with its low-velocity load it would be useful in a pinch, although it couldn't be fired accurately on full automatic without the rudimentary stock attachment. He tramped up the dunes to a vantage point overlooking the villa, spread himself flat in the unpleasantly spiky dune vegetation. But there was a cool sea wind, an occasional long drift of spray from the waves. The two Land-Rovers were still parked outside the villa's gate; the mercenaries squatted in the shade they afforded and played gambling games without much show of interest.

Belov didn't have to wait long. Kumenyere came out of the villa at a little past three. He'd changed clothes again, this time looking as if he were journeying into bush country. He carried the laser rifle case which Belov had presented to him, and a tote bag. The mercenaries scrambled to attention when he appeared. Kumenyere exchanged a few words with one of them and climbed into a Land-Rover. Both vehicles then roared off toward the highway.

It was futile to try to follow the doctor in his own

car. From the looks of things he was going after Henry Landreth; the rifle suggested the possibility of a night ambush somewhere, although that didn't seem to make sense. If Kumenyere had protected him before, why should he now want to kill him? Unless Landreth had been a prisoner, under house arrest.

Belov was unhappy with this turn of events, but there was nothing he could do yet. Only the girl could be of help to him. He wondered if he should risk returning to the villa in the Mercedes, claiming he'd left something valuable there. But the absence of the chauffeur would be suspicious. Trying to sneak in by broad daylight was foolhardy. He would, in time, get his hands on the girl. But patience was required. Annoyed by the biting heat of the sun on the back of his neck, and the forty kinds of flies with which he shared the dunes, he prepared to wait until nightfall if necessary, hoping there wouldn't be periodic patrols by the villa's guards which he would have to go to the trouble of ducking. But with the master temporarily away he doubted they would stir themselves.

"No, no, you must come at once," Lady Hecuba ha-Leví de Quattro-Smythe said on the telephone to Nyshuri. "Poor darling. I'm outraged! He had no right to do that; it's not as if you had any control over what that foolish Dr. Landreth has done. If Robeson Kumenyere has damaged your lovely face I shall kill the swine. He might as well have struck *me*. There is no difference in the way I feel about this brutal assault, and you know that I bear grudges forever. How badly does it hurt? I can barely understand you. Oh, *dear*. Do you think you can drive? Then jump into your little blue car and try to hurry—I'll be in agony until I see you, my sweet."

* * *

Michael Belov returned to the abandoned TANU camp to check on the chauffeur.

He was semiconscious in the trunk of the Mercedes, breathing in moans, sweating rivers. Belov hauled him out of there and walked him to one of the buildings. The chauffeur's knees buckled and his feet wandered and he cried like a baby. He had a goose egg on his temple where he'd been struck, perhaps too hard. Belov gave him a drink of water from a trickling standpipe, found rope. He tied the man and gagged him with half his shirt to stop his whining. Eventually, if his head cleared and he worked hard enough, he would be able to get his feet free and walk down the road to the villa. If not, he would die there.

Belov walked outside just as the blue Toyota hatchback rattled by, taking him by surprise. He had a glimpse of Nyshuri's face, badly swollen on the left side. Probably the eye was swollen almost shut too, or she would have seen him peripherally as she passed the hutlike buildings, which stood close to the villa road. She was traveling fast, slewing from side to side on the rutted track, raising a sandstorm that glittered in the sun.

Belov hesitated, looking back to see if she was being pursued. Then he ran for the Mercedes. It was a piece of luck; if he hadn't come down from the dunes to make a better disposition of the chauffeur, he would have had no hope of getting to the car in time to follow her.

She was out of sight already, en route to the highway, but he easily caught up, with a notion of cutting her off.

But at a bend of the track he encountered men in Chinese coolie hats and native *kekois*, a skirtlike garment, walking goats and zebu to the commune across the highway. By the time he got around them his chance was gone. Nyshuri turned north, taking the road to Bagamoyo. Traffic was light. She was a very fast and brainless driver, oblivious of the poor condition of the highway. He was content to stay well back, so she wouldn't recognize the car if she happened to notice it, and wait for the further opportunity he knew would develop.

"If you will kindly leave Nyshuri to me," Hecuba said to Jan-Nic Pretorius, "in due course she will tell me everything she knows. All you need to do is conceal yourself, and listen. Perhaps this is a function you can fulfill without clumsiness. She may be able to tell us what has become of Henry Landreth. She wasn't clear about that. But let me make myself clear. I am fond of Nyshuri. Her childlike eroticism revitalizes me. I have no intention of delivering her into your incompetent hands."

"She's coming with us," Jan-Nic said grimly. He had flushed a dirty red color from his shirt collar to the roots of his hair, a threat display Hecuba calmly stood up to, looking him in the eye and smiling faintly. "This way," Jan-Nic concluded, "I can be sure there's no risk of further betrayal."

"You mean to convey that the inconceivably stupid business at the hospital was *my* fault. And to whom did I betray you?"

"I only had a glimpse of one of them. He spoke English, with a decided American accent. A voice I've heard before, I know, it haunts me. But I can't recall—"

"Perhaps he was a house guest."

"Who also happened to be a professional assassin. I've only just learned how Bendert was killed. A very thin curved knife was thrust behind his eye and into the brain. The autopsy in Johannesburg revealed this. He must have been taken completely by surprise."

"How fortunate you were alert enough to escape a

similar fate. You must be very fast on your feet, like the racing dog you somewhat resemble."

The implication of cowardice caused Jan-Nic to tremble; Hecuba saw that he was pressing too hard, aware of his limitations and mistakes and desperate to make up for them. They had put the wrong man in the field, she thought. She caught a whiff of something else that depressed and worried her. An odor of fear and death. His. Others'. Let them take the girl, then. She wanted no more of this tainted and deadly business.

But Jan-Nic had already revised his strategy.

"It's quiet here," he said, walking to the seaward side of the courtyard terrace. The courtyard was fully in shadow, the tables bare. He looked out at the spume of breakers behind the seawall. "Isolated. I couldn't help noticing you've let your servants go for the day. You're not entertaining tonight."

"No."

"*Ach*, this might be the best place after all, if the girl needs persuasion . . ."

"Not in my house! Do your filthy butcher work somewhere else; I'm not paid to—"

Jan-Nic looked around at her, pleased to have uncovered a weakness.

Hecuba's pulse pounded but she said, more reasonably, "You're making a mistake. Nyshuri is coming to me beaten, hurt. Whatever she knows, she won't respond to you, a *mzungu*. Let me try it my way."

"But I don't trust you," Jan-Nic said with a cutting smile. "Who knows what passes between the two of you that an outsider would miss? As for pay, you'll take anyone's money. Perhaps Dr. Henry Landreth has found it prudent to bribe you already."

"How ridiculous. I've never met the man."

"Still I think it would be better if, when she arrives, the girl sees nothing of you at all. Willem!"

A stocky man with a bland fair face, small eyes, and sun-whitened brows appeared from a corner of the courtyard where he'd been patiently waiting.

"Take Lady Hecuba upstairs to her rooms. Stay with her. Remember that she is completely treacherous." To Hecuba he said, "Willem would be the first to admit that he has no imagination. He is sexually neuter. He follows instructions faithfully. He can't be distracted or diverted from his duty. But he can be annoyed. If you annoy him, you'll regret it."

Hecuba looked curiously at Willem, who was easily twice her size, and smiled, shrugging her bare shoulders in surrender.

"Do you play gin, Willem?"

"*Ja.*" Willem looked at Jan-Nic, who nodded his approval.

"Then the evening shouldn't be a *total* loss," Hecuba said. "Come along."


Henry Landreth's head ached severely from the long jarring trip by Land-Rover to the base of Kilimanjaro. His driver, an Army sergeant named Humbert Kivinje, was one of those who drove blithely, at fearsome speeds, using his horn instead of his brake pedal to bail him out of the inevitable tight spots. All along the highways of the country one could see the rusting hulks of vehicles come to a smashing bad end, but they provided no object lesson for Sergeant Kivinje. On several occasions, faced with what he thought was disaster, Henry had demanded, and finally pleaded shamelessly, for a reduction in speed. Kivinje had merely grinned at him.

"Sir, you have safe-conduct from *Jumbe*," he shouted, as if the letter which Henry carried placed them all on the side of the angels, including the people and animals who sauntered obliviously across high-velocity thoroughfares whenever it pleased them to do so.

After that Henry sat with a good grip on the Rover, his eyes closed, until he heard a distant rumble of thunder and looked up to find that they had nearly arrived. Kilimanjaro was directly ahead. It was about five in the afternoon. He could see nothing of the upper reaches of the mountain. To the south and west the skies were clear, an ashen blue over the rainless land. But ominous storms, with flashes of lightning, rumbled over Kilimanjaro. The huge mountain, gradually heating up, spewing invisible gases into the atmosphere, was making its own weather. He felt sick again; but this time it was from the excitement of having returned.

The town of Moshi, between the plains and peaks of Kilimanjaro, had been taken over, at Jumbe's order, by the military: Families were being relocated from the *shambas*, small homesteads, and *ujamaa* cooperatives on the rich slopes of the lower mountain. The roads in the area were jammed with cars, trucks, and livestock.

The Land-Rover was stopped at a checkpoint on the highway a few miles east of Moshi. An officer in sunglasses and faultless dress greens told them they could proceed no further. Sergeant Kivinje hopped out with his hand suggestively placed on the butt of his pearl-handled revolver and launched a tirade in Swahili, confident that Executive Order had precedence over rank. He jabbed a finger at his passenger in the Land-Rover, imperiously offered the document signed by Jumbe, and promised the officer he would be executed before sunrise if he detained them a moment longer.

How they loved their petty exercises of power, Landreth thought, watching the scene expressionlessly. It was one of the reasons they would never amount to anything.

The officer held the letter gingerly; it was pregnant with the seal of government. He peered at Henry Landreth and shrugged.

"You are going up Kilimanjaro? It is foolish. Above eight thousand feet the tracks are no good. There have already been floods near Marangu. You may not come back alive."

"I know the mountain and its moods very well," Henry said impatiently. "Do you wish to speak to Jumbe himself? He would be very unhappy taking his valuable time to speak to *you*."

The officer sighed and ostentatiously stamped a document of his own; they were allowed to pass. Sergeant Kivinje returned to the Land-Rover chuckling, and handed Jumbe's letter back to Henry.

"Where to now?"

"Take the Yingi road to the Nyangoro Coffee Cooperative. The manager will still be there. I'll stay the night and outfit myself from their stores."

The trip into Moshi was unavoidable but tortuous, the din terrific. A well-settled, prosperous area of nearly fifteen hundred square miles had been emptied by troops who were too few to do an adequate job, public servants cowed by the size of the ever-swelling mob. Nearly everyone was angry. Loudspeakers on public buildings blared confusing instructions to the refugees. Rumanian-built buses expelled quantities of oily smoke. The displaced persons who had relatives elsewhere were trying to cram themselves aboard the buses or into jitneys, locally known as *matatus*. Owners of private vehicles, even motor scooters, were charging exorbitant fees for transportation.

With the thunder of the mountain in the background, rumors of a cataclysmic eruption imminent, the swirling gray clouds pressing down toward the town, lightning like cannonfire in the gloom, Henry Landreth was reminded of the Malay Peninsula before World War Two, of a panicked populace fleeing the Japanese. But all this was happening at *his* instigation, arising from his obsessive need to stand, alone, on the threshold of the Catacombs. Discoverer of the great achievements of the Lords of the Storm. *Possessor*. As close to the infinite and the godlike as a man can come. When the Land-Rover was rocked in the street, when anxious black men attempted to come aboard, Henry ordered Sergeant Kivinje to draw his pistol and shoot the next man who dared.

Fortunately no homicides resulted from their ordeal. West of Moshi traffic quickened, though it remained heavy going to Arusha, where more accomodations were available in the abandoned towers of a noble but failed experiment, the East Africa Community. They soon reached the Yingi road, meeting another barrier. But their documentation was accepted without question by the soldiers stationed there, and they were waved through a crowd of evacuees waiting for transportation, carrying everything from babes in arms to zinc washtubs.

Not far along the Yingi road, in the cultivated foothills, they were jarred by an earth tremor of short duration. It was the first real evidence of what might be seething deep within Kilimanjaro.

Sergeant Kivinje pointed solemnly in the direction of the invisible summit of Kibo.

"Not so good for you to be up there if the mountain explodes."

"The mountain will not explode," Henry said calmly.

Above their heads a helicopter flapped. He looked up and caught a glimpse of it circling above the treetops at six thousand feet, just before it vanished in a drizzling mist.

* * *

"Why do you have so many snakes?" Willem said, looking around at the terrariums in Lady Hecuba's boudoir. Some of them were brightly lit, simulating desert sunshine; others were as shadowy as a jungle.

"I'm fond of them," Lady Hecuba said. She placed a sealed deck of cards on the little baize-covered game table. "They make intriguing pets."

"Dangerous, no?"

"Some are. You recognize the infamous boomslang, of course."

Willem grunted.

"And the saw-scaled viper."

Willem broke open the cards; he frowned and placed a finger in the crook of his elbow. "I saw a man die once. Bitten here. Thirty seconds he lived, no more."

"An extremely venomous specimen, no doubt. Only one milligram of the venom of the krait is enough to kill the average man."

She studied Willem for a few moments, wetting her frosted red lips, smiling. He was wearing a loose-fitting shirt with belled sleeves; the shirt was unbuttoned to the shiny notch of his diaphragm, and tucked into his trousers. His chest was bare, hairless, well tanned.

"Will you excuse me for a few moments? I have a rather sick *Boaedon libeatus*. He has nematodes, I'm afraid, and he's also having trouble molting. I'd hate to lose him—they are rather difficult to come by."

Hecuba selected drops from a medicine cabinet and opened the cage of the African house snake, a three-foot specimen, its skin half peeled, its color a brownish black. She picked up the snake from its bed of rocks, holding it with one hand just behind the head.

"He's not dangerous at all," she assured Willem.

"But he hates to take his medicine. Would you lend a hand? Just hold him carefully about the middle and I'll do the rest."

Willem gingerly accepted responsibility for half of the snake. Hecuba measured and squeezed two drops of viscous liquid into the open mouth.

"Good. Now if you will *gently* take him behind the head, just as I am holding him, and keep his head up so the medicine goes down in good order, I'll ruck out his cage."

With a little cordless vacuum cleaner Hecuba removed the rock-hard crystals of uric acid and bits of shed skin that had collected in the cage. Then she changed the drinking and bathing water.

"You're doing *very* well," she said to the stolid but perspiring Willem. "Now just lay him back on the rocks, poor old darling, while I swiftly attend to another matter."

As soon as she was certain that Willem was fully occupied with the business of getting the large and unyielding house snake back into his habitat, Hecuba slid open the door of another terrarium which, on casual inspection, looked empty. But she knew just what she wanted and where it would be concealed. She reached in and withdrew the coiled, beautiful banded little thing, bracelet size and small enough to fit in the palm of her hand. At a glance its head was indistinguishable from its tail.

Hecuba took two quick steps and with the stealth of a pick-pocket reached deep inside Willem's unbuttoned shirt. She deposited the snake in a loose pouch of silken material, inches from his liver.

Willem dropped the African house snake and straightened with a snort of surprise and fear as Lady Hecuba stepped nimbly back out of his reach. His lit-

tle eyes widened as he felt the body of the wormlike
snake against his flesh. His hand jumped to the opening of his shirt.

"NO!" Hecuba said. "Don't make any abrupt moves.
Do nothing to startle him. He is a little sluggish from
having been kept a degree or two colder than he likes.
But he will soon warm up from your body heat. Then
he will be unpredictable."

"What is it?" Willem said in a strangled voice.

"A coral snake. Highly venomous but not unusually
disagreeable. As long as you are very careful you may
coexist with him indefinitely. But if you try to remove
him, unless you have exceptional nerves you will undoubtedly botch the job. That means death."

She saw, in his eyes, the momentary urge to kill her
that was almost stronger than his fear of the lethal
nudging coldness. His sweat had begun to run in
streams. Hecuba smiled, thinking that a muscle might
soon begin to twitch uncontrollably and attract the re-
primanding sting.

Then she heard Nyshuri crying for her outside the
villa, a desperate, wounded cry.

She had wrecked the Toyota, almost within sight of
Villa Bib-Shala. Run off the road by a grimy hooting
tanker coming around a stalled vehicle abandoned in
the southbound lane, the car had caromed and
smashed its way down a slope paved with a jumble of
rocks strewn there during construction of the highway. Everything from a front wheel to the oil pan, the
transmission, and the tailpipe assembly was ripped
away, but the Toyota didn't roll over, nor did it meet
a rock big enough to punch the engine back into the
passenger compartment. The gas tank remained intact, but there wasn't enough gas left to consume the
wreck even if it had caught fire.

Nyshuri sat perfectly still for thirty seconds, bruised

and shaken, a death grip on the wheel, staring at a wedge of blue sea visible through one side of the smashed windshield.

The door on her side grated open. She felt a hand on her shoulder.

"How badly are you hurt?" she was asked in English.

Nyshuri turned her battered face slowly to Michael Belov. Her vision was blurred; she ought to have recognized him, but saw only that he was nicely dressed, deeply tanned, from his manner a man of substance, perhaps a diplomat.

He seemed truly concerned. She tried to answer him, but no words came out.

"Your car's a total loss, I'm afraid. Where are you going? Can I take you?" He touched her face. Despite the angle of the late afternoon sun her skin was cold, dotted with pinpoints of perspiration. Then his hands were all over her, feeling her bones, pressing gently into the muscled areas of her stomach and abdomen.

"Does that hurt? Here? Good. Listen to me. You've had a narrow escape. I don't think your injuries are too serious, but there's a danger of shock reaction. I want you to come with me."

Nyshuri licked her lips. "No. My . . . friend's house. Expecting me."

"Where?"

She nodded fractionally toward a fingerlike oasis of trees between the blazing land and the foaming edge of the sea three hundred yards distant.

"Just there."

"I'll take you."

"Thank you. Kind."

Belov reached around Nyshuri to get a hand under her arm so he could help her out of the car. Her head drooped. Looking down, she saw the pistol tucked into his waistband beneath his striped jacket. She was turning numb, and felt colder still.

"No . . ."

"Don't worry. The trick is to get moving. Lean against me. Have a go at it. There . . ."

"W . . . are you?"

"Your friend. Don't talk. Conserve your strength. Breathe deeply if you can."

They left the wreck behind. She was a big girl and she wore platform shoes, which were of no use in negotiating the rocky downslope. For the better part of the way he had to haul her along, her head nodding vertiginously against his shoulder. But when they reached a narrow track winding through groves to the wall of Hecuba's villa, she seemed slowly to come around.

"I know you," Nyshuri said suddenly.

"Do you?"

"Saw you . . . with Robeson." She had begun to walk by herself in the shallow sand, but she still held on to his arm, breathing rapidly, filled with tremors.

"That's right. I was there this morning."

"Are you his friend?"

"I'm a journalist."

"*My* friend—has sworn that she will kill him for what he did to me."

"Nyshuri—is your head clear now?"

"Better," she mumbled.

"It was really Henry Landreth I came to see this morning. But he was gone. Can you tell me where?"

She stopped near the gate and made a half turn, unsteadily.

"Straight to hell, when Robeson catches up with him. I don't care. I always hated being with him. His white skin, like worms in spoiled meat. I only want Hecuba. I will never leave her now."

Nyshuri ran, a hand on the wall to guide her, and tottered through the gates to the villa.

*"Hecuba, Hecuba, help me!"*

She was halfway to the house when Lady Hecuba appeared on her third-floor terrace.

"Nyshuri, get away from here. Run!"

Nyshuri stopped. Her brain simply refused to work anymore. She looked back at Belov, then again at Hecuba, who seemed no longer to be her friend. Nyshuri threw up her hands, wailing.

Jan-Nic Pretorius came outside on the verandah with a gun in his hand, one of the old reliable PPKs.

Belov drew his own weapon and slipped up close to Nyshuri, putting her between Pretorius and himself. There was no other suitable cover in the spacious yard. The sun was sinking low in the trees beyond the wall, random patterns of light and shade splashed across the pink facade of the house. Nyshuri, clutching her head, started to one side, then zagged the other way as Belov shadow-dodged along with her. Pretorius dropped down on one knee trying to draw a bead on Belov that wouldn't also include Nyshuri.

Belov said in John Wayne's familiar voice, " 'Fill your hand, you son of a bitch.' "

In Lady Hecub's boudoir Willem screamed, so high on the scale he sounded like a woman.

"Jan-Nic! Jan-Nic!" he cried, more recognizably. "God in Heaven, I'm a dead man!"

Jan-Nic, unnerved, allowed his gun hand to waver. In Afrikaans he shouted back, "Willem! What's wrong, man? I need your help!"

As Hecuba turned around on the terrace, Willem ruuhed out and lifted her high. Her own scream ended abruptly as she smashed down headfirst onto the verandah wall, overturning a stone urn planted with oleanders.

Belov dived into the grass, clamped a hand on Nyshuri's ankle and spilled her flat in front of him. He let off a rip of bullets from the Skorpion, elbow braced against the ground.

Enough of the bullets hit Jan-Nic to kill him.

Belov got up quickly, his eyes on Willem. The snake-bit man was staring down at the ruins of Lady Hecuba ha-Leví de Quattro-Smythe, his head lowered, his chest heaving. He began to shudder and buck as if a horse were kicking him. His eyes were unfocused. Belov, taking no chances that it was an act of some kind, raised the Skorpion and emptied the magazine in Willem's face.

Keeping low, Belov ran up to the verandah and looked into Jan-Nic's untouched face. But his throat was shattered. Around his neck he wore, on a gold chain, a medallion locket. Belov, strangely, wanted to open it. But he was afraid of what he might see: a glimpse of a life before death. The faces of children.

There was still a stink of battle on the warm air. He helped himself to Jan-Nic's Walther. There had been shouting, screams, gunfire, over in a few moments. How many others might be around? Where were the servants Hecuba needed to run a house this size? He stayed with his back pressed against the wall beside the high carved ebony front doors, listening, watching.

Nyshuri crawled to the edge of the verandah and pulled the loose body of her lover down into her lap, commenced lamentations in a musical, clicking tribal tongue.

Belov decided to make a move before she was too far gone in grief. He went to Nyshuri and crouched low beside her, where he could watch both the house and the road leading up to the gates.

"Nyshuri!" He had to shake her to get her to lift her head and regard him with a red-veined eye.

"Robeson Kumenyere is to blame for this," he said.

She agreed with him, nodding ecstatically. She started on another low moan of mourning. Belov cut her off by slapping her hard where her face was most tender.

"Listen. I will go after him and kill him for you. Is that what you want?"

"Yes . . . *yes.*"

"Tell me where he's gone."

"To the big mountain. To Kilimanjaro. After Henry."

"Where on the mountain?"

"Nyangoro . . . Coffee Cooperative." She raised bloody hands and smeared her face. "Oh, my Hecuba! *My life is gone.*"

"Kilimanjaro. You're certain of that."

She looked down at Hecuba's grossly misshapen head, a spilled jelly eye. She nodded.

"Thank you," Belov said to Nyshuri. "I'll keep my pledge to you."

He stood. He stepped behind her. He put the muzzle of the Walther close to the brain stem at the base of her skull, and pulled the trigger.


The road to the nationalized coffee-growing plantation on the southern slope of Kilimanjaro was a ribbon of broken bitumen that ran through irrigated acres of fruit trees and vegetable gardens, plots of grass where cattle still grazed despite the declared emergency. The orange corrugated metal roofs of the coop buildings, surrounded by thousands of Arabica coffee bushes, were close to the fringe of the montane forest belt, the beginning of Kilimanjaro National Park and game reserve.

Because of the threatening weather surrounding the mountain, it was nearly dark when the Land-Rover driven by Sergeant Kivinje bumped across a cattle guard and entered the Nyangoro Cooperative. There appeared to be no one around, but the helicopter Henry Landreth had observed earlier was parked near a long storage shed. Now the property of the Tanzanian People's Defense Force Air Wing, it was an old U. S. Army Raven with a Perspex pod jutting forward from the fuselage.

Kivinje slowed to make the right-angle turn to the lodge. Another quake jarred the ground beneath them. It was over in a few seconds, but it left Henry with a lingering uneasiness. He pondered the darkness of the lodge, the presence of the old helicopter. He had misgivings that refused to take any definite shape. Impulsively he reached out to Sergeant Kivinje.

"I've changed my mind. I won't stop here after all. Up ahead is the track to the nine-thousand-foot level. It's suitable for four-wheel-drive vehicles. We can make it to the climbing hut there in a couple of hours."

"But you have no food! No warm clothes. Very bitter at night on the mountain."

"I'm bloody well aware of that. We had one of our camps a little farther up, on the moorland. No one takes that route to Kibo—it's too difficult for inexperienced climbers. Our caches of food and clothing should still be there."

Sergeant Kivinje had the Rover down to a crawl. He looked anxious.

"Not much petrol, sir."

"Oh, very well. Pull over to the pump there by the garage. But be quick."

Henry brooded in the front seat while the sergeant cranked the pump, which someone had forgotten to lock, and inserted the nozzle into the Rover's gas tank. The liters rang off. A flash of red appeared on the dirty windshield and trembled there, then steadied to a hot perfect circle about the size of a shirt button. It crept slowly in Henry's direction. He stared, entranced, wondering what the light could be, what the source was.

The light was just at the outside of his reflection on the glass when the windshield began to fly into fragments, chewed up by a short burst of .22-caliber bullets. Bits of glass were dashed in his face; he heard one of the slugs ricochet off the steel handgrip of the seat behind him.

Henry let out a howl of dismay and jumped into the driver's seat, banging a bare knee on the gearshift knob. He turned the ignition key, saw another spot of red light traveling across the webbed glass, ducked, threw the Rover into gear, and pulled away, leaving Sergeant Kivinje hosing gas into the dirt.

No new holes appeared in the windshield. One appeared instead in Sergeant Kivinje's chin as he lifted his head in surprise to see where Henry was going. The impact of the lightweight bullet caused his head and torso to jerk back three or four inches. The bullet went down through his throat and tore the jugular vein. As Henry glanced back, he saw a stream of blood pumping in a corollary arc to the wasted gasoline. Kivinje collapsed slowly, his eyes like yellow fog, releasing his grip on the handle of the nozzle.

Bullets began to pierce the Land-Rover. Henry made a sliding panic turn to the left, then another, sharp right turn to avoid an area of piled-up brush and small trees ready for burning, and almost ended, wheels up, in a drainage ditch. The rear tires spun on a rain-softened embankment and bit deep, catapulted him forward as the windshield took another hit. He lost his hat and his bearings trying to crank the steering wheel from below the level of the dashboard, but in truth there was no place to hide: The big grayish-green Rover was an easy, flimsy target.

An open gate appeared and he barged through it, banging one side of the vehicle hard against an iron post; then he was traveling uphill through shrub country, the Rover blending in the rainy dusk with the color of the tidy, uniform coffee trees. Nothing lay ahead but a wide thick forest half smothered in ground fog. He heard no more bullets plinking metal. Sobbing from relief, Henry floored the accelerator and straightened himself behind the wheel. Nothing was blocking the track ahead. Soon it would be dark and not even the helicopter, if they dared to send it up, would be able to find him within the tall trees, unless they had heat-sensing equipment aboard, or night sights for their weapons. The latter might be a possibility; he realized now it was a laser beam that had sought him as he sat waiting for the gas tank to be filled. A new and terrifying adjunct to the sniper's art.

But who were they, and why did they want to kill him? He was still mindlessly in flight, too rattled to think it through, to accept the obvious answer: Robeson Kumenyere had decided to do away with his co-conspirator. At the moment nothing mattered but the nearness of sanctuary. A few hundred yards more. The plantation was well behind him, the big trees were springing up left and right, a deepening tangle of bramble defined the track. Some bush pigs fled from the sound of the Rover bearing down on them. A bend in the track, a wall of fog, he had to use his lights. Safe at last.

The Rover's engine, however, had begun to sing some wrong notes. It was developing what might prove to be a fatal cough. The odor of escaping motor oil was sharp in the windless air.

\* \* \*

In the lodge of the Nyangoro Coffee Cooperative, where the lights had been turned on, Robeson Kumenyere cleaned his new rifle meticulously before packing the components away in the presentation case.

"When you have the part you need, how long will it take you to repair the helicopter?" he asked the pilot who had flown him to Kilimanjaro from the airport in Dar es Salaam.

"Three hours, I should think, sir."

"Then you'll be ready to leave tomorrow afternoon."

"Yes, sir."

"Good. I'll be back by then."

"Going up the mountain now, sir?" the pilot asked incredulously.

"Of course not. Let Henry spend the night in the forest alone. He's ill equipped for the adventure. Of course he won't sleep a wink, he'll be afraid to doze off and risk a surprise. By morning he'll be nothing but a mass of exposed nerve endings." Kumenyere yawned and stretched his big frame. "Let's give the poor bugger I shot a proper burial, then see what's for supper in this place."

# KILIMANJARO

Makari Mountains, Tanzania
May 19

A Cessna Skylane belonging to a company owned by
Akim Koshar, the spice merchant and Soviet agent,
left Zanzibar at seven thirty in the morning, flew due
north and low about ten miles off the coastline of
Tanzania, crossing the Pemba Channel. They raised
the mangrove-dotted coast of Kenya fifty-nine minutes later and the pilot made a course correction that
would take them over the southern dogleg of Tsavo
National Park and then to the Kenya side, the northern slopes, of Mount Kilimanjaro.

Michael Belov rode in the right-hand seat of the
Cessna. He had brought with him gear sufficient for a
week's stay on Kilimanjaro in the rarefied atmosphere
above fourteen thousand feet. He was also carrying
two Polaroid cameras, a dozen film packs, and a lightweight machine that was capable of rapid transmission of the developed prints to a third-generation Molniya ("Lightning") satellite in a highly elliptical,
inclined orbit above the earth. The satellite made a
twice-daily run down the African continent from the
Nile Delta to Cape St. Francis, reaching a perigee of
310 miles very near the equator and only 37 minutes
of latitude from Kilimanjaro. He could quickly let his
superiors know what, if anything, they would find in
the Catacombs.

Midmorning the pilot circled to avoid a flock of
buzzards, the greatest hazard to small planes in the

airspace over bush Africa, and set the Cessna down on an unlicensed landing ground south of the Tsavo River. They were within a few miles of the invisible, unpoliced border, on a windy burned-up plain. There was high cloud cover on Kilimanjaro.

A bearded full-bellied man named McVickers, an old Africa hand, was waiting for Belov with a Toyota Land Cruiser station wagon. McVickers helped Belov transfer his backpack from the aircraft.

"Couldn't return home without climbing the mountain, eh?"

"Because it's there," Belov explained with utmost seriousness.

"Why the Nyangoro approach to Kibo?"

"It's highly touted."

"Aye, but difficult. At the best of times." McVickers had been looking over the alpine equipment which Akim Koshar had secured for Belov on short notice. "Looks like you know what you're doing. Wouldn't set foot up there myself now. Kibo's got the shakes. She's too hot." He offered a tin of snuff, which Belov declined. "Well, let's hump it, shall we? No roads the way we're going."

"Any trouble crossing the border?"

McVickers indicated the vast dusty space around them with a broad gesture.

"That diplomatic rubbish means nothing out here. But you're wise to avoid the Moshi area. Bit of a crush what with the evacuation order. Harebrained nonsense, of course. Unless the mountain blows herself sky-high, the lower slopes are safe enough."

"You don't believe there's a chance of a major eruption?" Belov asked him as they drove away from the landing strip.

McVickers took off his hat and scratched his balding head. "Well, man. Kilimanjaro's always been an active volcano. I've lived around her all of my life. Felt her tremble. Seen her belch smoke and grit. The inner crater of Kibo—the ash pit—that can be a deadly place at any time. Fumarole gases. But this past month she's been intent on self-destruction. Throwing up old ash to seed the clouds, which has resulted in some terrific rains. Meanwhile she's heating inside and melting her glaciers. I was at seven thousand feet just the other day and heard the ice cracking. There's a good deal of electrical disturbance in the air. Washes out radio and telephone transmissions."

He tapped the gimbal compass mounted on his dashboard. "Compass has gone off, and we're not close yet. And the quakes—they're not the sharp jolts you have sometimes, a few seconds and all back to normal. They continue rhythmically for up to half an hour. Harmonic tremors, they're called. I'm told that type of movement is caused by the flow of molten rock underground. Perhaps there will be a pop-off of some sort, or a slow leak. But if 'twere me going to spend a night or two near the moraine I'd be more concerned with the rotten glacier falling down round my ears. Quite probably it's a good approximation of hell up there already. But of course you've made up your mind."

"Sounds just the sort of thing I've been hankering after," Belov said with a smile.

Raun Hardie awoke about midafternoon to the familiar vibrations of four powerful engines mounted on the overhead wings of the C-130 transport. Her mouth was dry, her lips painfully cracked from the absence of humidity. She threw off the blanket and got up from the narrow strip of canvas seats in the front of the cabin. A portable head, like a closet, had been installed against the front bulkhead, mostly for her convenience. She unzipped and used it, then coated her lips with Chapstick and peered out a round window.

They were, according to the flight plan, at twenty thousand feet, in pale-blue but turbulent air. Much lower she saw gray, packed-down clouds on to infinity, an occasional breakthrough glimpse of jungle, solid green except for the gut loops of a chocolate-brown river. Her teeth chattered from a kind of morbid excitement she hadn't been able to escape for the past twenty hours, even when catnapping. In her dreams she jumped repeatedly from the big plane; each time her parafoil boomed open faultlessly above her head. But then she would drift and drift, never coming close to the ground, drift serenely toward the nearer stars.

Raun went up to the crowded flight deck before she could bedevil herself unnecessarily trying to interpret the dream.

Five men were there: Jade and Lem Meztizo, still pale and rabbity-eyed as he tried to shake off the lingering effects of the drugs in his system; the two American pilots flying this charter freight run for Air Nigeria from Lagos to Dar es Salaam; and a navigator.

Jade and his team were sharing the plane with a full load of machinery ticketed for Tanzania: a palm-oil press, assorted hydraulics, and some reconditioned earth-moving equipment. Their own gear took almost no space in the rear cargo area. There were three Triumph dirt bikes (Jade had obtained the bike she was most familiar with—she had owned a similar model during her years on the lam in Iowa), unbreakable jerrycans of gasoline, freeze-dried food packets, clothing, lightweight camping equipment, some microelectronic communications gear. Everything had been packed into two small pallets that would be parachuted ahead of them when they reached the drop zone.

Raun patted Lem softly on one cheek. He was

wearing a big patch of bandage where he'd been shot in the head with the tranquilizer dart.

He smiled and poured for her a mug of orange juice laced with glucose, which they had taken aboard during an hour-long and dispiriting layover in Lagos. She drank it greedily and watched Matthew Jade, who was leaning over the nav station punching updated meteorological reports onto a computer console screen.

"Where are we?" she asked Lem, heartened and steadied by the rush of glucose through her system.

"Ninety miles west of Kisangani, over the heart of the Congo Basin."

"Are we close?"

"Maybe two hours."

Jade straightened and turned around. From his expression she knew the latest report wasn't all that good. That morning, waiting in the incredibly soppy heat of the West African delta, they had heard such discouraging news from Africa's preeminent meteorologist, a Nigerian, that Jade seriously considered postponing the mission—although he realized that a run of bad weather could hold them up for a week or longer, time he obviously felt he didn't have to waste. But there were dense low clouds over the Makari, ceiling nearly zero at the summits of the mountains. And, according to reports from Kigoma, a hundred miles to the north on the shore of Lake Tanganyika, a severe dust haze from the steppes had been a problem for several days.

Updated satellite photos came through just in time. They showed an appreciable thinning of the cloud cover above the eastern lakeshore, just enough of an edge to decide Jade in favor of taking off, minutes before it would have been too late to make the two-thousand-mile run across the continent by nightfall.

"How does it look?" Raun said.

"That low-pressure system in the Mozambique Channel is on the move again. It could have just enough effect on the weather to the north to sock in the Makari by the time we get there. We might have to jump fifty or a hundred miles out of our way."

Raun nodded; it was one of the reasons they had the bikes with them. They would also be of limited use on the high moors of the target area, the southeast slope of Mount Kungwe where, down around five thousand feet, she had suggested the Catacombs were to be found.

Raun had been astounded and dismayed to learn just how accurately multispectral scanners in reconnaissance satellites one hundred miles high could map any area of the earth's surface, even if it was permanently under cloud. NSA also had in some of its satellites "close look" cameras which had a ground resolution of twelve inches. She was compelled after many hours spent at the Warshield poring over hundreds of images, to commit herself to a site for the Catacombs. Raun, uncomfortably aware of Jade's unsmiling scrutiny and obsessed with the notion that he was picking her mind apart and would discover the fact that she was a bald-faced liar, exclaimed over tiny landmarks and obscure trails and eventually settled for a spot that looked hellishly difficult to reach. He was satisfied.

The mountain was distinguished by its deep ravines, which were forested, on the lake side, below five thousand feet. Most of the ravines looked alike and seemed to share a common attribute: impenetrability. The montane forest sheltered abundant animal life. Many of the images showed, in sunny meadow pockets and along streambeds, herds of bushbuck and families of chimpanzee. Even a rare gorilla troop had been detected, in awesome detail, stripping shrubs of their favorite fruit.

But now they were almost there. Soon the reckoning.

How would Matthew Jade react when he finally learned that she had taken them all for a long and expensive ride? She knew only the size of his obsession, not the reasons for it. He could be violent and shockingly cruel—the thought made a coward of her. They were all going to be very much alone, in a savage place. If Jade tried to kill her, Lem couldn't stop him. Raun wasn't sure he would want to. He was also a victim of her hoax, and he'd already had a narrow escape at the hands of the men who had taken over the ranch with their dart guns and efficient ways. A miracle Lem was still alive.

It was difficult to keep her unhappy thoughts from her eyes, so she sat in the flight engineer's seat just behind the pilots and concentrated on the bleak view forward. The copilot handed her his headset and she listened for a while to some terrible rock music from Zaïre, then nodded off.

Raun was awakened by Matthew Jade's hand against her cheek. He was down on one knee, his face a foot from hers; she looked directly into his eyes. The man she hated, and feared.

He had never touched her like that before. She felt the most explosive sexual desire she'd ever felt for any man.

"We'll be over Lake Tanganyika in fifteen minutes," Jade said. "It's show time, Raun."

Henry Landreth crouched in a drenching rain on the bleak Shyira moorland of Kilimanjaro, shivering in the thin air, and wept to discover that everything he'd counted on—the shelter, food, and clothing he needed to survive another day on the mountain—was gone.

The shelter itself, the climbing hut, was still recognizable but the roof had been knocked askew by boulders bounding down from the alpine moraine nearly three thousand feet above, and the walls were half buried in an ice-studded mud flow a hundred yards wide and six feet deep. A trickle, really, compared to what it could be. But the flow had covered the cache of supplies left, months ago, by the Chapman/Weller expedition. On the moor the tussock grass was flattened by the unusual rains, the landscape of giant lobelia and groundsel trees divided by the mud.

He saw at once that it was not an eruptive flow; then the mud would have been heated almost to the boiling point and moving over a wider area at terrific speed, up to fifty miles an hour. But this was bad enough. He was still nearly a mile from the entrance to the Catacombs. An impossible distance under the circumstances. He had dozed fitfully the night before in the bullet-damaged Land-Rover, dry but cold. At first light he had struck out boldly for the moor, thinking of the meal he would have in a few hours, the tins of milk and juice and beef that would sustain him. The warm clothing. A fire. Rain deluged him while he was still on the track in the forest. And by then he was being stalked.

Henry didn't have to see the distinctive red circle of the laser to know that. But he was spared, partly because of the twists and turns of the track through the forest cover, and because a continuous earth tremor of twenty minutes' duration had recently put the gunman at a disadvantage. It was difficult to stand your ground and shoot while that ground was rolling beneath your feet in waves that eventually numbed the fingers and toes and caused extreme nausea.

From Shyira the way ahead was progressively steeper and the footing bad. Kilimanjaro was trembling again. Henry heard rumbling, the shots of the glacier calving in the clouds that obscured Kibo's summit.

No use going on. Henry's strength was almost gone.

His thin clothing was soaked, his boots waterlogged. He had torn the flesh of his palms and the pads of his fingers on brambles; the skin of his knees and elbows was almost completely worn away and they still bled, running pink with the rainwater down his arms and legs.

He hid low behind one of the cactuslike, brown-bark groundsels, which seemed, in his incipient delirium, more like a headless creature than a tree, with fleshy light-green rosettes and purple flowers at the end of each upstanding arm. He had picked up a stone the size of a doll's head. He waited for a glimpse of his pursuer.

Henry didn't have long to wait. A family of duikers, small mountain-dwelling antelopes, burst across the heath below, at the edge of an elfin forest. He focused his attention on the bordering *Hagenia* trees, dense with hanging moss, from which the duikers had bolted. He saw Robeson Kumenyere, laser rifle in hand, just at the edge of the heath, moving around it with the stride of a confident man. He wore a rain hat with the brim turned down and a slicker and high boots. In emulation of Jumbe Kinyati, he had a Kiko Rough Meerschaum pipe clenched between his teeth. The doctor might have been on a Sunday outing rather than a mission of cold-blooded betrayal.

Henry, shivering, was flooded with anguish and loathing.

As if he felt something, perhaps the full power of Henry Landreth's tormented psyche screaming at him from a thousand feet away, Kumenyere stopped and looked up searchingly, the rifle moving slowly to the level of his shoulder. Even if he had located Henry, he was still several hundred feet beyond the effective range of the weapon. What he saw interested him more, for the moment, than his quarry. A river of mud, rock, and ice was slowly on the move across the moor, crushing everything in its path, piling up now with increased speed due to the pressure of immeasurable tons of moraine mass displaced by cascading glacier ice and huge boulders and thinned to a molasses consistency by the incessant rain.

In his hiding place, waiting intently for Kumenyere to come close enough so he could leap up and knock his brains out with the stone in his hand, Henry was unaware that the mud had begun to creep again. He felt it first as a clammy tentacle slopping over one bare leg and looked around in surprise, then horror. He pulled his leg free, but a wave-surge of mud into the hollow behind the groundsel tree buried him nearly waist deep. Terrified, he twisted and dragged himself free of the sucking mud and rolled downhill for a dozen yards. He hit his head on a rock, sat up dazed, staggered blindly to his feet precious seconds later. The river of mud, gaining impetus as it pushed downhill, caught him again and threw him against the silky nightmare of an ostrich-plume lobelia.

He screamed. This time he could barely claw his way out of danger. And by now his weight had doubled from the clinging mud, his steps were clumsy. The head of the long slide sucked and slobbered after him, lurching along the ground; the body followed with a massive fluid grace. Henry's enormous feet became entangled; he crashed down and was gobbled to the elbows as he struggled to stay upright. This time he was too weak to escape. He was pummeled and pushed along. With his arms free he was able to make frantic swimming motions, thrusting his head high.

The pressure of the deep mud threatened to cave in his chest. He screamed again, hopelessly, as the mass, spreading over an ever-widening area, came to a precarious standstill. But Henry was phasing into shock, and he had difficulty breathing. His skin was white, his lips blue. He made a final sorry effort to heave himself free, and fainted.

Robeson Kumenyere found Henry faceup, three-quarters immersed in the thick motionless river. He aimed his rifle and clicked on the laser; the red spot appeared perfectly centered on Henry's closed right eye. The eyelid twitched, flickered, rose partway. Henry stared unseeingly at the muzzle of the rifle, and lapsed again into unconsciousness.

Kumenyere found he couldn't, needn't, pull the trigger. He gazed at the enormous tide of mud and rock poised at Henry's throat. In a matter of a few hours, depending on the rain, the flow would continue, instantly pulling Henry under. A new series of earth-shocks would certainly do the trick. And if for some reason the slide abated, in time he would still be picked clean to the white skull bones by the first passing animal or bird with a taste for human meat.

"Have an interesting death, Henry," Kumenyere said gently.

He put his rifle on his shoulder and walked back down the mountain.

Raun Hardie felt her ears pop as the C-130 descended more steeply to eleven thousand feet above Lake Tanganyika. The starboard cargo door was open. She was about to make the third parachute jump of her life, and she couldn't see much of anything down there yet, although the dense gray mat of cloud just beneath them was thinning rapidly, to the consistency of heavy cigar smoke. She picked up a weak glitter of sunlight on water. Leaning forward, she thought she could see the pale-green slopes of the Makari headland, familiar from all those hundreds of photos. And the dun-colored, rounded summit of Kungwe.

The pilot was now altering course slightly. Too bad if something went wrong, she thought, and they wound up in the drink. It was the seventh-largest and second-deepest lake in the world. Almost a mile deep. Closer to shore it was shallower, but then, of course, you had the crocodiles to contend with.

Raun was first in line—she would go just after the cargo master and his crew unloaded the pallets. All of the parachutes should come down within a radius of three hundred yards, with split-second timing. That is, if everyone did his thing correctly.

Lem Meztizo tapped her shoulder, and Raun looked around. He held up four fingers. And counting. She tried to swallow, and chewed the wad of gum in her cheek more ferociously. Behind Lem, Matthew Jade was plugged into the flight deck, talking to the pilot. She couldn't hear anything above the whistle and roar of the big engines up ahead. She turned back, facing forward, flexing her knees. Something in the sky caught her attention, but it disappeared from view so quickly she didn't know if it had been another plane, a large bird, or just a shadow on the clouds—their shadow.

Nothing else to do but wait, and try not to count off the seconds, Raun checked and rechecked the parachute harness, the static-line hookup, then watched the crew chief, who also was wearing headphones. The land was nearer, the surface of the lake rushing away beneath what had become a yellowish particulate haze. But the plane had slowed perceptibly.

It happened with the suddenness of being shot from a cannon. Green lights flashed, the cargo master and his team lunged synchronously, pallets tumbled one after another out the door. It was her turn. Raun took two running steps and leaped, doing a half twist away from the fuselage as she cleared the door space.

The slipstream blow, the quick surge of falling,

then the great booming canopy overhead. Nothing to
it. Raun got her breath back, shot a look at the receding Hercules, saw Lem's chute open, then Jade's. They
were strung out like trinkets on a necklace about a
quarter of a mile apart. But the two men were already
maneuvering, closing the distance between them and
the landing zone.

Raun looked down to orient herself, and was grateful for the excellent color photographs Jade had insisted she study. Despite the bothersome haze it was
all very familiar: the rugged contours of the land she
was drifting to meet; semiarid highlands and the jagged treeline below. Off to her left she had a glimpse
of the shore. The wind was taking her north at almost
ten knots. She pulled at the lift webs to alter the
shape of the canopy and compensate for drift, glanced
up again.

It was coming very fast, straight at her out of nowhere, and there was no sound. All the thunder of the
Tumansky turbojet engine was well behind the MiG
Fishbed fighter-interceptor. For three terrifying seconds she descended into its path, totally helpless,
while the delta-wing jet closed from one mile away
with a gradual sound of the sky tearing open. The jet
had a black pencil-sharp nose and two Atoll AAM's
mounted on wing pylons. She could clearly see the
head of the pilot inside the canopy. He had to have
seen Raun, no way to miss her. Therefore he intended
to run her down.

But before this flash of thought and her mounting
terror could crystallize into the certain knowledge of
her imminent death, the Fishbed barrel rolled and
flashed by over the lake almost too fast for her brain
to register the image. Then she was buffeted by a severe shock wave that came close to collapsing the
chute overhead. Her eardrums ached.

Adrenaline was still pumping madly as she hit the

ground and tucked and rolled and was dragged thirty yards by an unexpectedly fierce gust of wind across the friable skin of the alpine plateau. When she had the sagging canopy under control and was out of harness, she stood trembling, her body streaming wet beneath the jump suit. She scanned the plateau and thought she saw someone else come down in a collapsing blossom of chute about two hundred yards over the crest of a ridge.

Raun was astonished to find that she barely had the strength to stroll a dozen feet to one of the pallets and sit on it. She took off her helmet and put her head between her knees and rested like that until she heard the unnerving scream of the jet coming back. Or was it a different one?

*Now what?* she thought, but she didn't trouble to look up.

"Stop here."

Michael Belov heard the sound of the helicopter's turbine engine in the yard of the Nyangoro Coffee Cooperative. They had approached the plantation circuitously from the west and were traveling along a muddy track between neat straight rows of coffee shrubs. When McVickers stopped the Land Cruiser, Belov got out and continued on foot until he could see the orange metal roofs of the buildings and the rotor blades of the Raven helicopter turning. They turned slowly and it was apparent that the pilot was not about to take off.

It had not rained for an hour. There were hot flashes of sun through the streaming low clouds. Belov found concealment behind a heap of irrigation pipe. The pilot cut his engine, climbed on top of the heilcopter with his kit of wrenches, and made more adjustments on the rotor hub. The helicopter had the colors and markings of the Air Defense Wing. A radio was playing music but the pilot was, as far as Belov could tell, alone on the coop.

A tremor ran through the land, causing the pipes to rattle. Thinking the pile might collapse, Belov backed off a little way. After three or four minutes the tremor subsided.

He found it reasonable to believe that Kumenyere, after leaving his villa, had been driven to the nearest airport, where the copter had picked him up for the flight to Kilimanjaro. Here the copter had been grounded, probably for repairs. But Belov recalled that the Raven had an operational ceiling of only about ten thousand feet. Therefore, if Kumenyere was not here, undoubtedly he had pushed on up the mountain on foot, to an elevation of ten thousand feet or better, where the cloud cover was heavy. And he must have had a good idea beforehand where Henry Landreth could be found.

About twenty minutes later Robeson Kumenyere came walking down off the mountain. Alone. His boots were caked with mud. He carried the laser rifle in one hand. He went directly to the helicopter. A few feet away he suddenly raised his rifle over his head, a gesture of exultation. He did a little tribal dance to emphasize his triumph. The hunter home from the kill. It sent a cold shockwave through Belov's gut. Then Kumenyere wearily let down his pack and climbed into the helicopter beside the pilot; Belov couldn't see him clearly any longer.

Within a couple of minutes the engine started, the rotor blades achieved lift-off pitch, and the copter rose slowly. Belov crept back to the pile of rust-pitted pipe. He watched as the helicopter swung around above the trees and then flew southwest, in the general direction of Arusha.

He went back to the Land Cruiser. It was two thirty in the afternoon. He had McVickers follow the track where he'd first seen Kumenyere. It was not much to go on, but the ruts told of a big four-wheel drive vehicle that had passed that way during the last twenty-four hours.

Twenty minutes' tortuous driving from the cooperative they came to the abandoned Land-Rover, which looked like the backplate in a target gallery. The holes were small enough to have been made by .22s, the caliber of Kumenyere's rifle. He had thrown enough lead to disable the Rover, but otherwise the ambush was a futile one. There was no blood anywhere inside. If Landreth had been hit it wasn't serious, at least not right away. The key was in the ignition. The engine was dead cold, so the ambush hadn't happened recently. A spider spinning its web from steering wheel to dash panel suggested the vehicle had sat there at least overnight. There were crushed cigarette butts on the floorboards, a pack of them. Perhaps he had sat smoking nervously in the dark all night while Kumenyere enjoyed a restful snooze back at the coffee coop's lodge. Which might have given him a head start at dawn.

Belov tried the ignition but the engine wouldn't turn over. He and McVickers couldn't push the Land-Rover far enough to one side to allow the Toyota to pass. The Russian put on his foul-weather mountain gear and shouldered his backpack, which weighed close to thirty-five pounds. McVickers backed slowly away with a wave of his hand, and Belov continued up the track.

After a few minutes rain set in, a blowing drizzle that seeped to his skin despite his weatherproof clothing and worsened the footing. He fell several times, and his progress at best was excruciatingly slow. The air was thinner, much colder; he could see his breath. When the track became steeper he used his alpine ax to keep from sliding backward. All along the way he could still make out two sets of slurred bootprints. Two going up, one returning. It would not have surprised him to come across Henry Landreth's body by the side of the track as he moved steadily higher. He thought he was somewhere around ten thousand feet. Visibility was poor. From time to time the earth was uneasy beneath his feet, not precisely shaking: It felt a little as if he were walking across the back of a living creature. He heard a low rumbling that prickled the hairs on the back of his neck.

Slowly the dense creeper, brier, and giant ferns began to thin and he had a glimpse of a moor half smothered in cloud. The forest trees became noticeably smaller, hung with Saint-John's-wort and orchids. They were more widely spaced, forming pleasant glades rather than dense impenetrable tracts.

He emerged onto a devastated landscape that was thick with mud as far as he could see; it was as if he were looking at the canted bottom of a lake violently and completely drained of its waters. The mud, called lahar, was piled up in places in a soft wall five or six feet high; it contained some awesome boulders and huge chunks of ice clear as diamonds, unimaginably ancient ice now being shed by the glacier somewhere above in blinding fog and cloud.

There seemed to be no way to get through the mudslide—he would have to feel his way around it. But he was tired now; he had to rest. His eyes settled on a raft of timbers that looked as if they had formed a roof of some kind, perhaps the roof of a climbers' hut. The timbers were about forty feet away in the morass. The mud had swallowed the rest.

Belov, cold and dispirited, poured a shot of brandy from a sterling flask, never taking his eyes off the glistening mud. He had the uneasy feeling that the entire mass might suddenly pour down, with a loud plopping sound, like catsup from an upended bottle.

He swallowed the fiery brandy, then suddenly and angrily put his hands to his mouth and shouted.

"Hello! Henry Landreth! Can you hear me?"

The echoes bounced cheerlessly, frustratingly across the wide moorland.

It was schoolboy's pique; he'd known from the beginning that the odds were impossibly long. From bootprints on the ground it was apparent that Robeson Kumenyere also had turned back at this point. But his brief celebration before boarding the helicopter was testimony to his success. Undoubtedly he'd overtaken Landreth here and left him dead, perhaps in a narrow vale now deep in gelid mud.

At the corner of his eye Belov saw a tiny flare of red. It was next to nothing, a pinprick of light, attractant because of its contrast to the monotonous mud landscape. It could have been a late shaft of sun striking a piece of quartz at a specific angle to bring out the refracted color, but although there was a glow of sunset in the west, the fading daylight was diffused by the cloud cover. He looked to his right but didn't see the light again. All he saw were rocks of all sizes, smashed and uprooted trees with skinny trunks and large crowns of green leaves, thousands of pieces of ice embedded in the lahar.

Still . . .

He took binoculars from his pack and straightened, but before he could raise the glasses to his eyes he saw the tiny blip of red again. He focused hurriedly on the quadrant from which the glow was emanating. He couldn't locate it. He began a search pattern, noting the almost jellylike consistency of the mud, the thin puddles of rainwater on the undulant surface, some torn blossoms, and the time: The time was five twenty-three. The date was—

Belov lowered the glasses disbelievingly, a rictus of a smile appearing. He raised them again and saw the uplifted hands and a bony wrist, the large black lozenge and stainless band of a quartz LED watch, the slant red numerals. A trembling finger depressed a button on the side of the case. The display vanished. Then it was on again. Five twenty-four. He cocked the binoculars a little to the right of the watch and brought into view the mummified head of Henry Landreth, mud everywhere except for the black holes of nostils, eyes, shrunken mouth.

"Hang on!" Belov called. "I'm coming!"

There was no immediate response; then he saw the blinking of a mud-thickened eyelash, the fingers of Henry's left hand closing weakly in a try at a clenched-fist salute.

*Alive.*

"I'll get you out!" Belov said reassuringly. But even as he spoke he realized how very near impossible it would be to effect a rescue without sacrificing his own life in the attempt. Still, without Henry Landreth he couldn't hope to get his hands on the red diamonds, and the FIREKILL formula.

He was already working as he tried to think of a surefire solution. Henry was some forty yards uphill and to his right, well into the flow of mud which Belov now perceived to be moving, very slowly, piling up more thickly in some places than in others. The depth of the mud surrounding Henry was difficult to gauge: perhaps five feet. He seemed to be buried in it on his back and at an angle, his head downhill.

Should Belov wade up into the mud, he might quickly become immobile. Perhaps, no matter how careful he tried to be, he would step into a depression in the uneven moorland and sink over his head.

He was carrying two hundred coiled feet of a light but tough Dacron rope, his best bet if Henry retained sufficient strength in the cold mud bath to seize it. In the late seventies Belov had spent eight weeks touring the United States, and had enjoyed a couple of days on a dude ranch in Arizona. There a sometime movie cowboy and stunt man named Zane Grey Glenburn had taught him how to make and throw a lasso. The rope he now had in his hands lacked the weight of the lariat he'd used on the ranch, and he wasn't sure he could reach Henry, but there was no other real hope.

"I'm throwing a rope! Hold up your arm as high as you can—give me something to aim at!"

He edged closer to Henry along the perimeter of the moving mud, and as he did so was distracted by an unexpected and unnerving sight. On the raft of timbers that had been the roof of the climbing hut a tawny cheetah was sitting, watching him. The cheetah's face, at a distance, looked as stylized as a Noh mask; typically feline eyes a vivid yellow in the dying light, black teardrop patterns bracketing the short nose from the inside of each eye to the corners of the mouth. The tips of the steely whiskers had a peculiar radiance, like St. Elmo's fire.

It wasn't possible to tell how the creature had so cleanly reached the raft; perhaps by springing from one boulder after another across the coffee-colored mud. And, he thought, sparing the matter a few moments, cheetahs were plains animals, common enough in the flatlands of the Serengeti, where their starling bursts of speed augmented their hunting skills. But probably a lone cheetah was unheard of at this altitude. What had brought it here?

His fascination with the animal was short-lived; it looked well fed and couldn't be any danger to him. And he had to be quick about getting Henry unstuck. There was very little left of him above the surface.

Henry had heard, and tried to obey, Belov's command. But the arm he thrust higher shook and fell back to the mud. Now almost all of his head was sub-merged.

"Here it comes!"

Belov made a big whirling loop to one side of his body as Zane Grey Glenburn had taught, and threw the lasso forty feet. The loop, six feet in diameter, landed around Henry and he began to draw it tighter. Henry still had his other hand free.

"Try to push it down under your arm!" Belov shouted when the mud-laden Dacron loop had drawn closer and tighter around Henry. Obviously Henry no longer could lift his head from the ooze; but his left hand felt slowly around for the rope and closed on it, drew it down to the elbow of his right arm, pushed it beneath the mud. Not very far. Belov gave a slow steady pull on the line, setting the loop around what he hoped was Henry's shoulder. When his cautious pull resulted in a taut line he was ready for the desper-ate business of trying to yank Henry home without suf-focating him along the way.

"We need leverage! Grasp the line above your head with your left hand!"

Belov waited impatiently for Henry to respond. Henry needed three tries to reach high enough to take hold of the line inches above his face.

Belov's breath was smoking; he felt the cold even through his mountaineer's sweater and knit cap and marveled at the spark that had kept Henry alive, even at this low ebb, for what might have been hours.

"Now! Give me all the help you can—you're dead weight!"

Belov belayed the Dacron line around his waist and chest; the line ran tight back over one shoulder. He heaved with what he thought was all his strength and felt no give, no momentum beginning, which shocked him; it was like trying single-handedly to yank a whale off the ocean floor.

He sobbed with effort, finding it difficult, even in nailed boots, to get a good purchase on the sodden heath. He bent nearly double, trembling violently, willing himself to sustain the effort.

Another man might have cursed, or prayed. Belov did John Wayne.

"Well, Pilgrim . . . don't know how you got yourself . . . pinned down in that hog waller, but . . . it's gonna be all right. . . . The Duke ain't lost . . . a poor wayward Pilgrim . . . yet, and he ain't . . . about to start now . . . ayuh."

The tight line around his chest was having the undesirable effect of cutting off some of his wind, and he felt as if he were drifting off into a field of sparkling stars, out of touch with his fingers, his stomping boots.

Then the line seemed to part behind him and, with no way to put the brakes on, he pitched head over heels down the slope.

It took him half a minute to get to his feet; his head cleared slowly. He had gashed his chin and blood dripped steadily. He shoved a gloved finger against the wound to stanch the blood and turned in despair.

He saw that it hadn't been the line after all. Nor had he pulled Henry Landreth's right arm out of socket. The mud had yielded Henry whole, and he had come skimming and slicking down the heath after Belov. He was lying motionless, faceup, in a freshened rain. There was not an inch of Henry uncoated with mud, hair and hide, but the rain began slowly to clean him up.

Belov fetched his canteen to help nature along, and the flask of brandy. Henry took a long drink of water, choked, spat and spat streams of brown water. His skin was too blue, and Belov was worried. He poured a few drops of the brandy at a time on Henry's tongue and began to strip him in order to wrap him in one of the wool blankets from his pack.

Henry put a hand on his arm, a gesture of gratitude. "Did you see them?" he whispered. Belov was astonished to hear any sound from him other than wheezing, choking, and gasping.

"What?" He looked back over his shoulder, at the raft of timbers. The cheetah had vanished.

*"They,"* Henry continued, as if it were of vital importance, "did not want me to die. I thought they would be angry. But they came down to watch over me. Otherwise, don't you see—I'd have given up."

"I haven't seen anyone."

"No?"

"Who are you talking about?"

"The Lords of the Storm," Henry explained, his voice almost inaudible. "They ruled the earth—or at least the continent of Africa—ten thousand years ago." Henry's dirty forehead creased in a frown. He tried to take a look around, but hadn't the strength.

Belov, sitting him up naked to get a blanket around him, could almost see the wild beating of his heart in the thin cage of bones that was his chest. As far as Belov could tell, Henry hadn't been shot. But he was having trouble breathing. He looked very ill from prolonged exposure on the inhospitable mountain, and apparently was delirious.

He could lose the Englishman, Belov thought, gritting his teeth. After years at his trade he had an instinct about the nearness of death. He began rubbing Henry's body furiously in an attempt to restore circulation, to draw some warmth from the tepid veins. After all the luck they'd both had, *bloody hell*, Henry just wasn't going to duck out on him now!

# MOMELA LAKES, TANZANIA

**Camp David, Maryland**
**May 20**

The four men from the Soviet Union met at Chanvai
with Jumbe Kinyati and Robeson Kumenyere at ten
thirty in the morning, following an all-night flight
from Moscow to Kilimanjaro airport. The delegation
had been handpicked by the thirteen members of the
Politburo to provide a convincing demonstration of
the faith they had in Jumbe's bloodstones.

Two of the men, scientists of formidable brilliance,
had never before been allowed to travel outside the
Motherland. Grigor Atunyan was director of the Center for High-Energy Physics in Protvino, and Ardalion
Udaltsov, known as the Russian Einstein, did his
thinking at an institute named for him in the city of
Obninsk, which was devoted exclusively to scientific
facilities.

They were chaperoned, so to speak, by Vasili Obadashev, a deputy director (First Chief Directorate) of
the KGB and a protégé of the director; and by Alek-
sandr Kekilova, head of the powerful Administrative
Organs Department of the Central Committee, also a
protégé—of the strongman of the U.S.S.R., the general
secretary of the Communist Party.

A full support group of interpreters, secretaries, and
KGB officers had accompanied them. A corollary purpose of the trip was to make contact with Michael Belov, who was known to have left Zanzibar on the morning of the nineteenth for Kalimanjaro. But where he

was now, and what he was up to, remained a mystery that irritated Vasili Obadashev. Particularly because it was now clear that Cobra Dance's mission to the Warshield ranch had been a dismal failure. Undoubtedly Matthew Jade was at this moment well on his way to Tanzania, or already in the country.

Obadashev was a small man with narrow shoulders and no meat on his bones, temples that stood out so prominently on a high forehead they looked like the bumps of horns about to sprout, accentuating a decidedly devilish appearance. He wore thick glasses that threw his eyes into unsettling relief, as if they lived independently of his face.

He said to Jumbe, "The red diamond which we have seen is a remarkable artifact. The etchings found on it are, according to our scientists, part of a stringent mathematical model that has to do with the fluid-dynamic stability of plasmoids."

"Interesting," Udaltsov said, with a nod. He was rough as a peasant, in stature almost a giant but with arms so short he had to bend over to unzip his fly.

"Interesting," Kekilova continued. In a black suit and sweater and tieless white collar, he looked rather like an Irish priest. "But hardly enough to persuade us to reach into our hip pockets and hand over IRBMs in barter for those diamonds required to formulate the antimissile device known as FIREKILL."

Jumbe, his eyes heavy lidded, let that one just hang there. It was hot in the room, with the louvers of the windows nearly closed to shut out the sun's glare. Jumbe had apologized; the air conditioner was not working. But perhaps he only wanted the unacclimatized Russians to sweat.

Robeson Kumenyere sipped iced tea and studied the faces in front of him, and kept an eye on his pocket watch as he had promised to do, because of Jumbe's delicate health.

Jumbe said finally, "I'm not surprised to hear this. Only that it required so many of you, on short notice, to tell me."

Obadashev smiled. "Obviously our reservations fall short of outright rejection of your terms. We would like, however, to propose a somewhat more equitable method of determining the . . . scientific value of the so-called FIREKILL stones. I assume we will not be allowed to speak to any of your own experts, among them Dr. Henry Landreth, I believe."

"Presently unavailable," Kumenyere said. His pocket watch chimed delicately. Rather deliberately he lifted his sable eyes to Obadashev's face, who steepled his hands and stared back, reading Kumenyere like a well-loved book. He wondered if Jumbe realized the danger he was in from this smooth dandy. But that, for now, was of no concern to the KGB man.

"We thought so," Kekilova said. "Therefore we propose to leave Comrade Altunyan and Comrade Udaltsov at Chanvai until the twenty-ninth of May, with the understanding that they will be allowed, under conditions agreeable to you, Comrade Kinyati, to examine a series—although not the complete series—of the relevant bloodstones, therefore arriving at some degree of certainty of their ultimate worth to us. They are, of course, among the great scientific minds in the world today. Their assurances will guarantee immediate shipment of the requested Scoundrel missiles, and the crews to launch them. These weapons are already being prepared for rapid delivery."

Jumbe celebrated this news with a glum shrug of his shoulders.

"It is a great honor to be afforded the opportunity of extending hospitality to such eminent men. As for allowing them access to certain of the bloodstones which make up the FIREKILL model, you know as well as I why that is impossible. It would be useless to withhold key stones from men of such dazzling ability. Even a hint or two could provide the theoretical links that would enable them to arrive at the correct formulations, and they are easily memorized. Which event, in less than ten days' time, would leave me holding several handfuls of beautiful rare red diamonds—and the bag. My eldest son, who spent some time in the United States a few years ago, could have best summarized my feelings with an expression I detest but which seems particularly apt now. Comrades, stop jerking me off."

Obadashev frowned and, although he prided himself on his command of English, he was forced to glance at his interpreter. Who shrugged, baffled. An oppressive silence followed.

Kumenyere snapped shut the lid of his pocket watch and got to his feet.

"That will do for today, I think," he said softly, smiling at the delegation from the U.S.S.R. Jumbe silently shuffled from the room.

Only the Americans were left to be heard from. And time was getting away from them all.

Luncheon at Camp David, on a screened porch amid gorgeous flowering dogwoods, consisted of a seafood sausage appetizer, sweetbreads in Madeira sauce, quail in pastry served with white grapes, wine to suit.

Nobody was hungry.

Boomer, his face more florid than usual, said to John Guy Gibson: "She's screwed us, hasn't she? But good."

"It looks as if that was her intention all along," Gibby said, looking at the other men on the porch. Stephen Gage, the president's national security advisor, was there. So was Morgan Atterbury, the secretary of defense; General of the Army John Crew Landis, chairman of the joint chiefs; and Secretary of State Robert Dilks. Gibby referred again to the report he'd received an hour ago from his office in Langley, Virginia.

"Miss Hardie has been careful about lying to us. In going over all the taped conversations she had with Matthew Jade, we found she never affirmed that the Catacombs were in the Makari Mountains. When pressed to designate a site from Landsat photos, she said, quote: 'This looks most like the area I remember.' But mountain terrain is mountain terrain, anywhere in the world."

"Some difference," Stephen Gage muttered. "So she didn't lie. She just let your superspy believe what he wanted to believe."

"I understand she was never told of the importance of the Catacombs," Robert Dilks said. He was a tall, inelegant man whose socks never seemed to reach high enough, whose tie was always unraveling, whose haircuts, self-administered, were a scandal. His virtues in international diplomacy were his tireless mind and a witty skepticism. He wished all people well, and expected the worst from them.

"That's correct," Gibby said.

"Her attitude might have improved if you'd been straight with her. Wasn't she entitled to know our little secret? It's her neck too."

Gibby grimaced unhappily. "She was, after all, in prison for crimes against the Federal government."

"How did you get onto her, Gibby?" General Landis asked.

"Our chief of station in Tanzania checked out Raun's story. It seems she was hospitalized briefly in Dar for treatment of a severely sprained ankle, as she claimed. But records of the flying medic service indicate she was flown to Dar from the base of Mount Kilimanjaro, not the Makari Mountains. The pilot, who is now employed by Saga Oil in Benin, was tracked down. He remembered both Macdonald Hardie and his daughter."

Boomer said, "So with all the trouble we've gone to, they're sitting on a mountain at the wrong end of the country. Have you been in touch with Matt?"

"Goddard Space Flight Center can't lock him. There's a solar jam on. Our communications satellites may be deaf and blind for the next twelve hours."

"In the meantime," Boomer said, "a delegation of Russians met with Jumbe today at four thirty A.M. our time. They may have struck a deal."

"I saw the South African ambassador at eight this morning," Dilks said. "He placed most of their cards on the table. They know about the bloodstones, but not what the symbols represent. I told him we were not prepared at this time to make any comment on Jumbe's diamonds. But I assured him that the United States had not offered, and would not offer in the future, tactical nuclear weapons to Jumbe. Ambassador Wolkers informed me that round-the-clock photo reconnaissance of Tanzania is being maintained. If the Russians attempt to deploy either men or arms in the country, the attempt will be repelled forcibly by squadrons of the South African Air Force."

Boomer glanced at General Landis. "What kind of strength are they dealing from?"

"They can hit any target inside Tanzania with a squadron of Buccaneers. Thousand-pound bombs, Bullpups. They have the transports available to put a force of one thousand commandos on the ground in the first wave of an all-out assault. It would be pretty damned effective."

"What bothers me," Gage said, "is how the Russians would take it."

"What could they do about it?" Morgan Atterbury said. "Declare war on South Africa? Why bother? That government has more problems now than it can hope to survive. The discontent of its own white population, indefensible borders, hostile neighbors, well-armed and sophisticated Umkhonto guerrillas operating throughout the Transvaal. The Russians would be more than willing to sacrifice a few IRBMs and personnel in exchange for the bloodstones. It's not inconceivable they would anticipate such a move on the part of the South Africans and send unusable or obsolete missiles, expecting that they'd be destroyed as soon as they were unloaded."

"For that matter," General Landis said to Morgan, "would Jumbe know a functional nuclear warhead if he saw one? Libya has been trying to buy nuclear weapons for years. Qaddafi has been stung twice by con artists a lot less sophisticated than the Russians."

"Any of the physicists Jumbe's detaining would be able to tell."

"What we can't ascertain at this point," Dilks said, "is Jumbe's response to the delegation of our Soviet friends. Was there a deal?"

"They beat it back home too soon," Boomer suggested.

"Probably they wanted to see more stones," Morgan said. "In exchange for the usual vague promises. If so, they misjudged Jumbe."

"How long will it take Matt to get to Kilimanjaro from where he is?" Boomer asked Gibby.

"It's six hundred miles. He's virtually on foot. If they're picked up in that part of the country, which is a war zone, they'll either be shot or put in jail."

"Can we support him? Helicopters from a carrier?"

"No. The Makari Mountains are just about unreachable from the sea. And any carrier movements off the coast of East Africa would be big news."

"Even if he gets to Kilimanjaro in time," Morgan said, "it's a big mountain. You ought to see it from the air."

"Hell, Matt has a week! He can do miracles in a week."

"What if Raun Hardie still won't cooperate?" Gage said, helping himself to a glass of Chateau Latour-Pauillac.

Boomer said grimly, "It'll take Jade maybe the better part of an hour to reduce her to a big quivering pile of wet snot."

"Just thought I'd ask," Gage said.

# IRINGA HIGHLANDS

Makari Mountains, Tanzania
May 21

For Oliver Ijumaa, the coming of dawn meant only another night he had survived, another day he must somehow live through.

He awoke, to the crowing of roosters, in a section of concrete drainpipe padded with folded cardboard cartons. He trembled from the cold at five thousand feet. His broken, festering fingers began to throb hideously. Blistered burns cracked and oozed at every movement of his body. He crawled to the mouth of the pipe and looked out at the corrugated iron roofs of Iringa, a town of twenty-five thousand people that sat on a high, gusty, rockbound bluff.

In two days he had walked and jogged almost ninety miles through nearly trackless bush country, through heat and dust and swarms of insects attracted to his suppurating flesh, walked unprotected in clothing that was nothing but charred rags. All of his possessions (except for the stolen gold) had been lost in the holocaust of Von Kreutzen's Shooting Palace.

But now he wore a black suit with pink pinstripes he had taken from a corpse in a Hehe village southwest of Iringa.

Only desperation that bordered on insanity had prompted him to squeeze through a window in the small back room of the house while the villagers gathered in mourning beneath the trees in the front yard. It was dusk. He was looking for food, just a little of

the abundance heaped on the family of the departed,
nothing that could rob another living soul of suste-
nance. He was not, by nature or habit, a thief, though
sometimes he made no distinction between scrounging
and thievery. When he saw, in the guttering candle-
light, the long gaunt old man with his hands folded on
his chest, despair had combined with fatigue and pain
to defeat reason. The suit would very nearly fit him:
He and the dead man were of the same length, and
Oliver could not be any skinnier if he had lain in his
own grave for the past three months. The suit was
going nowhere but into the ground. And the magnificent shoes—

The wing-tip, black-and-white perforated shoes,
perhaps more than a quarter of a century old, were
too narrow and tight to walk in for long distances, but
they were necessary to complete the illusion of an appearance. Completely outfitted, with the ruins of his
bush shirt well concealed, standing downwind of anyone who might smell his wounds, he looked like a man
who had a life to go to.

But it was another man's appearance, he now realized, as he crouched on all fours looking out at the
still-sleeping town. A harsh wind was making a shoal
of rubbish along the tree-lined main street. The pipe
in which he had spent the night was for a culvert under construction, which would divert the waters of a
river beneath the highway. He was safe here until the
road crews reported for work. In town, by daylight, it
would surely be another story. The disappearance of
the suit and shoes, thus robbing the dignity of the
dead man at his own wake, undoubtedly had caused a
tribal uproar.

Last night, hanging around the back steps to the
kitchen of the Lions' Club in Iringa, where the annual
dinner-dance was in progress, Oliver had eaten his
first meal in days—a plate of *machicha na nyama*,

beef and spinach, slipped to him by a sympathetic waitress he had chatted up and who liked his style. She would certainly recall him if she heard about the stolen suit of clothes. Following any kind of hue and cry, the trigger-happy local People's Militia, thirsting for blood to relieve their boredom, would shoot him on sight.

Oliver had no wish to stay in Iringa a minute longer than necessary. But he had only a sketchy idea of where he was. He had left Bekele Big Springs knowing only that Kilimanjaro lay far to the north along Tanzania's Great North Road—and that road ran through Iringa. But it was much too far to walk. He had no money for bus fare, no identification. He was afraid to expose himself to hitch a ride.

He didn't know how desperately slim his chances were, even if he reached Kilimanjaro, of finding the man who had stolen his gold, broken his fingers, cruelly left him to burn to death. Oliver didn't have the name but he would never forget the face: the mane of black hair, the sullen grin, the look of vacancy which came into Tiernan Clarke's crafty eyes just before his spells of walking about and mumbling to himself. The calculating sag of Clarke's eyelids at the mention of rare red diamonds. Not a good man for Erika to be with, Oliver was sure of that. The man would want the diamonds; something else Oliver was sure of. He would force Erika to take him to where the diamonds were hidden.

Oliver had no concept of how enormous Kilimanjaro was. In his mind it was simply another mountain. He had climbed many mountains looking for gemstones; he would climb this one until he found Erika and the man he was going to kill.

He had nothing going for him but this obsession, which had been powerful enough to see him through two and a half days of incredible hardship. But the early morning was cold, he was hungry again, and probably in danger. For all of his trekking he was still approximately nowhere. His spirits were not high, and falling like a barometer before a bad blow. There was no traffic on the highway that was being improved just a few yards from where he was holed up. The pressure of leaning on his hands was almost unbearable in the crooked mangled sticks of two broken fingers.

Oliver backed slowly away from the opening of the drainpipe, until cardboard crumpled beneath his knees. He lay down again, sadly, eyes open. Before long they blinked slow tears. He gradually slipped into a stupefying depression, from which he was unable to rouse himself.

Day Three, Makari.

Raun Hardie awoke in her sleeping bag inside the small tent on Kungwe's south slope, hearing the barks and grunts of early-rising chimpanzees in the forest nearby. She'd observed a family of chimps near dusk the night before, in the glade where they were camped. The chimps were adroitly "fishing" in a termite mound with blades of bamboo for the toothsome grubs. After eating their fill, a couple of the chimps, one a big male who would weigh more than a hundred pounds, had reconnoitered the encampment, pausing to deny their curiosity by doing backflips. In this remote place they might never have seen another human being. They were good company, and Raun had always enjoyed having them around. But she didn't try to get too friendly. The chimpanzees could, for no apparent reason, become hostile, and one of them might remove part of her face with a single powerful swipe of a long forearm.

She sat up, propping herself on one elbow. She

smelled coffee. Already! The knowledge that she would soon have to face Matthew Jade again took her mind off the chimps' conversation.

On arrival they had quickly been sealed off by clouds, and the jets (Jade had spotted more than one during his descent) were no longer a problem. But obviously their arrival in Tanzania had been noted and reported. He decided to move their projected campsite as far away as they could walk before dark, carrying on their backs just the necessities. The bikes would leave tracks too easy to follow, so they abandoned them.

He selected a site with a steep wall of rock at their backs, an exposed heath between them and the lake, a trickle of a stream on one side. Continuing clouds would make it impossible to find them again from the air.

After gulping reconstituted meals that were hot but not particularly palatable, Jade and Raun shared a tent just big enough for the two of them to sit with their knees touching and a lamp between them. They reoriented themselves according to the photomaps Jade had brought. Lem stood guard with an Israeli-made Galili assault rifle until Jade could relieve him.

Raun's head was heavy with fatigue. A leopard screeched, elephants flatted their trumpet solos. She wondered what it would be like to put her head in his lap and go to sleep. The desire for sex with him was the same as the desire to be punished, she knew that. Odd how she could be thrilled and scared pea green at the same time. She wanted to touch him, to somehow let him know how confused she was. But she couldn't.

Day two had been sullen but rainless. Jade spent the first daylight hours exploring, alone, and came back with bad news.

"This isn't the place, Raun."

She summoned the necessary surprise. "It isn't!"

"The elephant track is just that. Nothing's been up here *but* elephants. A major expedition involving dozens of people would have left plenty of traces, no matter how thoroughly the Tanzanian government tried to clean up after them. This is virgin bush."

"I was so *sure*."

"We'll look around," he said encouragingly. "It'll come back to you."

"I hope so."

It was a miserably hard day. Purgatorial. Because there was nothing to do but climb up and down dry streambeds that at times were almost vertical. And look perplexed and crestfallen. And suffer the added stress of his growing disbelief. By day's end Raun was grim and shaking. She felt, self-righteously, that she was earning her pardon through hazards and labor so unremittingly difficult it made the standard prison rockpile seem by comparison a nap on a featherbed. She went to her tent immediately after eating and fell asleep as if she'd been knocked in the head.

Now she needed a good bath, which she couldn't have, and a shampoo, which she might be able to manage in the little bit of water available on the mountain. She crawled out of the tent, stretched and shivered. She took with her toilet articles, a small tube of biodegradable shampoo, and the precious towel she had made room for in her pack. Lem was tending a small fire, getting ready to make breakfast. She didn't see Jade. It was still dark on the heath. A stiff breeze came down from the heights. The sky had begun to lighten over the lake, but the clouds were still solidly there. Daybreak would be gray and cheerless.

Raun took a lantern and a long stick with her, whisking it through the scrubby vegetation on her way to frighten snakes and scorpions, a precaution she'd learned as a child. She had returned easily to the daylight-dark cycle of wilderness living. It had been like stepping back into the past. She was half dreaming, her mind on her father, wondering what he would have thought of Matthew Jade. They had much in common. Her father was bright but eccentric, indomitable, a loner, stubborn, secretive. She'd rebelled against him often, and loved him without reservation. There was one critical difference. Macdonald Hardie had had a genuine reverence for human life. He could never have killed anyone in cold blood.

Near the stream she selected a suitable place for her toilet, then went on down across flat bare rocks to the water's edge. She had company on the far side of the strream, near the forest: Several varieties of bucks were licking at small pools beneath the aerial roots of wild fig, which had strangled the host trees and left them like skeletons beneath a curtain of flourishing green leaves. There was a strong odor of fresh animal dung. Raun took off her long-sleeved shirt, wet her hair, and applied a little shampoo. Scrubbed her scalp. The wall of forest, coming clearer from the dark, was stirred by the wind. Her nipples drew tight as knots in a rope.

As she rinsed her hair she felt the helicopters rising from the level of the lake before she distinguished the reverberating chop of their four-bladed rotors. The powerful turbine engines produced a resonance in the stones on which she crouched, as if heavy machinery were coming to life in the earth. Wrapping the towel around her head, she looked up and saw the bright landing lights of the lead copter, a West German-built light troop carrier. The copter slanted in across the heath, twin machine guns strafing the campsite. Another helicopter appeared a hundred yards behind the first, then another, adding to the intolerable racket.

Raun grabbed up her shirt, was stunned by a burst

of light in her eyes as the third helicopter swerved in her direction. She began running upstream, dodged behind a pile of boulders as the pursuing copter slashed by overhead. It banked steeply to avoid the escarpment two hundred feet away and came in for a landing on the heath. Clamshell doors opened at the rear of the fuselage and five armed soldiers jumped out. Raun heard small arms fire from the campsite. Another copter was landing in a swarm of dust.

It was total confusion; she ran headlong across the streambed toward the forest. Behind her an automatic weapon chattered; she heard what might have been bullets flicking off rocks behind her. Then there was only the sound of the remaining chopper aloft, casting around with its dual searchlights. One of the beams picked her out, bare to the waist, ducking into the trees like a bashful stripper on amateur night at the VFW smoker.

A strong hand grabbed her and neatly threw her to the ground, half knocking the breath out of her. Jade's hand tore the towel from her head and pressed down across her mouth.

"Stay there!" he demanded. When he took his hand away she struggled to get her breath. He was on one knee, looking back, listening. He had his rifle in the other hand. The helicopter flew almost at treetop level, lights blazing. Jade snatched Raun up and ran with her along the trail, threw them both down behind a big rotten windfall as machine-gun fire pattered through the leaves overhead. Behind them shouts were raised. The copter quit firing and backed off.

Jade got up and ran them again, through the half dark. A panicked antelope barged across their path and nearly hit them; Raun screamed.

"You're a big help," Jade muttered. He pulled her off in a different direction. He seemed to be able to find his way very well where there was no recognizable track. But the soldiers had penetrated the forest; they were close behind. One of them saw something and started shooting. A bullet whizzed through the vines. Jade stopped short for just a moment. He seemed about to lose his balance. She felt a slight tremor running through his body, as if he'd brushed against a charged wire. Then he recovered and ran as swiftly as before, dragging Raun with him.

The helicopter was back, just overhead. It sank dazzling shafts of light through the dense foliage. The forest had become a lush, infinite stage setting, a masterpiece of shadow and light with vaulting trees and fuzzily luminous, dangling creeper. Raun looked up and saw blood running down Jade's face.

"Oh my God!"

At the same time they reached an impasse; a sudden drop, rock studded, forty feet or more. Jade backed off, turned, blood masking the pain and frustration he felt. He sagged down onto one knee and tried to clean out his eyes. He pitched his rifle away.

"How's your Swahili?"

She stared at him. She could never have imagined him wounded, giving up.

"I can—I can make myself understood."

"Tell them I've been hit. They don't have to shoot anymore, they've got us."

"Matt!"

"Get on it, Raun, it'll be a bloodbath here in another half a minute!"

Raun found the appropriate words in her memory and began to shout. There was no answer. The helicopter had retreated again. From the heath came the sounds of voices; languages she recognized but couldn't speak. Desert French; Arabic. Light had begun to seep into the forest, which had a drowned look, as if it were covered by a shallow sea. The forest was

utterly still; there was no wind. Raun shuddered and
repeated their desire to surrender.

Soldiers wearing dark berets and jungle camouflage
began to emerge. They carried assault rifles: Kalash-
nikovs. One of them darted in, retrieved Jade's rifle,
and disarmed it. Raun kneeled and put her arms
around Jade, looking at the welling of blood from a
wound that might have been scalp deep, or much
worse. It was causing him tremendous pain. She
stared up at the faces. Only one African, the others
with lighter skin. Asian mercenaries. She singled out
the one with rank.

"Get us a doctor," she said in English. "Do you have
a doctor with you?"

He shook his head, flicked an indifferent glance at
Jade, motioned for the two of them to get to their feet.

Raun felt a surge of relief. They weren't going to be
killed, at least not right away. This was the logical
place for it, blast away and tumble the bodies down
the cliff. She swallowed most of the lumps in her
throat.

Another of the mercenaries moved in, poked at her
shirt with the muzzle of his rifle until he was convinced it contained no concealed weapons. He hooked
it by the tall front gunsight and tossed the shirt to her.
Raun put it on.

"Stand aside," said the patrol leader to Raun. He
pointed to two of his men. "Go with them."

She glanced in horror at Jade. He nodded reassuringly, his eyes on the patrol leader. Raun walked
slowly to the soldiers, who fell in behind her, rifles
leveled at her waist. The others surrounded Jade.
They marched their prisoners back through the forest
that way, widely separated, Raun in front, Jade behind.

It was dawn on the heath. There was no sign of
Lem Meztizo. Raun looked frantically for him until

she was prodded into one of the helicopters. They led Jade to a different helicopter. She saw him stumble going in, and knew he was badly hurt. She wondered if Lem was already in the other copter. But she had a sick feeling he wasn't.

One of the soldiers flying with her had an odd-looking ring on one finger. He was showing it to the others, in the meager light. Raun leaned forward to try to get a better look, was roughly thrust back into her seat and held there by the flat of a rifle against her breasts.

"Where did you get that?" she said angrily to the soldier.

He turned, grinning, and held out the long finger. But she'd already recognized what he was wearing: Lem's mummified tarantula, with the vivid collection of precious stones.

The soldier raised his other hand and made an unmistakable motion with his trigger finger.

Raun turned away in anguish, tears running down her cheeks. The clamshell doors at the rear of the fuselage closed, and the helicopter lifted slowly from the ground.

# LAKE MANYARA

Iringa Highlands, Tanzania
May 21

Tiernan Clarke's house was large but crudely made and without style, knocked together like a packing crate. It was a clubhouse, a den of boyish men. On the front porch Erika leaned against a post and shielded her eyes. The day's glare had diminished, but what was left of the light sapped her strength. She heard men at work on the game ranch, the harsh bray of an animal, a truck motor racing.

The ranch was located atop the Great Rift Wall, one thousand feet high at this point. The forest going down to the bottom of the rift was turning gray from drought and dust. The glass shard of Manyara lay below; a hundred concentric wrinkles of dried soda measured the almost daily retreat of the shoreline in this dry year.

Hundreds of thousands of flamingos had arrived to take up temporary residence on the frothing shore. They made a great blushing-pink scrawl of bird life, unbroken for miles, fading into the shimmering distances. When they arose in pinpoint flocks to cross the open lake, they flashed like stars returning home for the night.

Her eyes were already tired. There was too much of earth and sky to see all at once. And she was still recovering from the shock of her own face in a mirror. At least her hair was clean, Erika thought. Her shirt and walk shorts were new.

"Erika!"

She turned and saw Clarke coming at a near run from the direction of the lion-fenced animal pens sprawled behind the house. He dusted his hat off on his hip, took a stale cheroot from between his lips and threw it away, ran a hand through his hair in a vain attempt to spruce up. He looked big and dark against the sunset, except for the pearly gash of his grin.

"Hello," she said, and dropped her hands, feeling the weight of the cast on her right wrist and hand.

"It's good to see you up and around so soon. I thought another few days—"

"No, I'm much better. I had to get up. I was worried—"

He joined her on the porch, and Erika caught the tang of sweat. His eyes were rimmed with the caked dust of the plains. The knuckles of his right hand had been skinned. Up close he made her head ache. Too much vitality. It forced sadness on her, whirling into delirium. She had to move off, turn her back on him.

"Brute of a day," he said, slumping into a chair and putting scuffed boots up on the porch rail. He snapped his fingers at a houseboy, who brought him, without having to be told, a fresh pack of his favorite smoke. "The Tanzanian government is making a gift of animals to stock a new park in Ghana. We have the licenses to supply those animals. Today on the Tarangire savanna we sighted a small breeding herd of Grévy's zebra. They're almost unknown this far south."

"That's what you do? Catch animals?"

He nodded. "Two of them gave us an all-day chase. Very hard on the vehicles. I spend nearly two thousand dollars a month to keep my lorries in running order."

"Hard on the zebras as well."

"We take pains with them. It requires ten men to

lasso a full-grown Grévy's and rope him before he
damages himself. We give them several injections:
tranquilizers, cortisone. Even so they often die in captivity. When you're up to it you might like to come
with us for a day, if there's time."

"If there's time? What do you mean?"

Clarke took the cheroot from his mouth, the sweet
smoke of which had given her sharp hunger for another man. He pointed with it in a northeasterly direction.

"Your mountain, Erika. It's just as you said. She
may erupt any day."

Erika was too deeply pained to speak. She had not
actively thought about the Catacombs for some time.
But images of the place—that everlasting moonglow,
spiral caverns of the yellow men—were always in her
mind, just at the level of sleep.

Clarke stood up. "We ought to have a talk about it.
Over dinner. I'm dead ripe and needing a shower." He
grinned. "I can tell you've enjoyed about as much of
me as you can stand."

Erika smiled too, but her reaction time was slow—
from all the medicine to dull pain, kill infections, give
her rest and peace. He was in the house before she
could stop him.

"Wait! I wanted to know—have you heard about
Chips?"

"Later," he promised vaguely. "Later we'll talk."

After sundown it turned chilly on the high escarpment, a shinbone of antiquity gleaming beneath a
three-quarters moon. They had dinner privately, away
from his raucous crew, in Clarke's sitting room and
office. Here there was a chimney of highly polished
stone, a fire of acacia wood. The table was set with
real silver; the chair backs were covered with lion
skins. The meal was served by the cook: roast Egyptian goose stuffed with bananas, rice, and ginger; cha-

pati bread; a maize dish with savory herbs. There were German wines of no real distinction. Erika was awkward with her left hand. She ate little but drank too much to fill a deepening depression; she drank until the fire blurred and she saw a nimbus around Clarke's combed-out mane. He was a compulsive talker and eater, attacking his plate, filling potential silences with anecdotes about wild animals and men. She knew she was, had to be, grateful to this peculiar black Irishman for saving her life, for continuing to protect her at a considerable risk to himself. She was still a fugitive. But he was treating her like a dull child.

At last his mood, on a full belly, became less hectic. He paused to light a cheroot. Erika, exposing terror in a quick lift of her eyes, said what she'd been saving up to say.

"Chips is dead, isn't he?"

He reached behind him for another bottle of wine, Madeira this time, poured it into a clean glass.

"Better drink this."

"I don't want it!"

Clarke pushed his plate aside and clenched his hands on the table.

"They're all dead, Erika. Ivututu Mission is deserted. The hospital closed."

She had two places to go to with her grief, back to bed or out into the luminous night. He let her go, allowed her a spell of privacy, then found her by one of the lion-proof fences at the back end of the ranch, where the air was warmer from the gamy heat of the pens. He put an arm around her. It was, unexpectedly, what she wanted.

"Erika, you are in no way responsible for the deaths of your friends."

She shook her head, the motion accompanied by little rusty cries.

"The government of Tanzania will be held accountable. You have the means to make them pay dearly."

"How?"

"They have attempted to conceal the existence of the Catacombs. Why, we don't know. But the Catacombs are an archaeological treasure, you say. You deserve to share the credit for discovering them."

"I have no proof of what we found there."

"Get more proof, Erika."

"I can't go back. You said the mountain—"

"Is touchy, yes. Even now it may be too late. But worth the gamble. For *his* sake. If you loved him."

"Putting together an expedition of any size would take—"

"No expedition, Erika. You. Myself. A couple of men we'll need to pack in gear. What would you require? Cameras?"

"Yes, and hundreds of rolls of film." For a few moments her eyes cleared, her face took on a shine. Then she held up the cast on her right arm. "But I— The climb would be too difficult, I don't have the strength. What am I thinking of?"

"You *could* locate the Catacombs again."

"Yes. The site is easily recognizable."

"How did you find your way in the first time?"

"With ultrasonic equipment that revealed the structure of the Catacombs inside the mountain."

"Ah." Clarke looked pleased. He backed off to light a cheroot. "The sort of thing used in oil exploration?"

"Yes."

"That *is* ingenious."

"The Lords of the Storm left symbolic messages, chiseled into a rock face that endured for ten thousand years on the mountain. Macdonald Hardie wasn't the first man to see the symbols, but he *was* the first to realize what was meant by them."

"In two days, three at the most, I can obtain everything we'll need. Beginning with a long-range helicopter that will set us down wherever you say. Erika, Kilimanjaro is less than an hour's flying time from here."

"So close!"

He saw her leaning, tense with the expectation of it.

"But if we don't make up our minds now—" Clarke rolled the murky cheroot between his fingers, letting her think about it just long enough. Then, casually, came the coup de grace.

"I think your Chips would have said—Go, Erika. Go to it, old girl."

Oliver stayed the day in his drainpipe, undetected, although construction work went on around him. At noon the machines were stilled and the workmen ate, then napped head to toe in the narrow shade of jacarandas across the highway. When they left for good he came out cautiously in the pink of sundown and found a swallow of soda left in a can, crusts of bread in a wrapper with a little meat and grease. The ants had got there first, but he brushed them off and wolfed the bites, sitting behind a piece of pipe while traffic went by on the unpaved highway.

At dusk a car came up the road with a tire flapping and pulled off at the construction site. Oliver stuck his head around the lip of the drainpipe just as a pair of headlights rounded on him. He pulled back quickly and crawled to the other end of the pipe.

A car door opened, closed. He heard footsteps. Then a gruff but feminine voice.

"You!"

Oliver started but made no sound.

The footsteps came toward him.

"I saw you when I drove off the roadway. Come

out, I won't eat you." She repeated this in Swahili, and added, "I have a flat tire. I am unable to change it myself. I have a shilling for you, if you'll be kind enough to lend a hand. But don't think you can take advantage of me because I'm alone, and a woman. I also have a rifle, and I am a crack shot. Now, if you don't show yourself promptly in order to earn a shilling for a few minutes' honest labor, I shall think you're up to some mischief. In that case I shall pot you now, and ask questions later. Am I understood?"

Oliver failed to move. A shot rang out, chipping concrete above his head. He sprang up instantly, raising his hands.

"That's better. Come around to me, now, slowly, and let's have a look at you."

He could see her in the beam of the lights from the car. She was a tall woman, almost as tall as Oliver, with a nose sharp as an elbow and high color in her cheeks. She had gray hair rather badly pinned up, so that strands of it fell over her ears and face. She was wearing a denim culotte, almost ankle length, and a cheap porkpie canvas hat with a red-and-green-striped band. Her rifle, steadily held, was an old Enfield.

"I am Emma Chase. From Njombe. Who are you?"

"Oliver, I."

As he approached with the wind she got a whiff of him, and frowned.

"What's this? Were you in a fire?"

Oliver nodded, dejectedly. Emma Chase set the butt of her rifle on the ground.

"Why didn't you say something? I'm a medical missionary. Go on, put your hands down, and come with me to the car."

She had Oliver sit on the front seat with his feet on the ground and take off his suit coat and shirt remnant. She used a flashlight to examine his skin and then his broken fingers.

"What a mess. I can clean you, bandage you, give you antibiotics and something for the pain. But those fingers should be attended to in hospital, otherwise I'm afraid they won't be of much use to you ever again. Did you catch them in a press?"

Oliver nodded; then his head remained bowed and he dripped tears.

"Not likely! These other marks—here, around your neck, on your wrists. They were caused by restraints of some sort. Oh, don't think I haven't seen it before. Uganda. The Central African Republic. You were tortured. Why? Was it the police?"

"No."

"You're in trouble, though, aren't you? Well. Tell me about it. You're my patient, Oliver, and I have sworn the Hippocratic oath. That is powerful *juju*. Should I betray you, my ears would fall off my head."

While she worked on him, and coaxed him, Oliver parted with bits and pieces of his story.

"So you want to kill this man. If you find him. Well, I don't think you will. It's a wild goose chase. You won't get to Kilimanjaro in the shape you're in, and penniless to boot."

She stood back, lips pursed, to look at him.

"There. You'll bear a few scars. Your hair will grow back in a few weeks where it was singed. Do you feel up to helping me with the tire?"

When they had the old tire off and the new one, nearly as bald as chicken skin, in its place, Emma gave Oliver his shilling, two sandwiches she'd brought with her, and a cup of hot coffee from her thermos.

"My advice is to forget about it. You're lucky to be alive. You'll find more gold. If you should catch up to this man, and I don't concede there is the remotest

possibility of *that*, you'd only be helpless again with
that hand as it is. At his mercy."

"No. Not helpless. This time, surprising him."

"So your mind is made up. You won't listen to common sense. I suppose you *could* ride with me as far as
Dodoma—I don't relish making the drive alone at
night. Dodoma will put you closer, but not all that
close, to Kilimanjaro. Tomorrow, if you'd care to stay
around until the end of our meetings, I might be able
to persuade another of our society's delegates to drive
you as far as Arusha. That's not a promise, but I—"

Emma was astonished to find Oliver on his knees in
front of her clutching at her hand, a sheen of fresh
tears in his eyes.

"Oliver, stop this ridiculous display! If I thought
there was any chance you might succeed in getting
close to this man, and be killed for your pains, I'd
leave you right here. Now get up. I'll need a full
night's sleep in the capital if I want to have my wits
about me in the morning."

Nine twenty A.M.

During the past twenty-four hours Henry Landreth had developed either pneumonia or a pulmonary edema caused by the altitude. His symptoms were fluid in the lungs, weakness, a bad and sometimes bloody cough, blue lips and nails, a pulse of 120 when he exerted himself even slightly. He had a fever. Henry's condition was a drain on the small cylinder of oxygen Belov had with him; but there was nothing else he could do for Henry except keep him warm and out of the weather.

They were at fifteen thousand feet, having spent most of the previous day inching past the treacherous, unstable moraine, putting distance between them and the wide path of the avalanche that seemed certain to come from the faltering glacier. But, according to Henry, they were still another thousand feet from the Catacombs. In this thin air it would be a difficult and perhaps fatal walk for the sick man. And they were now isolated on the high moor by a thick soup of fog and particulate matter sifting down from the caldera of Kibo. Belov found it increasingly difficult to leave the immediate vicinity of the camp in order to gather groundsel bark for their fire. If the fire should go out while he was away, he would lose his bearings and find himself marooned.

He cleared his throat, which felt gritty, stooped for

another chunk of the bark, and put it into a makeshift
bag, made from a shirt, with the other pieces he'd collected. The mountain boomed and shuddered almost
hourly, and the cracking of glacier ice had him jumpy.
His hair was stiff as cement from the sifting-down,
slightly moistened ash; he had to keep wiping his face
clean. They were not entirely out of the zone of maximum avalanche danger, although the steep granite
face Belov had pitched their camp next to had looked
smooth and free of loose rock and significant icefalls.
He looked back and saw the reassuring flicker of his
fire through the shadows and dream shapes on the
moor, and continued slowly uphill.

Unless he was imagining it, the fog, which had been
unmoving as a wall, now seemed to have a slight eddy
and flow, as if a wind had come up. That was encour-
aging. With visibility better, it might be worthwhile
getting Henry up and trying to improve on their position, while he was still lucid enough to direct them.

More bark. He reached for it.

By this time he was accustomed to the glow around
his gloved hands, the blade of his alpine ax, and the
plants that grew to human size from the deep grass. It
was St. Elmo's fire; the entire side of the mountain
seemed to be electrified. The radiance had a pecu-
liarly enlivening effect on the ghostly, graceful giant
lobelias, which resembled tall posts covered with
coarse angel hair. They loomed, like sentient creatures, everywhere in the fog.

The mountain shook him and he slipped down, his
feet going out from under him; he self-arrested with
the ax and pulled himself to his knees, caught his
breath. He looked, instinctively, for the fire. Saw it,
not much brighter than the flare of a match. He had
wandered a little too far. But he was now near a large
level area where the tussock seemed beaten down, or

worn away entirely. Groundsel and lobelia were missing, even large rocks had been removed.

He aimed his flashlight for a better look and discovered what could have been an old deep bootprint. He moved the light. There was a dull gleam of metal on the ground. He walked over to it and dug around the metal with his ax, unearthing a small aluminum foot pump for inflating pneumatic shelters.

Belov was sure he had found the base camp for the Chapman/Weller expedition.

He began chopping, at random, into the ground, searching for midden, and found, without too much trouble, some rubbish which hadn't begun to decompose: bits of foil-lined food packaging, exhausted fuel cells, an extensive compost of rinds, vegetable pods, and coffee grounds. The charcoal from many campfires.

So they were closer than Henry had thought. Excitement pinched his throat. Now if the fog would lift, for even an hour . . .

Belov hurried back down to his own campsite, homing in on the yellow pinprick of fire in front of the domed silvery shelter.

His mind was on his discovery, on the nearness of the Catacombs; the news, he was sure, would get Henry on his feet quickly. If he had to, Belov thought, he would *carry* the old man the rest of the way.

There was something in front of the shelter, behind the fire but unilluminated, a lithe dark shape with four legs and a high haunch. Even that much was hard to distinguish, and he'd been seeing too many anthropomorphized shapes on the moor that morning to trust his eyes. His rational mind told him it had to be Henry, that he had crawled out of the shelter on all fours in a delirium.

"Henry!"

But the head was small and catlike; it couldn't be a man. When it moved, Belov decided from the stride that it was a cheetah, like the one he'd seen on the afternoon he had pulled Henry from the mudslide.

Then his senses totally betrayed him: because the cheetah, in a kind of flowing elongated movement, appeared to rise from the ground and walk like a man. It walked away from the shelter and the trace of light that was repeated in the orb of a masked and flaring eye, and vanished in a split second.

As he was getting to the shelter, another earth tremor had Belov swaying on his feet. He ended on all fours himself and crawled inside almost in a panic. Henry Landreth was faceup in the sleeping bag, his eyes open, his mouth open; Belov thought he had died. Then he heard a bubbling breath that Henry dragged from his chest.

"Henry."

"Ahhh," Henry groaned, in obvious distress. The trembling of the mountain ceased. A few bits of detritus pattered above their heads on the Mylar shelter and Belov flinched, anticipating a Big One, a fifty-ton boulder hurtling noiselessly from high above. Time passed without mishap and his nerves settled down. He poured a drink for Henry, a mixture of brandy and water from melted ice. He helped the sick man to sit up, held the cup to his lips. The bubbling sounds in his chest were ominous. Belov gave him a liter of the precious oxygen.

"What—were we talking about?" Henry asked, as if hours hadn't lapsed since their last chat.

"We were talking about FIREKILL," Belov said with a smile. "And I told you I found it difficult to believe that a ballistics missile could be rendered into atoms in space by the force of electromagnetism. The earth's electromagnetic field—"

"Has been in existence—for at least two point seven

billion years. During those eras the field has fluctuated in magnitude countless times. The secret to FIRE-KILL—is to control the fluctuations, increasing their strength at will."

Henry suffered through a rugged coughing fit, and Belov eased him flat to rest.

"You were gone a long time," Henry complained. "I was afraid—something had happened to you."

"Henry, I may have found the site of the Chapman/Weller base camp. Only a few hundred yards from here. You were right. This *is* the way to the Catacombs. Can we be far?"

Henry was silent for so long Belov thought he hadn't heard. Then a faint smile appeared.

"No. Not far. With your help—I'll make it now."

"Henry, I think you've given it your best try. But you're a very sick man, and as soon as the weather breaks I'm going to bundle you back down the mountain—"

"No! I must—reach the Catacombs. They're depending on me!"

"Who?"

Henry turned his simmering eyes on Belov, and was silent again.

"Why don't you rest, conserve your strength. I'll fix you something nourishing."

"A little bouillon, that's all—I want. Right now—must talk to you, dear fellow. Convince you—I'm not a madman."

"Oh, I'm sure I haven't given you the impression I think you're insane, Henry. You're just overtired, and we both know you need medical attention."

Henry plucked at the sleeve of Belov's down-filled jacket.

"My friend. Listen. If I—I don't survive, then it will be up to you. You will be the caretaker of the secrets of the Catacombs. The great secret of FIREKILL."

"Not sure I'm keen on having the responsibility," Belov said lightly.

"Remember everything I tell you. It's of—critical importance."

"You shouldn't strain yourself like this. . . . All right, if it's so important to you. I'm listening."

"The earth itself," Henry said, "is an enormous magnet. This has been known—since the early seventeenth century. But no one in modern times has been able to conclusively identify the source of the magnetic field. The Lords of the Storm, however—knew everything there was to know about it."

"What is the source?"

"The very core of the earth. It is nothing less than a fluid dynamo, a huge metallic sphere—almost the size of the planet Mars. It has nearly a sixth of the earth's volume, one third of its mass. Around the core—there are highly charged fields, called toroidal fields, whose lines of force lie parallel to all spherical surfaces. They are—much stronger than the dipoles on the surface of the earth, the north-south alignment of the lines of magnetic force with the earth's axis of rotation."

"I don't think I understand what the core of the earth has to do with FIREKILL."

Henry smiled. "It is what can so easily be made of it that matters."

"The Lords of the Storm must have used the electromagnetic power of the earth's core to greatly intensify the toroidal fields around the earth."

"In effect they created—new fields, to save themselves from heavy bombardments of meteors, a storm of destruction from space."

"And FIREKILL worked?"

"Oh, very well. But that, of course—is the great joke—the cosmic joke—they were forced to play on themselves."

Henry began to laugh, and plunged into a coughing fit. The effects of it withdrew heavily from his small reserves of strength. Belov gave him oxygen. Then he went outside to rebuild the fire and heat beef bouillon in a pan for the Englishman. Visibility was improving; there was a hint of sunlight above the dreary moor.

Henry might have hours left; he might have a day. Belov was chafing with impatience, but he hoped that Henry's intense will to reenter the Catacombs, after Kumenyere's efforts to kill him, could keep him alive where even antibiotics, at this point, would fail.

The mountain shook; the bouillon was almost emptied from the pan. Henry was calling him, by his Swedish name. *Ket. Ket.* It sounded like another spasm of coughing. Belov waited for the tremors to subside, then went back inside the shelter with the bouillon he had saved.

"Good news, Henry. The fog is thinning."

Belov helped him to sit up again; Henry's color was shockingly bad and his eyes rolled back in his head. Belov forced him to swallow all of the bouillon.

More earth tremors; Henry had to lie down. Belov was dismayed.

"Henry—the tremors are more frequent."

"I know. There could be tons of ash—at any moment. Toxic gases. A pyroclastic venting from the crater. Disaster. Nothing would be left alive—on the mountain. The Catacombs will be lost forever."

"Then we certainly ought to hurry."

In a moment of insight, his gaze lucid, Henry said, "FIREKILL must be built again. The Lords of the Storm are with me. They wish to know—if it will happen again."

"I don't understand. Is there someone else on the mountain with us?"

"Win or lose—there is no way *I* can fail, is there?

England will realize, too late, my true worth. It's been thirty years. But revenge is a dish—"

"Best eaten cold. *What* revenge, Henry?"

Henry smiled enigmatically, then lapsed into a fretful silence. His breathing was rapid and shallow.

Belov sighed. "Can you make it, Henry?"

"Yes. Let's go—at once. Give me a hand, my boy."

Belov helped Henry from the sleeping bag, guided him outside the shelter. There Belov put on his pack, which was considerably lighter now. Besides the cylinder of oxygen, he took with him only emergency rations and his fluid recycler; Dacron rope; his cameras and film; and the powerful miniaturized photo transmission unit, which was about the size of a desk-top calculator. It was packaged with a detached, fully collapsible dish antenna the size of a beach umbrella. The ensemble weighed less than seven pounds.

Henry had on Belov's alpinist's sweater and knit cap, a pair of ill-fitting trousers, and cleated Dacron sneakers Belov had brought along to wear around the camp at night. Henry clung to him through another earth tremor. Particulate matter—tephra—was falling all around them, picking up some of the glow of St. Elmo's fire. But it wasn't a heavy fall, and the hazy orb of the sun could be detected for moments at a time through the ash-laden clouds and fog.

Belov carried the ice ax in his right hand; his left arm was around the coughing, chill-wracked Englishman. They made slow progress to the old Chapman/Weller campsite, where Henry had to rest. He sat on the ground and looked around him almost sightlessly. Belov had to keep a hand on him or he would have fallen over. He forcefed Henry a few bites of chocolate bar, got him up and moving again, following an uphill track still visible through the stunted tussock.

In the hours since he'd awakened, Belov had seen

few signs of animals and had not heard the cry of a bird, although at these altitudes (he knew from his mountaineering days) one could still expect to find hyrax and duiker, eagle and ibis. The threat from within the mountain had frightened most of them away.

His own lungs were straining for oxygen, his legs had begun to ache. Henry labored painfully against Belov's side, all but dragging his feet. Belov was so accustomed to the deep-down rumble of the mountain that he didn't consciously hear it anymore. But the noise and the frequent and lengthy harmonic tremors took their toll of his strength. His eyes smarted from high altitude, from the fog and grit.

He had thought Henry was nearly comatose. He was surprised to hear him speak.

"If only you could appreciate—the breathtaking purity—of the equations that govern the models of the gravitationally powered dynamo beneath our feet. Have I—did I tell you about the bloodstones, dear boy?"

"Yes, Henry. They're red diamonds. Etched with mathematical formulae. I can hardly wait to see them. But Henry: How can you be certain that FIREKILL works?"

"Because of the ancient chronicles. And because of—more recent developments, included in—Tesla's diaries. Tesla knew all about the stupendous power of electromagnetism—eighty years ago. Given the time—the need—he would have evolved something similar to FIREKILL."

The track was becoming stony, steeper.

"Are we going the right way?"

"It must be. Hard climbing now."

"Do you want to rest again?"

"No."

"Who is Tesla?"

"Nikola Telsa, a great genius. The most significant inventor of the nineteenth and twentieth centuries. Others—stole from him, profited from his ideas. But it was Tesla who gave us—the world as we have it today. He first conceived of alternating current. Three of the prototype generators he constructed—at Niagara Falls in 1896 are still working. His inventions include—X rays, radar, sonar, lasers, guided missiles."

"I've never heard of him," Belov admitted.

"In nineteen hundred, in his laboratory in Colorado Springs—Tesla succeeded, by using generators of no more than three hundred horsepower, in drawing electricity—from the earth. He used the earth as an enormous condenser and coil, to build up a surge of energy with a potential of—more than one hundred million volts."

"In *nineteen hundred?*"

"In effect he—he achieved a method of virtually free, wireless distribution of electrical power over the entire surface of the earth. All the power—that mankind would ever need. Constructing FIREKILL, from the models provided by the Lords of the Storm, would have been child's play for Tesla. But even if he—had realized what he *could* do, so long ago, there was no need for FIREKILL then. Only now is it worth the price we shall inevitably have to pay."

Henry's voice, not strong to begin with, had faded to a whisper.

"I'd better—sit down now."

Belov gave him more brandy and water to drink. The old man was shuddering, as if he were about to convulse. Belov held him tightly against his own body. Henry groaned, his eyelids fluttering.

"Don't give up, Henry."

There was an orange light above them, as if the sun had broken powerfully through the clouds. Belov looked up at it, and thought he was hallucinating. The radiant object floated slowly down through the fog toward them, coming near the ground. He felt the hairs on his head beginning to stir, to stand on end. He started up as the object floated closer, then seemed to bounce and change direction, coming more quickly and straight at them.

Henry opened his eyes and saw it.

"No—don't move," he said to Belov. "It won't hurt you."

The fireball was now only a few feet away from them, but Belov still couldn't judge how large it was. Perhaps the size of a basketball. All motion was suspended, for almost a minute. He heard a faint crackling, as if the air were being charged with electricity. Then the orange ball suddenly swung to the right of them, making almost a ninety-degree turn, and moved on downhill through the fog, bouncing again and again, slowly losing its radiance and bright color.

"What was it?" Belov asked, his blood beginning to flow freely again.

"Ball lightning. One of the strange phenomena of this place. They appear—out of nowhere. Some drift, some bounce like a child's ball on a banquette. They are—a total enigma. No known laws of science can account for their propulsion. They have never been duplicated in a laboratory. Except by Nikola Tesla. He produced—fireballs of extreme density, with a strong surface tension. And a temperature—seven times hotter than the sun. They may well be—a life form which we lack the senses to perceive."

Henry made an effort to clear his congested lungs. He was left with blood on his lips. He looked drearily at Belov.

"Well—my boy. If only—I could stop trembling. Draw a decent breath. But there's no use—lying about. I won't get any better."

Belov smiled. His own head felt as if it had been

split by an ax, but he tried to make it look easy as he hoisted Henry to his feet. They struggled on. This time neither man had the breath for talking.

They saw more of the curious fireballs: small blue ones appearing out of thin air and dropping to the ground, playful red and white balls that revolved slowly around each other until their formidable energy was slowly dissipated.

Twenty minutes had passed by Belov's chronometer. He'd lost all sense of where they were, where they'd come from. He couldn't believe they had progressed more than a hundred steps. Lack of visibility was discouraging and frightening. What if Henry had become confused at a turn somewhere below, and they were on the wrong track? Walls seeemed to be closing in. Each step was higher and more precarious than the last.

A conventional earthquake sent them sprawling; they were bombarded by small rocks from the heights. Belov lost his grip on Henry and felt himself carried away by the violent washboard motion of the mountain. He was as helpless as if he had been in the riptide of an ocean. Instinctively he seized a huge cabbage groundsel and hung on. Then he made the mistake of lifting his head, trying to find Henry. A glancing rock struck him in the left temple. He was aware of nothing until well after the quake ceased, and debris stopped pelting down.

He got slowly to his knees, gagging. His lungs felt packed with dust, and he smelled rotten eggs: Hydrogen sulfide gas was leaking from a seam of the mountain. He gagged and spat. Blood was trickling into one eye. Awkwardly, with numbed hands, Belov knotted a handkerchief around his head just above the eyebrows.

"Henry!" he called.

The fog was transformed by a vivid blue glow, arcs of lightning crackling in several places at once. The lightning was a result of electrostatic discharges caused by ash particles rubbing together in the dense air. His hair was on end again. It was terrifying; but the lightning flashes afforded him glimpses of large areas of the mountainside.

He looked around, but didn't see Henry anywhere. Had he been carried down the mountain, fallen into a crevasse below? Before the quake they seemed to have nearly reached a hoof-shaped cul-de-sac that was unlike anything he'd seen on the mountain. Towering, forbidding walls on three sides enclosed an unusually rich alpine meadow of perhaps four rugged acres, where the grass was nearly knee high, the crowned lobelia and groundsel huge. Heaps of lichen-encrusted stones—some of them must have weighed a ton—were everywhere. They looked like cairns. A gully split the hoof between the walls, becoming a chasm at the granitic end of the cul-de-sac. Plumes of gas or smoke were vented from the gully; they merged with the fog.

Belov staggered on uphill, frequently falling flat as lightning crackled low over the meadow. Finally he stopped and huddled at the base of a cairn, his chest heaving; he was afraid that further movement through the coarse ash-laden grass might attract a bolt to him. The mountain was still now, blessedly quiet; the fallout of old ash from the caldera another three thousand feet above him had lessened.

Unexpectedly the weather on the vast mountain began to change, for the better. A strengthening wind attacked the thick mantle of summit clouds. The rays of the sun struck the sheer granite of the cul-de-sac. The walls glittered like metallic mirrors. Looking up through a haze of tephra, Belov saw the dirty white summit of Kibo, a gray-blue sky above. The fog dissipated rapidly in the warming sun, which was now past its zenith. Looking down, he could see as far as the montane forest belt, the dark-green tops of trees still nearly buried in furrows of white fog. The lull, after a morning of tension and hazard, was almost enough to put him to sleep.

Belov shed his pack and stood wearily. He put his hands to his mouth and called.

"Hen-ry!"

The cul-de-sac reverberated with the echoes of his voice. He was nearly startled out of his boots when Henry's voice came back to him. It was little more than a strangled whisper, but he heard every word clearly, as if Henry were just a few feet away.

"No need to shout. I hear you perfectly. It's—the peculiar acoustics of this place."

Belov looked around in amazement. And saw no sign of the gaunt Englishman. Impossible for him to have traveled any significant distance on his own. The strengthening sunlight was hurting Belov's eyes. He took out glasses with gray polarized lenses and put them on. His hands were trembling from excitement.

"Henry—where are you? I don't see you."

Again he spoke loudly, unsure of his own senses. In reply he heard only the chilly wind sweeping through the cul-de-sac. The hairy, cigar-shaped lobelia stirred like apparitions. His head throbbed where the rock had struck him. He began to wonder if he'd suffered an auditory hallucination. Then came the unmistakable sounds of a desperately sick man coughing, gasping for breath.

"Don't know—how I got here. I blacked out—during the quake. *They* must have found me—brought me inside."

"Inside? What do you mean?—Where are you?"

"In the Catacombs, dear boy. Waiting—for you."

# MOMELA LAKES

Chale Point, Tanzania
May 23

After lunch at Chanvai Robeson Kumenyere joined
Jumbe on the verandah of his house. For the first time
in several days the summit of Kilimanjaro, still intact
despite the recent jolts and jettings of ancient ash
from the fumarole, could be seen clearly. Jumbe was
slightly cheered. For him the mountain was a symbol
of the potential greatness and unity of Africa; the
threat of a destructive eruption that might blow the
famous peak sky-high and leave scars that would endure for a century was an omen too obvious to ignore.

He had had no visitors since the Russians; he had
accepted few phone calls. Kumenyere sensed in him a
vital weakening of resolve.

The two men lit their pipes and smoked in silence
for a while. Some vervet monkeys, white hoods
around their black faces, sat grooming and chatting a
few feet away, in the crook of a giant heather tree.
Over the dwindling wetland of Big Momela a close-
knit flock of marabou storks arose, disturbed by a
midday prowler.

"Do you think the danger's over?"

"I've never thought there was any real danger of an
eruption," Kumenyere replied. "The mountain is always talking to itself. I'm told it may go on like this
for another month. There have been a few small ava-
lanches and mudslides. Nothing serious." He reached
out and clasped Jumbe's hand. "You mustn't look this

way. Tired, old, defeated. You are *Jumbe Kinyati*, the greatest leader Africa will ever know. You are on the verge of a spectacular success. The news is all good, Jumbe."

"Is it?"

"The doctors from Houston are very optimistic about the outcome of your surgery. I spoke to them again only this morning. And in less than two weeks black men everywhere will be rejoicing in the freedom of their brothers in South Africa."

"So many other men will die first. Why can I find no other way?"

"It's better *this* way. Two swift, powerful strokes. Remember. If you had had missiles six years ago, your sons would not have died in Rhodesia."

Pain; anger—Jumbe was predictably aroused. But only for a few moments. Then he slumped back in his chair.

"I don't have missiles now."

"The Russians will deal with you, Jumbe. You've manipulated them with great skill, left them eager but without a choice."

"And the Americans?"

"But we never counted on them; they were necessary only to bid up the game. They have reacted in a typical fashion—by sneaking CIA agents into the country and attempting to steal the bloodstones."

Jumbe looked at him in astonishment. "Why wasn't I told about this?"

Kumenyere laughed. "Don't worry. The bloodstones are safe. The Americans didn't steal them. They didn't come close. Nor will anyone else. I simply didn't want to bother you this morning with trivial matters. The two Americans were picked up by our soldiers in the Makari Mountains the day before yesterday. They are being held at our Chale Point base on Lake Tanganyika. No identification. But from the description I received, one member of the team has to be Raun Hardie."

"Then why were they looking for the Catacombs in the Makari Mountains? She knows better."

"I have an idea that Miss Hardie deliberately misled them about the location of the Catacombs. Remember, she was imprisoned by the U.S. government for alleged subversive activities. Some say she was unfairly treated. I would enjoy talking to her about her possible motivation for misleading the CIA. But it doesn't seem worth even the slight risk of letting her live another day. Of course the decision is up to you, Jumbe."

Jumbe thought about it. "Whatever Miss Hardie's motives were, she has not done us any harm. Perhaps we owe her her life."

"There are six days left before the twenty-ninth of May. Other CIA agents may be in the vicinity of Tanganyika, or on the way there. If a signal went out before their capture, there could be a rescue attempt. If this attempt succeeds, and she has a change of heart—"

"Yes, I see."

"How much trouble is it to dispose of both of them, in such a manner that no trace can ever be found?"

Jumbe bit down on the stem of his pipe and sat staring at Kilimanjaro.

"Handle it your way, then."

For fifty-six hours Raun Hardie and Matthew Jade had been imprisoned in a square windowless metal storage building with a concrete floor. The building was about seven feet high. The only air and light came through four horizontal louvered vents at the top of the barred and padlocked door. Each vent was half an inch wide and six inches long. The sheets of metal were corrugated, bolted together, bolted to the floor. The roof had a slight pitch to it; there was a difference of less than a foot from front to back. The building was not quite large enough for either of them to lie flat on the evil-smelling floor; but they couldn't have done this if they'd wanted to because of the way in which they had been handcuffed together: her left wrist to his right wrist, and vice-versa. They could stand, facing each other like partners in a bondage dance; sit cross-legged or yoga fashion, a position at which Jade was much more adept than Raun; or lie, fetally, on their sides with their arms against their chests, a position which allowed them to catch an hour or two of shallow sleep at a time.

Their clothing had been taken from them at the outset; except for a bloodied twist of bandage around Jade's head they were naked. Clothing would have slowed the rate of evaporation of precious moisture from their skin, but in clothes they couldn't remove they soon would have fouled themselves unendurably. Even so sanitation was something of a problem: The only outlet was a rank hole in the middle of the concrete floor, and tactful cooperation was required by each partner.

Total nudity also helped ease a more critical problem: getting enough fluids to stay alive in the miserable heat of the metal box. They were near the lakeshore, they knew that much: Jade had identified the sounds of an engine and bucket line as a dredger in operation, but the door of the box faced away from the lake and the potential of cooling breezes during the long days.

From the moment the door had been locked it was not opened again. They had neither food nor water. Twice a day—after shivering on the cold floor all night, and broiling under the tropical sun—the nozzle of a hose was thrust against one of the vents and they were drenched with chilly or tepid water from the lake. They quickly learned to lick each other to slake their thirsts and replenish some of the salts leeched from their bodies by profuse sweating, but the gains were always marginal. Their lips swelled, their throats ached from dehydration, palpitations of cramps were common—at least for Raun, who screamed often from the pain of knotted calves and thighs.

During the day they heard the sounds of drilling soldiers, the siren of a lake ferry, helicopters arriving and departing, the whistling scream of MiG fighters overhead. At night they heard laughter from a bar, the lap of waves against the shore, hippo and crocodile in reedy coves.

Raun had passed the initial hours of confinement in a state of shock that was expressed as gritty good hopes, then embarrassment at their mutual predicament, then nagging fear of being suddenly taken from captivity and turned over to a barracks of bored men for a gang rape. When nothing at all happened she decelerated through morbid self-pity and a bout of hysteria, bottomed into a torpid depression.

Jade, his normally sharp eyes milky with the pain from his wound, which had not been looked at by a doctor, said little. His mood was even, thoughtful, almost placid. He betrayed no anxiety. He insisted on dragging her around the small prison several times to study it minutely, and for the second time smashed her expectations of Jade the miracle worker by finding it, under the circumstances, escape proof. Thereafter he sat as quietly as possible, hurting, nauseated by the pain, conserving his energy, letting Raun run through her cycle of emotional adjustments.

After the physical shock of their first, sunset dousing, and the additional shock of being quickly persuaded to lick every inch of his skin which she could reach with her tongue while he did the same to her, and seeing him sexually aroused while being aroused herself, Raun had a second, inappropriate reaction: a fit of giggles. It exhausted her. Desire dwindled but the bath, the drink, the inadvertent sensuality, restored her wits.

They were both tired. They lay down together, arms cramped, faces a few inches apart.

"Matt."

"What?"

"Sorry for today."

"You did okay."

"Just okay?"

"Pretty damn good."

"Thank you. Matt?"

"Uh-huh?"

"Are they going to kill us?"

"I don't know."

"What do you *think*?"

"Too early to tell. Right now they're checking us out with a higher authority."

"They haven't questioned us."

"They probably will," he said.

"Will they get—rough?"

"Yes, they will, Raun."

"Oh. God."

"Easy now."

"I'm okay. I think. Matt, how's your head?"

"I'm trying to forget about it."

"That bad?"

He didn't reply. She closed her eyes, sighing. It was still damned hot in the box, but the wet floor felt good. So did being near him, with their knees touching, arms tightly linked, even though her fingers kept getting numb.

"This is my fault," she said. "I want you to know that."

"I'm the one who got shot."

"No. No. It's my fault we were there at all. It was the wrong place, Matt. I lied to you, all along."

He whistled dismally. "Jesus."

"This must be your lucky day," Raun said, and began to cry.

"So where is it, Raun?"

"K-Kilimanjaro. High up. About sixteen thousand feet. Sort of a cul-de-sac. You get to it from the Nyangoro track, which is too difficult above twelve thousand feet for all but experienced climbers. When you get there—it's really tricky the way the Catacombs are hidden away, but I meant what I said—nothing but mummies."

"Much more to it than that, Raun. Your father made an extra discovery, he just couldn't tell you about it; probably for reasons of security. The Chapman/Weller expedition found the remains of a highly technical civilization that flourished in the area ten thousand years ago. They had the Bomb, pop-up toasters, everything that makes life worthwhile. Including an anti-ballistics missile system that might really work. The mathematics of it are preserved on red diamonds. I've seen one. We want the rest of the diamonds. So do the Russians."

"The diamonds are in the Catacombs? I really did us in, didn't I?"

"Why tell me now?"

"Because I wanted—*want* to make love to you, and I couldn't, *can't,* want a man I'm not totally honest with. Does that make sense?"

"Yes." He studied her for a long time and didn't say or do much, just linked a little finger with hers and held on tightly. "We could probably work something out even handcuffed like this. But to tell the truth, Raun, I've had a hard day and I'm not up to it."

"I'm not either."

"Thanks for telling me anyway. I was wondering if you would."

"You *knew?*"

"I knew that you had a lot on your mind and that something wasn't kosher when I took my first look around day before yesterday. I just had a bad feeling."

"Now, l-look at us." Raun sniffed back more tears. "Matt, what about Lem?"

"If he isn't here, he's still there."

"But did you *see* him?"

"No."

"One of the soldiers on my helicopter had his—you know, that dead shellacked tarantula he was so proud of, and there were some blond hairs clinging to it—"

"Okay," Jade said, after a dismal silence broken only by the faint strangled sobs in her throat as she tried to keep her grief to herself. "They got him, then. Try to get some shut-eye, Raun."

" 'They got him, then.' Is that all you're going to say?"

"Do you want me to try to make you feel less guilty? Not tonight, Raun. Probably not ever."

After that she thought he wasn't going to speak to her again. She drifted off to sleep, dreamed fearfully of helicopters like giant insects pursuing her.

He woke her from a nightmare some time during the night. He had something urgent to tell her. His speech was a little slurred.

"Raun?"

"Yes, Matt?"

"Lem knew the risks. I don't blame you. Don't take it the way I made it sound."

"I'm a stupid cunt and I'm sick of myself."

"But you're not a quitter. Not by a long chalk, as

the—limeys say. I want you to know that I admire that. Were you always such a tough kid?"

"Damn—right."

"So you held off a couple of maniacs with knives back there in prison. You took a stiff jail sentence when all you had to do was whine and grovel a little bit. What I'm saying is, it's—balls against the wall again. Even when it looks like you're down to a minute to live, half a minute maybe, don't quit trying to find a way out."

"Just whistle up a guy with a big S on his sweat shirt."

"That asshole's never around when you want him. Try going crazy. I mean it. Twitch all over. Fall down. Foam at the mouth. Make strange noises. You're dealing with men who may be reluctant to pull the trigger on somebody who looks and acts possessed. The one who kills you could be afraid of having the evil spirit in you fly up his nose. Do you follow?"

"Don't make me laugh, it hurts."

"Think about it."

"You're a long way from my dreamboat. You have some personal idiosyncrasies that worry me. I love you anyway."

"Since we're being so gut-level sincere with each other, I think I ought to tell you you have great tits."

"I know it."

Later she awoke shivering and heard Jade moan, just once, through his teeth. Her hands, up to the manacled wrists, were like blocks of wood. She slept again. In the morning they were both flogged awake by water spurting through the vent.

There was something different about Jade, a difference that scared her. His movements, under duress, were slow and awkward. With his face close to hers as he licked slowly she saw that the pupil of one eye was larger than the other. She knew this meant something was seriously wrong inside his head: a hemorrhage beneath the skull, pressure, brain tissue dying off. He seemed to hear only dimly when she spoke to him; she had to repeat questions two or three times.

Now Raun was in charge. Her teeth chattered. She made him get to his feet. He looked and acted doped. The left side of his face was slack, the mouth pulled down in a funny way. He admitted, without distress, that he couldn't feel anything there. The rush of blood to Raun's hands was agonizing, but at least they were alive.

For ten minutes she screamed, until she was hoarse, for a doctor, paused, repeated herself in every language she knew. No one came to find out what she was carrying on about.

When she wasn't calling futilely for help, she spent the rest of the stifling day talking to Jade, trying to get him to respond. He had a few short lucid periods; then he seemed to disappear into a haze. All he wanted to do was sleep, hunched against her. She wouldn't let him go to sleep. She rocked him and shouted in his ear. When he lifted his head enough to look at her, the enlarged pupil of his eye seemed huge compared to the other one.

Finally, too dehydrated to utter more than a croak, her nervous system drained, she slept herself until the nightly hosing. Nearly forty hours had passed since they had been locked away. She nuzzled against Jade, licking the water from the hollow of his throat, catching the precious drops as they ran down his chin from his soaked hair. He tried to lick too, responding to the body's mindless instinct for survival. His lips were puffed and scaly. He soon gave up the effort and sat trembling randomly against her. Broken speech patterns became isolated bits of nonsense.

"Pubby," he said.

"Matt."

"Luxaweep."

"God damn it, no. *No!* You can't die like this! It just can't happen. Not to me. Not again. Don't you understand how much I love you and need you?"

His mouth stretched softly, like warm taffy, into the approximation of a grin. Saliva roped down from the lower corner of his mouth. Urine puddled beneath his slack penis; he'd become incontinent. The brain continued slowly to deteriorate. He panted.

"Warcricken?"

"Three goddam months! That's how long it took Andrew to die. The same cancer that killed his father and grandfather. How's that for fair, huh? How's *that* for a break in life? I had just six months with him, Matt! We counted on a year at least. But I'm glad there was that much time, because otherwise he would have died in jail and I would never have seen him, touched him again. While he sat there on trial, day after day, he'd look back at me; I knew he was starting to die, but what could I do about it? I thought it would be easy. It was a *good* plan. I never dreamed anyone would be hurt or killed. I thought we were all on the side of the angels. Life isn't like that, is it? Life is so goddamned messy and full of accidents and wrecked schemes. We do ourselves in. We do others in. And *sorry* doesn't get it. Not anymore."

He made it through the night. His withdrawal was steady but almost unobtrusive. First the galvanized twitchings ceased; he became leaden, unmoving. His breathing was so shallow it was nearly undetectable. Raun lay down with him when she could no longer endure the strain of holding him upright anymore, but she didn't close her eyes through the dark hours.

She talked almost without pause, whispered when she couldn't talk, murmured old songs of childhood. When his breathing seemed to have stopped for good she shook him frantically like a wind-up toy and was rewarded by a long-drawn convulsive breath that somehow got his lungs going again. She frequently put an ear to his chest; the machine ground on. He had a remarkable body; it just wouldn't quit. But she realized in her heart that almost nothing of Matthew Jade remained in the vital areas, the links and circuits of the grossly insulted brain. All this from a head wound he had told her was superficial.

He cooled during the night and stayed cold. No perspiration. She tried to feel a pulse in his throat but her fingers were numb again, receiving no messages.

The morning gush of the hose had no effect on Jade. His eyes were closed. She screamed for a doctor again, and was ignored. She was too stunned to cry anymore.

Despite her best efforts to stay awake she dozed off. It might have been for five minutes, or an hour.

When Raun awoke the box was heating up. Her tongue was thick and sluggish in her mouth. Outside the soldiers were drilling, she heard shrill commands in Swahili, the slap of palms against rifle butts. She stared at Matthew Jade's gray face. His body was inert. There was an ant on his forehead. She tried to brush it away but couldn't reach it. Then she made the effort to listen for his heartbeat. There was no heartbeat.

She sat up, struggling for balance as she dragged his body after. It was awhile before she could utter more than primitive, screechy, inconsolable sounds. Then the words burst clear from her throat.

"He's dead dead dead dead dead dead dead dead DEAD!"

Maybe now they would come. Too late.

The scout helicopter of the Jeshi la Wananchi la Tanzania, the People's Defense Force Air Wing, flew north from Chale Point along the shoreline of Lake Tanganyika at an altitude of three hundred feet. Aboard was the pilot, a Libyan named Habib, and a Tanzanian Army corporal, George Asani, who was the lookout. Corporal Asani carried a Kalashnikov and the helicopter, an old Cayuse, was armed with a machine gun and a grenade launcher.

Only a little dust haze from the steppes beyond Makari marred an otherwise perfect day, and visibility was good. At the base of Mount Kungwe, Habib headed inland, rising over the forest; mud-brown elephants fled ponderously, ears flapping, from the shadow of the copter as the noise interrupted their feeding and socializing. The forests of Kungwe, scored by deep defiles and occasional pockets of meadow, teemed with animal life, which Corporal Asani saw without seeing: wildebeest, warthog, baboon, gorilla.

Halfway up Kungwe but completely enclosed by forest canopy was what appeared from the air to be the glittering rusty-black pupil of an eye, almost surrounded by a sclera of small pieces of gray-white granite which was too porous to support any but rudimentary types of vegetation. The meteor was a big one; if fully excavated it might have weighed twenty tons. It was one of the recent—in terms of thousands of years—meteors that had fallen on Tanzania, probably about the time the Lords of the Storm conceived FIREKILL.

The whole of the eye, looking like a three-quarter moon with a black hole in it, was perhaps one hundred feet long and sixty feet wide. The exposed part of the meteorite was a ragged irregular mound about eight feet in diameter. They had flown over the

eye numerous times on patrol. But today Corporal Asani noticed, near the outer corner, a teardrop: what
was unmistakably the facedown body of a man in
boots and paramilitary uniform. His blond head was
uncovered to the sun. Crooked-neck buzzards were in
attendance, already beginning to feast.

The corporal tapped Habib on the shoulder and
used sign language to indicate that he wanted him to
circle and come in lower, hover at treetop level. He
took his binoculars from their case and raised them to
his eyes.

"I don't want to get too close," Habib complained
loudly. "Who knows what the buzzards will do? They
are stupid birds. They have killed too many pilots by
flying where they shouldn't."

"Then stay away; just let me have a closer look."

Corporal Asani focused on the body, the gleam of
nearly new boots. Too many buzzards had come to
the party. One of them had fingers, a hand, in its
beak, and was tugging, trying to rip off meat. He
couldn't see the dead man's face for the jostling and
the feathers. The body seemed small, foreshortened,
but that might have been from the distortion of his
angle of view.

At any rate, positive identification was called for.
He ordered Habib to set the chopper down.

"The rock is no good; too loose."

"Find a level place. You shouldn't have any problems. Do what I say."

Habib landed gingerly but without incident. He cut
the engine, and the rotor blades slowly wound down
to a stop. A few of the brown buzzards had flapped
into nearby trees at the appearance of the helicopter,
but now they were hopping down again and running
gruesomely toward the body, their heads a little like
the heads of reptiles, darting in to snatch at spoiled
meat.

Corporal Asani got out of the helicopter and one-handedly fired a burst from his Kalashnikov over the heads of the buzzards. It succeeded in scattering them again. Habib also got out of the chopper for a stretch and a smoke.

The corporal walked around the mound of the meteorite, boots crunching through the sharp pieces of granite, a rock that had to be almost as hard as the meteorite itself to have resisted the soft erosions of time, the rains of millennia. It was a mini-desert in a jungle, able to stop the encroaching power of roots, repress the fertility of seeds in bird droppings. Some toxic chemical leeched from the meteor might have held off the forest. For Corporal Asani the eye of Kungwe was unremarkable in a land where major quirks of nature abounded.

The closer he came to the corpse, the more puzzled he was. The uniform, he could see now, fit very badly, particularly below the waist. The man had had very short legs. But his arms were long, the backs of his hands exceptionally hairy. He was not a black man, not with that garish blond hair, but his complexion was dark brown. He seemed to be bearded. And he had tufted ears. . . .

Grimacing, unable to assimilate what he was seeing, Corporal Asani extended his rifle, caught the gunsight in the blouse collar at the back of the neck, lifted the head and torso, and found himself staring at the fly-covered face of a dead chimpanzee.

Almost beneath his feet there was an explosive upheaval of granite pieces and soupy buzzard shit and feathers, and a hand with a hunter's skinning knife appeared. Just as he glanced down with a flash of horror going off in his belly, the mirror blade lanced into his groin, ripped upward to his belt buckle, stuck there, and was withdrawn as the rocks continued to fly. The naked barrel chest and broad shoulders and finally the dust-gray spooky face of a man with gold-lined teeth rose from the shallow grave.

Asani's assassin plunged the knife into him again just below the breastbone, the blade angled to split the heart in two. Another hand shot up to take posses-son of his rifle and then Corporal Asani, spouting blood, was shoved violently backward, head whip-lashing, eyes flung open but blinded by the hard dazzle of the sun; he was dead a moment after he hit the ground.

Lem Meztizo the Third rose full length beside the body of the chimp. He wore nothing but underwear shorts and boot socks. He was spotted with the blood of the man he had just killed. His hair had been shorn nearly to the roots by his own hand. His teeth glinted in the light, his eyes were fiery from dust and a fever. He trained the Kalashnikov on Habib, who was mov-ing with commendable swiftness trying to get back into the helicopter, and nearly blew him apart at the base of his spine, taking care to keep the train of fire low so as not to seriously damage the helicopter.

He paused long enough to retrieve his boots from the chimpanzee, which he had found dead, of fifty-caliber machine-gun fire from a helicopter gunship, on the perimeter of their Kungwe camp the evening of the day the patrol carried off Raun Hardie and Mat-thew Jade. He put the boots back on. He took Corpo-ral Asani's garrison cap and put that on too. With most of his hair gone it wasn't a bad fit. Then he carried the Kalashnikov rifle to the helicopter, limping heav-ily on a sprained ankle, pulled Habib from the copter doorway, and climbed aboard.

There was a water bottle under one seat; he drank less than he wanted and put it back. He had never flown a Cayuse, but all helicopter cockpits are alike: A copter is flown by means of a cyclic control stick, rudder pedals, and a collective pitch lever at the pilot's right hand. The radio was squawking; he ignored it and turned the engine over, scanned the gauges. The gas tank was nearly full—they hadn't come far: about thirty miles. They had come in from the shore of the lake. The only thing he didn't know was whether they had traveled north or south to get to Kungwe.

Lem took off and at two hundred feet went straight out over open water, the flaring lake surface. He grabbed for sunglasses in a case on the instrument panel. To his right he saw a crowded lake steamer abeam the Makari headland. He fine tuned the high-frequency direction finder and locked into a strong signal almost immediately.

Now at least he knew where he was going: south, along the shoreline. It was all he knew, except for one thing: The chances of finding his friends alive were almost nil. The curious buzzing sensation he got at the top of his spine, around the occipital bulge, when Matt Jade was desperate and trying to home in on him, had faded early that morning.

But he had a machine gun, he had an armed grenade launcher, and it could be some consolation, if he located the base from which the airborne raid on Kungwe camp had been launched, to complete an exchange of surprises and tear the bastards up.

The sound of a key in the padlock; the metal bar on the outside of the door sliding back.

The sudden burning blast of blue daylight as the door opened almost made Raun sick to her stomach. She turned her face away, eyes tightly shut.

Hard-heeled shoes or boots on the concrete; someone stood over them both for nearly a minute. She smelled his high-powered shaving lotion. She opened her eyes as much as she could and saw him leaning over Jade, thumbing back an eyelid. He was a muslim mercenary in the Tanzanian Air Wing. He had the rank of colonel. He wore a short-sleeved blouse, walking shorts, knee socks, a spotless lime-green turban.

He turned his head slightly and their eyes met. His were like polished brown stones. The whites of his eyes were very white, and there was a rim of sclera beneath the dark irises and darker pupils. His face slanted down to a Van Dyke beard. He looked like the high priest in a grade-Z movie about mummies.

"Heh deh," Raun said, and tried to lick her swollen lips, the cracks of which were filled with dried blood like nail polish.

The colonel didn't reply. He put two fingers where the carotid pulse should be in Jade's throat, just below the jawline. He did not feel a pulse, and straightened up again. Still he didn't seem convinced. He took out a clasp knife and opened it, squatted beside the body. With the sharp, three-and-a-half-inch blade he made a slashing incision across Jade's chest. The flesh gaped open, but there was no welling of blood. The colonel grunted, put his knife away, and didn't look at Jade again.

He had a key ring with him. He found the keys that would unlock the handcuffs, and with them he separated Raun Hardie and Matthew Jade. She felt a small jolt of terror, of unbearable grief. She had buried Andrew Harkness herself, taking two days to dig the grave, sewing him snugly with an awl into an orange-striped awning. Saying her long good-byes in solitude, gaining strength from the self-imposed chores. Now she could only crouch by her man, reduced to the margins of an animal in a cage, helpless and condemned.

The colonel's every move seemed slow and ceremonial to her, freighted with significance. He removed the steel bands from around her wrists. Her hands looked as if someone had forced gloves onto blood-filled balloons. Raun's eyes bulged from the pain. She screamed, or tried to scream, but nothing came out except a high-pitched wheeze.

Four black soldiers were waiting in front of the corrugated metal shed. The colonel stepped outside and spoke to them. Two of the soldiers came in, took hold of Jade's ankles and dragged him out. The body was stiffening, his neck was inflexible. They just left him on the bare ground, naked, faceup in the searing sun.

It was Raun's turn. She tried to get up, to emerge with a show of dignity, but her knees wouldn't support her and her face was contorted from the grisly pain in her hands. They pulled her along on her knees, which were already raw from getting up and down on the rough concrete for fifty-six hours. She also had raw places on her hips, thighs, and elbows.

She was too dazed to take in much of her surroundings. A few low buildings, mountains in the distance, helicopters, landing strip along the water. A military transport truck was backing up to the shed. The truck bed was covered, canvas over metal struts. They picked Jade up again and threw him into the truck, facedown. Two of the soldiers climbed in and reached down for Raun. The colonel rode up front with the driver. The truck started, made a bumping turn.

They made her crouch on the floor between parallel benches. Two of them sat behind her, two in front. They had rifles with them. They were young soldiers. When she looked up at one of them while the truck jounced along a washboard road and caught him staring at her, his eyes jumped away. They were all nervous, but excited too. Raun was an event in their lives. They knew that she knew she was about to die.

The ride was a short one, less than a mile. The noise of the bucket dredger operating from a barge on the lake was louder. A cloud of dust hung around the truck. They lifted Raun over the tailgate and dropped her on sandy ground; she twisted an ankle and screamed. Her hands were still engorged, not quite so painful but nearly useless. She looked at the nearby dredger and smelled the heaps of gassy, lakebottom sand and mud it was spilling into mounds onshore.

The colonel had stepped down from the cab of the truck, where he stood watching Raun with a slightly sour expression. The soldiers had surrounded her but gave her room, eight to ten feet. They had an air of expectancy. They kept glancing at each other, rubbing their balls suggestively, pumping their fists in the air. They all spoke a native dialect Raun couldn't fathom. One of them, a big pleasant-looking kid wearing a beret, was the butt of the others' jokes. He grinned and shook his head and backed away from Raun, and Raun was perversely irritated. Did she look so terrible that no one wanted to rape her? It was a time-honored tradition, the musky swaggering males with their big guns, the cowering female captive. Not that she was looking forward to it, but rape would help stretch the time; and despite the grossness of assault perhaps it was a more human thing than merely pointing a gun and emptying her brains all over the lot.

Raun had an astonishing vision of Matthew Jade standing before her, fresh as a daisy, wearing a cowboy shirt with real mother-of-pearl buttons, his bull-dogger Stetson camped down over his shady eyes.

"Ya-hooo!" he went.

She was more irritated than ever.

"Fuck you. I'm the one's in trouble here."

He winked, the bastard.

"Fly up their noses, Raunie."

*What*? she thought, but then his face dissolved in the dust haze. Just a tantalizing mirage, but she remembered then what he had told her during the middle of their first night together about scratching around and trying to stay alive when Superman was out to lunch and God wasn't returning your calls.

Raun sat on the ground and began to laugh. She raised her head, looked at each of her captors in turn. She brayed like a donkey, snorted like a pig. She picked up handfuls of dust and sand and flung them into the air above her head. She rolled on the ground and came up well powdered and panting, with her dried tongue protruding between her teeth in a parody of lasciviousness.

She lunged at the tall boy in the beret and tugged at his trousers, mashing her face into his crotch. He pushed her away hastily, then slapped at her. His fingers stung her forehead but she kept boring in, backing him toward the dredger and away from the truck. The other soldiers were convulsed. Raun growled, reared up on her knees, waggled her breasts at her chosen victim. In her desperate playacting the distinction between the real and the mad blurred; she felt as if she were detached from her body, standing aside as coolly as the colonel and watching her crazed antics. But there was no way she or anyone could hope to stop it now, not until the order was given and their bullets smashed into her.

Unfortunately the colonel had a low threshold of boredom. He walked toward Raun and the soldiers and cracked out a command.

The spell was partly broken, but Raun wouldn't give up. One of the soldiers had to kick her hard in the stomach to knock the breath out of her and quiet her down. She lay on her side clutching her stomach, rolled onto her back.

The colonel repeated his order to shoot her. The soldiers reluctantly clicked off the safeties of their weapons, and moved side by side into the truck's parabolic shadow.

The tall boy dried his sopping brow on the sleeve of his shirt. Each of the soldiers waited for the others to commence firing. One of them heard a helicopter and glanced up to see where it was coming from. The colonel heard it too, and was momentarily distracted. Raun's left foot slid a couple of inches in the dirt and was still.

Flies buzzed inside the truck and crawled on Matthew Jade. In the few minutes the soldiers had been occupied with Raun there had been some changes.

First his respiration, *huiksi*, which had been down to a shallow, undetectable four breaths a minute, began to increase. His heartbeat also picked up slowly, and the induced, severe depression of the autonomic nervous system was reversed. A thin red line of blood appeared within the gash on his chest; a couple of drops fell to the floorboards of the truck before he shut off the flow with his mind. His eyes opened; the pupils equalized. His skin, which had been very cold to the touch, now warmed. His fingers moved first, curling lightly into the palms. Then his feet, his shoulders; his head lifted a fraction as he recovered from the state of tonic immobility he had willed hours ago. But despite his proficiency, there was no way to hurry the process of awakening the body from the Long Sleep Like the Dead without causing severe and possibly lethal strains on his vital organs. Just as there were no shortcuts along the road to *pavásio*, the state of deepest concentration from which he could gently sever all connections with the apparent world while remaining in touch by means of his spiritual, third eye—called *kataimatoqve* in the Hopi language.

Since achieving *pavásio*, he had been aware of everything that was happening to him, including the knife slash across his chest, which made no more impression than a pinprick. He had closely followed Raun's efforts to prolong her life and now, having heard the colonel's repeated command to his soldiers to shoot, he felt a stab of regret that he probably wasn't going to make it all the way back in time to save her. Even at a peak of physical efficiency there was no hope he could overwhelm four men with automatic rifles. He was completely naked and had no weapons.

He did, however, have a voice, and he was just able to stand up now without support as his heartbeat continued to accelerate. He felt a shock of adrenaline which would be useful.

Rising, turning, Jade willed his facial muscles to sag. His eyes were far back in his head. From deep in his throat came a hideous sucking, moaning noise. He walked stiffly and slowly to the tailgate of the truck and gave them all a good look at him.

The soldiers were a study in petrifaction. Jade was dead, they had been certain of it. Cold and unbreathing in the harsh sun. His body, when cut open, had not bled. So his appearance now, a raging, moaning, walking corpse, was beyond their ken. He was something out of a fell corner of their bush childhoods. In their minds they made of him a giant, come to gobble them up, tear them limb from limb.

Jade, noting an itchy trigger finger, an impulse to lift a Kalashnikov and fire wildly at him, concentrated his attention on the potential danger and moaned again like Marley's ghost, pointing a trembling finger that was as effective as a gun. The soldier he singled out dropped his rifle with a sharp cry of terror and trod on his fellows as he tried to get away.

They were all a split second from total panic, or recovery. The colonel, not so easily fooled, yelled a warning at his men. But his words were drowned by a helicopter flying over the truck, its shadow sweeping in like a dark wave of the sea. There was a momentary whistling sound, followed by a crumpling explosion as one of the mucky sandhills by the dredger blew apart, showering them with debris.

Raun was sitting up, staring at Jade. His eyes were on the helicopter as it banked left a couple of hundred yards downwind and started back. He motioned sluggishly to Raun.

"Get under the truck! Hurry!"

He didn't wait for her response; he dropped over the tailgate of the truck, landed awkwardly, got his balance, and picked up the abandoned rifle. Everyone, including the colonel, was now concentrating on the incoming copter. Two of the soldiers were prone, sighting on it. Jade knelt and in what seemed to him to be slow motion squeezed the trigger of the Kalashnikov in one-second bursts. Plum-sized holes ran up the colonel in a drunky line from his left kneecap to his right eyebrow. Before he fell Jade had already killed the big shy kid with the beret, who had not been properly taught to get his head down when armed helicopters zoomed in at him. Now his head was on the ground and several feet away from the rest of him. The unarmed soldier was off and running. Jade saw a quick burst from the pod of the inboard machine gun on the copter; heavy fifty-caliber slugs swatted the runner like a fly.

Raun came humping and crawling on her bloody dark elbows and bad knees and burrowed past him with a sob, huddled beneath the rear axle of the truck. Jade fell back a little himself.

In the helicopter Lem Meztizo answered ground fire from the two remaining soldiers with another burst from his machine gun. He missed, but as the copter swept by overhead, one of the soldiers lost his nerve and struck for cover. Jade dropped him, then sprayed the heels and soles of the other one until he let go of his rifle and rolled over screaming in pain.

"You're alive? You're alive?"

"Didn't you ever play dead when you were a kid?" Jade said to Raun. "I was just better at it than most. Stay here."

He crawled out from under the truck, holding the rifle in two hands across his chest. The helicopter, in Tanzania's colors, was turning before the sun, which was now halfway to the horizon over the lake. But he didn't know who was flying the copter; he'd had only a glimpse of a swarthy tense face, sunglasses, a fatigue cap pulled down tight. Gibby might have had a backup team handy, in case something went sour, but he doubted it. The helicopter stormed in again and he ducked his head to avoid the blast of grit stirred up by the rotor blades.

Lem got out grinning, and although most of his clothes and hair were missing, there was no mistaking his general contours, the twenty-four carat artistry in his mouth.

Jade threw his hands into the air in an ecstatic, silent gesture of celebration and welcome. Lem couldn't resist swaggering a little.

"Where'd you get the helicopter, stud?" Jade yelled at him. Lem had left the engine on.

"Took it off a couple of guys."

Raun let out a shriek of joy and scrambled from beneath the truck. The three of them merged, like aborigines, in a communal embrace.

The dredger had stopped running after the rocket-powered grenade exploded near it. The soldier Jade had shot in the feet was still writhing on the ground in pain; he was no problem for them. It was quiet there in the sun; no one had come from the base, which was out of sight behind a low ridge, to see what the grenade was about.

"Pick up some guns," Jade said, "and let's go. We'll get sorted out while we're still in the air."

"Where to?" Lem asked.

"Kilimanjaro."

They were aloft, approaching the Ugalla River Game Reserve at a thousand feet, the sun like red wine in the sky behind them. Lem was at the controls. Raun had found an extra water bottle in the cab of the truck at Chale Point and brought it along. There was a large first-aid kit in the helicopter, a pint of *konyagi* the pilot had stashed. With the water and the gin as a mild antiseptic, she and Jade had taken sponge baths and attended to each other's wounds.

He closed the slash across his chest with butterfly bandages and told Raun the wound would heal without a scar. He had been knifed before, and shot; there were no signs of such wounds on his hide, and by now she was familiar with every inch of it. He had an almost boyish build and a fair, downy skin. Just a small birthmark at the base of his spine.

"No scars?"

Mind over matter, Matthew Jade said.

"It started a long time ago. I found out I could wish away warts, stop nosebleeds, control pain by concentrating on it. I healed a broken ankle in two weeks, and the sucker was in pieces. I scared hell out of both my parents by going into a deep trance at a Hopi mystery play. John Tovókinpi of the Black Wolf Society recognized that I had a talent, and assigned himself as my guardian and mentor to instruct me in the wisdom of the *powáqa*—the Hopi sorcerers. I was also nuts about Harry Houdini when I was a kid. I set out to duplicate as many of his feats as I could."

"You do magic?"

"There's no magic involved, it's a matter of *pavásio* and plain hard work. Houdini was a gifted contortionist who could readily change the shape and dimensions of his body."

"Then why couldn't you get out of those handcuffs?"

Jade had a swig of the *konyagi* and passed her the bottle, but the fiery stuff aggravated her already sore throat, and she refused.

"It would have taken me all of thirty seconds," he said.

"But you let us suffer like that!"

"Out of the handcuffs didn't mean out of the box. That was a roughie. I couldn't be sure when or if they were watching us. If I was loose they could have decided just to crack the door a few inches and roll a grenade in. But I knew they wouldn't worry about a dead man."

"You might have told me what you were up to," she said, sulking.

Jade put a hand on her shoulder. "Sorry, Raun. I wanted your reaction to be genuine."

"It tore my heart out," she said simply, and blotted at tears on her lashes. She sat quietly for a time, looking out at the blurred pale bush passing below, the copter's streaky shadow, a herd of white-striped antelope on the run, veering one way, then another, as stylish in movement and spacing as a chorus line. Talking hurt her throat. The chill of their modest altitude gripped her and she shuddered; she wasn't wearing anything except a grimy blue nylon flight jacket that fit her like a shortie nightgown. Jade was still buck naked and unconcerned about it.

"Matt!"

Jade moved forward to the copilot's seat. Lem pointed out what looked like a permanent camp on the shaded bank of a sand river. There were two frame buildings, bungalow size. Behind the bungalows was a long shed with a metal roof and a livestock corral. Opposite the corral was a landing strip with a gasoline pump and a 350-gallon silvery tank with a BP shield emblem on it. A single-engine biplane that looked like a crop duster was staked down just off the landing strip. In front of one of the bungalows a pickup truck and a safari wagon, called a *combi*, were parked.

Jade signaled to Lem to set the helicopter down. They had only about a quarter of a tank of fuel left.

Jade and Raun, each carrying a Kalashnikov, walked along a path from the landing strip to the bungalows. There was low water along the river track, flashes of sun, the bracing scent of *leleshwa* leaves on the cool evening wind, blood lilies in the dusty yard. No one had come out to see who they were or what they were up to. Raun smelled food and salivated.

There was a sign by the track in front of the bungalows. U. S. DEPARTMENT OF AGRICULTURE, it read. UGALLA CENTER FOR DISEASE CONTROL.

"Home sweet home," Jade murmured.

They followed their noses to the second bungalow, went up the creaking steps of the verandah and through a screen door.

Inside, four men and two women were eating. They ranged in age from thirty to sixty. They were all white. They broke off their conversation and looked up warily. Two black houseboys and a cook peeked around the jamb of the kitchen door, and vanished like smoke. Ten seconds later they were herded in at the point of Lem Meztizo's rifle. Lem had them sit cross-legged on the floor with their hands on top of their heads.

The leader of the research team, a man with a bald

liver-spotted head and a white handlebar mustache, relaxed his grip on the edge of the table and said, "We don't have much money here. Petty cash. And some equipment for studying the mating cycles of tsetse flies that you wouldn't be much interested in."

"May I ask your name?" Jade said politely.

"Donald McKenzie, Duke University."

"Mr. McKenzie, despite what we look like we're not thieves, murderers, or escaped crazies. There are good reasons I can't establish just *who* we are, or what we're doing here. But if you have a radio—"

"We do."

"—I want to give you an encrypted message to relay to the U.S. Embassy in Tanzania. The message will be transmitted to the Operations Center at the State Department in Washington, and then to the White House Communications Agency. If you'll be patient and stick by your radio for an hour or so, we should have a reply confirming the urgency of our requirements and requesting your full cooperation. Do you know anyone in Washington?"

McKenzie raised an eyebrow, looked at the other faces around the table. A thin man who couldn't control his twitching lips said, "My c-college r-roommate is an undersecretary at H.E.W. C-C-Collins P-P-Patterson."

"You come along too," Jade said, "and we'll get Mr. Patterson on a radio hookup for additional verification."

"Hold on," McKenzie said. He stared at Jade with bright shrewd eyes. "I don't know who you are. Refugees from a damn nudist camp, is what it looks like. But you're Americans, in trouble, and I guess we can help, all right. I'll send your code message. In the meantime you'd be doing us a kindness to put those damn guns away. We don't have guns ourselves. The six of us together couldn't overpower one of you, if it came to that. Now, the girl there looks half starved. So let's all try to act like sensible adults. We'll get you into some clothes and fix you something to eat."

Jade returned their stares with a slightly glazed, thoughtful expression. Then he took the rifle, put the safety on, and leaned it against one wall. Lem and Raun did the same. Jade stepped forward and offered his hand to McKenzie. They took each other's measure, and smiled.

"This must be my lucky day," Jade said. Raun didn't know whether to laugh or hit him.

# DODOMA

Oliver Ijumaa spent the better part of two days in Dodoma, a city with severe growing pains on the Central Plateau of Tanzania.

Dodoma, primarily an agricultural center and wine-growing region, was gradually being transformed into the seat of Tanzania's government. A new parliament building had been erected, and the National Housing Corporation had put up some large apartment buildings for government workers. New construction made the task of getting around the inadequate streets by car formidable; a dust haze hung over the hot city and everywhere people were listless and irritable, staying indoors as much as possible.

Oliver took advantage of the circumstances by running errands for members of the medical missionary societies having their combined annual meeting in the city. He picked up quite a few extra shillings this way, enough money to purchase a second-hand white shirt and used sneakers for his abused feet, and two pairs of socks. He had been told it could get quite wet and cold on Kilimanjaro at night, so he prudently invested in a yellow slicker with a drawstring hood to keep the rain off. That left him with just enough money for sandwiches and beer. He slept nights in Emma Chase's car and pestered her remorselessly to use her good offices to provide him with transportation the rest of the way to Kilimanjaro.

On the afternoon of adjournment she brought to him a tall Englishman in ragged bush drill and dilapidated penny loafers. He was a little taller than, and almost as skinny as, Oliver himself.

"This is Phillip Goliath. He is a zoologist, with an obsessive interest in the rutting instinct of lesser kudu. He is returning to Arusha this afternoon by way of Kilimanjaro."

Oliver, in his ecstasy, did a little springy dance. Phillip Goliath grinned at him.

"I have told him something of your own obsession and predicament. Naturally his sense of fair play was outraged."

"I hope you get the bugger, Oliver. I'll help you if I can. Kilimanjaro airport is quite near the mountain."

"Walking far?"

"You can reach the lower slopes in half a day."

"One warning before I leave you in Phillip's care. He is a stupendously bad pilot, with an utter disregard for the demands of gravity."

Goliath grinned complacently and took Oliver's arm.

"We just have time for tea before we depart."

Tea was at the Dodoma Hotel. There, with a zoologist's passion to uncover the minutest truth about the subject under observation, Phillip Goliath soon had the full story of Oliver's travail.

"You've never been to the mountain? You've no idea where these explorers were mucking about?"

Oliver shook his head in bewilderment.

"Kilimanjaro's sheer size is against you from the start. And there have been rumblings, there might be a lava flow. Oh, there's plenty of danger. I bloody wish I could go with you, but I'll be fired from my post and lose my grant. Well, I've some gear in the plane you might find useful. An old sleeping bag and an ice ax, belonged to a chum of mine. But he won't be back for it—he's still hanging from the Eiger in a rather inaccessible location. Let's be off, shall we?"

Phillip Goliath's airplane was one of the famous old staggerwing Beeches, circa 1940. It still had the original engine, but it was a far cry from the pristine models that nowadays fetch one hundred thousand dollars or more from well-heeled aviation buffs. This one had a propeller that was too short to take advantage of the available 310 horses. It was patched and rusted and missing a good many instruments, such as the altimeter.

"I always know when I've strayed above ten thousand feet anyway," Goliath said cheerfully. "I get a little short of breath and my nose starts to bleed." He slammed his plane through some tricky air currents at the western edge of the Masai Steppe and grinned when Oliver clutched his seat with both hands and moaned.

"I've crumped her twice," Goliath shouted. "Rebuilt her the last time from the ground up. Had a hell of a time figuring what goes where. It's only the hard lesson in life you profit from. And where else in the world can you have the freedom to be a self-taught flyer?"

A little before seven o'clock Oliver had his first look at Kilimanjaro, nearly cloudless in the northern sky as they approached the airport on the Sanya Juu plain. The ash-tainted snowcap of Kibo was glazed red by the sun, and there was a low boil of smoke like a funereal boutonniere on the rim.

Oliver, although he had been warned, was depressed by the breadth of Kilimanjaro, from the wheat-covered slopes in the northwest to the coffee plantations south, the hundreds of square miles of forest belt and windy moorland.

"Suppose I should get on the radio and let the tower know I'm coming in," Goliath grumbled. "Otherwise there's all kinds of flak. Hello, hello? Kilimanjaro tower? Do you read me?"

When he had the formalities out of the way Goliath flew straight in and at rather a steep angle. Oliver stared in fascination and dread at the runway rushing up beneath the nose of the staggerwing and averted his gaze. To his right, three hundred feet below and a quarter of a mile away, a JetRanger helicopter was parked on the apron near the terminal building. Three men and a woman were walking from the building to the copter. The three men carried a large assortment of baggage. Two of them were black, the other white.

Oliver's sharp eyes singled him out. He had shoulders out of proportion to the narrowness of his body, and a wild shock of black hair. The woman also was unforgettable, though Oliver had only a glimpse of her reddish short hair, the cast on her right arm.

He clawed at the glass of the window as if he were trying to throw it open.

"Errrrikkkaaa!"

"What? What's that?" Goliath said, distracted from the landing he was trying to make.

"There is Erika! There is him, stealing my gold, he!"

"Just a moment, just a moment." The little plane leveled off with a wobble of wings, touched down, bounced on its large front wheels, came down again one wheel at a time as Goliath sought to keep the craft in a straight line down the runway.

"Bloody old dame flies well enough, but she's a bitch to control on the ground," he said, applying the brakes gingerly. "Here we are! Now what's the ruckus?"

Oliver was pounding his shoulder, pointing back at the terminal.

"Erika! Erika!"

"Are you certain? Let's just pull off on the taxi strip, then, and go have a look."

On the radio Oliver heard Tiernan Clarke's voice as he contacted Kilimanjaro tower; he tried to leap out of his seat without unfastening the lap strap. He shook the whole plane.

"It's him, is it? Uh-oh, they're departing. Can't roll along any faster, Oliver, she ground loops too easily."

From half a mile away they saw the JetRanger rising above the tarmac. Oliver clutched the sides of his head in dismay. The helicopter was stationary for a few moments, then turned in the direction of the mountain and flew away.

"No, no! Erika!"

"Of all the rotten luck. And my fuel reserve is low." Goliath took a fast look at Oliver's devastated expression, made up his mind, turned back to the long runway, swung the Beechcraft into the wind.

"November Kilo Tango Juliet Bravo, what are you *doing*?" the air traffic controller demanded.

"Nipping down to the corner for a bloody loaf," Goliath mumbled, and failed to reply to the tower's inquiry. He applied power, and took his foot off the brakes.

"They have a couple of miles on us and their cruising speed's a bit faster than we can manage," Goliath said as they sped snarling down the runway. "I daresay they can climb higher in that JetRanger. Still, we'll give it our best shot and hope they don't run us dry in some vertical spot. See him, Oliver?"

"Yes."

"Good, we're off." At almost as steep an angle as he had landed the staggerwing. Two hundred feet above the ground he banked sharply and the plane juddered and faltered momentarily, not having enough airspeed to support the maneuver. Goliath put the nose down and the plane shot ahead. The cabin was filled with a hot golden light.

"Yes, I have them too. They look to be at six thousand feet and climbing. That little cloud of dust, or whatever it is at the summit, seems to be growing. Little blue veins of lightning in it. God, it's a wonderful time of evening to fly! Just look around you, Oliver. The beauty of this land is like a narcotic. Who was it said 'Life reveals itself only in retrospect'? You see I figure, Oliver, if I stuff myself with living now, I'll be the wiser for it in my old age. Expect to need all that wisdom too; I won't have any money. If I hadn't met you this afternoon, I'd be missing all this. We'll just tag along back here; reckon we won't lose them if the light holds out."

Two thirds of the way to the summit the engine of the Beech began to labor as the small propeller failed to take a satisfactory bite of the thinning air. They saw the running lights of the helicopter winking against the dark face of Kibo a little below the glacier, at about sixteen thousand feet. The boiling upstanding cloud from the caldera now blotted out a fourth of the sky overhead, and there was a haze of fine ash at this altitude. The sun was going down; they were buffeted by strong winds. Goliath winced anxiously and tried to climb as the copter disappeared from view.

"Well, that's it," he said with a slight frown. "They've set down somewhere under the glacier." He wiped blood from his upper lip and nose and pleaded with his old dame.

"Just another couple of hundred feet, you can do it, sweetheart, you goddamned well *will* do it for me." To Oliver he said, "I've a splendid idea. See the bare place just ahead? That's the saddle between Kibo and Mawenzi peaks. It's possible to land an airplane there; at least I've heard of one bush pilot who pulled it off.

But he had a few hundred more hours in the air than I do. I shall be very disappointed with myself if I don't give it a try, having come this far. While we still have the light I'll just set her down and put you off with your gear. Then if I take off at full power I think I can climb high enough toward the scarp to sight the helicopter. When I have done, I'll wag my wings so you'll know where to climb in the morning."

Goliath looked at his gauges, including one that told him his oil pressure was on the low side and another that his fuel wasn't stretching.

"Hmmm. A good teacupful left, I suppose. Wind seems to come from several directions at once. Just like Serengeti at certain times of the day. We'll just crab right on down then, no use beating around the bush. Here we go." Oliver swallowed hard and lay back in what appeared to be a faint. "Two . . . hundred feet . . . one hundred . . . and . . . fifty . . . and . . . bloody . . . *Guinness* . . . *Book* . . . *of* . . . *Records*, I'll bugger all!"

The Beech, as if suddenly unsupported by the air, came down hard enough to blow a tire, but didn't, rebounded from the short tough grass and patches of scree, barreled down an irregular alley of giant lobelia. Goliath applied extreme rudder to avoid a towering rockpile, steered into more of the thick grabbing grass, touched the brake lightly several times. The plane wallowed and slid across the undulant saddle and stopped seven hundred feet after touchdown. Just ahead of them was a depression like a gravel pit, twenty feet deep.

There was sweat on Phillip Goliath's forehead and more blood on his upper lip, which ran down his chin when he smiled.

"Just between you and me," he allowed, "that was a spot of luck. We took a walloping, didn't we? Oh, well. Let's see if there's damage."

He inspected his plane thoroughly, paying particular attention to the struts, then frowned at the mist of ash building up on the windshield. The light was fading quickly from the sky, the snows of Kibo.

"Sorry to drop you and run," he said to Oliver, wiping a finger across the glass, "but this sort of thing is not so good for internal combustion engines. Best of luck. Keep your eye on me when I climb up there." He pointed to the three-sided, in-slanting gash in the rock below Kibo peak, where they had last observed the helicopter.

Oliver had made a small pile of the sleeping bag, ice ax, and three small plastic water bottles. He was wearing his hooded yellow slicker. He stepped forward, grasped Phillip Goliath's left hand with his two hands, and hung on wordlessly, gazing into the younger man's eyes.

"Working for you, every day of my life. No pay."

"Oliver, that isn't necessary. I've had loads of fun. Looks as if it'll be three against one up there, do watch yourself."

Goliath climbed back into the plane. The engine roared. Goliath brought the nose around as Oliver lifted the tail, and then he took off the way he had come, with a wave of his hand.

The staggerwing had trouble picking up speed in the grass; it rose, just missed some tall lobelia, fell back into the saddle, bounced, and rose again a little higher into the air, perhaps sixty feet. Oliver watched it crawling for altitude in the darkening sky, wing-tip lights flashing. His fists were clenched. Goliath flew toward the basaltic crag of Mawenzi, the noise of the engine fading quickly. Then he banked and came back, well above Oliver's head. He was climbing toward the scarp, rising to meet the down-shifting cloud of gases and ash from the crater. Oliver stopped breathing.

He saw the Beech catch the light of the dying sun, just for a moment; high up against the chiseled gash in the rock it glowed as if it were incandescent, and the wings dipped in acknowledgement of the hidden helicopter. Wind brought tears to Oliver's eyes. He couldn't hear the popping hum of the plane's engine anymore. As he watched, the left wing dipped too low. Goliath attempted to level off, to glide, and then the plane just plunged out of the sky, powerless, and was torn to pieces on the jagged slope of the mountain.

There was no noise of crashing, no fire, no sign of Phillip Goliath's "old dame" or of Phillip himself: the happiest man Oliver had ever met, and one of the bravest. Oliver continued to stand there, his chin lifted, choked with tears, the wind whipping the drawstrings of the slicker's hood painfully across his cheeks.

# TWO

# *THE CATACOMBS*

May 23

Erika was standing less than ten yards from the helicopter, which Tiernan Clarke's men had finished unloading, when the small plane appeared overhead, its engine sputtering. She looked up, a hand shielding her eyes from the brassy glare of the sunset, and saw the pilot dip his wings as if he were in trouble. Then the left wings dropped precipitously as the engine quit. Although he seemed to be attempting to glide down to the moor nearly three thousand feet below, where he had some hope of landing without cracking up, he abruptly lost control.

The plane struck the mountain and blew apart, a flashless, almost noiseless explosion of metal fragments, pieces of trees that were in the way, and human remains; some of the fragments had a momentary brilliance as they carried into the lightsea from the west.

She turned; she was already pale and gulping from altitude sickness, and shaky on her feet. Clarke had come up behind her in time to witness the accident. He put out a hand to steady her.

"My God! What can we do?"

"Nothing, Erika. There's no hope for anyone who was in that plane."

"But what was he doing up here?"

"Having a close look at the volcano, I suppose,"

Clarke said, barely concealing his indifference. He brushed at the tephra collecting in his hair, and hers, looked up at the mushrooming cloud over Kibo. There was a deep rumbling from inside the mountain, which was trembling slightly again.

"That can't be good," he said forbodingly of the cloud. "You'd better lead us inside, Erika. Is it far?"

"No . . . just there, through the gully. A hundred yards or so." She licked her lips. Her eyes looked vague. He saw she was going to faint and bellowed for oxygen. The two black men he'd brought with him, Simon Ovosi and Ned Chakava, came running with a big cylinder between them and Clarke placed the transparent cone over Erika's nose and mouth. A few deep breaths, and some color seeped into her cheeks.

They went then into the Catacombs, Erika leaning on Clarke's right arm, Simon and Ned bent over with the weight of the packs and cylinders of oxygen which they would all need from time to time at this altitude, even inside the Catacombs.

Soon the walls of the gully rose steeply above their heads; the path at the bottom, worn smooth by the feet of the explorers less than a year ago, wound tightly between outcrops of rock and occasional stunted groundsels that had somehow taken root and refused to die despite the near absence of sun during the day.

On the walls black markings appeared, randomly at first. They seemed to be cracks in the granite, but the light from Clarke's powerful flashlight bounced back dazzlingly.

"It's obsidian," Erika explained. "Volcanic glass, and nearly as hard as the rock itself. In a few moments you'll see that it hasn't occurred naturally—we think the obsidian was placed here by artisans."

She aimed Clarke's flashlight beam for him; a wall on their left, chiseled nearly smooth over an area ten feet square, was like a mosaic, the space filled with bold curving strokes and geometrical figures.

"Those are pictographs; what do they remind you of?"

"I don't know." Clarke looked more closely. "That one is almost a face—an animal's face."

"A cheetah, to be exact. The black arabesques and spots are simply the facial markings of cheetahs, which emphasize their everyday expressions and facial moods. The people of Zan, you see, were part cat."

"For the love of— What is this, Erika, your little initiation joke? New boys at the digs, and all that?"

"Not at all," Erika said, with a broad smile. "We're part ape, aren't we? You'll soon see for yourself what I'm talking about. This is how their written language evolved, pictographically, from the numerous subtle differences in mood that all faces, animal and human, express. Their ability to evolve symbolic notation came much later, of course."

Erika was feeling stronger, Clarke noted with satisfaction. She went on eagerly a few steps ahead of the others and came to another, large pictograph, some vertical slashes in the stone which also appeared to be obsidian. But one was not: It was a dark cleft only three feet wide. Erika simply walked into it and was swallowed up.

"Hey, Erika!"

"No need to yell," she said calmly, her voice sounding as if she were still standing next to him. "Even if we were a hundred yards apart I could hear every word you say. The acoustics are uncanny. It has to do with the placement of the clefts in the walls of the gully. Come on, we're wasting time."

"Amen to that," Clarke said, and followed her.

Without the flashlight beam he would have found himself, within a few steps, in complete blackness. The walls on either side were rough but not jagged, and inches from his shoulders. He felt uncomfortable in such close quarters; he began to sweat. His heart thudded from the exertion. He looked back with a sweep of his light to the entrance, where Ned and Simon were squeezing in with the packs and tanks.

"Erika?"

"I'm up here." Her voice was just a whisper.

It was a bit of a climb, and the ceiling soon dropped, forcing him to hunch along. No wonder the Catacombs had remained inviolate for so many thousands of years. In modern times Kilimanjaro had been climbed only since 1889. The way up from Nyangoro was not difficult enough for serious alpinists, who preferred to inch their way up Mawenzi, and too tough for the ordinary run of tourists.

Clarke negotiated a tight turn, his mouth open as he struggled to breathe. Behind him he heard the other men panting, and a canister of oxygen rang against one wall.

"Careful, you bloody idiot!" he shouted, and pressed on.

Another, hairpin turn to the shrinking passage; he was forced, cursing, to his hands and knees. As he rounded the bend he lifted the flashlight in his hand; light was reflected back brilliantly from obsidian strips along the walls of a small chamber. All but one. Erika stepped into view, beckoning to him.

"This way."

Another ten yards and there was head room. As he got to his feet, the mountain shook and rumbled. He braced himself, a hand against each of the side walls. The tremor lasted twelve to fifteen seconds, but it seemed much longer as he considered the possibility of the passage collapsing on him. He tried to be realistic. This couldn't be the first time in ten thousand years there had been serious seismic activity on Kilimanjaro. And he wasn't planning to stay around for very long.

When the tremor ended he made his way to the cleft where he'd seen Erika and aimed his flashlight beam through it. The beam picked up a gruesome sight; some sort of gargoyle on the wall of a cave. He went in, and felt Erika's hand on his arm.

"Is this it?" he said, casting the light around. The room had a low ceiling. It was about thirty by twenty feet. There was a crude stone altar of some sort, and more of the dark, fierce-looking creatures that at first glance had seemed to be carvings, leaning down at an angle from the walls. They were mostly feline, but they had certain human features: clawlike hands instead of forefeet, for instance.

"What are they?"

"Mummies, but nearly hard as stone. They're remote ancestors of the people of Zan. They had language, rudimentary skills with simple tools, a culture of sorts. From carbon dating we estimate their ages at about one hundred thousand years."

Clarke whistled.

"Don't do that!" she said sharply.

"What's the matter?"

"And keep your voice low. I told you about the way

sound carries, from the top to the bottom of the Catacombs. That's a distance of almost a thousand feet."

"What difference—?"

"Look at this," she said, and directed the beam of
his flashlight to the small cylinder of oxygen she was
holding in one hand. "It's empty. Someone just threw
it aside."

"One of your own explorers, more than likely."

"Not at all," Erika said, sharp again. "We were here
for months. Have you seen one scrap of trash, one
stone out of place anywhere? No archaeologist or serious explorer will leave debris at a valuable site. It's a
cardinal sin; unforgivable."

"How did you find the cylinder, Erika? Can't see a
thing in here without my light."

"Yes, you can. Switch it off."

Clarke did so. For nearly half a minute the chamber
was in darkness. He heard his men stumbling up the
passage behind them and, speaking quietly, his voice
carrying, he told them to freeze in place. He put an
arm around Erika, felt her heart beating savagely.

And then he discovered he could see her face very
well, as if it had developed its own source of light.
The floor, which had seemed to be made of solid
rock, was now translucent. Every object in the chamber stood out in the shadowless illumination.

"Amazing," Clarke murmured.

"The light is from the solid central core of the Catacombs. You'll see it in a few moments."

"Central core? Just where are we?"

"In the first of two antechambers which represent
the dawn of their culture. We're just above the first
level of the Catacombs. There are seven circular levels
in all, seventy huge chambers like slices of—angel
cake, I suppose. But each slice is nearly a hundred
feet high, measuring two hundred feet around the cir-
cumference of the wheel. There's no way to describe

the immensity of the Catacombs. You have to experience it. And then you won't believe your eyes. But there is something we should take care of first."

"What?"

She held up the tapped-out oxygen bottle, the dangling inhaler.

"I think I know who discarded this. He's totally indifferent to everything but his own greed. That's why he came back. He may still be in the Catacombs. If so, his greed has trapped him."

"Who are you talking about, Erika?"

Her voice thinned as she tried not to sob. "Henry Landreth. He's responsible for the deaths of more than thirty of my colleagues and friends. He'll be in the Repository, of course. Stealing all the stones he can carry."

"The red diamonds?"

"Yes. How did you know—?"

"Oliver mentioned them to me. If we find Henry Landreth, Erika, is he worth taking alive?"

Her fingers gripped his arm with surprising strength.

"No. But I want him to live, long enough for the rest of the world to get a good look at him, to hear about his treachery."

"Where is the Repository?"

"On the lowest level."

"Is there a way out of the Catacombs from that level?"

"The only way out we could find is the way we came in," Erika said.

"Suppose I leave Simon here with our equipment and one of the guns. Ned will come with us. How long does it take?"

"Half an hour going down; much longer coming up, of course. It would be wise to carry a cylinder of oxygen."

"Why don't we get started, then? If you're sure you're up to it."

"Meeting Henry face to face will make it all worthwhile."

In the bungalow on the Ugalla River, Raun Hardie had been asleep for only a couple of hours when Jade shook her awake. She rolled over and looked up hazily at him from the borrowed bed. The only light in the room was the light of the moon.

"Matt?"

"Sorry, Raun."

She smiled, thinking he had come to sleep with her. She was much too tired to do anything other than close her eyes and snuggle against his body and fall hard asleep again, but he was certainly welcome . . . She blinked and realized he was fully dressed, and not doing anything about it.

"Oh no!" she groaned. She pulled the pillow over her face.

"We've gassed up the helicopter. I want to leave right away."

"You said—in the morning!"

"Raun, listen to me. The news on the radio isn't good. Kilimanjaro's blowing its stack, a cloud of gases and ash thirty thousand feet high. Seismic activity has picked up again. It might be the prelude to a cataclysm."

"And you want to go *up there*? In the dark? That's crazy!"

"There's a full moon. If the fallout from the volcano isn't too heavy you might be able to locate the entrance to the Catacombs tonight. I could be in and out of there in a few hours. And I have a feeling tomorrow will be too late."

"*You* could be in and out—? What are you saying?"

"There's no need for you and Lem to gamble your lives on the timetable of a volcano. You'll drop me and take off again. Lem can pick me up at dawn. Pull your pants on, and let's get going."

There was something almost jaunty about him, she thought, with a dismal sinking feeling. He was manic. The nearness of death was the only thing that really mattered to him, the touch of a bony finger was like a needle loaded with heroin. Dear God, he hadn't had enough yet, *he couldn't get enough.*

In the Repository of the Catacombs Michael Belov stifled his own anger and marveled at what the tonic of rage had done for Henry Landreth.

For the first time in more than a day the desperately ill man was on his feet, suffused with a glow of false vitality. He stood in the hollow core of one of the three rock-crystal diamond vaults on the floor of the Repository, each a transparent replica of the Catacombs. The vault had been all but emptied of bloodstones. His howls echoed.

This chamber of the Catacombs was, in general dimension, exactly like the others Belov had explored and photographed. It had the height and breadth of all but the largest cathedrals of Europe. It was a tomb, immaculate despite its antiquity, without the dust of millennia lying thick on the floor. The rock walls and floor had been fired by some mysterious means and finished to a dull tan glaze. The inner walls of all the chambers, nearly eight feet thick, were perforated like Swiss cheese, allowing for a draftless circulation of fresh air.

The source of this air and the source of the perpetual light, like moonlight, was the core, a smooth round column that rose, seamlessly, from the depths of the mountain to the roof of the Catacombs. In the farthest corner of every chamber of the Catacombs there was light from this unearthly column—nearly enough light for one to read a newspaper by without suffering eyestrain.

The intermittent fireballs also gave off light—it hurt to look directly at them. The ball lightning was unpredictable. Sometimes hours passed between occurrences. Then, with a slight crackling, hissing noise one would appear, red or orange or bluish-green, out of thin air, and hover near the floor or high above their heads. It might be the size of a grapefruit, or a beach ball.

Most of the time the fireballs drifted only a few feet, but one of them had appeared to follow Belov like a watchdog as he toured several of the chambers on other levels with his camera while Henry slept. When Belov betrayed no anxiety, the glowing plasma came within a few feet of his head. All of his hair stood on end and he received, in only a few seconds' time, a painful burn on one side of his face.

*Don't worry,* Henry had said. *They won't hurt you.* He seemed to regard them as something alive, intelligent. Belov wasn't so sure of the benign intent of the fireballs, and hated to see them floating around, carrying power enough to light up a city the size of Stockholm, or vaporize anything they might touch.

"Robeson!" Henry screamed now. "He did this! He came here and took the FIREKILL stones! That's why he was trying to kill me!"

Belov joined him in the vault. Henry was snatching up the remaining diamonds, staring at them, throwing them down as if they were worthless glass beads when he failed to discover equations that satisfied him.

"How do you know?"

Henry stared at him, his blue underlip quivering.

"Couldn't be anyone else! I brought him here, don't

you see, weeks ago, to complete my translation of the essential equations. That was—Jumbe's idea. Neither of them trusted me."

"I wonder why not," Belov said with a sardonic smile.

"What? What?"

"Is it possible the stones are missing because they were never here in the first place? I've begun to think that you sold them a hoax, Henry. There is no such thing as FIREKILL. You've made the whole thing up."

Henry's rage and frustration found a new target, and with only a moment's hesitation he turned on his companion, hands shooting out to seize Belov by the throat. He had the extraordinary strength of a maniac. There was no room to maneuver in the hollow center of the vault. Belov slipped on one of the stones Henry had thrown down; he fell, wrenching his knee painfully, with Henry on top of him. The back of his head hit one of the rock-crystal shelves that held the diamonds in display sockets. Cloudy red pain flared in his mind. He couldn't breathe and began to panic, tried, too late, a badly aimed blow at the nerve center in Henry's armpit, a strike which might have killed him.

As it missed, Henry screamed and lifted the Russian's head. He hammered it against the shelf, again and again. After the third or fourth repetition Belov didn't feel the impact anymore. The red pain in his head turned into a pulsating, suffocating blackness.

Oliver was halfway up a long steep pitch of Kibo, on an approach to the sixteen-thousand-foot level where he had last seen Phillip Goliath's little airplane. The slope, without significant vegetation, totally open to the blasting winds, was an unstable mass of gravel and clay held partly in check by the remains of a glacier that had once extended to the saddle between the peaks of Kilimanjaro, a solid monolith of ice thirty feet deep and a thousand yards wide.

The moon was above and behind him, but a pall of ash was drifting over it, dimming the light. Soon he would be climbing in Stygian darkness and gloom. Almost directly overhead the stars already had been blotted out by the towering column of smoke and ash and bits of fiery rubble, some of which was falling out of the cloud. So far the prevailing wind had kept most of it from Oliver's side of the mountain.

But the noise, the shaking, had cost him some of his precious strength. It was like creeping in a space between railroad tracks while two endless, heavily loaded freight trains thundered by in opposite directions. He had already done some serious backsliding as sections of icy scree, shaken loose by the action of the volcano, fell apart beneath him in miniavalanches. Also it was bitingly cold on the mountain, and the wind, snapping from one direction and then another, froze the sweat on his face when he stopped to rest and lifted his hooded head more than a few inches from the ground. His hands had little feeling left, although he'd used a spare pair of socks to fashion fingerless gloves.

Oliver carried the bedroll, with three plastic water bottles inside, across his back. Without the ice ax, which he had lashed to one wrist—his miner's habit that had proved worthwhile already on the slippery peak—he could not have gone any distance at all.

But four hours of clawing, groping, and inching hand over hand toward the top had exhausted him. He crammed the sleeping bag into a space between some boulders that he hoped would not crush him if an especially strong tremor hit. There was no other way to anchor himself on the steep incline. He crawled, shivering, into the bag and rinsed his mouth, having inhaled more fine ash than he thought, then drank as much of the water as he could retain with his stomach cramping from nausea. He lay down on his side, gulping air, hands thrust deep into the bag to find warmth. They hurt him ferociously. In spite of his discomfort and altitude sickness, he dozed.

Something awakened him a little later; perhaps it was only a lessening of the volcano's amplitude as it rested between eruptions of steam and ash. The freight trains were rolling to a stop and he heard a different, reverberating sound: a helicopter beating its way up the slope. It seemed to be only a few hundred feet overhead.

Oliver sat up in time to catch a glimpse of the copter's running lights as it hovered in a dense cloud from the crater. The moon's light had been dimmed by the same murky cloud. Oliver couldn't make out the helicopter, which seemed to be dropping slowly to land beside the other one he knew was up there, beneath the sheer rock face by which he had guided himself since the beginning of his climb. Then, in a brilliant blue-tinged flash as lightning arced dramatically out of the fulminating cloud and struck the tip of a rotor blade, he saw the copter and everyone in it clearly.

Four seconds later, after the helicopter had fallen out of sight, he heard a crash.

Erika, Tiernan Clarke, and Ned Chakava were on Level One of the Catacombs when they heard Henry Landreth screaming dementedly in the Repository far below.

They were still in one of the diorama chambers they'd had to pass through in order to reach the pathway that spiraled around the central core. It was a typical room of the Catacombs, familiar to Erika; but the two men, of course, had never seen anything remotely like it. They couldn't be budged for more than half an hour, although the black man at first was in great fear of the creatures that stood, fixed for the ages in lifelike death, in upright tombs of rock crystal which were pure in their transparency but so hard the faceted surfaces couldn't be scratched with a knife. These men, more catlike in appearance than human, were among the elite of the early civilization of Zan, which had stretched in a wide belt across what was then the fertile heartland of Africa. They had flattened but shapely skulls; large, rounded, upstanding ears; blunt noses; and beautiful, yellow-gold, sensitive eyes.

Erika warned both men not to gaze directly into the eyes of the cat people, and explained why.

"How did they get this way?" Tiernan Clarke asked. "How did jungle cats turn into men?"

"I don't know yet. But the answers are here; all that's needed is the time to do the research. The civilization of Zan lasted for a thousand years. Everything they learned and experienced during that time is stored here in the Catacombs. This is more than just a burial place; it's a complete time capsule. Look at that diorama."

The diorama, a convex three-dimensional mosaic of colored crystals, took up all of the back wall of the chamber, about a hundred fifty feet from where they were standing. It depicted, with startling clarity and attention to detail, an entire city on a tropical seacoast, the center of which was a plaza composed of numerous platforms of smooth white stone, pyramidal and arrowhead-shaped buildings—also in white—and extensive terraced gardens. The plaza was well populated, and the people, if observed long enough, seemed to be moving. So did men flying above the great plaza in what looked like horseless chariots.

Other men and women, at a construction site, controlled with beams of light from headdresses huge dressed blocks of stone suspended in the air.

The effect of the diorama, of a world slowly in motion as it had been ten thousand years ago, was hypnotic.

"If you watch long enough," Erika said, "it changes from day to night and back again, over a period of about two of our weeks. We decided that the crystals are activated by vibrations from the central core, trillions of vibrations a second, too fast for any of our instruments to detect."

"How in hell," Clarke wondered, "did they excavate a room this size from solid rock?"

Then his head shot around at the first scream.

He thought immediately of the man they had left behind in the antechamber, Simon Ovosi—it was impossible to tell where the sound had come from. Ned Chakava dropped the rifle he was carrying, as if his hands had turned to stone.

"For Christ's sake!" Clarke said angrily; Ned retrieved the weapon immediately and cocked it. There was another scream, and another, abruptly choked off.

"Something got him, Guv," Ned Chakava muttered. "Something in this evil place got that man!"

Clarke shook his head. "Don't be a bloody fool! That wasn't terror we heard. It was—" He glanced at Erika, who looked horrified herself, drained of color in the eternal moonglow of the Catacombs.

"Rage," she said holding her head. "Frustration? He sounded as if—he were about to go mad."

"If that was your colleague Henry Landreth," Clarke said, "then he may not be alone. I think we should play your hunch, Erika, and search this Repository you told me about."

"We don't know—what's going on here—"

Clarke was wearing a .44 magnum revolver in a shoulder holster. He patted the butt with his right hand.

"We can take care of ourselves, Erika. Let's all have a whiff of oxygen before we start down—my head is splitting."

They were still gulping the much-needed oxygen when the second volley of screams reached them. This time the tone was unmistakable, and even more chilling: There was howling murder in his voice. Erika's eyes grew big above the clear plastic mask of the inhaler. Clarke got up restlessly from one knee, lips clamped on an unlit cheroot, and motioned to her.

The three left the chamber through one of the round ports, about five feet in diameter, that opened directly onto the central core. The path between the great core and the wall was about seven feet wide, spiraling at an easy angle down to the six remaining levels of the Catacombs. The path was not stone but made of a synthetic material that gripped the soles of one's shoes or boots. Yet it was hard enough to resist a knife point.

As for the core, the faintly blue-tinted energy source which Ned Chakava eyed with suspicion and avoided, pressing close to the wall as they descended, Erika was unable to say what it was or how it was charged. You could touch it, embrace it, fall asleep against it without ill effect. There was no measurable electromagnetic pollution inside the Catacombs, ruling out any known type of generator—except, possibly, the human mind. The core seemed inert, but it provided illumination for many thousands of square feet of chamber on each level; it also provided, mysteriously, for the circulation of the air. And it produced fireballs, attracted them. Again Erika was unable to say how or why.

They were halfway to the sixth level when an earth tremor jolted the Catacombs. A bad one; unlike other tremors this one seemed to be centered very near the core.

There was a sound of stress in the rock walls, and the core helix appeared to twist and stretch like ropy candy. They were thrown against one another, against the wall, against the core, then to the path where the tremor sent them bowling. Ned Chakava, who was carrying the bulky oxygen tank on his back, cried out in pain. There was a blushing red shadow deep within the core, pulsing swiftly from bottom to top and back again. It was like a convulsion.

When the tremor ceased, Clarke pulled Erika to her feet. Ned Chakava had a bleeding head where the oxygen tank had banged against it. He pressed a sodden handkerchief against the wound.

"Be all right," he said. "But I want to get *out* of here, Guv."

"So do I. *After* we visit the Repository." He glanced at Erika, who was studying a long crack that had appeared in the wall. Her expression was grim. He cocked his head and smiled tensely.

"Are you thinking there's a chance the Catacombs could collapse around our ears?"

"That's the first crack I've seen anywhere, but there must have been earthquakes in the past as powerful as this one. Their entire civilization vanished in a cataclysm, yet the mountain—and the Catacombs— survived."

"What sort of cataclysm?"

"A violent change in the earth's electromagnetic field resulted in a shift of the poles about ten thousand years ago. But they had no choice, really. It was that or—"

The crackling sound of a fireball interrupted her.

Erika looked around and saw it bounding slowly down the path toward them.

It was one of the largest plasmoids she'd seen, and even as she realized the potential danger she was fascinated with the glowing beauty of the yellow-orange ball. No laws of science could account for the way this one was moving, or dribbling, toward them; although it left no marks on the path or walls it was intensely hot, like the plasma of the sun.

Ned Chakava wailed as Erika felt her face glowing from the closeness of the sphere, which had a diameter of at least three feet. It bounded over her just as Tiernan Clarke snatched her roughly to one side, and hovered several feet above their heads. Then it continued on with a sound of bacon frying and settled down, just inches from the path, a few feet below them.

Ned backed up slowly, forgetting his pain, and bumped into Erika and Clarke.

"Now what?" Clarke asked.

"It's ball lightning," Erika explained. "We learned to live with them, but they *are* scary. This one will just float up against the core after a while and dissipate its energy."

"What if it doesn't?" he said unhappily. "It's in our way."

"We'll just have to wait."

"Until another shaker comes along? I don't think so. Ned, fire into it."

"No!" Erika said.

"Why not? That may be a way of getting rid of the damn thing . . . dissipating it, as you say."

"But—we simply don't know what it is. Matter in some inconceivable state. Some of us used to speculate—that they had intelligence."

Clarke gave her a jaundiced look. "Ned!"

The black man reluctantly raised his rifle and fired three quick shots at the fireball. There was no apparent effect as the shots echoed though the Catacombs. And there were no ricochets from the walls. The bullets just disappeared. Ned looked back slowly at Clarke, and shook his head.

As he did so the fireball began to shrink, and its color changed from a pumpkin color to a dull red. It was a new phenomenon; Erika had never seen one of the plasmoids change shape or color. She felt her heart begin to pound, and it wasn't just the effect of the thin air in the Catacombs.

The fireball suddenly shot toward Ned.

There was a popping sound as it touched either Ned or the barrel of his rifle. Ned's eyes stood out in his head. A blue flame like that from a gas jet appeared momentarily around him, like a halo, then the fireball zipped away and Ned collapsed, smoking; the back of his shirt and bush jacket had been burned away, the skin and flesh were crisp. The fireball had passed through him. The barrel of his rifle had fused into a bulbous lump.

Clarke went down on one knee and tried to find a pulse. There was none. Ned Chakava was dead.

The trembling of the Catacombs brought Michael Belov around. As soon as he moved, he threw up. Black waves of nausea continued to roll through him even after the tremors of the mountain stopped. There was a roaring in his head that had nothing to do with the lava gases forced through subterranean crevices and into the vents of the crater.

He didn't know where he was. His eyes wouldn't focus. He turned blindly around and around on the diamond-strewn floor like a lumpy animal trying to be born. Eventually he located the keyhole entrance to the crystal vault and crawled outside. Blood circulating in his head made it ache horribly, but his vision was improving. He sat up, fell over, sat up again.

Belov looked around the huge chamber—like so many others he'd seen—with its moody sepulchral lighting in which all flesh was the color of bone, and the faces of entombed creatures took on a life of the imagination. His head was exploding with each convulsive breath, but still there wasn't enough air for his lungs. He thought he might be dying. Like Henry.

Or was Henry already dead? Belov saw him lying, sprawled on his back, just a few feet away.

Needed oxygen, Belov thought. But the oxygen was exhausted. They'd come a long way since using the last of it, Henry dying with every step. But somehow he'd made it—here.

To the Repository.

Belov rose on one knee and waited until a surge of dizziness receded. He wondered if he was actually hearing gunshots, or if it was just a hallucination produced by his battered brain. A clock ticked inside him, faster than his frantic pulse, urging him on; getting close to panic time. But what did it mean? There was a deadline to meet, an appointment to keep—he couldn't remember. Something big, however.

He staggered half a dozen steps and went down on all fours beside Henry Landreth.

There was a great deal of blood on Henry's face, his clothes, the floor. He'd been coughing and spitting blood for more than a day, fluid from the drowning lungs, bits of lung tissue as well. But this had been a catastrophe, a final hemmorhage.

Belov tried to locate the pulse in Henry's slack throat. Bad news. Henry had been about to do something vital for him. It had to do with the red diamonds. But they were all gone, at least the ones that mattered. Plenty of red stones secure in their crystal sockets, only they weren't the right stones, and this discovery had sent Henry into a rage. What a pretty picture the stones would make for the satellite if only—

The Russian held his whirling head, and rested. It was almost clear to him now what he was doing here, but focusing precisely on his task still required too much of an effort. The odor of congealing blood sickened him. Too late for Henry, but all appointments had to be kept. Tomorrow was another day, of course, but never postpone until tomorrow what you can do today, particularly when there's only a few hundred feet of cracking, heaving granite between oneself and an unimaginable quantity of gaseous magma.

He looked at the face of his chronometer, trying to cencentrate. The dial was readable. The date was the twenty-third. Of May, he remembered, and almost grasped the significance of it. But he was distracted by another scattered piece of memory falling into place. Henry trying to strangle him, his surprise at the devastating strength of a man who should not have been able to stand unaided. The power of rage. And Henry had nearly succeeded in killing him. He'd been a total fool. Off guard.

So if it was nearly ten o'clock at 37 degrees and 39 minutes east longitude, three degrees south latitude, seven o'clock Greenwich, then what time was it in Moscow? And what did it matter?

The satellite, of course!

The satellite was coming, the sophisticated Molniya with multiple antennae capable, in perigee, of scooping up the myriad tiny signals from his phototransmitter and, hours later over Moscow, in the early morning, reproducing in excellent detail the series of photos that proved the existence of the Catacombs.

He would have, he recalled, from 1:06 to 1:18 A.M. to relay the photos. He had also hoped to send a message that he'd found the bloodstones they desperately wanted. But Kumenyere had them now, according to Henry, and Moscow would just have to pay his price.

Belov had all of his equipment with him, and the photos he'd taken in other chambers. They were in the pack he'd carried with such difficulty down seven levels to the Repository, along with Henry Landreth. His problem now was to get out of the Catacombs in time.

He knew he was deep in the mountain, and he had no idea of what lay beneath him. But the floor was hot. He didn't think it had been this hot to the touch an hour or two ago. The big pancake of blood Henry had spouted onto the floor had not fully coagulated.

Overhead three fireballs had appeared, shedding light. He was accustomed to them by now. They hovered twenty feet off the floor over Henry's body, varying in color from pale blue to red. He looked again at Henry's pinched face, at the bloody fingertips of one hand, and saw that Henry had been writing something on the floor when he died.

Belov took a close look at the symbols Henry had scrawled, childishly large, with his own thick dark blood. Three long rows of equations which Belov was unable to decipher. But obviously Henry had thought that it was important enough, as he lay gasping and vomiting his lungs out, to get it all down.

This had to be Henry Landreth's translation of the FIREKILL formulae.

Belov, sufficiently excited to overcome his pain, went for his pack and took out a Polaroid SX-70 camera with flash attachment. He photographed the equations from every angle, made certain that the prints were sharp and he hadn't missed anything. Let the physicists of the U.S.S.R. figure out what was meant. But Belov had his hunch: This was Henry's ultimate vindication, and the only revenge he could take on Robeson Kumenyere.

He had not paid much attention to the fireballs since their appearance, but their light seemed brighter. When he looked up he saw them circling each other, a display he found somewhat ominous but fascinating. He picked up his pack and put it on, adjusted the straps. This effort almost sent him reeling with dizziness again; he was in precarious shape for a long walk up and out of the Catacombs.

He sat down until the black corona around his brain receded and the pounding of blood in his temples became bearable. But the floor was hot, too hot, he had to get up again. He knew he should rest, despite the counterurging of his internal clock; but he decided to push on to the next level, and away from the danger he sensed here.

When he got to his feet and turned around, he saw a man with a shaggy mane of black hair standing fifty feet away, near the central core, leveling a big revolver at him.

"Good thing I hurried down," Tiernan Clarke said breathlessly. "So you made it without me, boy-o. Good enough, but I'll relieve you of your pack now. Which I assume you've stuffed with all the good things this treasure chest has to offer."

In the hour Simon Ovosi had been left alone in the antechamber of the Catacombs, armed with an ebony-handled knife with a five-inch lock blade and a .458 Winchester magnum rifle, he had stood his post despite the screams and gunshots emanating from below, the half-seen company of petrified creatures hung by their necks and tailbones from the crudely squared walls, the earth tremors that made him sweat-

ingly sick. He survived even the lengthy silences that
had him straining to hear footsteps, the familiar voice
of Tiernan Clarke confirming his return.

But his mind wasn't equal to the sight of the fireball; when it appeared a moaning babble escaped his
lips. The fireball was ovoid, bluish-purple in color,
about the size of one of his own fists. Attracted to
him, it moved slowly along beneath the low ceiling,
crackling faintly. He backed up and raised his rifle
and fired two roaring, deafening shots. The second of
the ricocheting slugs, flattened and jagged, hit him
below the right knee and cut deep, crippling him.

Simon fell back on the translucent floor as the fireball swooped and touched the muzzle of his gun.
There was a flash and a bit of smoke and he was left
holding a piece of smoldering stock; the rest of the
heavy rifle had vanished, along with the fireball.

Simon rolled over, still moaning, and saw the creatures stirring on the walls, eyes flashing to life, jaws
gaping, narrow feline heads switching side to side.
Two of them were tensing to jump at him. He pulled
his knife and hitched his way backward across the
rough floor on the seat of his pants, sobbing in terror,
slashing wildly at each threatening move.


As if she'd seen it yesterday, Raun had picked out
the cul-de-sac from the air, although the moon's light
was drastically cut by a cloud of grit by the time they
ascended to the 16,000 foot level.

The Cayuse helicopter, rated for 15,800 feet maximum altitude, was already above its limit and difficult to maintain in ground effect, a condition made
worse by the whiplash air currents, as heat from the
mountain caldera and expanding gases collided with
the cold air mass three miles above sea level. There
was a danger of being flung against one of the trip-

tych wall faces, and danger from the swarming ash that seeped hotly into the cockpit through the slightest aperture. Within minutes the fine grit could ruin the helicopter's hydraulic systems.

And the only good place to land was already occupied by another, larger helicopter.

Jade briefly debated turning over the controls to Lem and climbing down by means of a rope ladder to within a few feet of the ground, but he doubted if the helicopter would hover long enough for him to accomplish this.

Then his mind was made up for him as a dazzling streak of lightning flashed from the darkness of the huge ash cloud descending on them and struck a rotor-blade tip. For a few moments the inside of the cockpit was whitely incandescent. Raun screamed. Jade had his hands full trying to prevent a crackup as the engine lost power. The rotor slowed drastically, winding down to a stop. When the Cayuse nosed steeply down he quickly set the blades at a negative pitch angle, catching the airflow through the rotor as the helicopter began to drop. The flow was sufficient to keep the blades turning, fast enough to hold them shakily in the gusting air.

They had only about a hundred feet to go, not much time for maneuvering. He tried to bank it down behind the other copter, raising the collective pitch lever, calling on the kinetic energy left in the rotor to give them a few urgently needed moments of additional lift to slow the big machine for touchdown.

But one of the rotor blades struck the tailfin of the JetRanger, shearing it, and they lurched hard and jarringly to the right. All the weight of the copter was balanced on one skid, the supports of which buckled as another of the decelerating blades struck the ground. Instead of snapping off, it dug in and kept the helicopter from flipping over and possibly exploding.

There was another bolt of lightning as they crawled out of the disabled Cayuse. The air was so thick with fumes and grit, they were choking almost immediately. The ground shook; the helicopter fell over gratingly, just missing Lem, the last man off. Jade motioned for them to wrap their safari jackets around their heads, which afforded some protection against the ash. He grabbed Raun, who was down on one knee and looked stunned.

"How do we get inside?"

". . . The gully."

"Come on!"


Michael Belov's head ached so badly he couldn't keep his eyes open for more than a few seconds at a time, and one ear was filled with blood.

Nonetheless he said calmly to Tiernan Clarke, "Those photos can't be of any use to you. What you want are the bloodstones. And as you can see, there are hundreds of them here."

"I can see," Clarke replied, lifting the photo transmission machine from the backpack. "They've waited ten thousand years, boy-o. They can wait another minute for harvesting." He stared at the machine, perplexed. "Now what would this be for?"

Belov was lying on his stomach on the hot floor, which had begun to move from slowly intensifying seismic waves that added to his suffering. After rapping him on the skull with the barrel of the magnum revolver, Clarke had hogtied him with strips torn from his cotton safari jacket.

"It's a photo transmitter."

"That doesn't explain much." Clarke sorted through the stack of Polaroid shots again, plucked one and flashed it at Belov.

"So this was all you were interested in? And what do these symbols mean?"

"They have no value for you, compared to what one of the bloodstones is worth."

"Is that so?"

"Clarke, don't you realize what's happening here? Can't you feel it—the heat, the trembling—there's magma under this slab, maybe directly beneath it, and it could come welling up at any moment, turning this chamber into a blast furnace. There's no need to keep me tied down. I have no use for any of those stones. You're welcome to leave with as many as you can carry. Let's just get out while there's time."

Clarke wiped his sweating face and laughed.

"Don't worry, I'll take good care of myself, as I always have. But why should I take any interst in your well-being? As for these photos—" He unbuttoned a cargo pocket of his jacket. "I'll just keep them for souvenirs, like; decide what to do with them later. Let us say, for instance, when I'm enjoyin' the first cool gin of the evening on the stern deck of the *gahr-jus* yacht I plan to anchor permanently off my own Greek island."

A violent tremor threw him down; they both heard the grinding of rock, the rumble of gas expanding through narrow crevices all around the Catacombs. There was an odor of poisonous sulfides in the air. If the gas found a suitable outlet into the Repository, it would come with a roar, at a volatile one thousand degrees centigrade.

Clarke's revolver fell from the shoulder holster; the photos were scattered, curling up on the hot floor. Clarke got up looking dazed. He ignored Belov, reached for the backpack and shook it empty, carried it with him at a staggering jog across the broad floor toward the three rock-crystal diamond vaults. Each of the vaults was ten feet in diameter, hollow at the center. A vault was entered by means of an opening which a man Clarke's size had to squeeze through sideways. Inside lay the diamonds.

Belov struggled against the knots Clarke had tied, and nearly fainted from the effort. He lay on his side, coughing, his head sticky from the blood of the scalp wound Clarke had inflicted. His ears rang distressingly.

He felt a hand brush his forehead and jerked his head up. He looked at the pale intent face of Erika Weller, her head nodding slightly with the impact of each shallow breath she drew. The air in the Repository was fast becoming unbreathable.

"Untie me!" Belov said thickly.

"Who *are* you?"

"A journalist. I came here with—Henry Landreth."

"Henry? Where—"

Anger flared in her dark glazed eyes. She looked up and around and saw the body forty feet away.

"Oh, God. *He's dead?*"

"Pulmonary edema. And we'll be dead too, if you don't hurry."

Her hands dropped to the tight knots in the twisted cloth, but fumbled there ineffectually.

"It isn't fair," she complained. "I wanted him to see me; and I wanted to see what happened to his face when he realized he hadn't got away with it, that I—*I* was still alive to expose him. The bastard. *The rotten bastard!*"

She was nearly to the point of a breakdown: sick, scared, and emotionally spent. He realized that. And she would be no good to either of them if the last vital supports of rationality crumbled.

Tiernan Clarke had emerged from the first of the vaults, having swept it clean of the red diamonds now bulging on one side of the canvas pack. He saw Erika crouched beside Belov.

"Erika!" he shouted across the chamber. "Let him alone, and come help me!"

"*Erika!*" Belov said sharply, and succeeded in getting her full attention. She glanced down at him, startled.

"Clarke hit me with his gun. Look at my head! Whatever he's represented himself to be, he's nothing more than a rogue and a murderer. He's here only to steal bloodstones, and he'll take no one with him when he leaves."

"Erika!" Clarke bellowed, and she looked up indecisively.

The chamber, large as an aircraft hangar, trembled. The air had worsened, and Erika choked on it.

"Erika," Belov pleaded, "we have to get out of here before we're poisoned or incinerated."

"No! It *can't* happen. The Catacombs can't be destroyed. He worked so hard, it was a great achievement for Chips—"

"Erika, I have dozens of photographs. *Proof* exists of what your team discovered here. But it's no good if the Catacombs become our tomb. *Help me.*"

She stared at him for a few moments longer, then nodded. Her fingers flew at the difficult knots.

A hundred feet away Tiernan Clarke reached for his revolver, discovered that it wasn't in the holster, hesitated, then turned and ran and squeezed inside the next vault, drawn to the irresistible deep-red glare of bloodstones. He had to pull them, one at a time, like eggs from tight nests. He was fully absorbed in the task.

Coughing, weeping, Erika struggled with one knot, undid it, attacked another.

There was a sound like the crack of doom and the portion of the floor they were on was heaved upward a good eighteen inches. A wave of suffocating heat like nothing Belov had felt before was accompanied by an intense glow from the molten heart of the mountain. Brilliant fireballs were jumping out of the air, revolving at incredible speeds, bouncing crazily from the walls, floating over their heads.

The noise temporarily deafened them. Erika's mouth was wide open; she was screaming as they slid slowly along the floor, which was now hot enough to singe exposed skin. Belov couldn't hear her, nor could she hear him shouting to keep working, to free his hands of the last knot. His precious photos were scattering everywhere, whirling upward in a hot draft, scorching at the edges. Heavy machinery groaned and slipped along the slightly tilted floor, huge sarcophagi vibrated like tuning forks.

The other part of the floor cracked again, tented from the pressure of magma that had the thickness of toothpaste. Tiernan Clarke was trying to edge his way out of the second vault when a section of floor the size of a basketball court heaved and tipped. The three vaults crashed together.

For several seconds they leaned precariously but in balance, forming a rough pyramid. Then the floor shuddered and the middle vault tipped, dropped out, and began to roll, slowly. It resembled a big hollow glass log with Clarke trapped in the middle of it. The vault rolled down a gentle incline toward a furiously hot mass of lavalike incandescent scar tissue running jaggedly through the chamber.

The tilt of the slab of floor on which Belov was lying shielded him and Erika from the worst of the heat from the magma scar. But as the massive rolling vault came within twenty feet of the glowing molten rock, taking on a glow itself, there was a puff of grayish smoke inside, as if someone had touched a lighted match to a moth in a jar. Clarke, suddenly a jet of flame from head to toe, was consumed in a matter of seconds. Moments after that the vault, containing an untold fortune in red diamonds, wallowed in the magma and slowly melted.

Erika's hair was smoldering, but she had freed his hands at last.

Their skin had begun to blister. Belov sat up and pushed her toward a port that opened onto the central core, shouting words neither of them could hear. He felt only the pain in his head, and heard nothing but a dismal low roar. Erika stumbled up, swiping at her hair with her hands, and ran.

Belov got his feet loose, wrapped the painfully hot photo transmitter in scraps of cloth and snatched it up, hugged it under one arm. He saw a block of photos on the floor; they had stuck together in the heat. He retrieved those, along with a few more photos that didn't look too bad, picked up Clarke's revolver by the butt, and ran after Erika. The soles of his boots felt sticky. He could no longer breathe in this inferno. His lungs were raw, they felt stuffed full of sandpaper. With each dragging step he expected to suffer Clarke's fate and burst into flame.

The port to the central core was like a chimney, roaring with hot air and bits of ash at almost hurricane velocity. He crept through on hands and knees, nearly blind and deaf, pushing the photo transmitter ahead of him, and tumbled out into the relative coolness of the core.

Erika was there, face blank as a robot's. Some of her hair was in char. Her face was a mass of blisters. Her lips had swollen to twice their normal size. She lifted him up.

"Look!" she said. He had to read her lips to understand her.

The dynamic core was glowing with a new intens-

ity, a deep pink blush. Hundreds of multicolored fireballs quivered around it.

Erika was trembling. She put her mouth to his ear.
He dimly made out what she was saying.

"It's as if—it's always been—alive—but dying now.
Like the rest of us."

"You're not dying, Erika!" Belov shouted. "And we'll
get out of here. Just walk!"

She shook her head sadly. Belov saw that she could
absorb no more of this particular ordeal, and he wondered what hell she'd been through in the past month
or so.

He twisted her arm painfully, but there was no response. He held her head up then, and made her look
at him. Then he kissed her swollen lips.

Where force had failed, tenderness took effect.
Something stirred in her eyes, a flicker of acknowledgment of the need to survive. Erika touched his
own lips with her fingertips.

*Yes.*

"Let's go then."

A temblor hit; they were shaken. They stood their
ground with only each other for support, then began
to climb the path winding around the core, one sore
dragging step at a time.


Raun, Jade, and Lem Meztizo pushed on into the
Catacombs despite the violence happening below,
which was transmitted in jarring waves through solid
rock, audible as a low tortuous booming that painfully
assaulted the eardrums.

But inside was better than outside, where a dusky
blizzard sharp as glass was blowing through the cul-
de-sac, illuminated by bitter blue flashes of lightning.
Raun went first, remembering the way, through the

twisting, cloacal passage. Jade had a flashlight; the beam filled the passage with light. Lem carried one of the Kalashnikov rifles, all he had salvaged from the wrecked copter.

"How far?" Jade asked, as they were slowed by a tight turn and a narrowing of the passage that forced them to their hands and knees.

"I think—just a few feet. Then there's—a little chamber, with more of the striped walls."

He held the light over her shoulder as she stopped to rest, saw the reflections from obsidian.

"There it is."

"My God, what if this place—falls in on us?"

"Seems intact so far. No loose rock. Now, let's move."

They crawled another twenty feet and were able to stand. The chamber had a floor that sloped gradually up to a dozen vertical arabesques, six or seven feet high, on the uneven face of the wall opposite them.

"It's one of those markings," Raun said, looking around. "Third from the left?" She went scrambling up the tilted floor toward the wall.

As Raun reached the cleft in the rock face, Jade swung his flashlight beam toward it. Something stirred inside the cleft. Raun screamed and backed away. Simon Ovosi, his clothing in tatters, bloody slashes on his body and face, lunged at her, the knife with the five-inch blade raised high.

Jade was too distant to be of any use to Raun. Behind him Lem said sharply, "Matt!"

He threw himself out of the way and the Kalashnikov in Lem's hands blazed for a second and a half. All of the slugs hit Simon in the head and chest, stopping him. The blade that struck Raun on the shoulder had lost much of its force, and it spilled from his hand as Simon made a half turn on rubber knees and collapsed, rolling downhill toward Jade.

Raun held her shoulder, grimacing, and leaned against the wall, staring at the body.

"Who is *that*?"

Jade got to her as she began to tremble.

"Hurt bad?"

"He cut me. But I don't think— No, it's not too bad." She took her hand away from the slash on the ball of her right shoulder. Her fingers were bloody.

"*What's going on here?*"

Jade threw the light into the cleft from which Simon had emerged. There was blood on the walls, as if he'd been lurking there for some time. On the other side of the opening his light picked up part of a wall of ancient mummies.

"Raun, take a look."

She glanced in, then turned her head sharply away.

"Yes. That's it. As much as I ever saw of the Catacombs. I wouldn't—couldn't go in there with those things."

She looked fearfully into Jade's eyes.

"So—do I have to go now?"

"We'd better stick together, Raun."

Lem was kneeling beside the body of Simon Ovosi. He looked up.

"Matt, these slashes—he might have done it to himself, with his own knife. I don't think he was in a fight."

"What about an animal?"

"Well, it's possible."

"Leave him and come on." To Raun Jade said with a slight smile, "Me first this time."

"*Gladly.*"

She was panting; they all were. It was difficult to draw a full breath. And, following the shock of the attack, the blood of her wound, Raun felt nauseated and light-headed. Her skin was dazzling cold.

Jade saw it coming on and made her sit with her

head between her knees. He left Lem to guard her with the Kalashnikov and proceeded through the final short passage into the first of the Catacomb chambers. The walls were ringed with hideous, not-altogether-human remains. His light gleamed on tawny faces, broken fangs, rudimentary claws.

It was hot in the chamber. His face was streaming. He stumbled across the big-bore rifle Simon Ovosi had dropped, and picked it up. The rifle had recently been fired. Three cartridges left. Along one wall there were some bulky field packs, one of which contained excellent cameras and miles of unexposed 35-millimeter film. Another contained water in canteens, a loaf of plastic explosive, and a timer-detonator. He also found two large cylinders of oxygen.

"Lem; bring Raun." He already had learned that it was needless to raise your voice here. A whisper carried surprisingly far.

He gave Raun oxygen from a cylinder, and went exploring.

There was a second chamber. A strong draft of warm air, faintly tinged with hydrogen sulfide gas, was coming from somewhere. He searched the oblong room carefully.

In an altar area littered with relics of prehistory he discovered a crude passage with stone steps that dropped fifteen feet, then widened and angled toward an unknown light source. The Catacombs shuddered and fumed. Jade turned his head away from the updraft of unhealthy air and coughed retchingly. When the mountain settled down again he thought he heard voices, but could not distinguish words, from below.

He started to descend into the tight stairwell, which had a diameter of less than six feet. He hesitated, then went back for Raun and Lem and the cylinders of oxygen. On impulse he also shouldered the pack which contained the water and explosives.

\* \* \*

Near the third level on their way up and out of the Catacombs, Erika and Belov found the cylinder of oxygen abandoned by Tiernan Clarke in his impatience to get to the bloodstones. Between them, they nearly exhausted the remaining liters of the life-preserving oxygen.

The air in the core, already thin, had steadily worsened in quality, but it was still breathable. But they were both so depleted by the physical ordeal that their limbs had begun to tremble erratically as they dragged themselves up the helical path. When they tried to crawl they found themselves going in blundering irrational circles like insects dazed by the power of the core, moving around and around each other instead of making steady progress toward the top. Their brains had been starved for oxygen.

Belov looked at his watch while they rested. There was time, but barely enough time, for him to make his rendezvous with the satellite. The volcano was still shaking the Catacombs. But he didn't believe there would be further danger from the viscous, slowly extruded magma that had split the floor of the Repository.

Erika, however, was staring at the core, her jaw sagging, her face almost a parody of stunned surprise. The core had changed, in less than half an hour, from pinkish-white to a claret shade. The light had changed accordingly; only the myriad swarming fireballs retained their plasmic brilliance.

Erika and Belov's faces, having suffered too much abuse, now looked sinister and ghoulish. And, mysteriously, the core, the path, the walls around them, appeared subtly misshapen. It was as if they had breathed in too much oxygen too quickly, precipitating hallucinations, a waking nightmare.

"What is it, Erika?"

Belov's ears still rang from the bludgeoning he had taken; he couldn't hear himself speak too well. His words sounded distorted, as if he were hearing a recording played, irritatingly, at slightly the wrong speed. When he raised a hand it felt heavier, weighted. The tilt of his head toward the core was a little ponderous. Only enough to puzzle, not frighten him.

"Do you think it'll explode?"

"I don't know. All the laws—of physics break down here. I told you—that the core was beyond any means of physical calculation. It's not made of any material we've ever encountered. It exists. It's here. But—what in God's universe can it be? And what is it doing now?"

"Obvious that it's reached some sort of crisis," he said dully.

"I think—the core must be vibrating tremendously faster, setting up a resonance that eventually could— vaporize tungsten steel. Or crystalline carbon. That's why we're—heavier. Slower."

"I don't understand."

"As the core vibrates—one hundred, two hundred trillion times a second, time and space and matter are distorted around it. Eventually—the core will simply vanish. Long before that happens, we'll be frozen in place, unable to move away from it. Then we'll be— pulled apart, separated into atoms. I thought the volcano precipitated this crisis in the core. But it could be—just the other way around. The crisis could have something to do with all the stones that are missing, or destroyed. We always felt that it was a—a very great risk to remove them from their vaults, even for short periods of study."

"Why?"

"You had to—live in here for a while, absorb the rhythm of the Catacombs, in order to understand. It's always been a living, not a dead place. Until now. We've destroyed it, somehow."

Belov stared at Erika's face, which looked as dark as if he were viewing it through an infrared filter. The waning of the light had been troubling him for some time. It was difficult to judge emotions in the flat red light, but she looked rational, just a little frightened by her own surmise.

When he moved to touch her, the slight bothersome heaviness, as if his hand were being held back by a puppeteer's string, caused a buzz of alarm near his heart. He pulled Erika to her feet and picked up the photo transmitter. Tiernan Clarke's big magnum revolver, the heavy chrome frame a smear of pink, was tucked into his waistband.

Belov saw, as they labored upward, that the fireballs clinging to the core had decreased in number and size. And the strangeness, his sense of distortion and dislocation, grew. Despite the brutal red glow of the core he felt drawn to it, as if every atom of his being longed to merge with it. He might have been experiencing the first stages of nitrogen narcosis—a heady, heedless rapture, subtly orgasmic.

At his side Erika must have felt something similar: Her feet wandered on the path, but her head was up. She breathed ecstatically, mouth open, eyes agleam. She would have walked right into the core if he hadn't kept a tight grip on her elbow.

He sensed, in the shape of shadows moving in the thick unreal redness down the path from the second level, another danger. The shadows materialized. Two men, both armed; a woman.

Everyone stopped at the same time.

"Who are you?" Belov asked. The solemn intonation of the slowed words. But he had a hunch. He'd been anticipating a confrontation, since that afternoon at the Kivukoni Five-Star Hotel when an emissary of

Akim Koshar had handed him a piece of jade with its representation of two great mythical creatures tumbling through the cosmos, locked at each other's throats—Yin and Yang.

Erika broke free of him and, pushing against the sticky tightening web of Time, struggled toward Matthew Jade and Raun Hardie.

*"Go back!"*

*Baaaaccckkk.*

The Catacombs shuddered; there was a low growl of solid rock under immense, twisting pressure. Belov followed Erika, sensing an opportunity. He didn't know if he could take advantage of the newcomers but they seemed at a loss, perhaps confused by the demands which the undetectably oscillating core made on all of them. His head, his bones, felt heavy; his heartbeat was massive, pumping blood with the specific gravity of molten lead. Each breath weighed a ton.

"You can *feel* what's happening!" Erika warned the others. "Go back! While you can still move!"

She came between Raun and Jade. She put a hand imploringly on Jade, blocking the rifle Lem Meztizo had turned toward them. Belov went up to him, drawing his revolver with the wrong hand. He hit Lem in the back of the head with the butt. There was a spray of blood, black as ink, in the red air. Lem was separated from the Kalashnikov rifle, which Belov grabbed. As Lem fell, Belov turned, pointing the rifle at Raun Hardie. He could kill them both before Jade pulled the trigger of his big-bore Winchester, and Jade knew it.

"Throw it away," he said to Jade. "Down there."

Jade hesitated only a moment, then turned deliberately and hurled the rifle down the path.

"Kneel. Hands behind your head."

Erika had turned and was staring at him.

"What are you doing!"

Belov ignored her. As Jade got down on his knees and laced his fingers behind his head, Belov backed up, set the photo transmitter down, and shifted the rifle to his right hand. Lem Meztizo, holding his head where Belov had cracked him, was down on one knee. No immediate threat.

Belov said, "You are Jade, aren't you? Matthew Jade."

Jade nodded.

Belov nodded back, formally. It was almost a bow.

"Your escape from Lefortovo was brilliant. You fooled some very thorough doctors. They still wonder how you faked death so convincingly, and revived yourself afterward. But there is no way—you'll escape from hell itself."

He turned the Kalashnikov on Lem Meztizo and fired two short bursts at a low angle. His finger felt clumsy on the trigger; the pull was hard. Lem, knee-capped, fell back with a long scream of agony. Belov shifted the rifle to Jade and fired again. But Erika had moved in the meantime, taken two steps toward him; his aim was disturbed by an impulse not to include her in the line of fire. And Jade was also moving, lunging up and to one side. Instead of being knee shot, as Belov intended, he took a hit on one thigh and spun around, falling. Raun dropped beside him protectively as he writhed on the path. Belov felt a moment's sadness that it had to go this way. Then he turned and hurled the rifle away and snatched Erika's wrist.

Her face was twisted in anger.

"*Whyyy?*"

"I still need you, Erika." She resisted him. "You want to stay here? To die? You know you'll die, Erika. Don't be foolish."

The fight went out of her. He pulled her slowly up the path with him, a decided burden. Her ravaged face looked dull, animalistic, pulled out of shape by the forces of the dying core. No reason for this, he thought. But, just as he couldn't easily kill a man when there wasn't an absolute necessity for doing so, he couldn't leave Erika behind after she'd fought the knots that bound him, risking her own life.

He'd forgotten just where he was in the Catacombs, how much farther they had to go. His nerves screamed; his mind, confronted by scientific paradox, had begun to betray him. Ahead of him, on the path, he saw his wife, poised on her toes on the stage of the Swedish ballet, her head in elegant profile, arms angled over her head. She began to spin, faster and faster. He was thrilled, overcome. He heard the sounds of applause, monstrous muffled handclaps. Then she vanished and he was walking in deep sand, pushing against a motionless wall of surf, crying for Ingrid. But the sounds coming from his throat were grotesque.

*"Gruhhhhhhhh . . ."*

He was down on his knees. He had dropped the vital photo transmitter. He saw Erika's face in front of his own. She was talking to him, pulling at him, pointing. Her mouth was distorted, her words just tones registering on the tympana.

Belov looked where she was pointing. It was the way out. They'd made it.

He gathered up the photo transmitter, hugging it tightly against his chest, and crawled awkwardly to the inclined passage. As they worked their way upward the red light from the core, thick as tomato soup, turned into total darkness. Although he was moving more easily, breathing normally again, he started to panic with this sudden onset of blindness.

Erika was ahead of him, and he lost contact with her. He came to the steps in the vertical well, hearing her now, clearly, panting as she climbed in the dark. He followed, awkwardly, afraid of falling and losing the machine. Nothing could have forced him to go back into the red light, the slow whirlpool of Time.

In the antechamber he gropingly found Erika face-down on the floor near the altar, spent and dazed. The Catacombs were shaken by a temblor. He sat down beside her. Her skin gave off almost enough heat to fry an egg.

"We can't rest now. Better get out," he said, his words sharp to his own ears after the growls and groans below. "No telling what will happen."

"Can't . . . see."

He set the photo transmitter between his feet, opened the metal case, and fumbled with the controls. There was a low resonant hum and tiny lights came on. When his eyes became accustomed to the low level of illumination he looked around and saw that it would be enough for them to find their way out.

"Why did you do that? Shoot those men?"

"Them or me," he said lamely.

"That doesn't make sense. They can't get out now. They're trapped like—flies on flypaper."

"We aren't so well off ourselves. Sixteen thousand feet up on a mountain trying to explode." He held the face of his watch near one of the small lights on the photo transmitter. His heart jumped shockingly. Either his watch had stopped, or there had been an actual dislocation of time deep in the Catacombs beside the core. He held it to his ear. Ticking. If his watch was to be trusted, then, he still had a few minutes to contact the satellite, send a rapid stream of photos on their way to Moscow. But he couldn't do it from inside the chamber.

He badgered Erika to her feet again.

"Hold on to my belt," he said. "I'll lead us out of here."

Lightning flashed above the cul-de-sac, as many as three bolts simultaneously. The air was turbid with ash—it had drifted two inches deep in the gully. Belov's hair stood on end as soon as they emerged from the cleft in the wall.

"How did you get here?" he asked Erika.

"Helicopter. It's just there, at the end of the gully."

"We'll run for it."

In the ashen meadow they found two helicopters, one wrecked. Belov saw that the tail assembly of the JetRanger was irreparably damaged; it would fly only in ungainly, unmanageable circles. He pushed Erika inside the helicopter anyway, out of the maelstrom.

She sank back in the copilot's seat, eyes closed. He began to go through the Polaroid shots of the Catacombs, separating them. Most of the photographs, including those of Henry Landreth's formulae, written in his own blood, remained clear.

Belov placed the collapsible silver-dish antenna on top of the helicopter and began sending at once, aware that the field of electrostatic energy surrounding them might ruin the transmissions, with the satellite receiving only indecipherable signals.

Erika looked at the photo transmitter on his lap as he fed in the Polaroids at twenty-second intervals. She saw the Cyrillic markings on the machine.

"What are you doing?" she asked, almost disinterestedly.

"I wanted to show the people back home what they're missing."

Her puffed lips formed the semblance of a smile.

"Why—should they be so interested—'back home'?"

Belov glanced at her. *No harm in it now*, he thought. What difference could it make if she knew?

Probably neither of them was going to get off Kilimanjaro alive.

With his free hand he showed her one of the photos of the FIREKILL formulae.

"Did Henry Landreth tell any of you about FIRE-KILL?"

She had to think about it. "Henry said it was a—a device, employed by the people who engineered the Catacombs so capably, for warding off destructive meteor showers."

"FIREKILL has direct application today as an antiballistic missile device."

Erika peered at the formulae, then slowly shook her head. She no longer had the energy for rage.

"Good God. Is that what—so many of us have died for?"

"I'm afraid so," Belov murmured, busy with the photo transmitter again. He glanced at his watch. Everything he had sent would be received. He hoped some of the equation photographs would be intelligible to the right parties. But all they really needed to know in Moscow, he thought, was that the Catacombs existed, that it wasn't an elaborate hoax. They would then deal with Kumenyere, who had the appropriate stones tucked away.

"Are you telling me," Erika said, "that your government is foolish enough to actually construct this device?" She began making some ragged, pathetic sounds. It shocked him to realize the sounds were laughter. He looked at Erika.

"What's the joke?" he said sharply.

He heard the cockpit access door on his side swing open, but thought only that it hadn't been properly latched, that the wind had caught it.

Then he smelled the man outside and, at the same time, as lightning flashed, saw reflected on the Lexan windshield in front of him a dark face hooded in yellow. A streak of fear shot through the Russian as he tried to turn and reach for the revolver in his belt at the same time.

The blade of the ice ax crashing down caught him just above the occipital bulge and nearly cut his head off. Blood shot everywhere through the cockpit as Erika screamed hoarsely.

Oliver Ijumaa stood rooted by shock, his hand still gripping the handle of the ax, blood from the dead man running down his filthy slicker, turning muddy from the ash. Oliver stared at Belov's face. The photo transmitter had fallen from Belov's lap as his body jerked and shuddered. Oliver slowly raised his eyes.

Erika was looking at him in disbelief. Oliver smiled timidly. There was another flash of lightning.

"Making big mistake," he said. "Oh, heavens! Sorry. Sorry!"


In the Catacombs Matthew Jade was losing his struggle with a power more fascinating than Death itself.

The red energy of the stricken core had done more than slow him physically; it had divided his will. The wound in his leg had only partly crippled him. The leg would still bear some weight. But Lem was helpless. He had fainted from the pain of his riddled knees.

Jade had only Raun to help him. Between the two of them they could barely inch Lem up the path. The attraction was all the other way. He had lost all sense of time, of urgency. There was a thrilling resonance in his body, a pleasantly compelling oscillation that dulled the mind. Each breath he took sighed in his ears like solar wind. In this phantasmagoria of red and black he heard siren songs and felt a longing to surrender, to be flung atom by atom into a primordial universe.

When it seemed to be too much trouble, he let go of Lem and fell back, turned over on his side, let himself drift in the compelling tide created by the core.

Raun's face, lugubrious as a clown's, was close to his. Her mouth moved slowly. The sounds she made bore no relationship to speech. He had to laugh. His head rolled slowly, drunkenly, on his shoulders.

So this was what it was all about. In the end, Death teased, cajoled, seduced. There was no trauma, no pain. All the psychic agony of his own grim advances, his attempts to push himself deeper into the mystery without forfeit, had not prepared him for the ease he felt at this moment of transition.

"*Noooooo!*" Raun screamed

She was pulling at him. Jade felt vaguely irritated, and opened his eyes.

The Catacombs trembled. The power of it, counter to the gradually increasing vibrations in his own body, the low hum of forgetfulness, disturbed him. He sat up. Raun's voice was a low-comedy basso.

"*Matt—commmmingggg—tooooo—helppppp—usssss.*"

Then he saw them: the woman with the cast on her arm, beside her a tall bony hooded figure. He felt his heart constrict. Here was Death personified. He looked again. Death was wearing mud-caked sneakers and carrying a flashlight with a vivid pink beam.

A flood of weeping burst from him; thick tears oozed down his face. He crawled to Lem and took him by one arm. Oliver Ijumaa grasped the other arm. Erika embraced Raun, then pointed the way they had come and shook her head. Raun didn't understand at first.

"*What's the matter?*"

"*Blocked. Rockslide. Can't get out.*"

Jade, realizing something was wrong, left Lem with Oliver and came slowly to Erika. She explained their predicament through gestures and groaning words.

"*Another way out?*"

Erika shook her head, a big lolling motion. "*Don't—knowwww.*"

"*Have to—get away from that,*" Jade moaned. He meant the mad redness of the core. "*How?*"

Erika plucked at his sleeve. "*One of the chambers. Inside. Maybe—a chance.*"

With a huge effort Jade and Oliver lifted Lem to one of the entry ports and dragged him through it to a second-level chamber. Erika and Raun followed. Inside there was almost no light at all. Jade, feeling his movements somewhat less restricted this far from the core, took the flashlight and shone it through the red haze.

He saw chaos. Sarcophagi were upended, the machines of a long-dead civilization had been jammed together by a seizure of the mountain. The diorama at the far end of the chamber was buckling, and razor-edged shards of crystal showered down at each new convulsion.

Erika touched him again. "Wait." Jade turned the light on her face.

"Who are you?"

"Erika Weller." Their speech was still distorted, but not as drastically as it had been close to the core. Still she had the feeling that it was only a matter of time, they would be caught again as the death throes of the core continued.

"What happened outside? Where's the Russian?"

She shrugged, too tired for lengthy explanations.

"Dead."

"The way out?"

"The gully is jammed with rock and debris. We barely made it back before—we were trapped."

"You spent a lot of time in the Catacombs," Jade said. "You must have found other entrances."

"No." She sagged. "There's nothing. God help us all."

He lost patience and shook her. "There has to be a way! How many rooms are there like this one?"

"Dozens."

"That's several million cubic yards of material. They may have been supermen, but they still had to have a way of getting rid of the excavated rock. Their best bet was just to dump it down the side of the mountain."

"I don't know how they did it."

Raun came up to them. "Matt? What are we going to do?"

"Stay here with the others," Jade said. He turned to Erika. "Do you have another flashlight?"

"Yes," Erika said.

"Okay. Don't use it unless you have to."

"Where are you going?" Raun asked him.

"Exploring." He had a coughing fit. "While I can still move." He had begun to feel the lethargy again, the longing for the peace of the oscillating core. He bit his tongue for the taste of blood, the mind-clearing pain, and set off, still carrying the pack with the plastic explosives and detonator.

A dozen feet away he could no longer make out the others, waiting behind him in the bloody darkness. The beam of his light wisped through the haze of the chamber. The floor was uneven, made treacherous by pieces of crystal that were sharp enough to slice through boot leather.

In sidelong tombs he saw imperial catlike faces, eyes that in a better light would have been amber. Erika had cautioned him; he avoided looking directly into those eyes. He was chilled. He came to a fallen tomb that had been cracked lengthwise, exposing a shaped cavity roughly the size of one of the small but princely men. The floor trembled; bits of pulverized glass pattered down and though he covered his face with his arms he felt the bite of hail on the backs of his hands, the welling of blood.

When Jade looked up again he heard the chirp-cry of an excited cheetah not far away. He swung the light to his left and had a glimpse of spotted hide, a feline grin, as the animal rose from the littered floor in a manlike playful leap and nearly disappeared behind a block of odd-looking metal machinery. All that remained was a tall twitching tail, two thirds the length of the supple body he had seen.

He advanced cautiously on that tuft of tail, which was motionless for eight or ten seconds. He felt a hammering excitement against the wall of his chest. If the cheetah was here, then it had sought shelter from the impending catastrophe outside. Which meant a passage of some sort. One way of finding it was to drive the cheetah back the way it had come.

The tail abruptly disappeared. Jade ran forward, stumbling, almost losing his balance, casting the light around. From the dark he heard a spitting sound, and momentarily was confused. Had the cat doubled back on him? It might have been half crazed by the continual shaking of the Catacombs. Perhaps it meant to attack him. He felt the hairs on the back of his neck going stiff with alarm. He stopped and listened, moving his light slowly. He was sweating heavily, losing strength as he neared the point of dehydration. Not much time, he knew. The odds favoring survival had become incalculably long.

Then he saw it again, the face this time, the small neat head, the alert rounded ears. The cat was looking down at him from a perch a few feet above the floor of the chamber, barred face inscrutable. Nothing frenzied about the way the cheetah sat and observed him. A kind of distant curiosity in the somnolent eyes.

Jade felt a dizzying apprehension, because he couldn't be sure that he wasn't hallucinating.

He pressed on, trying to keep his light on the face of the cheetah. Its eyes became slits. It snarled at his approach but rather half-heartedly, and showed no signs of tension or a willingness to bolt.

When he was within ten ten feet, the big cat, with the deftness of a stage magician, went almost straight up in the air again. It came down facing away from him then leaped sinuously over a crooked line of sarcophagi, a jump that might have taken it ten feet from the floor, and just vanished, despite his efforts to keep the light trained on the tawny body.

He was sure then that he was in a dreaming state of shock, that nothing he'd seen for the last few minutes was real. He was as lost as if he were shipwrecked on a vast stretch of sea, with no hope for salvation. But he approached the massive wall of sarcophagi, some of which had been jarred out of place by the repeated quakes. Perfectly preserved cat-men looked down on him. He felt humbled by their immortality.

Jade felt too tired to continue. The flashlight in his hand dipped. The beam picked out a shaft in the floor partly uncovered by the movement of one of the sarcophagi, not quite enough space for a full-grown man to squeeze into.

In the shaft he saw the glowing upturned face of the cheetah, a wide-open, toothy snarl that was like a soundless command.

He made his way back across the floor to the others.

"I found something. Don't know what. It may be a chance."

Lem was semiconscious, helpless. Jade gave him oxygen, then Oliver carried Lem on his back. Oliver's sneakers were in shreds, his feet bleeding. He uttered no word of complaint.

When they reached the tomb that had concealed the shaft, Jade had Oliver put the wounded Lem down.

He put a hand on the crystal tomb that still blocked most of the entry to the shaft. "We have to heave it over," he said to them. "All of us together might be able to do it." Along with the offensive line of the Pittsburgh Steelers, he thought. The tomb was a monster. He hoped that fear would give them strength. He hoped for a miracle.

They all had enough left for one desperate try. For four or five seconds the sarcophagus withstood their screaming, grunting efforts. Then it moved. Six inches, eight. The four of them collapsed in a dazed heap beside the opening to the shaft. The Catacombs trembled anew. The diorama above their heads cracked loudly; the air was filled with flying shards.

"Inside!" Jade grabbed Raun and then Erika and pushed them down into the shaft, which descended at an angle of thirty degrees to the horizontal. Jade and Oliver passed down equipment, including the remaining cylinder of oxygen. Then they wrestled Lem into the hole. Lem screamed dismally and passed out again.

There wasn't room to stand in the shaft, but they could crouch, an agonizing posture to maintain while they pushed and dragged a prostrate and crippled man. The shaft was an obvious construction, about five feet square, close and very hot and frightening inside. They had no idea of where they were going, or what would happen if the shaft had been destroyed farther along by an earthquake. The air might give out, they could suffocate or bake to death. But going back was out of the question. Jade had staked everything on his glimpses of the will-o'-the-wisp cheetah, which was nowhere to be seen now.

"Has to be—the way out," he gasped, when Raun began to sob in terror. She froze up in front of him. He pushed her jarringly.

"Just keep moving!"

"How f-far?"

*"How the hell do I know?"*

"Matt, I can't breathe! I'm choking!"

He paused to let them all have a few whiffs of oxygen. Lem's eyelids fluttered, but he seemed to be sinking deeper into shock.

"Go on, go on!" Jade shouted, shoving the women ahead of him.

He guessed that they had progressed two hundred feet or more through solid rock; at least they were going down and not up, which made it easier. He was convinced that it was one of many shafts through which excavated material had been removed during construction of the Catacombs. The thought of the lone cheetah was the only thing that gave him hope at this point. *But how long was the shaft?*

He and Oliver made one of their frequent stops with Lem. Erika and Raun went ahead. He heard their sobbing breaths. And then Raun screamed.

"Matt!"

He looked back over his shoulder and saw a smear of light on a gleaming wall of obsidian, and knew they had run out of luck.

"Matt, it's blocked, *it's blocked!*"

He crawled down to the women, saw that the builders had plugged the shaft when it was no longer needed. Jade rocked on his heels angrily, staring at the barrier. What had happened to the cheetah? It had to have come this way. He wasn't crazy, he'd seen it. He looked around, and saw a red gleam on the floor of the shaft. Reached for it. He had one of the bloodstones in his hand. It felt as hot as a living heart. He wondered if Erika had dropped it. But Erika wasn't paying attention to the red diamond. She covered her face with her hands, gasping. Raun began to cry hysterically.

Jade slapped her hard. She stopped crying and looked dully at him.

"Get back out of the way! Both of you!"

He threw the red diamond down, tugged at the straps of the pack, and tore it open. He pulled out the plastic explosives and the timer. He was nearly reeling from lack of air. He crawled forward to the obsidian wall and ran his hands over it. The obsidian wasn't smooth; he found bubble-sized hollows and crevices, a couple of them deep enough for shaping charges.

"Careful, boss," Oliver warned him.

"I know, I know." Frantically Jade packed crevices with the explosive, all that he had. No way to judge if it would be enough. Working in the feeble glow from Raun's flashlight, he set the timer of the detonator. Two minutes. They had no more time left in this world. Either they were going to suffocate, or be crushed by the collapsing walls of the shaft if he had miscalculated the strength of his charge. Either way, it no longer mattered.

Raun and Erika had moved slowly back, but not far enough. He went after them, shoving, pushing, whacking them with his hands.

"Get down—lie down!"

Oliver bent over Lem, shielding him with his body. Jade piled on top of the women.

The explosives went off with a concussive roar. The shaped charges fragmented a chunk of obsidian the thickness of a bank vault door and fired those fragments as if from the muzzle of a cannon several hundred feet down the flank of the mountain.

When the survivors rose shakily to their knees, the shaft was flooding with the thin cold air of the high mountain, and with a refracted light that blinded them.

They followed the light to the sharp jagged hole that had been blown in the obsidian plug and looked out, still dazed, at a clearing sky and the sun rising over an alpine meadow. Water trickled nearby, runoff from the glacier. They were below the fulminating cloud at the summit and Kilimanjaro, for now, was quiet. All around them was space, air, light, and freedom. They had nowhere to go but down.

# EPILOGUE:
# CHANVAI

## May 29

From his office at the Kialamahindi Hospital in Dar, Robeson Kumenyere walked to the inverted pyramid and took the elevator to the top floor. It was seven o'clock in the morning, and the arbovirus lab was deserted. He locked the door anyway and set to work, removing with a screwdriver the enameled front panels from the computer-run board that kept track of the complicated experiments and programs of analysis.

On the backs of the panels were the twenty-four FIRE-KILL diamonds he had substituted for ordinary red glass reflectors. He opened an attaché case fitted with a piece of socketed Lucite for the stones and placed them inside. He put the reflectors back where they belonged and screwed the panels into place.

A military helicopter was waiting for him on the landing pad outside. He climbed in through the crew entry door of the Sikorsky and settled down in the cabin, alone, for the three-hundred-mile journey upcountry to Chanvai.

As the helicopter soared away over the hospital complex, Kumenyere looked down nostalgically but without regrets. The excellent health-care facility had been his inspiration, his achievement, but after today one of his associates would be in charge. Kumenyere's true destiny was about to be fulfilled. A metamorphosis from a little-known hospital administrator to the powerful leader of a bloc of African nations, forged by swift masterstrokes that would have the rest of the world gasping—he smiled and relaxed and let his imagination play at will for a few minutes. It was pure delight. Washington, London, Paris—he envisioned crisis meetings at the highest levels, emergency sessions of the U.N., the clamor from the press for official policy statements. Only the Russians would not be caught out, wondering what he was up to. Their missiles were making it all possible. They ultimately would have all the benefits of his control of the vital sea lanes around the Cape of Good Hope. Without a steady stream of supertankers from the Persian Gulf ports, a steel artery of oil, the giants of the West would be, in a few years' time, shriveled mummies, relics of capitalism.

From another case he removed the documents and manifestos he'd prepared, messages for heads of state in Africa and abroad. He reviewed the anticipated sequence of events for the next forty-eight hours.

IRBMs and the crews to man them were now on their way from the U.S.S.R. to Tanzania. Expected time of arrival, 1600 hours. All of the resources of the Jeshi la Wananchi la Tanzania had been concentrated at Kilimanjaro airport in anticipation of military action by South Africa. SAM missiles secretly obtained from Libya would be employed for the first time against attacking bombers.

Shortly before 1600 hours Robeson Kumenyere would release the terrible news that Jumbe Kinyati had died in his sleep, and announce that he was temporarily assuming control of the government for the duration of the crisis.

His first official act would be the offering of a conciliatory proposal to Zambia to settle their desultory border war. Then would come a communiqué announcing hostile action by the South African government, and an impassioned cry for help from other African nations, particularly the well-armed Zaïre air force.

An IRBM with a nuclear warhead would be launched against South Africa, resulting in a minimum loss of life but maximum panic.

With more warheads of devastating power at his disposal, the IRBMs dispersed and invulnerable to further raids by the South Africans, Robeson Kumenyere's ultimatum to the Pretorian government would be broadcast, along with his modest proposals for a workable coalition government of blacks and whites in South Africa.

Great pressure from the superpowers, particularly the Russians, would be brought to bear on the Afrikaners to accept the proposals of the charismatic new president of Tanzania.

Meanwhile he would be consolidating his power at home through the time-honored methods of persuading the weak and intimidating the strong.

Perhaps another launch would be needed to convince the Pretorian government of the wisdom of this course of action; Kumenyere wasn't sure about that. He knew only that eventually they would have to give in.

Black nationalists imprisoned in South Africa would be released. They would emerge like moles from the darkness of their confinement into the light, momentarily confused and in need of well-thought-out plans for the immediate future, which Kumenyere was ready to provide.

He would be, simultaneously, the iron fist and the voice of moderation willing to harmonize with other voices of moderation in Africa, those leaders whose cooperation he knew he could count on, and who would support his ambitious project.

It would be no secret that the Russians were deeply involved in the South African coup. He would announce, within a few weeks, that the Russians were leaving Tanzania, and would be congratulated for his courage and statesmanship. The Russians would eventually build FIREKILL, and start making some horrendous demands of their own.

It was a calm, clear day at Chanvai. The recent eruptions of ash from Kilimanjaro, now peaceful and smokeless, had largely been carried away on easterly winds to fall on prime agricultural areas of Kenya, heavily damaging the wheat crop. The rest of the ash had been dispersed over the Indian Ocean.

From the helicopter Kumenyere went directly to Jumbe's quarters in the main house. The louvers were nearly closed; little light came in. Jumbe didn't care for air conditioning, and his bedroom was stifling. Kumenyere found him propped up in a basket chair, eyes vacant as if he'd been dreaming before the knock on his door. He focused on his visitor.

"Good morning, Jumbe." Kumenyere smiled at the man he had come to murder.

"Good morning," Jumbe said spiritlessly.

Kumenyere put one of the attaché cases on an onyx tabletop, opened it.

"The FIREKILL stones."

Jumbe looked at them for a long time. His lips began to quiver.

"You should be pleased," Kumenyere said, still smiling. "It's a great day, Jumbe. The day you've lived all your life for. I understand how emotional you are. But it isn't good for you." Jumbe seemed not to be listening. Kumenyere opened his medical bag and took out a disposable hypodermic syringe, a mislabeled ampule containing a drug that would bring on a fatal heart seizure within thirty seconds. He drew some of the liquid into the syringe.

There was another knock at the door; Kumenyere looked up, frowning.

"I don't think we should be disturbed."

"Come in," Jumbe said, his voice suddenly strong.

The door was opened by the bearded General Timbaroo, who carried one of the little Ingram machine guns that were so deadly at close range and could be fired with one hand. There were some people behind him. Kumenyere stiffened at this unprecedented intrusion.

"Bring them in," Jumbe said to General Timbaroo.

Erika Weller entered the bedroom, followed by Raun Hardie and Matthew Jade, who was leaning on a crutch. Lastly Oliver appeared, peering first around the jamb of the door at Jumbe, who smiled a little and nodded. Oliver crept into the room and stood in one corner.

They all wore clean clothes. They had had medical attention. They had bathed, slept, and eaten. But they still looked as if they had just been salvaged from the hands of skilled torturers.

"Jumbe, what—" Kumenyere began, but he instinctively moved a step closer to the old man, placing a hand lightly on his shoulder. The other hand still held the almost unnoticeable syringe.

"The Russians," Jumbe said, "are not sending missiles. I'm afraid I temporarily misled you about that, Robeson."

"But—" He glanced at the table, where General Timbaroo was opening the second of the two attaché cases. "Don't touch that!"

"But we'll be needing it," Jumbe continued. "As evidence at your trial for sedition, and other crimes against the government of Tanzania."

"What do you mean, there won't be missiles? Have you forgotten who the enemy is? You stupid old fool! *Amani haija ila kwa ncha ya upanga!*"

"FIREKILL is too dangerous a toy, even for the Russians," Jumbe said, and nodded his head at Erika. "This is Erika Weller, of the Chapman/Weller expedition."

Despite his shock, Kumenyere was still able to smile at Erika.

"I see. You have—a remarkable faculty for survival."

"Fortunately," Jumbe said. "Or I might have continued on a course that would have resulted in certain catastrophe. Erika—would you explain?"

"Henry Landreth was right about FIREKILL. It works. It can stop meteors—or nuclear warheads—by atomizing them through an enormous buildup of electromagnetic waves. The technology is relatively simple, drawing on energy that is always available in the earth. But these waves subsequently have a damaging effect on the earth's natural magnetic poles, causing them to shift. When that happens, and it happens in the blink of an eye, the earth wobbles in its rotation, slows, then resumes rotating at a somewhat different angle. The result, on the surface, is always cataclysm. Huge tidal waves, walls of water a thousand feet high, rolling halfway across continents. Enough volcanic activity to throw a pall across the sun for a century. Civilizations destroyed. Almost all of life wiped out. The Lords of the Storm knew what the results might be when their physicists constructed models of FIREKILL. They had a terrible choice to make: to be devastated from space, or risk a cataclysm of their own making. They lost their gamble."

General Timbaroo was busy looking through the papers in Kumenyere's attaché case, his eyes alight. Erika cleared her throat. Jumbe breathed raspingly. Jade's crutch squeaked as he shifted his weight.

Jumbe said, "By the way, I had another medical examination yesterday."

Perspiration gleamed on Kumenyere's forehead. He

said in a small sad voice, "I would have been a great leader. A great man."

He clamped his left arm around Jumbe's head and placed the point of the syringe in his other hand against the carotid artery in Jumbe's neck.

"Your heart may be sound now," he said softly, "but it will stop seconds after I inject this. General Timbaroo! Push your submachine gun across the table toward me. I want a Land-Rover, fully fueled, waiting outside the door in five minutes, a 707 ready to depart Sanya Juu in one hour. *Get moving, man, and give that order!*"

"Robeson," Jumbe said, "for once consider what you're up against. *Haiwezekani.* Enough people have died already."

"I don't wish to be included in that tally." He glanced at Raun. "Close the attaché case. The one with the diamonds. Hold it until I tell you what to do next."

Raun swallowed and glanced at Jade, who nodded. General Timbaroo was at the bedroom door.

"Speak clearly, so I can hear every word!"

General Timbaroo spoke to a subordinate, who could then be heard running through the house. Jade relaxed on his crutch with a slight smile, apropos of nothing. A fly was buzzing around his head but he didn't make the mistake of trying to wave it off. Raun closed the attaché case, filled with diamonds that could be worth sixty million dollars to collectors who would not be particular about provenance, and stepped back slowly from the table.

In just under five minutes a soldier came running back to the bedroom. General Timbaroo had remained by the door. The Land-Rover was ready.

"The plane, the plane!" Kumenyere said impatiently.

General Timbaroo queried the soldier. Yes, the airport had been contacted, the aircraft was being fueled.

"Get up," Kumenyere said to Jumbe. The old man rose slowly, his head still at a wry angle in Kumenyere's embrace.

"General Timbaroo, go and stand beside Miss Weller. Don't anyone in this room move until I am outside with Jumbe."

He shifted the syringe adroitly to the other hand, aiming the point up under Jumbe's chin, and pulled the submachine gun off the table with his left hand. He looked at Raun.

"You first. Straight outside to the Land-Rover. Don't get too far in front of me."

When Raun had left the room, walking as deliberately and self-consciously as a bridesmaid at a wedding, Kumenyere followed, keeping a firm hold on Jumbe as they went down the hall, yelling a warning for everyone to clear out of the way.

Jade looked at General Timbaroo.

"Can you get me a rifle?" he said. "One with a good scope? I saw a Heckler-Koch in your arsenal yesterday, the G3SG/1. It ought to do."

"What are you thinking about?" Erika said. "You can barely walk!"

"But I can shoot," Jade said. "And the son of a bitch took Raun. General, we don't want them to get too big a lead on us; it can be tough to pick Kumenyere off once he reaches the airport."

"*Hasha!*" General Timbaroo said furiously, and ran from the bedroom with Jade stumping along behind him. Erika looked at Oliver, who shrugged, and they followed.

The engine of the Land-Rover outside was running. Guards armed with Ingrams stood at discreet distances.

"Put the case in front," Kumenyere said to Raun.

She did so.

"Now drive!"

Raun looked around as Erika and Oliver appeared on the verandah. She didn't see Jade. She looked back at Kumenyere, shaking her head in dismay. Kumenyere was wild with frustration and anger.

Jumbe smiled at her. "Do it for me," he said. "I would enjoy having your company on the way to the airport."

Kumenyere pushed Jumbe to the Land-Rover and climbed into the cramped backseat with him. Raun got in on the right, started up with the brake on, released it too fast. Gravel sprayed from the back wheels; the Rover bucked and almost died. Kumenyere screamed at her.

Jade appeared, empty-handed, on the verandah, leaned his crutch against the house and shielded his eyes as Raun drove away in the direction of the lake.

As the Land-Rover disappeared into a stand of trees, leaving a motionless haze of dust in the air, a Jeep came around the corner of the house with General Timbaroo driving; a van full of soldiers was just behind the Jeep. Timbaroo had the Heckler-Koch rifle with him.

Jade hopped down the steps and piled in beside Timbaroo.

"Is there a checkpoint on this road?" Jade shouted as they shot after the Land-Rover.

"About five miles north, at the edge of the park!"

"What's the terrain like?"

"Brush and grass."

"Dry enough to burn?"

"Instantly." He realized what Jade was after, and reached for the microphone of the radio slung under the dashboard of the Jeep. When he had contacted the checkpoint he ordered brushfires to be started on either side of the road.

Jade hung on to the bouncing, careening Jeep and muttered, "Fly up his nose, Raunie." He had the sniper's rifle cradled in one arm, but it would be useless to him until both vehicles came to a crawl. Then he was complicating his task by adding fire and smoke in a dry wilderness, perhaps endangering Raun and Jumbe all the more. But it was the only thing he could think of to slow the Rover down long enough to get off a shot at Kumenyere.

In the Land-Rover Kumenyere had discarded the hypodermic syringe, which was of less value to him under the circumstances than the stubby Ingram. He had the muzzle pressed against Jumbe's side. Jumbe sat quietly, distressed by the dust and the sun beating down on the open vehicle, the rough ride.

"*Kwa nini?*" he said dispiritedly. "How could you use me so cruelly? After Rhodesia you were the only son I had. We built a fine hospital together. I would have done anything for you."

"I'm a better man than you, Jumbe. And I will prove it yet."

After that Jumbe said nothing, but sat with his eyes half closed, wincing at the jolts from the road.

Kumenyere was aware of the smoke boiling over the road as soon as Raun was. He stood up in the Rover as she began to slow.

"I can't see!" Raun yelled.

He looked back and saw the Jeep and the van in pursuit, the hard glint of light off a tilted windshield.

"Get off the track! Go around the fire!"

Raun cocked the wheel hard left and drove between a couple of umbrella thorns, crackled through tall caper and toothbrush bush. A leopard tortoise, caught in the open, was crushed by the offside front wheel. They rebounded from flat rocks and found a natural tunnel paved with dung in the thick browning bush. A termite-riddled hulk of a stinkbark lying in the way exploded into sawdust as Raun drove across it. A change of wind brought the taint of smoke.

And suddenly there were elephants, elephants everywhere, in shades from toffee brown to rusty gray, huge beasts wheeling and snorting in a double panic from the approach of fire, the roar of the Land-Rover's engine.

"No!" Kumenyere screamed. "Stop! Get us out of here!"

Raun hit the brakes on ground hammered hard as concrete in the drought by ponderous feet. The Rover slowed, stopped, stalled beneath trunks raised in alarm like cobras in baskets, the lethal slant of old ivory. Raun ground the starter and the engine spun, five seconds, ten, but nothing happened.

The Rover was bumped, bumped again. There was nothing but elephant hide all around them, rage, flailing trunks, fear, dust. The windshield was shattered as Raun ducked beneath the dashboard, getting as low as she could. Kumenyere screamed, firing his machine gun to little effect. Blood sprayed down, but the Rover began to rock until it turned over on its side. Both Kumenyere and Jumbe were spilled from the backseat.

As Jade and Timbaroo came bouncing through the brush to the clearing where the Land-Rover had stalled, two of the biggest elephants Jade had ever seen were trying to crush the Rover with their feet. It was, already, very nearly unrecognizable.

"Jumbe!" Timbaroo cried, and he jumped out from behind the wheel, rushing fearlessly into the churning mass of elephants.

Jade took aim from the Jeep and shot one of the elephants in the eye.

The huge animal staggered back, almost going

down on its hindquarters. It turned, lumbered trumpeting toward deeper brush, but suddenly fell. Timbaroo appeared, dragging Jumbe with him, through the smoke and haze. An elephant was on a collision course with them. Jade turned on the Jeep's siren and began firing the rifle to get the herd moving away from them.

Most of the elephants swung away from the threat of fire and the surging siren. But one, a matron with a shattered tusk, stayed behind.

Jade saw Robeson Kumenyere moving, in a crouch, through the haze toward General Timbaroo and Jumbe. They had their backs to him. Kumenyere raised the submachine gun. Jade realized he had abandoned hope of getting away, his vision of life had receded to a narrow focus. All he cared about was killing Jumbe before he was killed himself.

Jade swung the muzzle of the Heckler-Koch toward Kumenyere and pulled the trigger. The magazine was empty. He yelled. Timbaroo heard him but reacted too slowly to protect himself. A rip of bullets across his back sent him sprawling and Jumbe, on hands and knees, was motionless, an easy target.

The female elephant loomed up behind Kumenyere and sent him flying, separated from his weapon, with a swing of her trunk. As he lay on his back in the dirt trying to lift his head, she swayed up to him and reached down with a certain delicacy, lifted him, held him dangling a few feet above the ground. Kumenyere screamed and struggled in her embrace.

She lifted one forefoot and began slowly to swing it from side to side, building momentum. Then with a quick dip of her trunk she lowered Kumenyere and sliced him across the middle with toenails sharp enough to separate a clump of coarse grass from its roots.

The lower half of his body sagged down in a long

stretch that almost touched his toes to the ground. Everything fell out of him in a gush of blood like water from an uncapped hydrant. His spine, along with the tough fibrous cord, held him together momentarily. Then she gave a little upward jerk with her trunk and the spine was severed. She threw the head and torso aside and moved off with a blast that sounded to Jade like sweet revenge. The matriarch had singled out Kumenyere, he was sure of that; it hadn't been a random attack. But he would never know why, and he had other things to think about.

Soldiers were arriving in droves. He got out of the Jeep and hobbled to the place where Timbaroo had fallen. He was badly wounded but conscious; he might live. Smoke was getting thick, the crackle of fire was closer. Jade grabbed one of the soldiers and pulled him toward the nearly demolished Land-Rover. Raun was upside down inside, cut and terrified. They pried her carefully out of the wreckage. More soldiers came running to lend a hand. A combi arrived and Raun and Jade were helped into it.

She was too stunned to speak. They were driven back to Chanvai. Jade declined Erika's offer of help and put Raun to bed himself. He sat with her the rest of the afternoon and gave her whiskey. He drank a lot of the whiskey himself, and kept an eye on her, and touched her when he thought she needed touching.

Jumbe came around dusk. He had a drink with Jade, and shook his hand. He said they were welcome to stay at Chanvai as long as they liked. If Jade wanted anything from the government or the people of Tanzania, he had only to ask. Jade had never seen a sadder face.

Jade left Raun sleeping and visited Lem, who was in an air-conditioned bungalow, flat on his back, still heavily sedated. Two nurses attended him. Both knees requred surgery, for which he was to be flown back to the States. Jade fed him, although Lem wasn't very hungry, and told him how Robeson Kumenyere had finished. Jade had a few more drinks and turned off a few more lights in his head.

About seven thirty Erika was summoned to the conference room at Chanvai.

For a few minutes she was alone. There was a fire on the hearth; it provided all of the light in the room. Erika sat in a zebra-skin chair beneath the flag of Tanzania, her somber eyes fixed on the flames, the play of light across the glistening onyx table. She didn't look around when she heard the sounds of Jumbe's sandals on the concrete floor.

He stopped near her, and held out a sheet of paper. Erika scarcely glanced at it.

"What's this?"

"It seems that Tiernan Clarke lied to you, in order to more easily enlist your aid in reaching the Catacombs. There *were* survivors at Ivututu. Dr. Poincarré did heroic work on behalf of all the victims. This is a list of those we have flown to the hosp—"

Erika lunged from the chair and snatched at the flimsy paper, scanned the eleven names with eyes that quickly scalded.

"Chips—" she moaned.

Jumbe shook his head. "I'm sorry. According to Dr. Poincarré, he died on the evening of May seventeenth."

Erika let the paper fall from her fingers; it drifted in the draft from the fire and came to rest under the table. She stared in bitter anger at the hunched old man.

"Of course we have notified his son, who is on his way to Chanvai. Now, I think we should talk. I want us to be in full accord as to what will be said, and not said, at the press conference tomorrow."

"Or there will be no press conference."

"To some extent I'm at your mercy," Jumbe said, with a smile that begged her indulgence. "You realize that. I have no wish to make life more difficult for you than it is already. But I can, if I must. You realize that too. In my opinion it will serve no useful purpose to dwell on the tragedy, and the treachery, we have suffered. You have lost someone you loved dearly; I have lost a man I thought of as my son. My reputation has diminished during the past year, but I haven't been hopelessly compromised through my folly. I believe I can continue to serve my country usefully. For your part, I would think you most profitably might apply yourself to the years of research that remain, the volumes you will write about the Catacombs and the people of Zan. In your work you will of course have the full backing of the government of Tanzania."

"The exclusive backing."

"Yes."

"And the funds to establish a museum, in Chips' name."

"That too."

"I find it distasteful—degrading—even talking to you like this."

He shrugged. "And how much satisfaction will you ultimately find in your bitterness, the slight revenge you may exact from telling the truth as you know it?"

"None, I suppose."

"I'm having a statement drafted," Jumbe said, "that I'm sure we can both agree on before the conference."

"Some things simply can't be explained away," Erika said tautly.

"Oh?" Jumbe smiled again. "You would indeed be surprised." He turned to go.

"There's one more thing," Erika said. "I'd like to talk to you about Oliver."

\*   ❈   \*

After her meeting with Jumbe, Erika spent a half hour roaming the grounds of Chanvai, trying to locate Oliver. She was afraid he had succumbed to his deep-rooted distrust of governments and authority figures and hit the road again, without a penny.

It was nearly dusk when she found him, in scrounged clothing that included a crinkly pair of plaid pants that ended above his ankles, and soiled white golfing visor. He was attempting to repair a bicycle he had pulled out of a shed. He'd adopted a new pet, another mongoose, one of scores that lived on the estate. It clung to Oliver's right shoulder and talked urgently in his ear at Erika's approach. Oliver didn't look around. There was a hot post-daylight glaze of silk and pearl and purple shadow across the land. He spun a tireless wheel of the upended bicycle; the spokes flashed in a mime of flight.

"Oliver."

He hunched his shoulders and covered his face with his long hands, shuddering a little in an agony of the soul. Erika stopped a few feet from him and studied him compassionately.

"It's all right, Oliver. You have nothing to blame yourself for."

"Your friend, dying. My fault."

"*No*, Oliver. Chips was very sick, even before I left Ivututu. His fate was never in your hands. You did everything humanly possible to help me. Performed miracles, really. I don't feel merely indebted to you. I feel about you as I would a brother, my own flesh and blood."

For a while he didn't move. It got swiftly darker. Then he spread his fingers, peering at her incredulously.

"I mean it, Oliver. You have saved my life, and

since I'm not what you'd call long in the tooth, I'm afraid you're stuck with me for quite a few years yet. I intend to devote as much time as necessary to seeing that you have what you need most in this life: your freedom. The freedom to do your prospecting utterly without interference from this government or special interest groups. I'm arranging for the necessary documents now. You will be provided with all the tools you require. To strike gold, or mine gemstones, or whatever. There will be a sizable subsidy, every year; and half of everything you discover is yours to keep. You could very well wind up a rich man, Oliver."

He lowered his hands. He trembled. His feet tried to caper, but for once in his life he was clumsy. He fell down in a heap.

"Well, I hope I'm not spoiling you," Erika said, with a smile and with tears in her eyes. She turned and walked back toward the main house.

"Erika! Going now?"

"Yes, Oliver. To Switzerland, for a few months. To see my family, and to rest. But I'll be back. I suppose I may be spending the rest of my life here. There's that much to do, you see. So very much to do."

When Lem Meztizo's nurse turned up to give him morphine so he could make it through the night without screaming, Jade returned, bottle in hand, to check up on Raun.

"Matt?"

"The one and only."

"Are you drunk?"

"Gosh no."

From outside came the sound of wind in the trees, the bark and yowl of animals in the wild. He sat down clumsily on the bed beside her and put the bottle to his lips.

"Have you had enough yet?" She sighed.

"Of whiskey?"

"No. I mean—enough of flying up His nose."

"Whose nose?"

"His. You know. Him with the scythe."

"Oh." He realized how hard he'd been thinking about that himself. "Yeah. Good odds, anyway."

"I'm glad," Raun said. "Matt?"

"Yes?"

"Take me home with you."

"Why?"

"It's time we got acquainted."

He thought about that too, and stretched out beside her, trying not to jostle his bad leg. He was too tired to tell himself anymore that it didn't hurt.

"This must be my lucky day," he said.

She smiled and moved her head against his shoulder and drifted to sleep again.

# AFTERWORD

In the preparation and writing of *Catacombs* I'm in-debted to more literary and personal sources than I can (or should) name here. At the risk of offending some of those I must leave out, I want to thank Dick Winston, of the firm of Harry Winston in New York, who has studied countless diamonds from all over the world. It was Dick who, in casual conversation, men-tioned the single red diamond he has seen in the course of his career, a diamond with strange and inde-ciperable markings, and thus unwittingly initiated the processes that became *Catacombs*.

For the reader who has more than a casual interest in Africa, and the dilemma its diverse peoples face in coping with each other as well as the demands of the present and future, two books are highly recom-mended. One is the E. P. Dutton & Co., Inc., com-bined edition of Peter Matthiessen's *The Tree Where Man Was Born* and Eliot Porter's *The African Experi-ence*. The text, by Matthiessen, is the result of a re-markable fusion of the naturalist's eye and the mind of a poet: Here is a formidable creative power at work, informed by rare intelligence. The photographs, by Porter, particularly of elephants in their habitat, have the unobtrusive impact of enduring art.

*Among the Elephants*, published in the U.S. by The Viking Press, Inc., is by Iain and Oria Douglas-

Hamilton. Their book, unfortunately, is not widely known. It vividly shares a life in the wild unavailable to the majority of us, and introduces two people with nerve, wit, and a passion for the huge beleaguered animal that is, like Kilimanjaro, a symbol of the magnitude and latent power of an entire continent.

JOHN FARRIS
NOVEMBER 1980